Larry's Party

Carol Shields

COMPASS PRESS

* OXFORD * MELBOURNE *

First published in Great Britain in 1997 by
Fourth Estate Limited, 6 Salem Road, London W2 4BU.
Compass Press Large Print Book Series: an imprint of ISIS
Publishing Ltd, Great Britain, and Bolinda Press, Australia.
This edition is published in 1998 by Australian Large Print
Audio & Video Pty Ltd, Melbourne, Australia and
ISIS Publishing Ltd, Oxford, UK with the permission of
Fourth Estate Ltd.

Australian Cataloguing in
Publication Data
Shields, Carol
    Larry's party / Carol Shields. –
(Compass Press large print
book series).
ISBN 1864422262
1. Large print books.
2. Flower arrangers – Canada –
Fiction.
3. Maze gardens – Fiction.
4. Men – Fiction.
5. Domestic fiction, Canadian.
I. Title.
C813.54

British Library Cataloguing in
Publication Data
Shields, Carol
    Larry's party
1. Men – Social
conditions – Fiction
2. Large type books
I. Title
813.5'4 [F]

ISBN 0-7531-6241-5 (pb)

Cover art reproduced with the permission of Fourth Estate Limited.

ISBN 1-86442-226-2 (ALPAV Pty Ltd)
ISBN 0-7531-5867-1(ISIS Publishing Ltd)

For Joseph, Nicholas, and Sofia

With thanks to a few men who have offered suggestions in the writing of this book: David Arnason, Tommy Banks, Tony Giardini, Jack Hodgins, Robin Hoople, Don Huband, Steve Hunt, Dayv James-French, the late Jim Keller, Joseph Krotz, Jake MacDonald, Brian MacKinnon, Don McCarthy, Bill Neville, Mark Morton, Doug Pepper, Gord Peters, John Ralston Saul, Donald Shields, John Shields, Harry Strub and Max Wyman.

Thanks, too, to Maggie Dwyer and Jane Gralen and to the staff at the Winnipeg Public Library.

What is this mighty labyrinth – the earth,
But a wild maze the moment of our birth?

("Reflections on Walking in
the Maze at Hampton Court"
British Magazine, 1747)

CONTENTS

CHAPTER ONE

Fifteen Minutes in the Life of Larry Weller
1977

By mistake Larry Weller took someone else's Harris tweed jacket instead of his own, and it wasn't till he jammed his hand in the pocket that he knew something was wrong.

His hand was traveling straight into a silky void. His five fingers pushed down, looking for the balled-up Kleenex from his own familiar worn-out pocket, the nickels and dimes, the ticket receipts from all the movies he and Dorrie had been seeing lately. Also those hard little bits of lint, like meteor grit, that never seem to lose themselves once they've worked into the seams.

This pocket – today's pocket – was different. Clean, a slippery valley. The stitches he touched at the bottom weren't his stitches. His fingertips glided now on a sweet little sea of lining. He grabbed for the buttons. Leather, the real thing. And something else – the sleeves were a good half inch longer than they should have been.

This jacket was twice the value of his own. The texture, the seams. You could see it got sent all the time to the cleaners. Another thing, you could tell by the way the shoulders sprang out that this jacket got parked on a thick wooden hanger at night. Above a row of polished shoes. Refilling its tweedy warp and woof with oxygenated air.

He should have run back to the coffee shop to see if his own jacket was still scrunched there on the back of his chair, but it was already quarter to six, and Dorrie was expecting him at six sharp, and it was rush hour and he wasn't anywhere near the bus stop.

And – the thought came to him – what's the point? A jacket's a jacket. A person who patronizes a place like Cafe Capri is almost asking to get his jacket copped. This way all that's happened is a kind of exchange.

Forget the bus, he decided. He'd walk. He'd stroll. In his hot new Harris tweed apparel. He'd push his shoulders along, letting them roll loose in their sockets. Forward with the right shoulder, bam, then the left shoulder coming up from behind. He'd let his arms swing wide. Fan his fingers out. Here comes the Big Guy, watch out for the Big Guy.

The sleeves rubbed light across the back of his hands, scratchy but not *too* scratchy.

And then he saw that the cuff buttons were leather too, a smaller-size version of the main buttons, but the same design, a sort of cross-pattern like a pecan pie cut in quarters, only the slices overlapped this little bit. You could feel the raised design with your finger, the way the four quadrants of leather crossed over and over each other, their edges cut wavy on the inside margin. These waves intersected in the middle, dived down there in a dark center and disappeared. A black hole in the button universe. Zero.

Quadrant was a word Larry hadn't even thought of for about ten years, not since geometry class, grade eleven.

The color of the jacket was mixed shades of brown, a strong background of freckled tobacco tones with subtle orange flecks. Very subtle. No one would say: hey, here comes this person with orange flecks distributed across his jacket. You'd have to be one inch away before you took in those flecks.

Orange wasn't Larry's favorite color, at least not in the clothing line. He remembered he'd had orange swim trunks back in high school, MacDonald Secondary, probably about two sizes too big, since he was always worrying at that time in his life about his bulge showing, which was exactly the opposite of most guys, who made a big point of showing what they had. Modesty ran in his family, his mum, his dad, his sister, Midge, and once modesty gets into your veins you're stuck with it. Dorrie, on the other hand, doesn't even shut the bathroom door when she's in there, going. A different kind of family altogether.

He'd had orange socks once too, neon orange. That didn't last too long. Pretty soon he was back to white socks. Sports socks. You got a choice between a red stripe around the top, a blue stripe, or no stripe at all. Even geeks like Larry and his friend Bill Herschel, who didn't go in for sports, they still wore those thick cotton sports socks every single day. You bought them three in a pack and they lasted about a week before they fell into holes. You always thought, hey, what a bargain, three pairs of socks at this fantastic price!

White socks went on for a long time in Larry's life. A whole era.

Usually he didn't button a jacket, but it just came to him as he was walking along that he wanted to do up one of those leather buttons, the middle one. It felt good, not too tight over the gut. The guy must be about his own size, 40 medium, which is lucky for him. If, for example, he'd picked up Larry's old jacket, he could throw it in the garbage tomorrow, but at least he wasn't walking around Winnipeg with just his shirt on his back. The nights got cool this time of year. Rain was forecast too.

A lot of people don't know that Harris tweed is virtually waterproof. You'd think cloth this thick and woolly would soak up water like a sponge, but, in actual fact, rain slides right off the surface. This was explained to Larry by a knowledgeable old guy who worked in menswear at Hector's. That would be, what, nine, ten years ago, before Hector's went out of business. Larry could tell that this wasn't just a sales pitch. The guy – he wore a lapel button that said "Salesman of the Year" – talked about how the sheep they've got over there are covered with special long oily hair that repels water. This made sense to Larry, a sheep standing out in the rain day and night. That was his protection.

Dorrie kept wanting him to buy a khaki trenchcoat, but he doesn't need one, not with his Harris tweed. You don't want bulk when you're walking along. He walks a lot. It's when he does his thinking. He hums his thoughts out on the air like music; they've got a disco beat: My name is Larry Weller. I'm a floral designer, twenty-six years old, and I'm walking down Notre Dame Avenue, in the city of Winnipeg, in the country of Canada, in the month of April, in the year 1977, and I'm thinking hard. About being hungry, about being late, about having sex later on tonight. About how great I feel in this other guy's Harris tweed jacket.

Cars were zipping along, horns honking, trucks going by every couple of seconds, people yelling at each other. Not a quiet neighborhood. But even with all the noise blaring out, Larry kept hearing this tiny slidey little underneath noise. He'd been hearing it for the last couple of minutes. Whoosh, wash, whoosh, wash. It was coming out of the body of Larry J. Weller. It wasn't that he found it objectionable. He liked it, as a matter of fact, but he just wanted to know what it was.

He whooshed past the Triple Value Store, past the Portuguese Funeral Home, past Big Mike's where they had their windows full of ski equipment on sale. The store was packed with people wearing spring clothes, denim jackets, super-flare pants, and so on, but they were already thinking ahead to next winter. They had snow in their heads instead of a nice hot beach. That's one thing Larry appreciates about Dorrie. She lives in the moment. When it's snowing she thinks about snow. When it's spring, like right now, she's thinking about getting some new sandals. That's what she's doing this very minute: buying sandals at Shoes Express, their two-for-one sale. Larry knows she's probably made up her mind already, but she told him she'd wait till he got to the store before buying. She wants to make sure Larry likes what she decides on, even though sandals are just sandals to him. Just a bunch of straps.

Dorrie knows how to stretch money. She saves the fifty-cents-off coupons from Ponderosa – which'll give you a rib eye steak, baked potato and salad, all for $1.69. Or she'll hear a rumor that next week shoe prices are going to get slashed double. So she'll say to the guy at Shoes Express, "Look, can you hold these for me till next Wednesday or Thursday or whatever, so I can get in on the sale price?"

It comes to Larry, what the noise is. It's the lining of his jacket moving back and forth across his shoulders as he strolls along, also the lining material sliding up and down against his shirt-sleeves. He can make it softer if he slows down. Or louder if he lifts his arm and waves at that guy across the street that he doesn't even know. The guy's waving back, he's trying to figure out who Larry is – *hey, who's that man striding along over there, that man in the very top-line Harris tweed jacket?*

Actually no one wears Harris tweed much anymore. In fact, they never did, no one Larry ever knew. It's vintage almost, like a costume. What happened was, Larry was about to graduate from Red River College (Floral Arts Diploma), just two guys and twenty-four girls. The ceremony was in the cafeteria instead of the general-purpose room, and dress was supposed to be informal. So what's informal? Suits or what? The girls ended up wearing just regular dresses, and the two guys opted for jackets and dress pants.

Larry and his mother went to Hector's, which she swears by, and that's where they found the Harris tweed, this nubby-dubby wool cloth, smooth and rough at the same time, heavy but also light, with the look of money and the feel of a grain sack, and everywhere these soft little hairs riding on top of the weave. The salesman said: "Hey, you could wear that jacket to a do at the Prime Minister's." Larry had never heard of Harris tweed, but the salesman said it was a classic. That it would never go out of style. That it would wear like iron. Then his mother chimed in about how it wouldn't show the dirt, and the salesman said he'd try real hard to get them twenty percent off, and that clinched it.

Larry wears the Harris tweed to Flowerfolks almost every day over a pair of jeans, and it's hardly worn out at all. It never looks wrinkled or dirty. Or at least it didn't until today when Larry put on this other jacket by mistake. So! There's Harris tweed and Harris tweed, uh-*huh*.

It was an accident how Larry got into floral design. A fluke. He'd been out of school for a few weeks, just goofing off, and finally his mother phoned Red River College one day and asked them to mail out their brochure on the Furnace Repair course. She figured everyone's got a furnace, so even with the economy up and down, furnaces were a good thing to get into. Well, someone must have been sleeping at the switch, because along came a pamphlet from Floral Arts, flowers instead of furnaces. Larry's mother, Dot, sat right down in the breakfast nook and read it straight through, tapping her foot as she turned the pages, and nodding her head at the ivy wallpaper as if she was saying, yes, yes, floral design really is the future.

Larry's father, though, wasn't too overwhelmed. Larry could tell he was thinking that flowers were for girls, not boys. Like maybe his only son was a homo and it was just starting to show. In the end, he did come to Larry's graduation in the cafeteria but he didn't know where to look. Even when Mrs. Starr presented Larry with the Rose Wreath for having the top point average, Larry's father just sat there with his chin scraping the floor.

Larry was offered a job right off at Flowerfolks, and he's been there ever since. Last October he got to do the centerpieces for the mayor's banquet. It was even on television, Channel 13. You saw the mayor standing up to give his speech and there were these sprays of wheat, eucalyptus branches, and baby orchids right there on the table. Orchids! So much for your average taxpayer. But Flowerfolks has a policy of delivering their flowers to hospital wards if their clients don't want them afterwards, so it's really not a waste. They're a chain with a social conscience, and also an emphasis on professionalism. They like the employees to look good. Shoulder-length hair's okay for male staff, but not a quarter inch longer. A tie's optional, but jackets are required. That's where the Harris tweed comes in.

Larry can't help thinking how this new, new jacket will knock their eyebrows off down at work.

Or maybe not, maybe they won't even notice. He hadn't noticed himself when he picked it up, so why should they? What happened was he went up to the counter to order his cappuccino. Not that he had to order it. He takes the same thing every day, a double cappuccino. He used to go to a bar for a few beers after work, but Dorrie got worried about all the booze he was soaking up. She was convinced his brain cells were getting killed off. One by one they were going out, like Christmas lights on a string, only there weren't any replacements available.

"Why don't you switch to coffee?" she said, and that's when Larry started dropping into Cafe Capri, which is just around the corner from Flowerfolks. A nothing place, but they've brought cappuccino to this town. Nobody knew what it was at first, and some people, like Larry's folks, still don't. Larry's tried it, and now he's on a streak with double cappuccinos. They start making it when they see him come through the door at five-thirty.

He likes to put on his own cinnamon. He likes it spread out thin across the entire foam area, not just sitting in a wet clump in the middle. You take the shaker, hold it sideways about two inches to the right of the cup and tap it twice, lightly. A soft little cinnamon cloud forms in the air – you can almost see it hanging there – and then the little grains drift down evenly into the cup. Total coverage. Like the dust storm in Winnipeg last summer, how it coated every ledge and leaf and petunia petal with this beautiful, evenly distributed layer of powdery dust.

Lots of coffee places have switched over to disposable plastic, but Cafe Capri still uses those old white cups and saucers with the green rims. You put one of those cups up to your mouth and the thickness feels exactly right, the same dimensions as your own tongue and lips. You and your cup melt together, it's like a kiss. Customers appreciate that. They're so grateful for regular cups and saucers that they carry their own empties up to the counter on their way out. That's what Larry must have done. Taken his cup back up, put his fifty-five cents by the cash, and picked up a jacket from the chair. Only it was someone else's chair. Or maybe the other guy had already made off with Larry's jacket at that point. A mistake can work both ways. Larry was probably busy thinking about meeting Dorrie, about the movie they were going to see that night, *Marathon Man*, their third time, and then coming back to her place after, his prick stirring at the thought.

When they first started going together they'd be lying there on top of her bed and she'd say, "Let's fuck and fuck and fuck forever."

"Do you have to say that?" Larry said to her after he'd known her a couple of months. "Can't you just say 'making love'?"

She got her hurt look. Parts of her face tended to lose their shape, especially around her mouth. "You say 'fuck,' " she said to Larry. "You say it all the time."

"No, I don't."

"Come off it. You're always saying 'fuck this' and 'fuck that.' "

"Maybe. Maybe I do. But I don't say it literally."

"What?" She looked baffled.

"Not *literally*."

"There you go again," she said, "with those college words."

Larry stared at her. *She actually thinks* flower *college is* college.

It was sort of a mistake the way they got together. Larry had taken another girl to a Halloween party at St. Anthony's Hall. She, the other girl, had a pirate suit on, with a patch over the eye, a sword, the whole thing. And she'd made herself a moustache with an eyebrow pencil or something. That bothered Larry, turning his head around quick, and looking into the face of a girl wearing a moustache. A costume is supposed to change you, but you can go too far. Larry was a clown that night. He had the floppy shoes and the hat and the white paint on his face, but he'd skipped the red nose. Who's going to score points with a red nose? There was another girl, Dorrie, at the table who'd come with her girlfriends. She was dressed like a Martian, but only a little bit like a Martian. You got the general idea, but you didn't think when you were dancing with her that she was some weird extraterrestrial. She was just this skinny, swervy, good-looking girl who happened to be wearing a rented Martian suit.

"You in love with this Dorrie?" That's what Larry's father asked him a couple of months ago. They were sitting there in the stands. As usual the Jets were winning. Everyone around them was cheering like crazy, and Larry's father said to Larry, not quite turning his face: "So, you in love with this girl? This Dorrie person?"

"What?" Larry said. He had his eyes on the goalie all alone out there on the ice, big as a Japanese wrestler in his mask and shin pads, putting on a tap-dance show while the puck was coming down the ice.

11

"Love," Larry's father said. "You heard me."

"I like her," Larry said after a few seconds. He didn't know what else to say. The question set a flange around his thoughts, holding back his recent worrying days and nights, keeping them separate from right-now time.

"But you're not in love?"

"I guess not."

"You just like her?"

"Yes. But a lot."

"You're twenty-six years old," Larry's father said. "I married Mum when I was twenty-five."

Like a deadline's been missed, that was his tone of voice.

"Yeah," Larry said. "Twenty-six years old, and the kid's still living at home!"

He felt his bony face fall into confusion. And yet he loved this confusion, it was so unexpected, so full of thrill and danger. Love, love.

"Nothing wrong with living at home," Larry's father said, huffing a little, looking off sideways. "Did I say there was anything wrong with that?"

Larry was running this conversation through his head while he walked along Notre Dame Avenue in his stolen Harris tweed jacket, seeing himself in his self's silver mirror. The fabric swayed around him, shifting and reshifting on his shoulders with every step he took. It seemed like something alive. Inside him, and outside him too. It was like an apartment. He could move into this jacket and live there. Take up residence, get himself a new phone number and a set of cereal bowls.

That's when he realized he was in love with dopey smart Dorrie. In love. He was. He really was. Knowing it was like running into a wall of heat, his head and hands pushing right through it. This surprised him, but not completely. You can fall in love all by yourself. You don't have to be standing next to the person; you can do it alone, walking down a street with the wind blowing in your face, a whole lot of people you don't even know going by and they're kind of half bumping into you but you don't notice because you're in a trancelike state. He forgot, suddenly, how Dorrie had this too-little face with too much hair around it and how he always used to get turned on by girls with bigger faces and just average hair size.

He looked at his watch, worried. He knew she'd still be standing there, though, next to the cash with her arms full of shoes and she'd be pissed off for about two seconds and then she'd get an eyeful of Larry's jacket and before you knew it she'd be rubbing her hands up and down the cloth and fingering the buttons.

The problem, though, was tomorrow. Larry and his new jacket weren't going to make it tomorrow. He could go to work in this jacket, but no way could he go back to the Capri at five o'clock. They'd grab him the minute he walked in. *Hey, buddy, there's a call out for that jacket. That jacket's been reported.*

Wait a minute, it's all a mistake.

A mistake that led to another mistake that led to another. People make mistakes all the time, so many mistakes that they aren't mistakes anymore, they're just positive and negative charges shooting back and forth and moving you along. Like good luck and bad luck. Like a tunnel you're walking through, with all your pores wide open. When it turns, you turn too.

Larry remembers seeing a patient in the Winnipeg Chronic Care Unit when he delivered the flowers after the mayor's banquet. This guy didn't have any arms or legs, just little buds growing out of his body. He was one bad mistake, like a human salt shaker perched there on the edge of a bed. Larry, set the flowers down on the table next to him, and the guy leaned over a couple of inches and brushed them with his forehead, then he smelled them, then he stuck his tongue out and licked the leaves and petals, all the while giving Larry a look, almost a wink but not quite. Larry took a lick too, lightly. What he found was, eucalyptus tastes like horse medicine. And orchids don't taste at all.

The sun was dipping low, and Larry was at the corner now, only half a block from Shoes Express. There was a great big rubbish receptacle standing there with a sign on it: Help Keep Our City Clean.

Larry unbuttoned the Harris tweed jacket, slipped it off fast and rolled it up in a sweet little ball. He stuffed it into the rubbish bin. He had to cram it in. He didn't know if he was making a mistake or not, getting rid of that jacket, and he didn't care. The jacket had to go.

And that's when he really knew how cold the wind had got. It puffed his shirt-sleeves up like a couple of balloons, so that all of a sudden he had these huge brand-new muscles. Superman. Then it shifted around quick, and there he was with his shirt pressed flat against his arms and chest, puny and shrunk-up. The next minute he was inflated again. Then it all got sucked out. In and out, in and out. The windiest city in the country, in North America. It really was.

There were plenty of eyes on him, he could feel them boring through to his skin. In about two minutes some guy was going to pull that Harris tweed jacket out of the garbage and put it on. But by that time Larry would be around the corner, walking straight toward the next thing that was going to happen to him.

CHAPTER TWO

Larry's Love
1978

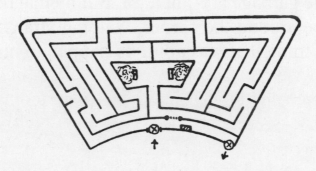

On a Wednesday in winter Larry walked over to a barber shop on Sargent Avenue and asked for a cut. "Just a regular cut," he told the barber in an unsmiling, muttering tone of voice that was altogether unlike his usual manner. This was after a decade of having shoulder-length hair. He came out of the barber shop half an hour later with hair that was short around the ears and cropped close at the neck. Even the color seemed different – darker, denser, and without shadows, a color hard to put a name to.

He was shivery with cold for hours after his haircut, lonely for his hair, shrunken in his upper body, but he also felt stronger, braver. The new look made him want to bunch his fists like a prizefighter or cross his arms over his chest. He stood in front of the bathroom mirror working on new expressions, moving his mouth and eyebrows around, and trying to settle on something friendly.

Vivian and Marcie who work with Larry at

Flowerfolks were both bursting with compliments. Vivian, the store manager, said the new cut made him look "younger and healthier," and that started Larry wondering about how he'd been looking lately. He was only twenty-seven, which was not really old enough to show up on his face and body – or was it? His own opinion was that he was in pretty fair shape what with all the walking he did to and from work, plus the weekend hikes out at Birds Hill with his friend Bill Herschel. Marcie chimed in then about how the new hairstyle made him look more "with-it." "Its 1978," she said. "The sixties are over."

What would she know, Larry thought – she was only a kid, seventeen, eighteen.

Larry, at twenty-seven, still lived with his parents, Dot and Stu, in their bungalow on Ella Street, but this was his last week; he was set to move out on Friday, at long last. Both Dot and Stu approved of their son's haircut. Not that they jumped up and down and waved their arms. It was more a case of pretend nonchalance. "About bloody time," Larry's father said, and started in about the number of times he'd had to open the bathtub drain and clean out all the hair and muck. "Why, you're handsome as can be," Dot said, reaching out and testing the flat of her hand against the new springiness of Larry's hair. It had been some time since she'd touched the top of her son's head, years in fact, and now it was like she couldn't stop herself "If this is Dorrie's influence," she said, "then I say more power to her."

On Friday afternoon – blizzards, high winds – Larry and his folks, and his girlfriend, Dorrie, and her family, went downtown to the Law Courts and got married. Dorrie (Dora) Marie Shaw and Laurence John Weller became the Wellers, husband and wife. And on Saturday morning the bridal couple boarded an Air Canada jet for London, England.

Most of the passengers on the plane were wearing jeans and sweaters, but Dorrie had chosen for her travel outfit a new rose-colored polyester blend suit. Now she regretted it, she told Larry. The suit's straight skirt was restrictive so that she couldn't relax and enjoy the trip, and she worried about the hard wrinkles that had formed across her lap. She should have invested in one of those folding travel irons she'd seen on sale. And she'd been a dope not to bring along some spot-lifter for the stain on her jacket lapel. By the time they got to England it would be permanently set. They put dye in airplane food, coloring the gravy dark brown so it looked richer and more appetising. One of the salesmen at Manitoba Motors, where she works, told her about it. He also told her not to drink carbonated drinks on the flight because of gas. People pass a lot of gas on planes, he'd informed her. It had to do with air pressure. Also, one alcoholic drink on land equals three in the air. This is important information.

If only someone had filled her in about what to wear for a trip like this. She'd never been on a plane before – neither had Larry for that matter – but somehow she'd got the idea that air travel was dressy, especially if you were headed for an international destination, such as London, England. She was all for being casual, as she told Larry, she loved comfortable clothes, he knew that, but wouldn't you think people would make an effort to look nice when they went somewhere important?

"Not everyone's on their honeymoon," he reminded her.

And that was the moment they heard a special announcement over the P.A. system, the pilot's chuckly, good-sport voice coming at them from the cockpit. "Ladies and gents, we thought you'd like to know we've got a brand-new married couple aboard our flight today. How about a round of applause, everyone, for Mr. and Mrs. Larry Weller of Winnipeg, Manitoba."

A stewardess was suddenly standing next to the bride and groom with a bottle of champagne and two glasses and also a corsage to pin on Dorrie's shoulder, compliments of Air Canada.

"Ohh!' Dorrie gave a little shriek. She glowed bright pink. She squirmed in her seat with pleasure. "This is fabulous. How did you know? Baby roses, I love baby roses, and, look, they match my outfit. It's perfect."

"I almost died of embarrassment," Dorrie would tell Larry's mother two weeks later, back home in Winnipeg. "I bet you anything I was blushing from head to foot. Everyone was just staring at the two of us, and then they started cheering and clapping and peering around their seats at us or standing up so they could see who we were and what we looked like. Was I ever glad I had my new pink outfit on. And Larry with his hair restyled. The newly-weds!"

The champagne sent Dorrie straight to sleep, her feet tucked up under her on the seat, and her head flopped over on Larry's shoulder. The sweet perfume of the roses, which were already darkening, got stirred in with the drone of voices and the dimmed cabin lights and the steady, sleepy vibrations of the plane as it nosed through the night sky.

A little drunk, stranded between the old day and the new, between one continent and another, Larry felt the proprietorial pleasure of having a hushed and satisfied companion by his side. He and Dorrie had boarded the plane under a weight of anticlimax, worn out after the wedding and the wedding lunch at the Delta and from moving his things over to Dorrie's apartment. And they were hollowed out too – that's how it felt – after a long, ecstatic night of sex, then the alarm clock going off at five-thirty, the last-minute packing to do, and Larry's folks arriving, too early, to drive them out to the airport. It was a lot to absorb. But now this unexpected tribute had come to them, to himself and to his wife, Dorrie. A wife, a wife. He breathed the word into the rubbery patterned upholstery of the seat ahead of him – *wife*.

A daze of contentment fell over him, numbing and fateful, and he shook his head violently to clear his senses – but in the excitement of the last few hours he had forgotten about his recent haircut. Instead of the movement of soft hair flying outward and then landing with a bounce on his neck, that comforting silky familiar flick against his cheek, he sensed only the abruptness of his cold, clean face, how exposed it was beneath the tiny cabin light and how stupidly rigid.

An hour ago he had felt the tug of drowsiness, but now he pledged himself to stay awake. Grief was involved in this decision, and possibly a crude form of gallantry. Staying awake seemed a portion of what was expected of him, part of the new role he had undertaken a mere thirty-six hours earlier, standing in front of a marriage commissioner at the Law Courts with his family and Dorrie's family looking on. "Marriage is not to be entered into lightly, but with certainty, mutual respect, and a sense of reverence." These words had been part of the civil ceremony, printed on a little souvenir card he and Dorrie had been given.

He was a husband now, and his chattering, fretful Dorrie, no longer a girlfriend but a wife, was slipping down sideways against his arm, her face damp, pared-down, and sealed shut with sleep. He felt her shoulder lift on every third or fourth breath, lift and then fall in a catching, irregular way, as though her dreams had brought her up against a new, puzzling form of exhaustion, something she would soon be getting used to.

For her sake he would stay alert. He would keep guard over her, drawing himself as straight as possible in his seat without disturbing her sleeping body. He'd clamp his jaw firmly shut in a husbandlike way, patient, forbearing, and keep his eyes steady in the dark. He would do this in order to keep panic at a distance. All that was required of him was to outstare the image in the floating black glass of the window, that shorn, bewildered, fresh-faced stranger whose profile, for all its raw boyishness, reminded him, alarmingly, of – of who?

His father, that's who.

"The very image of his mother," people used to say about Larry Weller. Same blue eyes. The freckled skin. Dot's gestures. That mouth.

Larry could not recall any mention of a resemblance to his father. He was his mother's boy. Heir to her body, her intensity, and to her frantic private pleasures and glooms.

But now, twenty-seven and a half years into his life, he found that his father had moved in beneath his bones. That nameless part of his face, the hinged area where the jaw approaches the lower ear – he could see now what his flowing hair had hidden: that his father's genes were alive in his body. Even his earlobes, their fleshiness and color What was that color? A hint of strawberry that spread from the ears up the veins to the cheeks, his father's cheeks, curving and surprisingly soft in a man's hard face.

His father's solid, ruddy presence. It arrived, sudden and shocking, and stayed with him throughout the two weeks of his and Dorrie's honeymoon. He met it each morning in the shaving mirror of the various modest hotels where they stayed. What kind of trick was this? He'd turn his eyes slowly toward the mirror, creeping up on his face, and there the old guy would be, larger and more substantial than a simple genetic flicker. His father's flexible loose skin pressed up against the glass, a fully formed image, yawning, hoisting up his sleepy lids, dressed in his work clothes with the bus factory's insignia on the pocket, *Air-Rider*, his broad shoulders and back bunching forward under Larry's pajamas, and his large red hands reaching out, every finger scarred in one way or another from the upholstery work he did at the plant. And Larry could hear the voice too, his father's high, querulous voice, with the Lancashire notes still in place after twenty-seven years in Canada.

Stu Weller. Master upholsterer. Husband of Dot, father of Midge and Larry.

It was Stu, with Dot's blessing, who had the idea of giving the young couple a package tour of England. A wedding present, gruffly, unceremoniously offered. "We did the same for your sister when she got herself married."

Never mind that Midge and her husband got divorced after two years. That Paul turned out to like men more than women.

Dorrie would have preferred a honeymoon in Los Angeles or maybe Mexico, somewhere hot, a nice hotel on the beach, but how can a person say no to free tickets, everything paid for, the plane fare, plus a twelve-day bus trip, Sunbrite Tours, breakfast and dinner, all the way up to the Pennines, then down to Land's End, the very south-west tip of England, then back to London for the final three days. Stu and Dot had taken a similar package tour a few years back, a twenty-fifth anniversary present to themselves, a "journey back to our roots," as Dot put it, though the real roots for both of them were in the industrial northern town of Bolton, not the green sprawling English countryside.

And when Larry and Dorrie got there it *was* green, unimaginably green – a bright variegated green that made Larry think of Brussels sprouts. Everyone back home had said: What? – you're going to England in March? Are you crazy?

But here they were, carried over England's green hills, ferried down into narrow green valleys, pulling up in the parking lots of green medieval villages where thick-towered castles threw greenish shadows across their squat Sunbrite coach (they had got over their terror of riding along on the left side of the highway with the traffic thundering straight at them).

The tour began in London and headed north-east. Rain, and then episodes of brilliant slanting sunshine accompanied them as they set off, then rain again, pelting the bare trees and hedges, bringing violent, pressing changes of light, as though the day itself was about to offer up an immense idea. They stopped at the picture-postcard town of Saffron Walden, where they were led on a quick march through the old twisted streets and served lunch in a tearoom called the Silken Cat. Dorrie was staunchly brave about the steak and kidney pie, leaving only a few polite scraps on her plate.

"Take notice of these ceiling beams," their guide instructed. His name was Arthur, a stout, broad-faced man, a Londoner with a beer-roughened voice and a school teacher's patient explaining manner. "Late fifteenth century. Possibly earlier."

Dorrie copied this information into a little travel diary she pulled from her purse – "Late 15th century."

Larry found his wife's note-taking touching and also surprising. Where had that diary come from? Its cover was red leather. The narrow ruled pages were edged in gold. One of her girlfriends at Manitoba

Motors must have given it to her, a going-away present, something she wouldn't have thought of herself, not in a million years. It moved him to see his Dorrie in a pose of studentlike concentration, pausing over her choice of words, and keeping her writing neat and small. That she would busy herself recording this chip of historical information – late fifteenth century – record it for *him*, for their life together, stirred a lever of love in his heart.

But he remembered from school that fifteenth century really meant the fourteen-hundreds, how confusing that could be, and he wondered if Dorrie knew the difference and whether he should clarify the point for her. But no. She had already closed the diary and recapped her pen. Looking up at him, catching his eyes on her, she sent a kiss through the air, her small coral lips pushing out.

The first night the tour group was installed in a hotel in Norwich (sixteenth century, more beams) which was said to have been visited on at least one occasion by Edward VII and a "lady friend." There were snowdrops blooming in the hotel's front garden. Flowers in March. This took Larry a moment to register, the impossibility of flowers – but here they were. Back home in Canada it was twenty below zero. "Snowdrops," Dorrie wrote in her diary when she was told what the flowers were called.

"Snowdrops are only the beginning," Arthur told Larry and Dorrie. "You'll be seeing daffodils before we're done."

The tour, it turned out, was only half booked. The other travelers were mostly retired New Zealanders and Australians, and an ancient deaf Romanian couple who never let go of each other's hands. "Everyone's so old," Dorrie whispered to Larry. She had a gift for disappointment, and now she was wrinkling up her face. "Everyone's old and fat except for us."

It was true. Or close to being true. The eighteen passengers, men as well as women, shared the spongy carelessness of flesh that accompanies late middle age. The white permed heads of the wives, their husbands' rosy baldness, framed faces that were, to Larry's eyes at least, remarkably similar, softened, and blurred in outline, with their features melted to a kind of putty.

"I'll bet we're the only ones who screw all night," Dorrie said, looking around. "Or screw at all."

"Probably." He smiled down at her.

"Notice I said screw and not fuck."

"Congratulations. "

"I'm a married woman now. Respectable."

"Ha." Still smiling.

"Ha yourself."

A white-haired husband and wife from Arizona had signed on to the tour. They were in England on their sabbatical leave. She, the wife, pronounced the word "sabbatical" as though the syllables were beads on a string. She explained to Dorrie, who had never heard of a sabbatical, that she and Dr. Edwards, her husband, had been to Thailand "last time" and before that to Berkeley in California. "We see these occasions as opportunities to replenish ourselves every seven years," she said, "and take stock."

* * *

26

The members of the tour group were wakened early each morning in their various freezing hotel rooms by a knock on the door, then Arthur calling out an upbeat "Morning!"

"Oh, God!" Dorrie came up from under the blankets.

Larry, shaving, washing, attempted to avoid his father's eyes in the mirror, that ghostly presence floating beneath the steamed-over surface. He tried, through the lather, to blink the face away, and by the time he was fully dressed, two sweaters plus a jacket, he had mostly succeeded.

Invariably he and Dorrie were the last ones down to the hotel dining room, and every morning they were greeted by the same teasing cries of welcome. "Here come the honeymooners." "Late again." "Hail to the bride and groom!" Dorrie, ducking her head, her mouth puckering up with happiness and embarrassment, slid into a chair, while Larry accepted pats on the back or thumbs-up signs from the men.

There were hot plates of bacon and sausages and egg – although Dorrie, who was feeling "off," made do with tea and toast. After that the tour members took their places on the coach and set off for the day's destination. The New Zealanders and Australians – Heather and Gregory, Joan and Douglas, Marjorie and Brian, Larry never did get all their names straight – preferred to sit near the front of the bus where they bantered genially back and forth, observing silence only when Arthur drew their attention to points of interest. The Romanians sat at the back, the same seat every day. Larry and Dorrie found themselves in the middle of the coach – Dorrie next to the window, taking it as her rightful place since she was shorter than Larry, and because the window seat made her feel less queasy.

Dr. and Mrs. Edwards sat across the aisle from them, their maps and guidebooks spread out on their laps. "We don't want to miss a thing," Mrs. Edwards told them. She had her suspicions about Arthur. He was lazy, she said. He "recited" instead of "interpreting." And he left items off the itinerary, a certain twelfth-century abbey that was definitely starred in their guidebook. She planned to write to Sunbrite's head office about it when she got home.

"Now, now, Sweetheart," Dr. Edwards said, patting her hand.

Dr. Edwards told Larry to call him Robin. He asked Larry what he did professionally, what his "field of endeavor" was. Larry told him about the Flowerfolks chain of florists back in Winnipeg, about how he'd got started in the business by taking a floral arts course at a local college. "Ah, botany!" Dr. Edwards said. "Or would that be horticulture?" He turned his body stiffly toward Larry, awaiting his reply. "A little of each," Larry said, thinking. "But not quite."

Dr. Edwards was a sociologist; population, urban patterns. A perfect dunce in the garden, he told Larry. Didn't know a primrose from a lily. He'd never developed an interest. He hadn't had the leisure. He and Mrs. Edwards lived in an apartment in Tucson, always had, so there wasn't the need. But someday, when he retired, he might look into it. A hobby kind of thing. A person had to keep learning.

"Maybe I should take up sociology as a hobby," Larry said. He meant it as a joke, but Dr. Edwards drew back, startled.

One afternoon the coach came to a halt beside a rutted field, the site of an old Roman town, its houses and temples and public spaces outlined on the grass with flat red bricks. Dorrie sat down on a corner of a house foundation and wrote in her diary: "Second Century." She underlined the entry twice, and looked up at Larry, blankly. He could see it was hard for her to believe that this ruined site had once been a real town bursting with men and women.

She was cold, she told Larry. She'd had enough for one day. More than enough. Later Larry thought of that moment of exhaustion, Dorrie huddled on the foundations of an ancient Roman dwelling, how it seemed to split their honeymoon in two.

They were ushered as the days went by through castles, churches, through stately homes and crumbling tithe barns, and they tramped one morning, in a soft grey rain, along the top of the medieval walls of the city of York. That day, in a vast museum, they looked at coins and furniture and agricultural implements and, spread out in an immense glass case, more than fifty different kinds of scissors for trimming the wicks of lamps. History, it seemed to Larry, left strange details behind, mostly meaningless: odd and foolish gadgets, tools that had become separated from their purpose, whimsical notions, curious turnings, a surprising number of dead ends.

* * *

But it was outdoor England that took Larry by surprise and filled him with a kind of anxiety as the coach traveled further and further north. This anxiety he identified, finally, as a welling up of happiness. The greenness of England. It seemed there was not one part of this island that was not under cultivation, not one piece of land so exposed or unfavorable that something could not be made to take root and grow. Their guide, Arthur, joked that in the city of Leeds the birds wake up coughing, but even there, between the factories and dark smudged houses, Larry glimpsed the winter trunks of oaks and chestnuts. Leafless now, thrust up against smoking chimneys and blackened air, these trees seemed to Larry magisterial presences, rich in dignity and entitlement. He thought, mournfully, of the spindly, skinny poplars back home, the impoverished jack pines and stunted spruce, their slow annual growth in a difficult climate and their lopsided, unlovely shapes.

But it was the hedges of England, even more than the trees, that brought him a sense of wonderment. Such shady density, like an artist's soft pencil, working its way across the English terrain. Why hadn't his parents told him about this astonishing thing they'd grown up with? The hedges were everywhere. Out in the countryside they separated fields from pasture land, snaking up and down the tilted landscape, criss-crossing each other or angling wildly out of sight, dividing one patch of green from another, providing a barrier between cattle and sheep and flocks of geese. These hedges were stock-proof, Arthur explained, meaning sheep couldn't slip through – they were every bit as effective as stone walls or barbed wire, and some of them had roots that were hundreds of years old.

In the towns the clipped hedges served as fences between houses, a stitching of fine green seams, and gave protection and privacy to tiny garden plots. Luxurious and shapely, they seemed pieces of tended sculpture, and now, late in a mild winter, their woody fullness was enveloped by a pale furred cloud of green. Buds in March. It seemed impossible. Young leaves unfolding.

Back home you hardly ever saw a hedge, or if you did it was only common spirea or the weedy, fernlike caragana, which was almost impossible to keep in trim. Larry's father had surrounded the Ella Street house with a chainlink fence, top quality – that was years ago. Like the aluminum siding he'd put on top of the house's old clapboard, it did the job and there was zero upkeep.

"What are all these hedges made of?" Larry asked Arthur, tossing back the hair he didn't have anymore. "I mean, what kind of plants do they use?"

Arthur didn't know. He knew history stuff, he knew his kings and queens, but he was a Londoner. He didn't know green stuff.

In a brilliantly lit bookstore in Manchester Larry found a book about hedges. It was in a bargain bin. Over a hundred colored, badly bound illustrations instructed the reader on the varieties and uses of hornbeam, butcher's broom, laurel, cypress, juniper, lime, white-thorn, privet, holly, hawthorn, yew, dwarf box, and sycamore. How to plant them, how to nourish

31

them, and tricks to keep them trim and tidy. How certain plants can be intertwined with others to make a sturdier or more beautiful hedge; plashing, this artful mixing of varieties was called. Larry studied the pages of *Hedges of England and Scotland* while the coach made its way south, heading toward Devon and Cornwall. In a mere day or two he was able to distinguish from the bus window the various species. This easy mastery surprised him, but then he remembered how he had won the class prize back in his floral arts course, that one of his teachers had commented on his excellent memory and another on his observation skills.

The clues to identifying hedges lay in the density and distribution of thicket, the hue of the green foliage, and the form of the developing leaves. He pronounced the names out loud as he spotted them, and then he wrote them on the inside of the book's cover. He'd forgotten in the last two or three years that he was like this, always wanting to know things he didn't need to know.

Dorrie, seated next to him on the coach, had fallen into the doldrums. She was homesick, she said. And tired of being stuck with all these old biddies. Their teasing at breakfast, always the same old thing, it was getting on her nerves, it was driving her bananas.

Each day was greener than the one before. One morning, halfway through the two-week tour, Arthur leapt from his seat at the front of the coach and excitedly pointed out a long sloping field of daffodils. "Didn't I promise you, ladies and gents, that we'd be seeing daffodils on this holiday! " Everyone crowded to the windows for a look, everyone except for Mrs. Edwards, who was sleeping soundly with her head thrown straight back and her mouth open.

Dorrie pulled her diary out of her purse and wrote a single word on the page: "Daffodils." (Years later when Larry came across the little book, he found three-quarters of the pages empty. "Daffodils" was the final entry.)

On the same day that they saw the daffodils Dr. Edwards bought Larry a pint of beer – this was in a pub early in the evening, a ten minutes' rest stop – and said, out of the blue, "Our sabbatical leave doesn't actually come up for another two years, but Mrs. Edwards has a problem with prescription drugs, also over-the-counter drugs. It's a terrible business and getting worse, and so it seemed a good idea for us to get away."

Larry peered into the remains of his dark foamless beer. He wished he were standing at the other end of the polished bar where the New Zealand and Australian couples were laughing loudly and arguing about how many miles it was to the hotel in Bath. Full of rivalrous good feeling, they liked to joke back and forth, shouting out about the relative merits of kiwis and kangaroos, soccer teams and politics. Larry was drawn to their good spirits, but felt shy in their presence, especially the men with their bluff, hearty conviviality, so different from Dr. Edwards' sly, stiff questioning.

And yet Dr. Edwards, Robin, had seen fit to divulge his unhappy situation to Larry, to a stranger young enough to be his son.

"She hides them. They're so small, you see. The pills. So easy to conceal."

"Is she addicted to them?" This seemed to Larry a foolish, obvious question, but he felt a response of some kind was required.

"Yes, addicted, of course. She can't help herself."

"That's terrible. It must be awfully difficult –"

"It's heartening to see a couple like yourself," Dr. Edwards said, steering the conversation in a more positive direction. "Just starting off in your life, free as a pair of birds."

Larry swallowed down the rest of his beer. "We're going to have a baby," he said. "My wife, I mean."

Dr. Edwards received the news politely: "I see," he said. His fingers twirled a button on his raincoat.

"Maybe you've noticed that she's not feeling all that great," Larry said. "In the mornings especially."

"I hadn't actually noticed."

"Morning sickness."

He and Dorrie had agreed that the baby was going to be a secret, at least until they got back home and told their families. It startled him now to hear the words running so loosely out of his mouth: the baby. He'd scarcely thought of "the baby" since leaving home. It was hard enough to remember he was a husband, much less a father. He had to remind himself, announcing the fact to the mirror every morning as he blinked away the ghost of his father's face. *Husband, husband* – one husband face pushing its way through another, blunt, self-satisfied, but never quite losing its look of surprise.

Lately he'd found he could dispel the face by filling

34

up his head with the greenness of hedgerows. It was like switching channels. Holly, lime, whitethorn, box, a string of names like the chorus of a popular song. He let their shrubby patterns press down on his brain, their smooth stiff dignified shapes and rounded perfection.

"We were going to wait and get married in June. But then – this happened – so here we are. March."

He could see he had lost Dr. Edwards' interest, and certainly the opportunity to offer comforting remarks about Mrs. Edwards' problems.

"Well," Dr. Edwards said. He spoke briskly now, more like a sportscaster than a sociology teacher. "Time we got back on the coach or we'll be left behind."

"We've been going together for over a year," Larry explained. He hung on to his beer glass. "We'd already talked about marriage. We'd already made up our minds, so this didn't make any real difference."

Dr. Edwards' face had pulled into a frown. He put his hand on Larry's shoulder, bearing down heavily with his fingertips. "About my wife?" he said. "I'd appreciate it if you regarded what I said as confidential."

"Why? " Dorrie yelled at Larry. "Why would you go and tell that old professor jerk about us?"

They were in Devon, in the town of Barnstable, the King's Inn. Their room was at the front of the hotel overlooking a street of busy shops.

"I don't know," Larry said.

"We fucking decided we weren't going to tell anyone. And don't tell me not to say fuck. I'll say fuck all I fucking want."

"It just came out. We were talking, and it slipped out."

"My mother doesn't even know. My own mother. And you had to go and tell that jerk. Did you honestly think he wasn't going to tell that snot of a wife? My 'condition' she said to me, I shouldn't be having a beer in my 'condition.' And now the whole bus is going to know. I'll bet you anything they already do."

"What does it matter?"

"We're on our honeymoon, that's why it matters. We're the lovey-dovey honeymooners, for God's sake, only now the little bride person is pregnant."

"No one even thinks like that anymore."

"Oh yeah? What about your mother and father? They think like that."

"How do you know what they think?"

"They think no one's good enough for their precious little Larry, that's what they think. Especially girls dumb enough to go and get themselves preggo."

"They'll get used to it."

"Like it's my fault. Like you didn't have one little thing to do with it, right?" She sank down on the bed, moaning, her head rolling back and forth. "I can just see your dad looking at me. That look of his, oh boy. Like don't I have any brains? Like why wasn't I on the pill?"

"We'll tell them as soon as we get back. It'll take them a day or two, that's all. Then they'll get used to it."

She turned and gave him a shrewd look. "What about you? When are you going to get used to it?"

"I am used to it."

"Oh yeah, sure. I'm like sitting there on the bus, day

after day, thinking up names. Girls' names. Boys' names. That's what's in my head. I like Victoria for a girl. For a boy I like Troy. Those kinds of thoughts. And you're jumping up and down looking at bushes. Writing them down. That's all you care about. Goddamn fucking bushes."

He pulled her close to him, rocking her back and forth, patting her hair.

Startled, he recognized that pat, its cruel economy and monumental detachment. It was the sign of someone who was distracted, weary. A husband's pat. He'd seen his father touch his mother in exactly the same way when she fell into one of her blue days. Only patting wasn't really the same thing as touching. Patting a person was like going on automatic pilot, you just reached out and did it. There, there. Looking covertly at his watch. Almost dinnertime. Pat, stroke, pat.

It calmed her. She collapsed against him. They lay back on the bed, hanging on to each other limply and not saying anything. In ten minutes it would be time to go down to the dining room. He was ravenous.

A single day remained – and one more major historical site to take in: Hampton Court.

"This palace is unrivaled," Arthur said, gathering his charges in a tight circle around him, "for its high state of preservation." He pointed out Anne Boleyn's Gateway, the Astronomical Clock (electrified two years ago), the Great Hall, the Fountain Court, the Chapel Royal with its intricately carved roof. "Note the quality of the workmanship," he said. "What you behold is a monument to the finest artists and artisans in the land."

The members of the tour group had taken up a collection, and the evening before they'd presented Arthur with a set of silver cufflinks. He had blinked when he opened the jeweler's box, blinked and looked up into their waiting faces. "For he's a jolly good fellow," one of the Australians sang out, trying to get a round going. The man's name was Brian. He was large, kindly, and elegantly bald. It was he who had taken up the collection for Arthur and passed around a thank-you card for everyone to sign. But he launched the song in a faltering key that no one could follow.

Surprisingly, it was Dorrie who moved forward and picked up the melody, drawing in the others with her strong, clear voice. She came from a musical family; her father sang baritone with the Police Chorale; her mother, after a few drinks, belted out a torchy rendition of "You Light Up My Life." And Dorrie's voice, despite her size, a mere one hundred pounds, was true and forceful.

> For he's a jolly good fellow
> Which nobody can deny.

At that moment Larry loved her terribly. His helpless Dorrie. He froze the frame in his mind. This was something he needed to remember. The upward tilt of her chin as she risked a minor feat of descant on the final words. The way her hands curled inside her raincoat pockets, plunging straight forward into a second chorus, as though she'd been anointed, for a brief second or two, Miss Harmony of Sunbrite Tours.

Mrs. Edwards had wondered aloud about the appropriateness of cufflinks for Arthur. "He doesn't look like a man who is particularly intimate with French cuffs," she whispered to her husband and to Larry and Dorrie. But this morning, following Arthur into Hampton Court gardens, Larry glimpsed a flash of silver at Arthur's wrist. "Before you," Arthur said, pointing, "is the oldest surviving hedge maze in England."

A what? Larry had never heard of a hedge maze.

"We've got three-quarters of an hour," Arthur announced in his jolly voice. "If you get lost, just give us a shout and we'll come and rescue you."

Later, Larry memorized the formula for getting through the maze. He could recite it easily for anyone who cared to listen. Turn left as you enter the maze, then right, right again, then left, left, left and yet another left. That brings you to the centre. To get out, you unwind, turning right, then three more rights, then a left at the next two turnings, and you're home free.

But on the day he first visited the Hampton Court maze, March 24, 1978, a young, untraveled floral designer from the middle of Canada, the newly married husband of Dorrie Shaw who was four months pregnant with his son Ryan – on that day he took every wrong turning. He was, in fact, the last of the tour group to come stumbling out of the maze's exit.

Dorrie in her perky blue raincoat was standing, waiting. "We were worried," she said to him crossly. Then, "You look dizzy."

It was true. The interior of the maze *had* made him dizzy. It was very early in the morning, a frosty day, so cold he could see his breath as it left his mouth and widened out in the air. It seemed a wonder that the tender needlelike leaves could withstand such cold. The green walls rose about him, too high to see over. Who would have expected such height and density? And he hadn't anticipated the sensation of feeling unplugged from the world or the heightened state of panicked awareness that was, nevertheless, re-pairable. Without thinking, he had slowed his pace, falling behind the others, willing himself to be lost, to be alone. He could see Mrs. Edwards ahead of him on the narrow path, walking side by side with Dorrie, their heads together, talking, and Mr. Edwards following close behind. Larry watched the three of them take a right-hand turn and disappear behind a bank of foliage.

He wondered exactly how lost a person could get. Lost at sea, lost in the woods. Fatally lost.

"You look lost in thought," Vivian had said to him on his last day at Flowerfolks, the day before he and Dorrie were married. He had been in the back of the store, staring into a blaze of dyed blue carnations. "I was just thinking," he told her, and she had floated him a lazy smile. "Communing with the merchandise?" she said, touching the sleeve of his jacket. "I do it all the time."

He had been reflecting, while staring at the fringed blue petals, about love, about the long steady way his imperfect parents managed to love each other, and about his own deficient love for Dorrie, how it came and went, how he kept finding it and losing it again.

And now, here in this garden maze, getting lost, and then found, seemed the whole point, that and the moment of willed abandonment, the unexpected rapture of being blindly led.

In the distance he could hear a larky Australian accented voice – one of their own group – calling "This way, this way." He shrank from the sound, its pulsating jollity, wanting to push deeper and deeper into the thicket and surrender himself to the maze's cunning, this closed, expensive contrivance. He observed how his feet chose each wrong turning, working against his navigational instincts, circling and repeating, and bringing on a feverish detachment. Someone older than himself paced inside his body, someone stronger too, cut loose from the common bonds of sex, of responsibility. Looking back he would remember a brief moment when time felt mute and motionless. This hour of solitary wandering seemed a gift, and part of the gift was an old greedy grammar flapping in his ears: lost, more lost, utterly lost. He felt the fourteen days of his marriage collapsing backward and becoming an invented artifact, a curved space he must learn to fit into. Love was not protected. No, it wasn't. It sat out in the open like anything else.

Forty-five minutes, Arthur had given them. But Larry Weller had lingered inside the green walls for a full hour.

"We were worried," Dorrie said. Scolding.

He followed her into the coach for the ride back to London. "How could you get yourself so lost?" she kept asking. The next day they boarded a plane that carried them across a wide ocean, then over the immense empty stretches of Labrador and the sunlit cities and villages of Ontario, an endless afternoon of flight. Frozen lakes and woodlands spread beneath them, thinning finally, flattening out to a corridor of snow-covered fields and then the dark knowable labyrinth of tangled roadways and rooftops and clouds of cold air rising up to greet them.

A sweet soprano bell dinged for attention. Seat belts buckled, tables up, the landing gear grinding down, a small suite of engineering miracles carefully sequenced. Dorrie gave Larry's hand an excited, distracted squeeze that said: almost home. They were about to be matter-of-factly claimed by familiar streets and houses and the life they'd chosen or which had chosen them.

Departures and arrivals: he didn't know it then, but these two forces would form the twin bolts of his existence – as would the brief moments of clarity that rose up in between, offering stillness. A suspension of breath. His life held in his own hands.

CHAPTER THREE

Larry's Folks
1980

Shortly before Larry's thirtieth birthday he managed to get enough money together for a down payment on a small house over on Lipton Street, a handyman special, just five rooms and a glassed-in front porch, and now he spends most evenings and weekends working on it. He and his wife, Dorrie, moved in two months ago, and ever since then she's been after him to lay new tiles in the kitchen, and after that there's the bathroom fixtures to replace, and maybe some ceiling insulation before winter comes along. A list as long as your arm. But this summer Larry's been using every spare minute to work on the yard, sometimes with the help of his friend Bill Herschel, but more often alone. Might as well do it while the weather's still good, Larry says. And he wants the whole yard closed in so Ryan can play out there next spring, unsupervised.

He'd be working at it today, only his folks have invited him and Dorrie and the baby over for the birthday festivities. Sunday dinner, opening his presents from the family, blowing out the candles, the usual. It's 1980; he's about to enter the decade of decadence, only he doesn't know that yet, no one does; he only knows he feels the good hum of almost continuous anticipation in his chest, even though Dorrie griped all the way over to his folks' place about how they were probably going to have a hot dinner, gravy and everything, when here it was, the bitch end of a sizzling day. Her own idea of hot weather fare is a big bowl of ice-cream and a glass of iced tea.

A brutal bored silence had fallen between them these last weeks.

A mere three years ago he was a young buck walking down a Winnipeg street in his shirt-sleeves. He remembers how that felt, no wife, no kid, no house, no yard. Now the whole picture's changed, but that's okay, especially his kid, Ryan. Another thing: he's supposed to be sunk in gloom at the thought of turning thirty, but he isn't. He's unique and mortal, he knows that, and he's got this sweet little babe of a house, and a yard that's slowly taking shape, all its corners filling up with transplanted shrubs from the wholesaler down in Carmen. There're some flowers too, and a few sweet peppers, but it's mainly the shrubs he loves. Dorrie keeps calling them bushes, and he keeps having to correct her. "You've got shrub mania," she says, but her lips smile when she's saying it. "You want to be the shrub king of the universe."

Maybe it's true. Maybe he wants to make his yard a real shrub showplace. Somewhere Larry's heard that almost everyone in the world is allowed one minute of fame in their lives, or maybe that's one hour.

Stu Weller, Larry's dad, got written up once in the weekend section of the *Winnipeg Tribune* on the subject of his corkscrew and bottle-opener collection, which included 600 items at the time of the interview, and has almost doubled since. Larry's older sister, Midge, won a thousand dollars last year in the art gallery raffle – enough for a trip to Hawaii with a girlfriend – and she actually appeared on Channel 13 talking about how surprised she was, and how she didn't usually waste money on raffle tickets unless it was for a good cause like expanding the gallery's exhibition space or something.

Larry's own moment of fame is still some years in the future, and that's fine with him. He's got enough on his mind these days, his young family – Dorrie, little Ryan – and his job at Flowerfolks, and his current preoccupation with transforming his yard. As for his mother, Dot, she's had enough celebrity for a lifetime. Don't even talk to her about being famous, especially not the kind of fame that comes boiling out of ignorance, and haunts you for the rest of your life. Dumb Dot. Careless Dot. Dot the murderer. Of course, that was a long time ago.

When Larry was a little kid his mother warned him about the dangers of public drinking fountains. "No one ever, ever puts their mouth right on the spout," she said, "because they can pick up other people's germs, and who knows what kind of disease you'll get."

This was bad news for Larry. At that age he liked to stand on tiptoe and press his lips directly on the cool silvery water spout, rather than trying to catch the spray in his mouth as it looped unpredictably upward.

Besides, his mother's caution didn't make sense, since if no one ever touched the spout, how could there be any germs? He recalls – he must have been six or seven at the time – that he presented this piece of logic to his mother, but she only shook her headful of squashed curls and said sadly, wisely, "There will always be people in this world who don't know any better."

He pictured these people – the people who didn't know any better – as a race of clumsy unfortunates, and according to his mother there were plenty of them living right here on Ella Street in Winnipeg's West End: those people who mowed their lawns but failed to rake up the clippings, for instance. People who didn't know any better stored cake flour and other staples in their original paper bags so that their cupboards swarmed with ants and beetles. They never got around to replacing the crumbling rubber-backed placemats from the Lake of the Woods with "The Story of Wood Pulp" stamped in the middle. That was the problem with people who didn't know any better: they never threw things away, not even their stained tea-towels, not even their oven mitts with holes burnt right through the fingers.

People who didn't know any better actually ate the coleslaw that came with their hamburgers, poking it out of those miniature pleated paper cups with their stabbing forks. Someone, their well-meaning mothers probably, told them they should eat any and all green vegetables that were put in front of them, not that there's anything very green about coleslaw, especially when it's been sitting in a puddle of wet salad dressing and improperly refrigerated for heaven only knows how many days. These people have never heard of the word salmonella, or if they have, they probably can't pronounce it.

Whereas Dot (Dorothy) Woolsey Weller, wife of Stu Weller, mother of Larry and Midge, grandmother of Ryan, knows about food poisoning intimately, tragically. She was, early in her life, an ignorant and careless person, one of those very people who didn't know any better and who will never be allowed, now, to forget her lack of knowledge. She's obliged to remember every day, either for a fleeting moment – her good days – or for long suffering afternoons of gloom. "Your mother's got a nip of the blues today," Stu Weller used to tell his kids while they were growing up in the Ella Street house, and they knew what that meant. There sat their mother at the kitchen table, again, still in her chenille robe, again, when they got home from school, her hands rubbing back and forth across her face, and her eyes blank and glassy, reliving her single terrifying act of infamy.

Even today, August 17th, her son's thirtieth birthday, she's remembering. Larry knows the signs. It's five-thirty on a Sunday afternoon, and there she is, high-rumped and perspiring in her creased cotton sundress, busying herself in the kitchen, setting the dinner plates on top of the stove to warm, as if they weren't already hot from being in a hot kitchen. She's peering into the oven at the bubbling casserole, and she's floating back and forth, fridge to counter, counter to sink. Her large airy gestures seem to have

47

sprung not from her life as wife and mother, but from a sunny, creamy, abundant girlhood, which Larry doubts she ever had. She smiles and she chats and she even flirts a little with her thirty-year-old son, who looks on, a bottle of cold beer in his hand, but he knows the old warnings. Her jittery detachment gives her away. She picks up a jar of pickles and bangs it hard on the breadboard to loosen the lid. She's thinking and fretting and knowing and feeling sick with the poison of memory.

This my mother, Larry thinks, my sad soft mother. Most of her life has involved the absorbing of her grievous history, of trying to go forward when all this *heaviness* lies inside. One ancient mistake, one hour gone wrong, and now she pays and pays.

She's a housewife, Larry's mother, a maker of custard sauce, a knitter of scarves, a fervent keeper of baby pictures and family scrapbooks, but this is her real work: sorrowing, remembering. The loose shuttle of her pain flies back and forth so that sometimes she seems just fine, just like anyone else's mother. Today she's made Larry a lemon meringue pie for his birthday instead of a cake; she could have made it yesterday and kept it on the top shelf of the fridge just under the freezer section, but with *her* history she wouldn't dream of taking a chance like that, and who could blame her? Her anxieties about food are built into the Weller family chronicle – as is Larry's passion for lemon meringue pie. Dot makes her son a big one every year on his birthday, with a circle of birthday candles poking up through the golden-tipped meringue. A sight to behold.

There'll be Lancashire hotpot too, that's what's bubbling away in the oven right now. It's a simple oldtime recipe that Dot's mother used to make on Saturday nights back in England: chunks of stewing lamb arranged across the bottom of a Pyrex casserole, then a layer of sliced potatoes, another of carrots, then more lamb, and all this topped with a handful of finely diced onions. Next you add plenty of salt, pepper, and parsley flakes, and a cup of Oxo, and bake covered for an hour and a half. Larry's crazy about Lancashire hotpot, or at least he pretends he is, for the sake of his sad and perpetually grieving and remembering mother. Mum, he calls her; he always has. Americans say Mom or Ma. People in movies and books say Mother.

She's set the dropleaf table in the living room for six, her best damask cloth and the good cutlery and china. There'll be just the family, her loved ones, as she likes to call them, as though they were characters out of an obituary – her husband Stu, Larry, Dorrie, and little Ryan in his booster seat. Her daughter Midge is coming too, but here it is, almost time to sit down at the table, and she hasn't turned up yet. Three years ago Midge kicked her husband out after receiving an anonymous note saying that Paul frequented a certain gay bar, and now she swears she's never going to get married again. She says, with her eyes rolling upward, that she knew something was funny-bunny about him from day one.

Larry worries about his mum. She's not getting out enough lately, hardly at all in fact, unless you call a trip to Sears' mattress sale "getting out." It also worries Larry that his mother frets so much about other people. She worries about Midge, that at the age of thirty-two she's starting to get bitter, always sounding off like a regular women's libber, going on marches and so forth. She also worries about Larry and Dorrie, the way they're half the time bickering, and Dorrie working full-time for Manitoba Motors instead of staying home with Ryan, who's still in diapers at twenty-three months, and she worries about her husband who right this minute is in the bedroom putting on a clean sports shirt because she nagged him into it, and is in a bad mood. As a matter of fact, he's done nothing but grumble all day, the heat, the mosquitoes, his lower back pain, not enough sugar in his afternoon coffee, the mess in the backyard because of the compost pile Larry's talked him into, and now having to eat at the dropleaf table in the living room instead of the kitchen nook. So far he hasn't even said happy birthday to Larry, to his own son.

She checks the oven, looks at the clock, glances out the kitchen window to see if Midge's car is coming down the back lane. Where is that girl? Next she pours boiling water over the silver pie server in case of lurking germs, then sets it on a paper towel to dry. Immaculate. So's the speckled linoleum. So is Dot's cutlery drawer. In this house you would never see a tea-bag tossed wet and leaking into the sink, or a pile of coffee grounds. People who let a skin of mold accumulate on the hem of their shower curtain are not her kind of people. This is a woman who carries her meat home from the butcher's and washes it at the sink. Larry is watching her rinse her hands under the tap, and at the same time he's kicking his foot against the table leg the way he used to do when he was little. The upholstered breakfast nook where he sits has the wiped hygienic smell of on old marriage. He's blowing a little tune into his empty beer bottle.

Is there room in the tilting, rotating world for a thirty-year-old man who sits blowing into a bottle? He thinks this, and so does his mother, who reaches over and takes it from him, not so much with tan air of rebuke as with resolution, and places it under the counter. What deprivation, her expression asks, what injury has stalled her son at the age of thirty? Something's been subtracted too soon, but what? And is it her fault?

Of course it's her fault.

Worry, worry, a circle of worry. And these are her loved ones, these five. Her grumbling husband, her errant daughter, her baffling son, and in the living room her daughter-in-law Dorrie, whose neatness of body, whose sharpness of eye and chin and shoulder, is bent over the weekend paper, scouting the ads and cutting out dollars-off coupons, while little Ryan sits on the floor and plays with the paper scraps, tearing them into tiny flakes. This small and insufficient family. This is all Larry's mother's got to cushion her against the damage of her own life.

The history of Dot Weller, and how she killed her mother-in-law, came to Larry in small pieces, by installments as it were. He can't remember a time when he didn't know at least part of the story, and he's not sure, in fact, if he's ever been presented with a full account, start to finish, all at once.

In one of his mother's albums there's an old photograph of Larry himself taken at nine months. Little Larry wearing a white smocked nightgown is wedged into an old-fashioned wooden highchair which for some reason has been carried out of doors. Blurred trees and a suggestion of lawn fill in a background lit with a glare of ominous light that falls across the infant's fine frizz of hair and on to the glossy wood of the chair. Can a head think when it's that size? Can a baby's face be this wise and unfoolable? His hands, which look like nothing so much as a pair of crimped shells, gripping the edge of the highchair's tray, and his expression is pulled into a knit of absorbed anguish. He can't possibly know at this age, or can he, that a calamity has occurred in his mother's life? And yet, the comprehending orbits of his soft eyes, the small roundness of his mouth, already hold a full level of bruising knowledge. He has a mother who cries in her sleep. A mother who's missing the kind of cold, saving curiosity that would hold her steady after a tragic event and whose contagion of grief has spread to him. Through her milk, through her skin and fingertips.

Or it may have been, in the beginning, no more than a series of silences that accrued around certain topics, which in the life of his mother could not be approached openly. Looking back, Larry seems almost certain that the story, when it came, was presented through the agency of intense whispering toneless voices – but whose? his father's? his sister's?

– and that behind the recital of events lay a sense of driving urgency: this was information that he was going to need in order to live in the Weller family, in order to walk around in the world. The calamity that occurred in the autumn of 1949, one year before he was born, was inescapable, housed as it was in the walls like a layer of formaldehyde insulation, an always present, tightly lashed narrative embracing everyone who lived under the family roof. And so Larry knows his mother's suffering. He's always known it, filling in around the known bits with his imagination. He would like to put his arms around her, and she would like this too. But he doesn't know where to begin, doesn't know if she knows that he knows or how much he knows or what weight he attaches to it. So he's silent and she's silent. He sits fiddling with his beer bottle, until it's firmly taken from him, and she checks the clock for the umpteenth time, as if each ticking minute places an extra weight on her sadness.

Dot Weller was twenty-five years old at the time of the accident and married to young Stu Weller who worked as an upholsterer for British Railways in the northern town of Bolton. Their infant daughter Midge, short for Marjorie, had just taken her first steps, a happy little kid tottering from chair to chair, and chortling in tune with her acrobatic daring. The most contented baby in the world, everyone said. A perfect sweetie.

The family lived in a newish council house, four airy rooms and a tiny garden where in the summer Dot grew lettuce, radishes, carrots, blackcurrants, and a wavy row of runner beans. She would have preferred a patch of fine lawn and a bed of flowers – she was partial to lupines – but an anxious, learned frugality kept her concentration on what she and Stu and baby Midge could consume. The blackcurrants she made into a rather sour jam, since sugar was still rationed and hard to come by, and the runner beans she stewed up and preserved in sealed jars. This made her happy, gazing at her row of bottled fruit and vegetables, twelve pints in all, the beans blue-green in colour, gleaming from the pantry shelf.

Stu was down at the Works six days a week, but on Sundays he stayed at home and made morning tea for his pretty young wife and himself. The least he could do, he liked to say. He tossed little Midge in the air, read the *Sunday Mirror* straight through, and cleaned out the grates, and just before noon went up the road to the pub for a quick gin and tonic, which he fancied in those days to be a gentleman's drink. After that he and Dot and their little dumpling of a daughter boarded a bus and crossed town to where his mother and dad lived in their two-up, two-down, and where a Sunday joint awaited them. These were happy days. Each of them felt the privilege of it. "But they ought to come to *us* for Sunday dinner the odd time," Dot said. "It isn't right, your mother doing all the work."

She prevailed on them, and at last they agreed. The Sunday journey was reversed, Mum and Dad Weller crossing town one late October morning on the number 16 bus and arriving at the door drenched from cold rain, but cheerful, and ready for a hot meal. There was roast beef and mash and gravy, and a choice of

Brussels sprouts or runner beans. There was horse-radish sauce served in a little sweet-dish, a wedding gift. And for pudding a homemade sponge topped with golden syrup.

It was a blessing, people said afterward, that they didn't all choose beans over sprouts. Only Mum Weller helped herself, and rather generously, to the beans. "And Dot here's the one who bottled them," said Stu, the proud young husband. "Have a little more, Mum, you haven't made but half a dent."

An hour later, drinking a cup of tea, the old woman complained of double vision, of having trouble swallowing. Nevertheless, Stu and his father bundled a sleepy Midge into her pram and wandered off to the stretch of waste ground by the railway yards, leaving Dot alone with her distressed mother-in-law. Dot offered more tea, but it was waved away. She produced a hot-water bottle and a blanket to fold over her mother-in-law's trunky knees. Mum Weller rocked back and forth a few times, then groaned suddenly, and fell forward with a crash on to the hearth rug, her head missing by an inch the metal fender. Dot ran to her side, kneeling on the rug. Mother Weller's head was twisted grotesquely to one side, and her face held a look of throttled purple. Dot remembers crying out, but doesn't know what she said. (Probably *help*, *help*, but who was there to help?) And then she passed her hand back and forth before the dead woman's eyes.

She was indeed dead. The young Dot had never seen a dead person, but she knew this bulky presence on her floor had passed to the other side, as folks said back then. There she lay, face down on the ash-strewn carpet, a heavy woman, stiffly corseted, and padded with layer upon layer of woolen clothes, her checked skirt immense across her buttocks and her knitted jumper rucked up. Her hips and calves were bunched clumsy and lifeless as meat beneath her, and the pink edge of her knickers obscenely revealed. A queerish smell of rubbish rose from the body. *It can't be, it can't be*, Dot remembers thinking as she tugged at the inert figure, its solid, unmovable heft. Then a thought occurred to her: heart attack. The words formed in her head, bringing a rush of relief – so this is what happened! – and, even in the midst of her comprehension, she experienced a whiff, no more, of shameful self-congratulations, for she had recognised and named the phantom before her. She had been witness, moreover, to one of the body's great dramas.

But it wasn't a heart attack that brought on her mother-in-law's cataclysmic end. Oh, if only it had been, if only! Mum Weller's death – as was revealed later through laboratory testing – was caused by severe type C botulism. The source of the botulism was Dot's stewed runner beans, inadequately sealed, insufficiently heated – the same beans that had been standing in their pretty glass jar for the last two months, as purely green and sweet as innocence itself.

Dot Weller is fifty-six now, and her husband Stu fifty-eight. Stu's parents died in their mid-fifties, his mother from the botulism, and his father, two years later, from rage – though the death notice specified a massive stroke. His rage, closer to biblical wrath, had bloomed into existence on that terrible Sunday when

56

his wife fell dead on the hearth rug, poisoned by her stupid imbecile of a daughter-in-law. Murder was the word Dad Weller used. Even, *deliberate* murder. He said as much to the reporter from the *Manchester Evening News* who sent a photographer to take a picture of the Wellers' garden, catching in one corner the dark row of beans that had been the agent of evil. There was no reasoning with him, although he'd been all his life a reasonable man. His world had been cleft in two by calamity, and he refused to put down the finger of blame.

In the end that blaming finger drove Stu straight to the immigration office in Stockport, and soon after he brought his pregnant wife and child to Canada where, in fact, thousands of other English workers headed in the late forties. There were factory jobs to be had in Winnipeg. It was possible to aspire to a house and garden of one's own, to buy a car in time, a washing machine, a refrigerator, to make a better life for the kids. And to escape the sourness of ugly scenes and family angers. When news came that the old man had died of a stroke, Stu didn't trouble himself to go home for the funeral.

Larry knows the poison episode in all its tragic rhythms and reverberations. This is what it's like to grow up with a bad chapter of someone else's story, in the toxic glow of someone else's guilt, a guilt that became a rooted sorrow. He's had his fingers in the mouth of his mother's sick grief and now it's his; every crease and fold belong to him. He knows about the offered cup of tea and the hot-water bottle; his ears can hear the precise sound of the body thudding on the hearth rug; he sees the inky photograph in the newspaper and its headline: "Bolton Woman Poisons Mother-in-Law." All this has entered the doors and windows of his childhood, without his really noticing. It was simply – there. Like the oxygen he breathed. Like a banked fire. And he can imagine even his mother's most covert thoughts, that which could never be said: thank God little Midge refused the beans. And even: thank God I passed them up myself.

And for Larry, who was born just two months after his parents settled in Winnipeg, the flight from the home country has the flavor of Old Testament exodus. He finds it hard to believe. He looks at his solid, slow-moving parents and tries to imagine the force that urged them to gather up their possessions and voyage, sight unseen, to a new country. They were eight days on a rusty Greek liner, then three days by train to Manitoba. Dot Weller was sick every mile of the way, and she must have looked back over her shoulder more than once and wondered what she'd left behind and why. Catastrophe drove them out, catastrophe coupled with guilt that was cut like an incision on his mother's brain. How were they to survive in the heat of a parent's punishing anger?

When Larry thinks about his folks, this is the piece of their life he can never quite take in: that his father, out of love, out of the wish to protect his wife, would uproot himself, and turn his back on a guaranteed job, a snug house, his weekly gin and tonic, and all that was familiar, that he might have elected freedom or forgetfulness, but instead chose to witness his wife's plodding, painful, affectless search for that thing that would pass as forgiveness. Larry glimpses something heroic at the heart of his obstinate and embarrassing father, who rescued his young wife, who stood by her. Stu Weller is a man who, without a gobbet of doubt, believes in bringing back the death penalty. He rattles on about welfare bums, and sometimes refers to blacks as nig-nogs, and maintains, somewhat illogically, that queers ought to be sterilised, the whole lot of them. Which is why it surprises Larry that his father has committed so manly and self-sacrificing an act, and he asks himself whether he could do the same for his wife Dorrie. Probably not. He admits his love will never be as pure as his father's, and certainly not as good as the scripted golden love in his head.

Not that his parents, Stu and Dot, managed to blot out all recollection of the tragedy, far from it. Anything, even after all these years, will trip a switch in Dot's head: the mention of Bolton, of food poisoning, of home preserving, of sponge cake, a reference to mothers-in-law, to hearth rugs, the specter of sudden death, the word beans – above all, the word beans, a substance banned from the Weller household and never, never spoken of. In all Larry's thirty years he has not once tasted that treasonous vegetable.

Stu Weller loves his job. For thirty years now he's worked as an upholsterer for a custom coach company in south Winnipeg, the largest of its kind in North America. He left school at fourteen, as soon as he legally could, and went straight on to the railways where he learned his trade. Right away he took to it, and it's served him well. Switching from trains to buses, when coming to Canada, was easier than falling off a log, and he's worked on some real beauties. A custom coach is a handmade object, that's something most people don't appreciate. You take a few basic sheets of metal, cut them, bend them, twist them, apply bracing and rivets, and there you've got something entirely different. Everything but the motor is built right on the Air-Rider factory floor, even the fuel tanks, even the decorative touches, which is where Stu Weller comes in.

It's a fact that some of North America's biggest and brightest names in the entertainment industry have ordered customized vehicles from Air-Rider, wondrous rolling homes and offices with white carpeting on the walls and Italian marble for flooring. A country-and-western singer – after a beer or two Stu Weller will drop the odd hint about who exactly this singer is – custom ordered a model with a bathroom floor that dropped open, bingo, to reveal a hot tub where the luggage compartment generally goes. A cool half-million dollars for that package. This same coach possessed a full kitchen with oak inlay cupboards and a hidden berth for the traveling cook. Last year Stu did the upholstery for a hospital coach, a traveling clinic for rural areas, and now he's working on a coach for relocating prisoners, each seat transformed into a separate little jail cell with bars going right up to the ceiling. Slash-proof vinyl is what he's installing at the moment, and the barest minimum of padding. Every order brings a new challenge. The floor supervisor always takes him aside and says,

"Look, Stu, you're the one with the experience. We need to have your particular expertise on this design."

On weekends Stu Weller naps or creeps around the house, waiting for Monday morning to come. His hands understand the secrets of foam and spring and frame, how to make the under-structure invisible and at the same time strong. There's a wide range of fabrics at his disposal, your velvets, your brocades, your suedes and leathers. For the president of an American television network he covered the coach walls with a shimmering mauve satin, and received a personal handwritten letter of thanks and appreciation. Next in the works is a special chapel coach for a well-known TV evangelist, and Stu's planning to go heavy on plum-colored velour and white leather for the doors that separate the public part of the unit from the private. He's learned that people are willing to spend money for quality; they want the best materials and they're looking for top-notch workmanship. Over the years he's been offered jobs in a number of Winnipeg's better upholstery houses, but he's never considered them for a minute. He knows the custom coach business inside and out, and can't imagine working all day on mere furniture, on simple sofas or chairs.

Of course, he's not above a weekend project at home. The breakfast nook in the kitchen, built in the early seventies, is his own design, a curving red vinyl bench with bright brass tacking. Smart, modern, comfortable. And last summer he took apart the livingroom couch, reglued the frame and reupholstered it in a midnight-blue textured nylon. Visitors to the house think they're seeing a brand-new piece of furniture. His wedding gift to Larry and Dorrie was a trip to England plus a first-class upholstery job on an old Hide-a-bed Larry had picked up at a garage sale. It looks good, too, done up in one of those abstract prints that're all the rage now, and it's Scotchguarded so that when Dorrie leaves one of Ryan's messed diapers lying around, as she tends to do, there's not too much damage.

He's offered to do another upholstery job for Larry's thirtieth. He could do a padded headboard, he suggested, in artificial leather, but Larry said no, he'd rather have a couple of loads of good topsoil for the yard. Well, if that's what the kid wants, that's what he gets. Christ Jesus. Dirt.

From the way Stu's scratching his shirt-collar you can tell he can't quite believe he's got a son who's thirty years old today. He doesn't, it seems, know what to make of his son and his slapdash wife (Dorrie, Dor, Dorable) and Larry's funny-bunny ideas about hiking and the environment and planting shrub "arrange-ments" in his yard and working in a florist shop year after year, fussing with little leaves and flowers all day long. But he keeps his mouth shut. The last thing Stu wants is a fight.

His son calls him Dad or Da; in return he calls Larry nothing, just *you*. Neither of them can remember when this started, but Larry recognizes his no-name status as a temporary form of shyness on his father's part; ha! temporary for life. But shyness is all it amounts to. After all, his dad lent him money for his down payment, didn't he? And he had a load of top-quality topsoil delivered to Larry's house yesterday morning before Larry and Dorrie were even out of bed.

Six o'clock. Larry's folks always sit down for supper at six sharp, even when it's a special occasion like today, and even though Midge hasn't turned up or had the courtesy to telephone. The drapes have been pulled shut all day to keep the heat down, and the light seeping into the living room is the color of dusty amber. It's crowded with the table pulled out and with having to squeeze in extra chairs and the hot dishes lined up on the sideboard. Little Ryan starts making a fuss, grabbing at the tablecloth, and Dot frets about him knocking over the glass dish of pickled onions. She's really worried about death, that her table of carefully prepared food will bring damage, not nourishment, to those she loves best in the world. "Sit down, Mum," Larry says, as he pulls out her chair – a rare gesture in this house, an unbelievable gesture – and helps her to settle comfortably. He'd like to lean over and touch his cheek to the top of her freshly combed hair. "Well," she says looking around, "pick up your forks, everyone."

At that moment Midge in shorts and an orange and pink T-shirt bursts through the back door, her car keys jingling from the fingers of one hand, a bag of dinner rolls in the other, her contribution. She drops the rolls in the center of the table, still in their plastic Safeway bag. The next minute she's dragging in an immense unwieldy wrapped parcel which is a birthday present for her brother, but which won't be opened until after dessert, after the candles are blown out and the pie consumed. Larry already knows it will be something for the yard, a piece of gardening equipment or an exotic plant maybe. His sister has always known how to read him. Mits, he calls her, or Mit-Brain or Pigeon.

She takes her place at the table, squeezing in between her mother and Dorrie, waving her arms. She's steaming with a jumble of excuses and fresh news, as well as with the humid heat of the day. Sorry, sorry, sorry, everyone, she says, but she's been away all weekend to an anger workshop at a Gimli resort. Two hundred women took part. If you signed up early you got ten percent off, but she only heard of it on Friday afternoon, so she knocked off work early, said she had a headache, then packed up the car and hit the road. No time to phone, just a spur of the moment thing, an opportunity she couldn't pass up. There was an anger workshop leader up from the States. Yeah, really, that's her specialty. What a woman! Gray hair down to her waist, barefoot, and she's got a PhD in something or other, she's a doctor, that's her title, travels all over the place, writes books, gives lectures, TV talk shows, Phil Donahue and so forth. Holler it out, that's what she demands of her anger groups. Scream, yell, weep till you pee, hang on to each other. Tell your story, then bury it, and that's what they did. They gathered on the beach early this morning, just as the sun was coming up over the horizon of Lake Winnipeg, two hundred shouting, half-clothed women, and in one orchestrated moment – there was a sort of drum roll provided and a loudspeaker – each of them threw into the mild waves a symbolic pebble, their compacted rage, their flinty little burdens of hoarded injustice. Oh, God, it was beautiful, the peace of it, the relief. Right there on the beach there were these gigantic urns of tea, it's called peace tea, it's made from apples and lichen, like it's from seaweed too. And bread, these great gigantic loaves just passed around and torn apart and eaten like that out of the hand, no butter or anything, just pure grainy bread and the breeze coming off the lake and all those stones buried under the water, out of sight, out of mind, gone forever, and women dancing on the sand with their arms around each other, singing too, or maybe just sitting quietly while the sun bobbed up, the stillness, the light on the water. And then the fucking traffic coming home – it was a nightmare, you can just imagine, and in this everlasting heat!

Dot takes Ryan on her lap – her little Rye-Krisp, her little Ribena, her Mister Man, her Noodle-Doodle – and settles him against her peaceful chest.

"So what were all these chicks so angry about?" Dorrie asks Midge. She can't stand her sister-in-law, and the feeling is mutual.

"Oh, God," Midge shakes her head, and reaches for a pickled onion. "Don't get me started."

And no one does. They talk about the heat instead, and the ragweed count, and whether or not Quebec should separate. They're trying to keep on being a family, after all. Nothing real will ever get said out loud in this house, though Midge will bleat and blast, and Larry will prod and suggest. It doesn't matter; Larry understood this years ago. Today his dad tells a joke he heard at the plant, a long story about a Newfie visiting Quebec and trying to buy some cod liver oil from a Frenchie. Dot Weller hums Ryan to sleep, and

Dorrie Weller tells everyone how she's found this place in the North End where you can purchase cleaning products at twenty percent off.

Larry listens. This is how he's learning about the world, exactly as everyone else does – from sideways comments over a lemon meringue pie, sudden bursts of comprehension or weird parallels that come curling out of the radio, out of a movie, off the pages of a newspaper, out of a joke – and his baffled self stands back and says: so this is how it works.

You would have thought Larry's folks would have turned themselves into a grief-hardened set of statuettes, but no. They're moving, they're breathing, they're practicing rituals of their own tentative invention, and Larry's sucking it up. His mother's gorgeous bloom of guilt, his father's stoic heart, his sister's brilliant jets of anger, even the alternate sharpness and slack of his wife's domestic habits – these burn around him, a ring of fluorescence, though the zone between such vividness and the plain familiar faces around the table seems too narrow to enter. He's thirty years old, for Chrissake, old enough to know that he can't know everything. All he wants is what he's owed, what he's lucky enough to find along the way. All he wants is to go on living and living until he's a hundred years old and then he'll lie down and die.

CHAPTER FOUR

Larry's Work
1981

Most of Larry's friends have had half a dozen jobs in their lives, and quite a few of the guys have suffered spells of unemployment in between. But Larry's been lucky. He's worked at Flowerfolks for twelve years now, ever since he completed his Floral Arts Diploma back in '69.

Flowerfolks is a small chain with a reputation for friendly service and a quality product. Usually you can spot a Flowerfolks arrangement by its natural appearance. For instance, they don't go in for bending stems into far-out shapes and positions, or for those Holly Hobby wreathes, et cetera, or weird combinations like, say, tulips and birds-of-paradise sticking out of the same arrangement. Even their Welcome-New-Baby floral offerings have a fresh earthy look to them. Larry says it makes him shudder just thinking about those styrofoam lamb shapes with pink and blue flowers poking out of their backs. Simplicity and integrity at a reasonable price – that's what Flowerfolks has always stood for.

Well, that's changed overnight.

All twelve Flowerfolks stores have been swallowed up by Flowercity, the California-based multinational. Suddenly there's a new logo. Suddenly there are dyed carnations all over the place, whereas formerly they were carried reluctantly, on special order only. Suddenly the staff, even the guys, are wearing blue-and-white checked smocks with their names pinned to little round Peter-Pan collars. Half the floor area in the various outlets is given over now to artificial flowers, something Flowerfolks has always looked down on. As Vivian Bondurant says, "Why have something dead when you can have it alive?" A good question.

Vivian, the branch manager, gave notice two weeks after the Flowercity takeover. She dreads what she sees coming in the eighties, and, besides, she's ready for a career change. "I've worked my tush off," she told Larry, "building this place up, establishing a loyal clientele here in the West End, turning out a reliable product. I've definitely decided to go back to school. Social work – that's where the jobs are going to be in the future. I was reading the other day about squirrels and I –"

"Squirrels?" Larry interrupts, scratching his chest through his checked smock. His wife's washed it twice now, but it's still stiff with sizing.

"Seventy-four percent of the nuts that a squirrel hides never get found. Amazing, isn't it?"

"You mean –"

"I mean I've been hiding nuts, too, in a sense. Forever making little improvements in the business?

Remembering people's names. Following up after weddings. Sending those little anniversary reminders. Bringing in white balls from Toronto at Christmas when no other outlet in town would touch them. All that stuff."

"And?"

"And where has it got me?"

"I thought you loved it here."

"Like now they want daily time sheets. The whole ball of wax. Wouldn't you think, if they kept up with modern management, that they'd have figured out that it's *people* who matter! Computerized inventory. Good God! Not that there's anything wrong with computers per se, but they want it just so. And I have to turn up every single day for work in this dumb schoolgirl get-up. A checked smock at my age. I mean!"

"What do you mean your age? You're talking like you're –"

"Like I'm thirty-eight years old. A mature woman. Ha! If I wanted to be Little Bo Peep I'd go work at Disneyland. It's different for you, you're –"

"I'm thirty-one."

"A mere babe."

"But social work, Viv! How do you know you're going to like social work?"

"I don't. I'll probably hate it. Poor people, sick people. Omigod. But at least I'll have my dignity. You know, doing something useful."

"Hey, Viv, wait a minute. You're the one who's always saying how flowers are important. Remember your Chinese story –"

"Chinese story? What Chinese story?"

"You know – about the Chinaman who has two pennies –"

"Two yen, you mean."

"And he spends one on a loaf of bread and the other to buy a flower."

"Listen, Larry, I've got to tell you something. I hope it won't hurt your feelings."

"Go ahead. Shoot."

"Look, you're a sensitive guy, you really, truly are, but there's something you've got to know, especially working in a business that's ninety-nine percent customer relations."

"I can take it. Just go ahead."

"Well, look, you just can't say Chinaman anymore. It sounds prejudiced. You have to say Chinese person."

"Oh."

"Saying Chinaman's like saying Wop or Honky."

"My old dad says Chink."

"Exactly. There you have it. We've come a long way, baby."

"I'll remember."

"You'll have to, Larry. 'Cause it looks like you'll be in charge here when I go."

"Me? Are you kidding?"

"It's not for sure, but there've been these teensie-weensie hints from the head office, those bastards. Little inquiries, you know? Like is this Weller person reliable? Can he make decisions? What are his interpersonal skills? That kind of thing."

"I can't believe it. I never thought –"

"Like those squirrels I was mentioning earlier? You've been burying your nuts all along – nothing personal, pal – and now it's time to go find a few. You deserve it, Larry. You'll be a great boss. I've written a recommendation, as a matter of fact. A whole page, typed, single-spaced. He's a great guy, I said, or words to that effect. With capital O-Original ideas. Does this man know how to make irises stand up or what? And he's well organized, keeps a neat work table, doesn't let the orders get backed up, doesn't play royal highness with the trainees. Hey, what gives? You're supposed to be looking happy. You're going up the ladder, my laddie-boy. What's the matter?"

"I just can't," Larry said, "imagine this place without you."

Larry doesn't talk much about his job, but he thinks about it a lot, and mostly he thinks he's lucky. Work for him adds up to a whole lot more than the feel of ferns in his hands or the sight of sprigged baby's breath gleaming through the glass of the cooler or even the green spongy cave of the store itself with its forest smells rising up to greet him when he comes in in the morning. How many people get to work in that kind of lushness, the air breaking out into fragrance and color all around you. The loose, light humidity of the place is part of being at work, a big part, but all these particularities are shaken loose by the good music of talk. He and Viv talk all day long. They've been talking for twelve years, an unceasing, seamless conversation.

There are always a couple of assistants around, but

they come and go: Wendy, Kerri, Dawn, Sidney, Brenda, Lou-Anne, two or three Jennifers, a big fat guy called Tommy Enns, an endless procession of them, trainees from Red River College, young and confused, eager, stumbling, shrill or shy, it all depended. A new apprentice on an eight-week work stint tends to turn the place really hairy, at least at first, but Larry and Viv hold it steady and fluid with their voices, his, hers – talking, talking, all day the two of them talking.

While they stand at the bench "backing" bridal bouquets or improvising a winter arrangement to deliver to Victoria Hospital's Palliative Care Unit or unpacking cedars (they come twenty bunches to a box) Larry and Viv discuss Michael Jackson's stage style or Margaret Trudeau's maternal instincts or lack thereof. Their fingers move and so do their mouths. Yammer, yammer. About economics they admit their ignorance, and their right to their ignorance. They talk about the penny shortage in the States, the danger of radon in basements, the inflated salaries of professional football players, and about the pros and cons of whooping cough shots – on this particular topic Viv managed to persuade Larry not to have his three-year-old son, Ryan, inoculated after all. The two of them reminisce about the time a guy walked in and ordered a dozen dead roses to send to his ex-wife, and how Vivian took the order, then calmly phoned the police.

They talk about the cost of air conditioners in the States versus the cost in Canada. About draft dodgers, whether they should be sent home. About pimples, whether to pop them or leave them alone. About mothers, their mood swings, their dumb sweetness. About Ronald Reagan, how good-hearted or stupid the man is. How hot it is outside, how rainy, how the back lane is blocked with snow. A whole decade has slid by, its weathers and transports and passing personalities, and all of it crystalized into the words that fly back and forth between Vivian Bondurant and Larry Weller. A million words, a zillion. Note for note, the biggest noise in Larry's life is the noise that comes out of Viv Bondurant's throat.

Her voice is a low, confidential rumble, but full of little runs and pauses. She knows how to build up to a story, and she knows exactly when it's time to throw the ball into Larry's court. "So what do *you* think, Lare?" What she brings him are bulletins from that layer of the world he seems doomed to miss, the anecdotes she gleans from CHOL's call-in show or *People Magazine* exposés. She passes on, generously, with unstoppable authority, such things as cough remedies from somebody or other's grandmother, the fact that Italians use mums only for funerals, or what can be said out loud these days and what's *verboten*. Chinamen are now Chinese people. Indians are natives. And so on and so forth.

Certain topics between them are off limits. For instance, they never, never mention Larry's wife, Dorrie; Viv, with her strong sense of intuition, probably suspects things aren't working out too well in that department. On the other hand, she can be surprisingly upfront about herself, making a point, for instance, of keeping Larry up to date on her menstrual cycle. "It's better you know when I'm having my rag

73

days, kiddo, then you can keep out of my way." In fact, she's blessed with a remarkably even temperament, a woman whose running commentary on the world is underpinned by an easy acceptance of whatever comes her way. What she collects in her life is information, and it's *information* too valuable not to be shared.

Larry's grateful. He owes Viv a lot, and yet he hardly knows her. She and her husband, Hector, live quietly in a house in St. Vital. Hector's older than Viv by a good fifteen years and he's been married before – this slipped out one day when Viv was sorting through a box of holly at the store – and has fathered a couple of kids who grew up to be whiners and grabbers, which is why he doesn't want to have any more, and that's okay-José with Viv. Larry has only been to their house once, a Sunday morning a few years ago when he dropped off some screwed-up billing statements.

He'd never in his life seen such an airy house, everything dusted and polished and in perfect repair, and the pale beige drapes hanging with their pleats just so. Viv, wearing jeans and a turtleneck sweater, made coffee which she served to Hector and Larry at a shining kitchen table. She was quieter than she was at the store, sitting back and letting the men get acquainted. Afterward, Hector showed Larry the basement where he repaired clocks.

This was his job, not just a hobby. Against one wall stood a long workbench for Hector's tools. They were astonishingly beautiful, these tools, brass tipped with dark wooden handles and a look of antiquity about them. A metal lathe gleamed, handsome as a museum piece, clean, polished, ready to go. A square of pegboard held drill bits arranged in the shape of a harp. "Every last thing you see here is European," Hector said proudly. "German, mostly. You can't beat the Krauts for machinery."

"Yeah," murmured Larry, his eyes on the metal teeth of a miniature saw.

Twenty or thirty clocks stood about the room or hung on the walls, some of them disemboweled, and others tagged and ready to be picked up by their owners. Hector explained to Larry, pointing out their burnished edges, how to tell a French clock from an English clock, how certain clocks have a regulator mechanism that allows for the expansion or contraction of their pendulums, and the reasons for the transition of pocket watches to wrist watches. Larry ran his hand appreciatively over the frame of a plain round wall clock.

"That's a Seth Thomas you're looking at," Hector said. "The real thing."

"Ah," said Larry, who had never heard of a Seth Thomas.

The two men stood together for a minute in respectful silence. The air was full of the loud busy sound of ticking, and then suddenly – Hector held up a finger to Larry; here it comes! – there was a brief concert of chimes and bongs; twelve noon. "That's my hourly concert," Hector said, and Larry could tell it was something he said often and each time with pleasure. "That's all the music I need."

Larry looked around, then, at the low-ceilinged room which was dark in the corners but whitely lit under the cone of a green work light. Here was the domain of a man who had his name and trade listed in the Yellow Pages. The pervasive tang of machine oil lay over his ticking, working kingdom, and there in the middle stood Hector Bondurant himself, with his arms folded across his stomach, tapping his elbows, beaming broadly, a monarch in his chosen sphere.

Larry felt a stab of irrational jealousy. For the briefest of moments he wanted to own this space, this spacious house with its neat drapes and its stern white coffee mugs, and he yearned for the daily descent down linoleum-clad stairs to this warm, snug hideaway and its waiting workbench covered with sorted parts and beautifully aligned tools. He wanted all these things, but most of all he wanted Hector's work, his clockmaker's hands and the intricate mechanical promise he coaxes from mere wood and metal.

In the same instant, lapping up against Larry's instant desire to become a clockmaker, was his longing to work side by side with his father down at Air-Rider Coach Works, transforming metal sheets into mobile palaces. The miracle of it, making something out of nothing. The pleasure at the end of the day to see what you'd constructed with your own hands.

And then there was his wife, Dorrie, who sold cars at Manitoba Motors – he'd never thought much about Dorrie's job, but now he wanted a portion of that too. Himself in a snappy sports jacket with "Call Me Larry" on his lapel button. The lingo, the come-on, the bargains teasingly offered and withdrawn, the intensity of the minute-by-minute shifts, the decisive moment, and the thrill: the final solemnity, of signing on the dotted line and pocketing a fat commission.

There's no getting around it: the rhapsody of work hums between Larry's ears, its variables and strategies, its implements and its tightly focused skills. Sometimes he tries to scare himself with thoughts of wordlessness, the long, vacant mornings of the unemployed – how would that feel? – and the mingled boredom and sadness of being broke and without accomplishment, without any way to deal with time. In the end, anything's better than nothing, even the working stiff's daily grind. Some work is graceless, he knows that. Work can be dirty, noisy, dangerous, degrading, but it's still work, and that's what turns the gears of life. He understands this spare, singular fact better than he will ever be able to understand the unguessable secrets of love and happiness.

Years later, when his life was going badly, he came to see work as the only consolation for persisting in the world.

Before Dorrie got married she was a clerk-receptionist in the parts division of Manitoba Motors. The pay wasn't great, but she had a reputation for getting along with the customers, always commiserating with them over the size of their repair bills, taking their side. They appreciated that. They nicknamed her Dorable. The head of auto parts, a man named Al Leonard, said she was the most efficient employee he'd ever seen. She had a knack for keeping track of details and for remembering what was where and which parts were out of stock. In those days she wore jeans to work and a thick sweater since it was always drafty, what with the door to the repairs garage opening and closing all day long. Besides, she was stuck behind the counter, so what did it matter if she went casual or dressy?

After Ryan was born, she stayed home for three months and earned the odd bit of money by making follow-up calls for repair service. The way it worked, Manitoba Motors sent her out a list of completed repairs once a week, and her job was to phone the clients and ask if they were satisfied with the work. A public relations kind of thing, making the customer feel valued and looked after. She got paid so much a call, and she was able to squeeze in maybe fifteen or so calls while Ryan napped in the afternoon. Even so, the pay was peanuts, and half the time no one was at home or else they chewed her out for disturbing them in the middle of the day.

She decided to go back to work full-time. Russell LaFleur, the head honcho, surprised her by asking if she'd ever thought of going on the sales floor. Times had changed. Women were out there buying their own vehicles now, single women with careers and money to spend on extras. Women valued the judgment of other women. They appreciated a woman's point of view. When Dorrie pulls out the literature showing the cross-sections of engines, they stand at attention, taking in every word. Type of transmission, power brakes, cruise control – she ticks these items off on the tips of her nicely manicured fingers. She is deeply sympathetic when it comes to color and upholstery combinations, and she's able to give complete concentration to seat comfort, leg room, the convenience of the glove compartment with its own little overhead light. "We all have to live within a budget," she says, prefacing her pitch on fuel consumption, and giving a resigned shrug and a wrinkling of her small nose, signaling complicity. *Hey, we're in this together, we can work this out, these are the figures, trust me.*

Right away she bought herself two perky little suits from a designer's outlet she knows, a soft grey wool flannel and a brisk blue houndstooth check. Professional apparel, she calls it. An investment. Women working for other dealers in town go in for pant suits, but Dorrie sticks to skirts and coordinated pantyhose. After all, there are men customers out there too, and with them, as well as with women, she has an enviable sales completion record. At the end of every three-month sales period, Mr. LaFleur takes the whole gang out for a steak and beans dinner at The Loft. The high-commission sales staff get served steak, and those on the bottom of the chart get a plate of beans. It's a riot, Dorrie tells Larry, but then she's always on the steak-eating end of things. Twice she's been salesperson of the month, and once, last April, she was tops in the city. For that she got a plaque with her name engraved on it and a weekend for two at the Hecla Island resort hotel. And she went straight out and bought a third suit, a raspberry linen blend, nice for summer, and a pair of high-heeled sandals.

She'd like another baby; she'd like to be a lady of leisure, so she says anyway, and she tells Larry she's going to quit Manitoba Motors and give her aching feet a rest as soon as they've got enough money in the bank. But how much is enough, that's the question. She can't wait to move off Lipton Street with its rinkydink houses and busy traffic. She's got her eye on the Linden Woods subdivision west of town, a double garage, en-suite bathrooms, a family room with fireplace and wet bar. And what she'd really like, even though it sounds crazy, is a spiral staircase with a wrought-iron railing. She and Larry saw one last Sunday at a real estate open house they attended, and she said afterwards that walking down that staircase with her hand on the rail felt exactly like being a movie star. "If we could live in a house like this," she told Larry, "I'd never work another day in my life."

Larry doesn't want to move out of his house. He admits it's no palace, but he's just finished insulating the basement and he's thinking about doing the roof. He's installed a new garbage disposal unit too. He points this out to Dorrie, what he's invested in terms of money and work.

"You just don't want to leave your crazy yard," she charges.

Sighing, shrugging, he acknowledges the truth of what she says.

He's worked hard on the yard. It's a small lot, thirty-foot frontage and ninety in depth, that's all, but there's nothing else like it in the city of Winnipeg, and probably not even in the province of Manitoba. Every inch of it is filled with hedges, and these hedges are planted in the intricate pattern of a maze. There's a direct access route for the mailman, of course, but there's also a sinuous alternate path that winds twice around the house with half a dozen false turning points.

Larry's maze craze (as Dorrie calls it) started three and a half-years ago when they got married and went to England for their honeymoon. The highlight of the trip was a tour through the famous Hampton Court maze outside London, and ever since then Larry's been reading library books about mazes. And adapting his classic maze design so that it's tailored to the size of the Lipton Street lot. He's acquired nursery stock from a cut-rate greenhouse and learned just what shrubs work best in this climate and how to keep them alive during a long winter by burying the young shoots under heaps of leaves. Right now the hedges are thinly distributed and so short they can be easily overstepped; it'll be another four or five years before the hedge walls get high enough for his liking, but meanwhile he's nursing them along. The last thing he wants is to move to Linden Woods, where he'd have to start over and where the by-laws probably prohibit eccentric gardening.

Whereas anything goes in this neighborhood. The people around here are a mixed bag. His friend Bill Herschel, who lives two streets over, works full-time for the Manitoba Endangered Species Alert and sometimes gives Larry a hand on the weekend. The Gilshammers across the lane (he's in cut-rate electronics; she works at a unisex hair salon) have just donated the raked leaves from their property. So have the two guys down the street. (Larry can't remember their names offhand, but he knows they do stage carpentry for a theatre downtown, which he figures must be a pretty interesting line of work.) Lucy Warkenten, who's got the upstairs apartment next door, doesn't have any leaves to offer, but she takes a keen interest in Larry's maze, and has walked through it half a dozen times, stepping along in her purple leather boots. (She's a self-employed bookbinder working out of her apartment.) Beneath Lucy live the Lees with their three little kids. Ken Lee delivers pizzas for Bella Vista and gives Larry all his leaves and grass clippings, and plenty of advice on the subject of propagating shrubs, which must be planted in a shallow but wide trench so that the roots can spread out sideways and help anchor the branches against prevailing winds. The Grangers, Gord and Moira, live on the other side of Larry's house. Moira's a housewife, a semi-invalid, with an interest in spelling reform (she'd like to see the letter X eliminated), and Gord designs ergonomic work gloves, his most recent breakthrough featuring reduced padding at the finger joints so that the gloved hand can grasp objects more readily in cold weather. The good-hearted Grangers, too, have contributed their fall rakings to the survival of Larry Weller's baby hedges, and now, with winter about to crash down, Larry's and Dorrie's yard looks like a series of Indian burial mounds with their mushroom of a house poking through.

In the dark November evenings people in this neighborhood tend to stay home with their families, enjoying their hamburger suppers and favorite TV shows. Generally speaking, the house lights go out along the street somewhere between ten o'clock and eleven-thirty. There are, Larry assumes, starbursts of sex or of hospitality or latenight comings and goings and probably even acts of violence, but nights in the neighborhood are quiet for the most part, and heavy with sleep. Under a depthless navy-blue sky, beneath a cold bone of a moon, this small segment of the world is renewing itself, restoring its emptied-out substance, getting ready for tomorrow. Ready to go back to work.

Working for Flowercity and married to Dorrie and living on Lipton Street, Larry had no idea that technology was about to bulldoze the job market. In the early eighties, that enchanted, stupid time, almost everyone had a job, or if they didn't they expected they'd find one any minute. No one dreamed of the redundancies and dehirings and downsizings the end of the century would bring, where in a mean, lean, bottom-line world, a day's work would become as rare and as exotic as the prized orchids Larry keeps swaddled in insulation at the back of the cool unit.

Larry, himself, was slow to wake up to the idea of work. At twelve he took over another kid's paper route and lasted a week. During his final year of high school, hungry for money, longing for name-brand jeans and a leather jacket, he worked at a neighborhood McDonald's, adding up orders, and ringing in cash, hating every minute of it. He didn't like to think in those days that he'd have to spend the rest of his life working. But then he got lucky. He fell into the right line of work: flowers, plants.

And now, ever since Viv Bondurant's left Flowercity, Larry's been in charge down at the store, and that means getting up at six o'clock three mornings a week and driving out to Stems Inc., the wholesalers. They're open for business at seven, and Larry likes to be in and out in half an hour. He's got his standard orders, of course, his poms, daisies, roses, carnations, and so on, and then he likes to spend a few minutes looking around at what's just come in from the flower brokers in Montreal. Stems has about 140 accounts, so it's not surprising he bumps into some of the other florists around town, Sally Ullrich, Jim Carmody, and catches up on what's new. Over in the corner there's coffee going and a basket of donuts – a nice touch, Larry thinks, since he skips breakfast at home these days, and Dorrie's too busy, anyway, getting Ryan ready for daycare, to stop and make coffee.

He's got a lot of wedding orders coming up, so today he picks up a good supply of baby's breath. He prefers the stuff from Peru, which is as pure a product as you can get. The wedding bulge across the North American continent is in June and July, but there's a major blip in the city of Winnipeg, where winter weddings have come to the fore. That way newly married couples can get away for a tropical honeymoon. Larry does a nice bridal semi-cascade; average price $120. Brides want roses nine times out of ten. You can't talk them out of it. They think flowers, and, bingo, roses come to mind. Roses are romantic, also generic. Winnipeg roses originate in southern Ontario, where they've got acres of them under glass.

The gingers get shipped to Manitoba from South Africa, freesia from Holland, and carnations from

California. People think carnations are a cheapy flower, but it's not true; sometimes, depending on weather fluctuations, they're more expensive than roses, and they last a hell of a lot longer. Some nationalities hate carnations, that's something to remember. Tree fern is trucked in from Florida in warmed vehicles. They're always good for funeral baskets. You don't see a lot of camellias anymore, that old corsage staple, but then Larry doesn't do anything like the number of corsages he did when he started in the business back in the late sixties. To tell the truth, corsages were old-fashioned even then, relics from the thirties and forties. How's a woman supposed to button her coat over a corsage? And what if it doesn't match her outfit? – actually, there's an old florist's law that says a corsage is doomed to be the wrong color, something women have always known, just as they know there's no way to secure a corsage without at least a small fuss, not to mention permanent damage to their silk blouses. If a customer absolutely insists on going the corsage route, Larry encourages them to think about a small wrist arrangement he's perfected, which is sturdy, attractive, and comfortable to wear.

He's happy to give advice about prolonging the life of cut flowers, but warns his customers that they mustn't have unrealistic expectations. Flowers are fragile, flowers are needy. There are people who put their flowers in dirty vases. You can actually see the green scum line from the last bunch. Would you drink out of that vase? No way. You want to put your flowers in a disinfected container; that's all the magic white powder in the little envelope is – a disinfectant.

Of course you've already cut your flowers with a knife and on an angle before putting them in water. Don't expect dafs to go more than three days, though, no matter what you do to them and for them.

Poinsettias will start selling in a week's time; Larry gets his delivered from Carmen, Manitoba, just an hour away. Then it's Valentine's Day, then your Easter lilies – they come from Carmen too. Mother's Day is crazy, the biggest day of the year, and right after that you're into graduation tributes, retirements, and a spate of summer weddings. It's a funny business with its ups and downs, but Larry's grateful for the way the main holidays are strung out over the year. He's always hearing about photo opportunities, but what about flower opportunities? They come and they go; they keep him buoyed up and alive and working, and he welcomes the noise of daily bustle in his life.

When Viv first left, she phoned the store occasionally to see how business was going. After a while, though, she stopped checking in. Larry's heard somewhere that she dropped out of the social work program and was selling flowers in a corner of a Safeway in North Kildonan. He's also heard that she's pregnant and has quit work altogether. He hasn't seen her for ages now, but he thinks of her at least once every day, and wonders what she's doing at that very moment. He didn't notice it happening at the time, but it must have been that they said goodbye to each other and really meant it, and maybe that's the way it goes with friends you have from work.

Sometimes down at the store he'll be holding a stemmed alstroemeria in his hand. More often than not, this will be the flamingo variety, his favorite, a rose color streaked with lavender, a floppy uneven head of fragile petals spread out to reveal a colony of tender stamen threads, their pinks, their golds. This flower, an herb really, started out as a seed way down in South America in Colombia. Some Spanish-speaking guy, as Larry imagines him, harvested the seed of this flower and someone else put it back into the earth, carefully, using his hands probably, to push the soil in place. They earned their daily bread doing that, fed their families, kept themselves alert. It's South American rain that drenches the Colombian earth and foreign sunshine that falls on the first green shoots, and it all happens, it all works.

And what next? Larry supposes that Spanish-speaking laborers equipped with hoes arrive to beat back the weeds, but are they men or women who do this work? Maybe both, and maybe children, too, in that part of the world. Larry wonders what goes on in their heads when they perform this tedious and backbreaking work, and whether they have any idea when they pack the cut flowers into insulated boxes, laying the heads end to end, that these living things are about to be carried aboard enormous jet aircraft, handled gently, handled like the treasure they are, that they will be transported across international frontiers, sorted, sold, inspected, sold again, and that without noticeable wilting or fading – except to an expert eye – they will come to rest in the hands of a young Canadian male in an ordinary mid-continental florist establishment, bringing with them a spot of organic color in a white and frozen country (where the mercury has fallen overnight to twenty degrees below zero and where the windchill factor has risen steadily all day so that no living matter has any right to exist, but it does and here it is – this astonishing object he holds in his grasp).

Larry thinks how the alstroemeria head he cups in his hand has no memory and no gratitude toward those who delivered it to this moment. *It toils not, neither does it spin*. It's sprouted, grown, bloomed, that's all. But Larry, placing it beside a branch of rosy kangaroo paw from British Columbia and a spray of Dutch leather leaf and a spear or two of local bear grass, feels himself a fortunate man. He's worried sick at the moment about the distance that's grown between himself and his wife, about the night terrors that trouble his only child, about money, about broken or neglected friendships, about the pressure of too much silence, about whether his hedges will weather the winter, but he is, nevertheless, plugged into the planet. He's part of the action, part of the world's work, a cog in the great turning wheel of desire and intention.

The day will arrive in his life when work – devotion to work, work's steady pressure and application – will be all that stands between himself and the bankruptcy of his soul. "At least you have your work," his worried, kind-hearted friends will murmur, and if they don't, if they forget the availability of this single consolation – well then, he'll say it to himself: *at least I have my work*.

CHAPTER FIVE

Larry's Words
1983

The word *labyrinth* has only recently come into the vocabulary of Larry Weller, aged thirty-two, a heterosexual male (married, one child) living in Winnipeg, Manitoba, Canada. He doesn't bother himself with the etymology of the word *labyrinth*; in fact, at this time in his life he has zero interest in word derivations, but he can tell you plain and simple what a labyrinth is. A labyrinth is a complex path. That's it. It's not necessarily something complicated or classical, as you might think. The overpass out on Highway 2 is a kind of labyrinth, as Larry will be happy to tell you. So is the fox-and-geese tracery he stamped into the backyard snow as a child in Winnipeg's West End. He sees that now. So's a modern golf course. Take St. George's Country Club out in the St. James area of the city, for instance, the way it nudges you along gently from hole to hole, each step plotted in a forward direction so that you wouldn't dream of attacking the whole thing backwards or bucking in any way the ongoing, numerically pre-determined scheme. And an airport is a labyrinth too, or a commercial building or, say, a city subway system. It seems those who live in the twentieth century have a liking for putting ourselves on a predetermined conveyor track and letting it carry us along.

A maze, though, is different from a labyrinth, at least in the opinion of some. A maze is more likely to baffle and mislead those who tread its paths. A maze is a puzzle. A maze is designed to deceive the travelers who seek a promised goal. It's possible that a labyrinth can be a maze, and that a maze can be a labyrinth, but strictly speaking the two words call up different ideas. (Larry read these definitions, and their relationship to each other, three years ago, in a library book called *Mazes and Labyrinths: Their History and Development*.)

If he had not married Dorrie Shaw, if he had never visited Hampton Court, his life would have swerved on an alternate course, and the word *labyrinth* would have floated by him like one of those specks in the fluid of his eye.

He finds it paradoxical that while his life is shrinking before his very eyes, his vocabulary should be expanding. It's weird. It's farout. It's *paradoxical* — that's the bouncy new word he's been saying out loud lately, not to show off, but because it "pops" on his tongue. It's a word he's only recently taken into his brain, last week in fact. "Isn't it paradoxical," his sister Midge said to him over the phone, "that I kicked my husband out because he was just plain queer, and now

I've moved in with him because he's queer and he's sick and maybe dying?"

"It's what?" Larry asked her, ashamed of his begging tone, his needy need to know what words mean. "What did you call it?"

"A paradox. You know, like ironic."

"Oh, yeah. Right."

He went the next day and bought himself a pocket dictionary and he keeps it down at Flowercity. It's on a shelf under the counter, handy. There are people, he's noticed, whose vocabularies stand a step or two higher on the evolutionary staircase, and he's had this idea lately that words can help him in the future or maybe even with his present difficulties. The empty white echo he sometimes hears can be calmed by words. It might be the solution: that all he needs are some new words, big or little it doesn't matter, as long as their compacted significance registers, in his head, on his tongue. He could increase his overall word power, add a new word every day. Who knows what's likely to happen if he sharpens up: the way he talks, the way he thinks. There are men and women who live by cunning and silence, but he doesn't want to be one of them, grunting, pointing, holding back. He wants to be ready when the time comes to open his mouth and let the words run out like streaming lava.

There are people out there who imagine they want to pass straight through language to clarity, but Larry Weller of Winnipeg, Canada, wants, all of a sudden, at age thirty-two, to hang on to words, even separate words that sit all on their own, each with a little brain and a wreath of steam around its breathed-out sound:

cantankerous, irrepressible, magnanimous. And, yes, ironic. You can discuss this idea of words, but you'll need more words just to get started: hypothesis, axiomatic, closure.

He was a dreamy kid growing up, and after that a dreamy adolescent, just letting his life happen to him. It took him years to get himself wide awake, and lately he's been feeling that he's dozing off again, collapsing inward like the shrink-wrapped merchandise on the rack at the front of the store, the little plastic bottles of Vita-Grow and Root-Start and Mite-Bomb. The music that pours out of the radio all day at the store has flattened his brain with its wailing. He's reached a dead end in his job – branch manager of a so-so flower shop – where he's been for fourteen years. An impasse. (That's another of his new words; he got that one from TV.) Besides his job stalemate, he's got a wife who won't sleep in the same bed with him anymore, at least not until he promises to sell their house and move upmarket.

Upmarket. He doesn't need to look that one up. He hears it all the time these days, and little by little he's absorbed more or less the sense of what it means. Last year he and Dorrie traded in their old Toyota and "moved upmarket" to a *brand-new* Toyota. Not a huge move, just a subtle shift upward. (The word subtle he can pronounce, but not spell, but then he doesn't need to spell it, does he?)

The florist chain he works for used to be called Flowerfolks, until *it* went upmarket, becoming Flowercity with a whole new clientele and a different product line: more exotics, more artificials and dried stuff. Ryan, his four-year-old son, has gone "upmarket" too, toddling off to junior-kindergarten in coordinated outfits manufactured by OshKosh and Kids-Can-Grow.

It's ironic, Larry thinks, *ironic* that his wife Dorrie grew up in a pokey little lace-curtainy house over on Borden Road, her mom and dad and six kids packed into four rooms, no basement, a garage full of junk, so that when she and Larry first bought the Lipton Street house, a fixer-upper if there ever was one, she thought they'd arrived at a palace. Well, not now. She's got her eyes on the Linden Woods subdivision, but she can't get Larry motivated to move out that way. He's worked too hard on the hedge maze in the Lipton Street yard, which is just beginning to take shape.

So who's going to buy a house, Dorrie says, that's got a yard choked to the gills with bushes?

One of these days she's going to get a bulldozer in there and clear the whole thing out. This bush business is driving her straight up the wall. That's an expression she's picked up from Larry's English mother, and these days just about everything drives her up the wall.

Or else drives her bananas. Like, for instance, the way her husband, Larry, talks. Those big words he's spouting. She hadn't figured him for a show-off when they first met back in 1976, so how come he's exploding these days with fancy words?

Is this a fair accusation? Well, yes and no. A lot of Larry's recently acquired vocabulary is clustered around his *preoccupation* with mazes. He's lifted his collection of new words from a series of library books, and they've stuck to him like burrs. Dorrie says he's trying to put her down when he uses these words. She says he always has his nose in a book. He used to be fun, he used to make her laugh, but now all he can talk about are such things as: turf mazes, shepherd's race, Julian's bower, knot garden, Jerusalem, Minotaur, *jeu-de-lettres*, pigs-in-clover, frets and meanders, the Trémaux algorithm, *pavi-mentum tessellatum*, fylfot, wilderness, unicursal, topiary, nodes, the Mount of Venus, *maisons de Dëdalus*, Troy-town, cup-and-ring, ocular or spiral, serpent-through-waist, chevron.

On and on. He's astonished himself to think he's taken in so many words in the last few years, harpoons aimed straight at the brain, and that he actually remembers them.

One of Larry's steady customers down at the flower shop is Mrs. Fordwich, who popped in the other morning, ordering flowers for the annual Chamber Music Fund Raiser, and, since it was getting Close to Christmas, Larry suggested a basket of mixed poinsettias. "I don't think so, Larry," she said slowly. "I mean, poinsettias at this time of the year! It's a little banal, don't you think?"

Banal. It seems to him he's heard that word before, and now, from Mrs. Fordwich, he detects, along with the word's lazy, offhand delivery, a shade of dismissal in her voice. He stares at her woundedly. But what exactly does banal mean?

Later, he reaches under the counter for his dictionary. The definition of banal is meaningless from overuse; hackneyed; trivial. There are punctures in Larry's overall perception, he sees, that will exclude him, cripple him unless he smartens up – and what else? He'll be left all his life with that drifting, stupid, *banal* crinkle on his puss: *Hey, would you mind running that by me one more time. I didn't quite catch–*

This is no one's fault exactly; this is what you'd expect, given Larry Weller's history, his background, his *banal* take on the world.

Carnations are probably banal too, he reasons. Asparagus fern sure as hell is banal. Chrysanthemums? Definitely, those poofy pots from Safeway with the bow stuck on the side. And maybe, just probably, he's a little banal himself.

A *spokeshave* is a cutting tool having a blade set between two handles, and it's used for rounding wood or other materials.

Larry had never seen or heard the word spokeshave until he and Dorrie and their little boy, Ryan, were invited, along with a few other neighbors, over to Lucy Warkenten's apartment for a Christmas drink.

Lucy lives next door to the Wellers on the second floor of an old house, and works as a bookbinder, using a screened-off corner of her living room for "a studio." Larry has always felt friendly toward Lucy, who is about forty years of age and lives alone. She wears long creased skirts and Mexican sweaters and lots of wooden jewelry. Artsy-fartsy, Dorrie calls her, one of your old-time cactus-cunt virgins.

The party was held late on a dark Sunday afternoon, and Lucy had candles burning all around the room.

Under a white-painted, sparkle-strewn twig of a tree she had placed wrapped toys for the Lee children who lived downstairs and for four-year-old Ryan: tiny windmills to construct, intricate puzzles, Japanese pencils. There was a bowl of spiced wine punch on the coffee table and plates of fruitcake and cookies. After everyone was served, eating, drinking, and chattering away to each other, Lucy Warkenten drew Larry over to the window and showed him how his maze looked when viewed from above.

His heart jumped to see that, even under a layer of snow, the maze's pattern stood out clearly. Its looping paths, doubling back and forth on themselves, possessed a tidiness and precision he hadn't thought to imagine. "Watching that maze take shape," Lucy told Larry solemnly, touching his sweater cuff with the flat of her hand, "has given me more pleasure than you can know."

"I think I do know," he said, and in saying so surrendered a secret he'd once thought necessary.

She showed him her own work corner with its range of tools. *Vellum tips*, marbled *endpapers, slips, cords, a lying press*, the stack of millboard, silky *headbands*. Tacked on the wall was a recipe for *glair*, an egg-white mixture that binds gold leaf to paper. A paged book was called a *codex*, she explained to Larry – the word comes from the Latin, meaning wood.

Larry had never heard any of these words before, at least not as they applied to the art of bookbinding, and it made him squint at Lucy through the late afternoon candlelight, seeing her suddenly as someone who lived every day inside the walls of a foreign language, only not really foreign at all. While the other people in the room chatted and snacked on cheese and swallowed glasses of wine, Lucy showed Larry her current project, which was putting between new "boards" an old volume, and covering it with pale grey goatskin. "The trick," she said, "is to make it look as though the leather has just grown there." The book was titled *Deep Furrows*, written some sixty years ago by a Canadian socialist called Hopkins Moorhouse.

"Is it any good?" Larry asked.

"What?"

"The book."

Lucy shrugged. "Dead boring. But one of Moorhouse's descendants wants it rebound." Then she said, "A good binding can preserve a book for hundreds of years."

Hundreds of years! Larry thought of his fragile floral arrangements, how he never holds out hope for more than a week.

"A work of art!" Lucy pronounced, and he thought at first she was talking about the half-bound book in her hand. In fact, she had put the book down and was looking out her window once again, gesturing toward the sight of his snowy maze, etched in shadow, a strange, many-jointed creature hunkering down beneath the cold moonlight, asking nothing of anybody, not even the favor of being noticed.

Larry's first word as a child was *pop*, and according to family legend he liked to say it over and over, a long sputter of happy pops with a punchy emphasis on the final *p*. Larry's folks, his mum, his dad, decided finally it was just a noise and not a real word, but Larry's mother, Dot, wrote it down anyway in Larry's baby book on the page titled "Our Baby Learns To Talk."

Larry's sister Midge, two years older than Larry, was credited with *dog* as her first word. According to family legend, she pronounced it clearly, cleanly, and then she barked a soft baby bow-wow to indicate that she connected language with content. Even at twelve months she was smart as a whip.

Once, years later, Midge said to Larry, "Maybe you weren't really saying pop at all. Maybe you were saying poop."

"Maybe you were saying God when you said dog," Larry told her. "Like those kids who get things backwards, what d'ya call that again?"

"Dyslexia," she supplied, somewhat sternly.

"Right," he said. "Dyslexia, dyslexia, dyslexia."

Sometimes Larry sees his future laid out with terrifying clarity. An endless struggle to remember what he already knows.

When Larry was a kid his mother was forever listening to the radio – while she cooked or ironed or did her housework – and sometimes, out of curiosity, she stopped the dial at a place where foreign languages came curling out of the radio's plastic grillwork: Italian or Portuguese or Polish, they were all the same to Larry, full of squawks and spit and kicking sounds.

"Jibber jabber," Larry's father called this talk, shaking his head, apparently convinced, despite all reason, that these "noises" meant nothing, that they were no more than a form of elaborate nonsense.

Everything ran together; and there weren't any real words the way there were in English. These foreigners were just pretending to talk, trying to fool everyone.

Larry knows better. Everyone in the world walks around with a supply of meaningful words inside their heads, bundled there like kindling or like the long-fibered nerve bundles he remembers from his high school general science class. At the very least these words possess the transparent clarities that point to such objects as floor, window, chair, ball. The more dangerous and toxic words came later and with difficulty, but everyone eventually got themselves equipped with a few. Bus route. Property tax. Paycheck. Pedestrian. Words were everywhere; you couldn't escape them, and along with the shape of the words came comprehension, like a gulped capsule. The world itself seemed to hold a word in its mouth, a single-syllable hum, heavy and vowel-laden and ready as a storm warning to announce itself.

As for himself, he doesn't have enough words yet, he knows that. Not nearly enough.

Larry's mum and dad came to Canada from England back in 1950, but after all this time they still say railway, for example, instead of railroad. Larry's mother calls her kitchen stove a cooker, and Larry's dad says petrol instead of gasoline. Larry wouldn't dream of saying railway or cooker or petrol himself, but the words coming out of his parents' mouths feel delicately edged and full, and give his heart, every time he hears them, a twist of happiness, as though his fumbling, stumbling mother and father have, if nothing else, improvised for themselves a crude shelter in an alien land. They can hide there. Be themselves, whatever that means.

"Mazel tov," says Larry's friend Bill Herschel, at weddings, birthdays, football games, at any festive occasion.

Larry, growing up next door to the Herschel family, has learned to say it too. The phrase sits on his tongue like a wad of soft caramel. *Mazel tov*. It pushes right past what he's capable of thinking or feeling, so that he opens his mouth and becomes an eloquent maker of fine sounds and of brilliant music. A celebrant, a happy boy; later, a happy man.

The word *sex*? What did it mean? "Well," Larry's mother said, plainly embarrassed (this was a long time ago), "it has to do with hugging and kissing and lying in bed." Then she said, "It's mostly for men."

Years later, when he was a man himself, in his mid-forties, his body softening, but his brain ticking along one more skeptical track, Larry Weller lay in a woman's warm embrace and heard himself instructed in what she termed the *tantric* mysteries. Tantric? Sex, she explained in her pebbly voice, could be deeper and more frightening than he knew. You could climb inside the word *sex* and grow yourself a new skin: rough, hairy, primal, unrecognizable. You could go right to the edge of that word and forget your own name, you could bury yourself in your body and find your way out to another existence.

What? Larry asked himself in his plodding,

stubborn, and possibly imperious way, what does any of this *mean*?

Damn, hell, Jesus, God, piss, shit, screw, fart, fuck, prick, cunt, balls, asshole, motherfucker.

Larry Weller knows all these words. How could he live in the world if he didn't? They're like coins, for carrying around in your pocket and spending when you feel like it. No one's going to put you in jail for what you open up your mouth and say. (Well, not around here anyway.) Larry's wife, Dorrie, says fucking this, fucking that all the time. It helps to keep her from going bananas, she says. Larry sometimes refers to something or other as being fucked up, but he's careful not to say it around his young son. One fuck-talking parent is enough for a kid to handle.

Sometimes people don't even know what they're saying. Words can slip loose from their meanings. There's a young, slender, and beautiful Vietnamese woman who comes into Larry's flower shop every Friday afternoon to take advantage of the weekly happy hour: all cut flowers at half-price between four and five p.m. She points shyly to what she wants, three tulips, say, some sprays of foliage or whatever – then she counts out her money carefully on the counter, picks up the wrapped flowers and says, bowing politely, sweetly, "Okay, I bugger off now."

There is in the English language a rollcall of noble words. Nation. Honor. Achievement. Majesty. Integrity. Righteousness. Learning. Glory.

Larry knows these words – who doesn't? – but

almost never uses them. These are the words of those anointed beings who take the long view. Whereas he lives in the short view, his close-up, textured, parochial world, the little valley of intimacy he was born into, always thinking, without knowing he's thinking. Living next door to the great words, but not with them. His share of the truth – what truth? – is going to come (when it comes) modestly packaged and tied with string, he knows that.

In the future, though, he'll learn to bring his words to conclusion, but then, sliding into a shrugging second gear, arrive at an abrupt half-embarrassed stop, as if to say: these words aren't really me, they're just the clothes I wear.

Like almost all men, Larry will be called upon in his life for a moment or two of genuine eloquence, and these instances will coalesce around that ceremony known as the marriage proposal. "Will you marry me?" he said to Dorrie Shaw back in 1978, his mouth full of sharp minerals. To a second wife, whom he has not yet met, he will say, simply, "I want to live with you forever."

He actually made these pronouncements, full of doubt and also hope. Full of amazement that he knows the words and that such simple words will suffice.

"I'm married to a maze nut," Dorrie used to say in the old days when she and Larry were newly married. She said it fondly, as wives do, shaking their heads over their husbands' indulgences, the way Larry's mother exclaims over her husband's corkscrew and bottle-opener collection, which has now reached 2000 specimens, and which she is obliged to dust and number and keep in reasonable order, a collection whose point she has never questioned, nor felt qualified to question.

Dorrie gave her husband, Larry, a paperback book called *Celtic Mazes and Labyrinths* on their first wedding anniversary, and inscribed it: "Happy memories of Hampton Court," calling to mind their honeymoon in England where Larry saw his first maze.

It's maze madness, she says now, that's what he's got. It's a form of insanity. It drives her crazy, sitting in the middle of a writhing forest. Mazes remind her of a bunch of snakes, and she hates snakes.

It's a passion, an obsession.

The word *obsession* feels too boxy and broad for the round cavity of Larry's mouth, so he simply says to friends or family or anyone who asks, that he's "into" mazes. A hobby kind of thing. He plays it down. He doesn't know why, but he'd rather not let people know how "into it" he really is, that it's like a ripe crystal growing in his brain and taking up more and more space.

It's not only mazes themselves he thinks of, but the *idea* of mazes, and the idea is a soft steady incandescent light bulb at the edge of his vision; it's always there, it's always switched on. He can turn his gaze at will and watch it, casting its glow on the supple sleeping aisles of shrubbery around his house, their serpentine (ser-pen-tine) allure, their teasing treachery and promise of reward.

The hedge maze in Larry's yard employs three varieties of plants. The hearty cotoneaster (*Cotoneaster horizontalis*) – which turns red in the fall and which lends itself nicely to pruning tools – makes up the outer ring of the maze. Common caragana (*Caragana arborescens*), feathery green and not quite so prunable – not at all, in fact – forms the walls of the middle ring. And alpine currant (*Ribes alpinum*) leads into the heart of the maze, where Larry plans to install a small stone fountain one day. (He's already sent off to a supply house in Florida for a design catalogue.)

He's put in his hedge stock bare root in the spring, which adds up to half the cost of waiting till summer and buying the individual plants in pots. Naturally he shops around and uses his florist's connections in order to get a good price. (After all, he's got a mortgage, he's got a little kid who's starting swimming and gymnastics lessons.)

There's a paradox – that useful word again – built into the shrubs he's chosen. He wants the plants to grow fast so that his overall design will be realized, but, at the same time, you can't have *really* fast-growing shrubs in a maze or you'll spend your whole life shaping and cutting back new growth. He's had to come to terms with that *dilemma*, he's had to *accommodate* that fact. (There's pain involved in these new words, the way they hint at so much time lost, time wasted, all those years of unknowing.)

Why has Larry committed to memory the Latin names for his shrubs? Because he senses – vaguely – that they deserve the full dignity of his attention. They've survived a couple of tough Manitoba winters, and they're looking good. Really good. So far, not one has shriveled and died. They seem, in fact, to love him. Shrubs, he feels, are shy exiles in the plant kingdom. They're not quite trees, not quite anything, really, but they have, nevertheless, been awarded by the experts out there, your professors, your writers of gardening books, full botanical classification. (He sees them even in the wintertime with a kind of love, their elegance and sprigged look of surprise.)

He loves the Latin roll of the words in his mouth – *Leguminosae* – and he loves himself for being a man capable of remembering these rare words, for being alert, for paying attention, particularly since he has not always in his life paid sufficient attention. This is something entirely new. His jittery spirits are soothed by the little Latinate sighs and bumps. He hopes, optimistically, that the words that live in his head will eventually find their way to his mouth. Perhaps he'll even learn to flip them off his tongue unself-consciously, to secrete them through his pores. What else, really, does he need in his life but more words? When you add up the world and its words you get a kind of cosmic sandwich, two thick slices of meaning with nothing required in between. Sometimes, though, he wishes he wouldn't: wouldn't try so hard. What did he used to think about before he tried? What was it that stood behind his eyes – before he figured out how to find the right words?

There are a few words that are missing even from Larry's new under-the-counter dictionary. His sister, Midge, for instance, is divorced from her husband, but she's living with him again. What's the word for her status now? And for her husband? And for what passes between them?

What can he call the feeling he has for his son, Ryan? That mixture of guilt and longing, that ballooning ever-protective, multi-limbed force that's too big to cram into the category of love.

When he hits a traffic light on his way home from work, sitting at an intersection in the near-dark, ten seconds, twenty seconds – what does he call the rapturous seizure he feels as he counts off on his fingers the essential description of where he is in the world? *Here I am, but no one knows my location at this moment. No one knows my eyes are blinking, adjusting, making leaps, asking the question inside the question inside the question –*

And what's the word for that spasm of panic that strikes Larry as he unlocks his back door on a winter night? He enters with his house keys in one hand, a boxed pizza or a bag of takeout chicken in the other. In the tiny linoleum-floored vestibule he stamps the snow off his boots, and stoops to remove them, feeling as he leans forward that the air has dangerously thinned and that he could easily topple over dead on the spot.

He hums Michael Jackson's "Billy Jean" to scatter the silence, an aerosol spray. The silence contributes to his plummeting faith in his own arrangements. Still air, empty rooms. It was as though he and Dorrie had never embarked on a life of house and children, but had been brought to this spiritless edge by force. The walls, the kitchen floor, the tight circle of second-hand appliances, the tiny corner table with its chairs pushed neatly in – these objects refuse to acknowledge him, though he's the one – isn't he? – who brought the scene into being, and who is now trapped in the bubble of his own dread. He ought to rejoice in the settledness of this room, but he doesn't. He should see it as a sequestered cave hidden away in the tall immensity of winter. What is the word for the slow, airless, unrelieved absence he feels? It's coming to him, this word, winging its way as though guided by radar, but it hasn't quite arrived.

Dorrie will be home from her sales job at Manitoba Motors in ten minutes, after she picks up Ryan from daycare. Her mouth will bear a mere trace of her Frankly Fuchsia lipstick. Her quick kiss against his cheek delivers the smallest of electric shocks. A shock of this order doesn't really hurt, but then it doesn't feel good either. Is there a word for a sensation as fleeting and as useless as this?

It strikes Larry that language may not yet have evolved to the point where it represents the world fully.

Recognizing this gap brings him a rush of anxiety. Perhaps we're waiting, all of us, he thinks, longing to hear "something" but not knowing what it is.

Down at Flowercity a guy's come in and ordered an immense gift bouquet of cut flowers for his aged aunt, and on the card he wants the words: Happy Spring!

And today *is* spring, March 21, the equinox. The strengthening sun, the melting snow. Everything on earth testifies to the newly arrived season, but Larry's been too sunk in gloom to notice. Things couldn't be worse at home. Dorrie's hardly spoken to him in the last month except to grump about the draft from the north wall of the kitchen. And the lack of closet space. And how she hates their hellhole of a house.

Solstice, equinox. He loves the sound of those words, and remembers how a teacher back in high school once wrote them on the blackboard, putting a slash across the middle of equinox, equal nights, night and day. What beautiful logic. The twice-yearly miracle. And here it is. Today. The vernal equinox. About time.

"Larry Weller?"
"Yes?"
"Larry. This is Lucy calling. Lucy Warkenten."
"Lucy!"
Larry's next-door neighbor, Lucy Warkenten, has never phoned him at work before. He and his latest trainee from Red River College, Bob Buxtead, are standing at the work counter doing centerpieces for a Lions' banquet. They've decided to go for a spring theme, even though the snow's still hanging on here and there, and the daffodils that arrived from British Columbia this morning look faintly puckered at the base of the petals.

Lucy sounds worried, and also excited. "I hope I'm not interrupting you," she tells Larry carefully.
"No, not at all."
"I was just wondering –"
"Yes?"
"Well, I was looking out my window just now, just a

few minutes ago, and I was wondering about your maze, Larry. If you've changed your mind or something."

"About what?"

"If you, you know, decided to start over or something? With a new design. A new concept?"

"No," Larry said, baffled, fiddling with a pile of bear grass on his work counter, their sharp green edges. "No, I'm thinking of maybe putting in a new node in the south-east corner when the weather breaks, something a little fancier that I've been working out, but for now –"

"Larry, listen." He heard her take a long breath before continuing. "Larry, there's a bulldozer in your yard. Or a, what d'ya call it? – one of those machines. It's been there for about fifteen minutes."

"A what? Did you say a bulldozer?"

"It's already – I'm so sorry to have to tell you this" – another sharp breath, a trembling inhalation – "but it, this machine, it's already dug up the whole front part of –"

"Never mind, Lucy. I'll be right there."

Traffic was bad, even in the dead-middle of a Monday afternoon. It was twenty minutes before Larry pulled up in front of his house on Lipton Street.

He saw the ruin of his front yard, the plowed-up furrows of mud and snow, the levered ground, and the thrusting image of his wooden front steps, suddenly, grotesquely, revealed. A yellow backhoe, not a bulldozer but just as purposeful, sat silent at the side of the house, and directly in front of it stood the wobbly stick figure of Lucy Warkenten in her flowered parka and purple skirt and boots, her arms held straight out sideways like a crossing guard at attention, the cold spring wind booming off her anxious face. Her posture was defiant and disturbed, as if she were a crazy woman, semaphoring for help.

He remembered later how he shut his eyes against Lucy, and against the pale sunlight coloring the flattened yard. It was not disbelief that assaulted him; on the contrary, he believed at once. He comprehended. He knew. What he felt was the steady, tough pummeling of words against his body: *knowledge, pain, shame, emptiness, sorrow*, and, curiously, like rain falling on the other side of the city, that oxygen-laden word *relief*. A portion of what he knew was over. *The end.*

Lucy was moving toward him then, the late afternoon sun striking her face, her eyes, her working lips and teeth. Sorry, sorry, she seemed to be saying through the width of empty air.

And Larry himself, stunned, battered, and opening his mouth at last, giving way not to speech, but to language's smashed, broken syllables and attenuated vowel sounds: the piercing cries and howls of a man injured beyond words.

CHAPTER SIX

Larry's Friends
1984

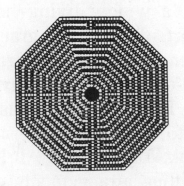

Emerging from the cramped crawlspace of his first marriage, Larry Weller was talked into attending his sixteenth high school reunion, which was to be a reception and dinner held in the school's newly spruced up gymnasium. He went along with his old classmate, Bill Herschel, and Bill's wife, Heather. Both Bill and Heather had been in the same 1968 graduating class with Larry at MacDonald Secondary.

Heather – she was Heather McPhail back then – had been class secretary, a member of the Honor Society, and a teenage beauty with flocks of good-looking boys vying for the privilege of leaning on her locker. She could have had any one of those muscular, lounging, spice-scented youths, but she opted instead for skinny Bill Herschel, math whiz and president of the Outdoor Club, whose clothes were never quite right and whose Jewish parents made him a problematic son-in-law for Heather's High Anglican family, and vice versa. They married the day after Bill finished his degree in Environmental Studies – neither set of parents attended the ceremony – and now they have two little girls, Chantal, six, and Sophie, eight.

The girls' babysitter for the evening of the reunion is a Mrs. Carroll, a widow living next door to the Herschels, a sort of honorary grandmother to the Herschel children, who has also agreed to look after Larry's six-year-old son, Ryan. Larry's arrangement with his ex-wife, Dorrie, is that he has Ryan weekends – Friday night to Sunday night – and she has him during the week. Larry hasn't told Dorrie about tonight's babysitting arrangements or even the fact that he's decided to go to his school reunion. She's being extra picky these days. She likes things done a certain way, no exceptions, and she'd be sure to get herself into a knot if she knew Ryan was going to spend the night on a fold-out couch in the Herschels' basement rec room. A damp basement was the last thing Ryan needed, with his runny nose and cough. Besides, the Herschel girls were little prima donnas, in Dorrie's opinion, just like their mother.

That part's not true. Heather McPhail Herschel is all gentleness – melting eyes, wavy brown hair, and an ample risen-bread look about her body – and she has extended to Larry Weller a thousand kindnesses since his marriage to Dorrie broke up a year ago. "Listen," she said in the first terrible days after Larry moved out, "Bill and I want to do everything we can to help you get through this. You know you're welcome here any time, night or day, and that goes for Ryan too. You can phone, drop in, whatever. We'll feed you, pour wine over your head, or you can just hang around and talk. You're going to need to talk, Larry, and we're here to listen. You can count on us, that's all I want to say. That's what friends are for."

Larry appreciates Heather's kindness, appreciates especially her refusing to badmouth Dorrie, for not saying he's had a lucky escape from a rotten marriage, which is what some of his other friends have hinted, have even told him outright. Back in high school he hadn't been able to look Heather McPhail in the eye, and he still can't quite manage it, even though she's married to his oldest friend and he sees her at least once a week. For some reason he's unable to wipe from his mind the fact that she'd been Heather McPhail in her former life, that terrifyingly popular school sweetheart and the second smartest and second-best looking girl in their class, second that is after Megsy Hicks, the number one queen of MacDonald's 1968 graduating class.

If Heather McPhail was soft and curved, Megsy Hicks was a hard, straight line. Megsy of the bold sexy sweaters and Cher-style hair, Megsy of the wide mobile lipglossed mouth in the middle of a face that was all quick sketch lines and strong severity – and attached to a moving, undulating, muscular woman's body. The fact that Megsy Hicks wore glasses and was still *popular* set her in another constellation of praise altogether. Larry had dreamed of her every night back then, but had never so much as spoken to her in the four years of high school, nor even breathed in her direction an anonymous "Hi" while passing between classes. She stared straight through him in those days, and he expected to be stared through. It was what he deserved. He was part of the jerk squad, president of nothing, member of no organization, unathletic, with barely average marks, the dreamy owner of an unreliable voice and a face that wouldn't behave; he was – he acknowledged as much – an unmemorable smudge in the 1968 yearbook, except for being a friend of Bill Herschel who had unaccountably landed Heather McPhail as a girlfriend.

Only in his boyish dreams – his daydreams that is, those soft-focused films he projected on to his bedroom ceiling before falling asleep – did Megsy Hicks reach out for his hand and cup it against her hard, sweatered breast. Her mouth pressed damp kisses down the length of his body, while her fingers grew busy with his pajama bottoms. "I've been waiting for this," she said over and over again, as if, with her glasses off, she didn't notice what a drip he really was, as though she was oblivious to the honking embarrassment of being Larry Weller and what that might mean. Her voice rang thrillingly, ticklingly, in his ear. "Again," she said in her bossy volleyball captain's voice. "Touch me here. And here."

He loved her. No one knew this, not even Bill Herschel, who'd been his best friend since they were seven years old, and what he felt for Megsy was not a simple crush, and not what his mother would have called puppy love, but the most radiant and tender of passions. Megsy, Megsy, sweet Megsy. Alone, he found himself deep in the schooling of love and love's impossibility. He wanted to protect her, and she yearned for that protection – never mind that she was

114

editor of the yearbook and class valedictorian. He, Larry Weller, would look after her. The silk of her dark hair fanned out each night on his pillow; her tiny exposed earlobes were starred with silver studs and these he lovingly touched, moving down then to her body, that long, elastic, tennis-toughened body that bent round him like a capital C – *Yes, yes, she cried* – warming the roughed, lonely sheets of his bed and holding him close.

This kind of love doesn't go away as easily as people think. It hangs in the head like a muzzy fog, sometimes for years. The only reason he'd gone to the fifth year reunion was to get a glimpse of Megsy Hicks, but she hadn't turned up. Someone, Heather probably, reported that she'd moved to Toronto and had married into money, which figured. She wasn't at the tenth reunion either, and Larry, who'd dragged his new wife, Dorrie, along, had spent a dazed evening, reworking through the filtration plant of his mind, just why his face should so suddenly lose its musculature on hearing Megsy Hicks' name, and revert to that wayward, flesh-betraying wobble of unreason. Megsy Hicks, he was told, had planned to come, but her husband had to go off to Paris – Paris, uh-huh! – at the last minute, on business, and she'd decided to go along.

There hadn't been a fifteenth reunion. Somehow it never got organized, but now there was to be a sixteenth, and Larry had let himself get talked into going. "It'll be fun for you to see some old friends," Heather told him, meaning it would do him good to feel himself part of the ongoing world once again. So what if he was divorced, she said. So were a lot of other people who'd be there.

And why, after all, should he worry? He was thirty-three years old, a father, a taxpayer, an employed citizen, the manager of Flowercity, a prospering florist shop which last week won first place in the provincial table decoration division. His foolish, puny body had filled out in his early twenties, and he'd learned, as most people do eventually, to fold his moments of terror into a wide and easy-breathing safety zone of his own devising. He'd made mistakes in his life, one big mistake anyway, his marriage to Dorrie, but he had prospects, he had a future, though he's not sure how much he really wants this new Larry self to come forward and identify itself. And most important, he had what really mattered in a person's life: he had friends.

A lot of friends or not quite enough? He isn't sure. He stands at the back of his crowded life and ponders this question.

One of his friends is a guy named Gene Chandler. Gene's a jock who likes a beer and a good laugh. The two of them got to know each other at Red River College, where Larry was studying Floral Arts and Gene was doing the Basic Communications course that later landed him a reporter's job at the *Free Press*. Now he's writing editorials, moving on. They still get together now and then for a cappuccino at the Capri or maybe a hockey game – someone down at the paper's always giving Gene free tickets. When Gene and his wife, Liz, heard about Larry's marriage break-up, they

116

had him over for seafood lasagna and urged him to share his feelings, which he tried hard to do, for their sake if not for his. He'd made a mistake. He'd married someone he had nothing in common with. He and Dorrie couldn't talk, not the way married couples needed to talk. And they had different goals, it seemed. "That's bad," Liz said, serving out forkfuls of green salad. "Having different goals can be tough."

It happened that Gene Chandler had a golfing buddy called Big Bruce Sztuwark, and it was through Gene Chandler that Larry connected with Bruce Sztuwark, who wanted a hedge maze constructed on his riverside property west of the city, and the word was that Larry Weller was into mazes. Big Bruce weighs a good two hundred and fifty pounds and possesses the untroubled bluntness of a man with pockets of dough. He and his wife, Erleen, had been over to England last year where they'd seen a terrific classic style maze, a beauty, somewhere over near Wales, he's forgotten the exact name of the place, but he was blown over by it, both of them were. Hey, Bruce said to Erleen at the time, we oughta get ourselves one of those for at home. Can't you just imagine it – a real live maze in Winnipeg!

As he talked to Larry, he rocked his magisterial chest rhythmically back and forth. "We don't need a contract," he said when they got together a second time to discuss the construction of the maze. "We've got friends in common. We can trust each other, right?"

Now Larry's spending his evenings drawing up plans, and as his 2H pencil moves over the drafting paper he's feeling himself coming alive again. The

117

apartment he's rented on Westminster Avenue is a dump, but he likes the neighborhood of worn-down early-century houses and small shops and brick duplexes. Across the street is the Tall Grass Bakery, where he buys warm bread and the city's best cinnamon rolls and where the gentle-voiced staff know him by name. *Hiya, Larry, what'll it be today?* Just like they've known him forever. Just like friends.

It was really Bob Buxtead, not Larry, who won the table decoration trophy at the Provincial Florists Association playoffs. Larry paid the registration fee and offered encouragement, and sat in the front row watching Bob, who stood in a glare of light on the stage at the Convention Center along with the other contestants. They were each given thirteen flowers to work with, a handful of dark glossy twigs, and a plug of florist's foam. An hour and fifteen minutes later, following a dramatic drum roll, Bob was declared the winner; the judges were unanimous, and now he's going off to Toronto next week for the nationals.

Bob Buxtead started out at the store two years ago as a temporary holiday replacement, just a kid, but he was so good that Larry decided to keep him on permancntly. He has a long oaken older-man's face, a square jaw carefully shaved, and a rich, strenuous way of concentrating on what his rather squarish hands are doing. He hums little encouragements to himself as he progresses on a piece, and this humming abruptly stops as he pauses to reach for a flower, a leaf, a width of ribbon, whatever he needs – and then resumes. The hum of creation. He's weird at times. Once he remarked to Larry that he saw flowers as a branch of poetry, and Larry hadn't known what to say or where to look.

Bob Buxtead brought a blue teapot to work and a box of mixed herbal teas, and he brings Larry a cup of lemon zinger or raspberry leaf in the middle of the afternoon instead of the usual bitter coffee, sitting in its pot all day. "Some people find caffeine a depressant, not a stimulant," he tactfully offered. Sports hold no interest for him – he admits it – and in fact he seems to have no aptitude at all for male joshing, for rough teasing or ongoing jokes. He arrives on time in the morning, works diligently on his orders, eats a packed lunch at noon, and breaks only for his three o'clock cup of tea. There are some days when he and Larry exchange only a few dozen words.

And yet, when Bob Buxtead announced that he was getting married to his girlfriend, a nurse at Winnipeg General, he asked Larry to serve as best man. "I can't think of a better friend," he said simply.

If friendship is a question of picking up the tune, then Larry has far from perfect pitch. But perhaps it was true that the two of them had become friends. The atmosphere at Flowercity has changed since Bob Buxtead arrived. Things are calmer, even on the busiest days, and in a curious corkscrewy way that Larry can't begin to articulate, sweeter.

Lucy Warkenten is one of Larry's good friends, although they've only known each other for a couple of years. Forty-one years old, unmarried, a bookbinder by profession, she balances a tender sense of courtesy with an impulse to lunge, lurch, and barge into the affairs of her friends, of which she has dozens. And yet, when she and Larry go off for their weekly Tuesday movie (half-price tickets for the early show) she is able to make him feel that he's her only friend, and that she is privileged to be seated next to so agreeable a person. Their after-movie pizza is accompanied by discussions on such subjects as social expectations, censorship, gardens, Egyptian labyrinths, papermaking and its place in the culture, the harm parents do their children, the futility of psychoanalysis, and the difficulties of battling grief and depression, those twin shadows. All these subjects are new to Larry, at least the expression of them, but Lucy has the ability, as he sees it, to place resonant phrases in his throat and the accompanying impulse to nod enthusiastically and say in her floating, forthcoming, ribbony voice "Exactly!"

"So, you're seeing a woman then?" Larry's mother said a few weeks ago, speaking shyly.

"Not the way you think," Larry told her.

When he's with Lucy, thoughts of age, sex, and failure slip away, and his own ignorance too. A curtain of transparency ripples between them, and he sees their friendship as a kind of enchantment he's fallen into, and knows enough to prize it. Between them they never speak of his marriage and divorce, nor of Lucy's living alone and the likelihood that she will go on living alone.

A pact between exiles?

Well, maybe.

* * *

120

Larry doesn't think of his folks as friends exactly, but in a way they are. He sees them once or twice a week, dropping in after work or bringing Ryan over for Sunday supper. They've been pretty good about the divorce, not butting in, and not coming down too hard on Dorrie. "She knows how to manage money," Larry's dad said, "that's one thing. She won't be bleeding you royal for the rest of your bloody life." Larry's mother, Dot, did say once, rather sourly, that she'd rather be a dot than a door, meaning she'd never thought much of Dorrie. "She's such a *tight* wound-up little thing."

Well, yes, Larry could see how she got that impression. Dorrie's squirrely little body seemed to be made of bundled wire. She was a natural keeper of strict schedules and hard budgets. A tireless seeker of bargains. Pitiless. (Who said that about being pitiless? Some friend of Larry's, but he can't remember who.) Once, in the midst of making love, she caught her breath and said to Larry, "Hurry up, can't you, I've got to be at work early tomorrow."

Larry's sister, Midge, who's been through the marital wars herself, is direct about Dorrie. "She's a total bitch. I mean! And on top of that she's brainless. And she tricked you into getting married. Why the hell wasn't she on the pill like every other woman in the universe? Because she's dumb, that's why. Dumb like a fox. Honestly, Lare-snare, you're well out of it. Good riddance, I say."

His son, Ryan? – is Ryan a friend? Fathers and sons are supposed to be pals. But Ryan's a little boy. He still cries when he's frustrated or frightened, and this ability to cry – and Larry's ability to comfort, at least in part – means that they're not quite friends. The footing's not equal.

He loves his child. But he was the one who walked out and left this small boy behind. That's what the crying's really about. That's another reason they aren't friends.

"A three-year marriage that doesn't pan out isn't a tragedy," said Larry's long-time friend Jim Carmody over a drink following the provincial floral competition. Jim is a flower consultant for Weddings Unlimited.

"Actually it was five years," Larry said.

"Well, whatever."

"To tell the truth, I used to wonder what you saw in her," said Sally Wolsche Ullrich, a woman who works in dried plants and flowers, and has been a friend of Larry's for some years. "Of course, no one ever understands other people's marriages, it's like those marriages are shielded from us, such terribly, terribly private arrangements when you think of it. But still! You and Dorrie always seemed to run on different gears, know what I mean?"

"Sort of," Larry said.

Ben Shaw, Dorrie's oldest brother, ran into Larry out at St. Vital Mall not long ago and said, "Hey, buddy, listen. I'm sorry as hell how things've worked with you and Dor. God only knows, she's not the easiest gal in the world – well, what woman is! Ha. Life's a bitch and then you marry one. But look, let's not let this get in the way of us being friends or anything dumb-ass like that, okay?"

Larry, who has never once thought of his brother-in-law as a friend, said, "Sure, yeah, I'm with you. Okay, Ben, okay."

"It's a rotten time," said Michael Kelly, one of Larry's neighbors on Lipton Street. Michael, who works as a stage carpenter, has just split up with his live-in partner, Scott Allyson, after twelve years. "Like, every relationship has conflict, and Scott and I hung on all this time because we were able to integrate our conflict. On the other hand, you've got to keep saying to yourself that it's damaging to live with someone who isn't the *right* person. A kind of poison creeps in, it can kill you in the end. I didn't know your wife all that well, but the one or two times we got together, well, she seemed kind of on another wavelength. Like another planet almost."

"Yeah," Larry nodded, "that's true."

"You loved her," Bill Herschel said right after the break-up. They were in Bill's car, which was piled to the roof with Larry's clothes, and they were on their way to the newly rented Westminster Avenue apartment. Larry was crying. He'd lost his son, his wife, his place on the planet.

The houses in old, narrow-streeted Winnipeg were often built in groups of three. Sister houses, they were called, double-story models whose cheap, plain

123

identical architecture was varied only by a gable or a veranda railing or a piece of gingerbread trim. The Herschels' house had been sistered with Larry's boyhood house, and between the two growing boys there had always been the airy accident and ease of friendship, which has continued into their adult life. Theirs is a friendship mitered and nailed down, and requiring not a word of analysis or effort of maintenance. Each would have been embarrassed to describe the bond between them, a bond that stretched easily over absence or confession and even, as on the day Larry left Dorrie, tears.

The crying started with nothing, just a sting behind his eyes as Bill's car pulled away from the curb, then a full-scale unstoppable propulsion of tears, and the next minute he was drowning, his throat, his lungs filling up. He was making a fool of himself, noisy and gulping for air like those heroes in movies who clutch each other in the big emotional scenes and sob out loud with their big hunky shoulders heaving. You were supposed to cry yourself watching those scenes, but Larry tends to squirm instead. And now, here he was, weeping his eyes out as the car spun on to Broadway Avenue, and here was Bill with one hand on the steering-wheel and the other on Larry's sleeve and he was saying, "You did love her. That's something you're going to want to remember. It'll make all this seem worthwhile in the long run, the fact that you really did love her in the beginning."

The final assault and mop-up of his marriage seems a blur to Larry, and he knows he has his friends to thank. His sadness was curbed, and surprisingly quickly, by the small gifts and kind words of those friends. His gratitude, though, was hobbled by the fact that he distrusted slightly the state of his own wretchedness, which felt mechanically induced and inflated, like something from a TV show. He eyed his responses skeptically, and found himself shaken by the fear of artifice, in much the same way he had been wracked by the slipperiness of his love for Dorrie during their English honeymoon, dismayed to find that love so freshly pledged and publicly sworn could keep rising up and then disappearing.

And so he wonders, looking back to the days following his leaving Dorrie, if his grief wore a kind of stage make-up that gave him away. His confusion, except for his grief over Ryan, felt bejeweled, unearned. Bill found him a lawyer, who got things rolling right away. Other friends lent him furniture, invited him to meals and football games, praised him for his so-called adjustment and offered cheerful unmocking compliments about his new growth of beard, the first serious beard of his life. Almost no one asked for the details of the break-up, and Larry was grateful for that, since he knows, even at age thirty-three, that discovery wears people out, and repetition has a way of enlarging the half-rehearsed acts that make up sad marriages.

Sometimes at night he woke from bizarre dreams and whispered to himself, "Careful, careful." Be careful of chaos, of silence, of words, of other people, of myself, that stranger Larry Weller. Sometimes, too, the felt he needed lessons in how to be a grown-up man. How do you learn to deal with the daily calendar,

125

a new red number every day, pushing you into the tunnel of an ever-receding future?

It's come as a surprise to Larry, considering the gaping hole at the center of his life, that so many of his old routines continue as before. Here he is, suddenly a single guy, a divorced man, living not in a house but in a one-bedroom apartment, but he nevertheless spends the same eight hours every day working in the same old florist establishment, taking telephone orders for the same bridal bouquets and centerpieces, and tallying up the bills at the end of the week. Flowers, their intricate waxy petals, keep him from thinking about wanting the life he wants. He still has Sunday supper sitting in his mother's padded breakfast nook, the unvarying roasted meat and potatoes and Brussels sprouts in their blue-and-white serving dish. Shame attends him, and loneliness, but there are days when he wants to say, "I'm in love," meaning in love with his new arrangements. On Saturdays he and Bill Herschel drive out to Birds Hill to spend an hour or two on the hiking trails. They've done this since they were young boys, telling each other dirty jokes, beneath which lay unlit embers of sex, what they needed to know or pronounce out loud. To Birds Hill they took a cheap Boy Scout compass and a map, and there they willed themselves to become lost, so that they could arrive, heroically, at a state of being found. It was a game; they'd invented it, its theatrics and rewards. You took a stream, you followed it closely; it would lead you somewhere; you could count on it. Larry sometimes felt that his body's essence, his sense of who he was, drained away between the bookends of those weekend walks.

Now they take their children along, Larry's son, Ryan, and Bill's two girls. Bill wears a pair of binoculars around his neck, and Larry carries a small and beautiful spiral notebook in his back pocket.

This notebook was a gift from Lucy Warkenten, she who believes so ardently in the power of books and their registered messages. "You just might want to jot down your feelings from time to time," she'd suggested shortly after the separation. "People under stress sometimes find they can discharge their feelings if they get them down on paper." This was just one of the many pieces of helpful advice Larry has received from his friends.

So far he's written only two words in the notebook, and these are on the first page. "Dorrie. Dorrie."

Often he hears of a divorced couple who become friends, and he finds himself wondering from time to time if this will ever happen to him and Dorrie. He doubts it. Some extravagant meltdown would be necessary first. Or a prolonged period of rainy stillness, leading to accidental laughter or a shared impromptu meal or an emergency of some kind or an old joke recalled, or perhaps the photographs from their English honeymoon brought out.

He's going on with his life, but at the same time he's deeply distressed, he knows he is. He reasons that being friends with Dorrie might take the edge off the panic he continually feels. But that's not going to happen; he feels pretty sure of that.

Something happened to Larry back in high school; some fever of discouragement came over him. His other, earlier self, the brave little boy standing at the edge of the playground and hugging the elbows of his woolen sweater – he had loved him better. That photograph self, posed against the green unfallen world.

But adolescent Larry Weller, that mediocre student at MacDonald Secondary in west Winnipeg, only son of Dot and Stu Weller, brother of Midge Weller – that Larry had found himself slipping backward and was too stupidly feeble to put up a defence, and too addicted to the luxury of dreams to wake up. He was condemned to daily humiliations – of not knowing how to position his feet under his desk in study hall, of accidentally slurping his soup in the cafeteria, and what made it worse was that he understood precisely how widespread, how dull, how ordinary these adolescent lapses were.

He had the wrong nose, the wrong shoulders. Once begun, the momentum of failure increased incrementally, and he was saved from real despair only by the certainty that the excruciating awe, pity, and embarrassment of his life would someday come to an end. He knew this without believing it, in the same way you know but can't believe the center of the earth is molten material. Maybe that's why he walked around wanting to punch someone in the nose. Anyone.

And yet, Bill Herschel had found his way out, why shouldn't Larry Weller? Bill had a girl, someone he took to movies, someone he kissed and whose sweater front he was allowed to touch. He'd found a way to warm his freezing limbs. Meanwhile, on Saturday nights, when his fellow students were out at a rock concert or gathered in someone's rec room to smoke, drink beer, and make out, Larry was at home reading old copies of *Popular Mechanics* or watching television with his parents, either the hockey game or the Saturday night movie. The living-room curtains were pulled snug; the furnace hummed. He felt his loneliness become a kind of embarrassment, and that embarrassment was eating his self away. Neither his mother nor father seemed to have any inkling about their son's failure to connect with the world, and, enclosed in the shell of their bland unawareness, he was safe, at least temporarily. Safety was one thing, but what he really wanted was to be electrified, to be wounded, to be cast into the wilderness, to be released, to be exalted, and most especially to be surrounded by the drowning noise and ebullience and casual presence of friends calling out his name, demanding his presence.

At ten o'clock on those long ago evenings his mother made tea and set out three mugs and a plate of fruitcake or buttered toast. No, they didn't have an inkling, and, as Bill Herschel liked to say, it takes a thousand inklings to make a clue. As long as Larry could keep his folks in a state of dumb innocence he felt he could get through it himself, this sinking hell, the slow torture of it. After that he would join the grown-up world and spend his time, legitimately, as his parents did, embedded in their cozy weekend evenings, their hobbies and TV shows. That was the future, the way out. This knowledge was stored coldly in his chest.

It seems now a long way back to those Saturday evenings, and Larry has made it a point not to relive his adolescent panics. Tonight, attending his sixteenth high school reunion, standing between Bill and Heather Herschel and joining in the school song – *Onward, onward, brave MacDonald* – he is stirred and grateful to find himself part of this celebrating crowd of men and women who are dressed for an evening of pleasure, suits and ties, short silky swinging dresses, bringing with them their grown-up regard for each other, and their newly evolved, kinder selves. Larry looks around at the singing faces and robust swaying shoulders, his classmates dwarfed in the tall shadowy gymnasium through whose open windows the fragrance of spring floats in. The old teenage sadness feels at this moment utterly displaced by the thundery weather of love, or, at the very least, good will.

The singing ends raggedly – more than a few have forgotten the words – and then, still standing, they hear from the platform a list of the deceased being read aloud, their dead classmates. Cameron Ford, Bruce Wilkinson, Shirley McGuinty, Clara-Jane Barber, Anita Beckerston, Kenny Charles, Bugsy Lambert. Someone, one of the men, moans when Bugsy's name is mentioned, a cry of shocked surprise, and then the flat unaccented reading of the list continues – Simon Lu, Charlotte Sawatski, Kay Armstrong. The dead, Larry thinks, don't have to remember names, shake hands, kiss or not kiss, or try to be funny or at ease, yet how could so many have perished in a mere sixteen years – car accidents? cancer? – and why doesn't the woman reading the names put a little bubble of tenderness around each one as she pronounces it?

Through a haze of sorrow, or was it a kind of respect

for those who'd let go of the world so uncomplainingly, Larry only gradually comprehends who it is who's rattling off the names of the dead as though they were items on a grocery list. It's Megsy Hicks.

Only she's Megsy Hicks Clarkson now, according to the program. Tall, bony, shiny-suited. Her round glasses twinkle intelligently under the lights, and her long straight hair holds flashes of gray. Just as she had once triumphed over the wearing of spectacles, Larry sees that she is now soaring above the humiliation of premature gray. There seems something magnificent about this. He feels his insides soften with remembered love and wonders, with a sidelong look in the direction of fate, if he will speak to her before the evening is out.

But the dinner places are assigned, and he finds himself at a table in the far corner of the gym. Seated next to him is Nancy Oleson, an outstandingly pretty girl back in high school, but now, in her mid-thirties, scrawny and sexless in blue stretch pants and a not very fresh cotton shirt. Her fingers play compulsively with her headful of stiffened hair. Divorced, she tells Larry. The guy was an asshole.

Bill and Heather are at the table too, and Larry would bet money that Heather's hand is resting on Bill's knee or else Bill's hand under the table has slipped between Heather's thighs. They are feeling the weight of their anointment: high school sweethearts, young love. And their faces have grown correspondingly soft, transfigured with nostalgia, radiant.

The heat catches. Skip Hurst, a former nerd like Larry, tells a long, funny story about having a flat tire in Thailand where he now lives. He's married to a Thai woman, a doctor, and he proudly passes around a photo of her holding their newly born baby. "I don't know why I came all this way to the reunion," he says suddenly, cheerfully. His skin has a capillary richness. "I hated every minute of high school."

"Oh, so did I." This, surprisingly, from Heather. Then she adds, "Until I met Bill that day in the cafeteria. He dropped his carton of milk on my shoe. The little pointy corner got me on my big toe. Yikes."

"Anything to get your attention," Bill says.

"I had a crush on you," Nancy Oleson tells Skip. She's on her fourth glass of wine, not drunk exactly, but warming up. "I guess I pretty well had a crush on anything in pants that moved."

"How about me?" Bill asks.

She gives a nice dirty laugh. "I think it was Larry I had my eye on. Yes, you, Larry Weller. You were so sweet and shy, and one day you lent me your colored pencils in geography. Mr Bailey's class."

"I remember," Larry says. It's true, he does remember.

"So why the hell didn't you ask me out, then?"

Everyone laughs. They either know the answer to this question or they don't, it doesn't matter.

They're served a tossed salad, then a plate crowded with chicken, rice, and hard peas, and for dessert a sweetly medicinal-tasting ice-cream concoction. With coffee, a hood of intimacy falls over the table, and the talk moves easily, touching on travel, children, marriage, divorce, work, disappointments. This talk is skewed with the remembrance of an old self-consciousness now banished, at least for this evening, and perhaps – who can tell? – forever. It's as though they know that the meaning of their lives is not a fact to be discovered but a choice they make, have already, in fact, made. Sixteen years have passed with their gaps and revelations. History has been laid down like paving stones, added up, subtracted, and lightly dismissed. Laughter flows, and Larry, only moderately drunk, feels blessed. If only they could go on like this forever, seated at this floating table with its covering of love. Friends, friends. Isn't this what he's longed for all his life, to be in the brimming midst of friends?

Then he feels the shadow of someone standing behind him and turns his head a fraction of an inch. It's Megsy Hicks. Her hands are actually gripping the rounded back of his folding chair so that he is in a sense in her embrace, doubly blessed on this night of rapture. Now she's leaning over him into the table's circle of warmth, her gray flecked hair swinging close to Larry's face, so close he can smell the spice of her perfume.

"Shame on you guys," she's saying, or rather barking out in her one-note student council voice. "We can't have this now, can we. How about mixing with the others. Moving around a little. Come on now, everybody, up on your feet. It's mingle time."

The invasion is so brutal and unexpected that for a moment no one speaks. Larry studies the winking surface of his dark coffee. His scalp freezes.

"I hope," Heather says carefully, "that you aren't scolding us, Megsy."

"I'm just trying –" Megsy snarls, vigorously, righteously, shaking her hair.

"Go fuck yourself, Megsy Hicks," says Nancy Oleson.

The words come lightly, sweetly, from Nancy's large droll mouth, but they are enough to blow the bad dream away. Larry is conscious of a displacement of air behind him, and the sound of the silk suit as it swishes from sight. Skip Hurst whistles a single low note. Bill and Heather Herschel turn to each other and stare, and brave, drunk Nancy Oleson has her hand clapped over her teeth. Her eyes are wild and goofy as she turns to Larry Weller, that former adolescent nobody, seeking his approval.

It takes a moment, two minutes, but what they all begin to feel is the welling up of laughter, gathering around the table like a bomb, doubling and tripling. It's going to burst the room apart when it comes.

Larry's brain sings, as though he has just worked out a long, difficult mathematical problem. And somewhere else, just out of earshot, he senses that his life is quietly clearing its throat, getting ready, at last, to speak.

CHAPTER SEVEN

Larry's Penis
1986

Larry loves to see a woman with raindrops in her hair.

And he loves to see a woman walking briskly while eating an apple, piercing the skin with her eager teeth. His first wife, Dorrie, was a daring eater of apples, grasping them firmly and gnawing them straight to their economical cores.

His now-wife – they've been married only a month – cuts her apples into wedges, then reassembles them in a Baggie for her lunch. She packs a second Baggie full of raw vegetables, carrots, celery, cauliflower, which she's washed carefully at the kitchen sink and cut, attractively, on the diagonal. A third Baggie contains a cube of low-fat cheese. These three little still lifes are created afresh each day and snugged in polyethylene covers, and Larry's wife gives a near-audible mew of satisfaction tucking these packets into her briefcase, substance transformed to abstraction, and abstraction a door to an invisible, orderly world. Things she can't see draw her closest attention, but she's vigilant, too, about the immediate details of her ongoing life. She turns and floats Larry a lazy, detached smile. The only child of elderly parents, she's learned early to take care of her external being, to be good to herself, hence her pristinely packed lunches, hence her well-pressed linen suit and beautiful, expensive shoes.

The name of Larry's new wife is Beth Prior, a twenty-nine-year-old woman who's writing her doctoral thesis on women saints.

Goodness is what she's really in search of, especially feminine goodness, that baffling contradiction. Why, in the centuries when women were denied, ignored, oppressed, and tortured, did they continue to fashion themselves into vessels of virtue? How, considering their ignorance and non-status, was it possible for them to get even a rudimentary purchase on the continuum of goodness and evil, to reflect on its meaning and to direct themselves so purely, so persistently, toward moral perfection?

Was it, Beth asks, that their smaller, more vulnerable body size drove them into wily strategies, so that by arming themselves with holy rectitude they were able to solicit the protection of men? Or, she speculates (speculation is her natural mode, as Larry more and more sees), did wearing a mask of intense goodness signal to these same men a complementary veiled intensity of passion, making these goodly women more desirable as bedmates, and thereby raising their value on the marriage market?

Or maybe – Beth does not discount the notion – women simply long to be good for the sake of goodness; maybe they're predisposed by evolutionary mapping to commit acts of charity so that a race commanded by men might not implode. For nothing, according to Beth, makes women more resistant to venal temptations than the lack of a penis and its attendant fluid and fluid sacs. Penis owners are more violent, their will more concentrated – that much is indisputable. (At this Larry blinks, but Beth hurries on.) Men are, in this respect, as much slaves to their biology as women, and cannot, therefore, be held to blame. "Don't you think," Beth asks her new husband, "that an uncontrollable rush of testosterone would impede the sort of moral deliberation required to, you know, achieve perfect goodness?"

"I'll have to think about that," Larry says.

They are having this discussion while lying on their wide white bed in a rented town house in River Forest, Illinois. The weekend sun shines through the sheer curtains, then bounces off the slick sheets on to their naked bodies.

> And so, good morrow to our waking souls
> Which watch not one another out of fear.

Earlier this morning Beth had wakened Larry by murmuring these lines in his ear. "That's John Donne talking, the horny old he-devil himself."

"One of your penis owners?" asked Larry, who has never heard of John Donne.

"Emphatically!" says Beth, taking Larry's penis

into both her hands and regarding it with curiosity, as though in search of its heartbeat. "He was a poet of the sacred who also happened to be crazy about the sexual act."

Waking up to poetry is something new for thirty-six-year-old Larry Weller, and he worries that Beth will grow tired of interpreting the literate world to him. Dorrie, his ex-wife back in Winnipeg, sells cars for a living. Mileage, cruise control, safety features, that's Dorrie's poetry. His new wife - his now-wife as he thinks of her – is a scholar, a lecturer in Rosary College's women's studies department, a specialist in holy saints and, like the poet she's just quoted, an avid sensualist-in-training. "Here it comes," she says to Larry's stiffening penis. Her voice curls back with childlike surprise. "Oh my, yes, it's coming, coming, coming, coming. Oh my, hello there!"

A tube of flesh, purplish in hue, veined, hooded, hanging there. Shaft and glans. A nozzle. A rounded snout. A cylinder wrapped like a wonton in transparent skin. Hanging there, always there, first thing in the morning, last thing at night. Trunk, stalk, drainpipe, pickle. A wagging horn strung between the legs, sewn into the body on a network of nerves and blood and cushiony scrotum. Lightning rod, rattlesnake, bum splitter. A knob, a swelling, pinky-blue, blood-filled, wormy white, its tip an open hole, leaking. A duct, a conduit, ribbed, fibrous. Dick, dink, ding-dong-bell. The family jewels. Tender, tight. A boner. A jack-hammer, a probe, a woodie. A banana in the pocket – now who said that? – someone famous, wasn't it? Mae West? The cow in the barn, and the barn door open.

(Holy embarrassment, Robin!) Cock, pendulum. Phallus. Prick. Engine. Sword, breadstick, crank and hammer. Your Henry, your Johnson, your John Thomas, your Ralph, your Charlie. Your pecker, Peter, your Billy-boy, your one-eyed-monster in his turtleneck sweater. Now damp, now dry, now itchy, now swelling, full of longing, rising, rising again, in search of, in search of what?

Larry Weller's penis is average in size. At least he thinks it is. It's widely believed that men using public urinals check out the size of the men standing next to them, but Larry's found this kind of covert comparison remarkably difficult to accomplish. Men tend to avoid staring at the penises of other men unless they are sending a direct invitational message. The penis of Larry Weller is circumcised; this was done right after he was born. The doctor had spoken to his still sore and swollen mother about male hygiene, about current thinking on the topic. The talk lasted maybe a minute and a half, but Larry will live with the decision forever, a little piece of himself missing, thrown away, returned to dust.

Larry left Winnipeg for Illinois a year ago. He loaded up his Audi 100 – his ex-wife, Dorrie, had got him a deal with one of her rivals – and drove non-stop through the long, bent, bushy state of Minnesota, its white-banked highways skirting a thousand little towns with their water towers and grain elevators shining under caps of fresh snow. He'd quit his job as manager of a Flowercity outlet. No one could believe it, his friends, his family. He'd been there seventeen years, since he was a kid straight out of the Floral Arts course at Red River College. Seventeen years on the job, the seventies, the eighties, while other guys his age were cruising the continent on motorbikes, living like bums, seeing the world.

It was three in the morning when he hit the Minnesota–Wisconsin state line. The bridge at LaCrosse was bathed in mauve light, and he drove across feeling himself a crowned monarch, propelled by the zing of his tires on the frozen bridge surface. He, Larry Weller, had been awarded a commission to build a garden maze in suburban Chicago, a rich man's toy. He was going to work under Eric Eisner, the renowned landscape architect. No wonder he drove with a sense of his own unannounced splendor, a single car alone on the bridge – his – under the singular cloud-smudged moon. Artie Shaw was on the radio with one of his golden oldies, "Begin the Beguine." Sexy. Larry's dad's favorite tune. A dumb song, but oddly, weepily, stirring. Maybe it was the music or maybe the moonlight or the thought that he was hinging his past to the present, but he felt sexy all over at that moment, even the points at the back of his scalp and under the skin of his fingertips. His penis jumped in his pants. His pisser, his pony, his jack-in-the-box. Why?

Why would anyone leave a perfectly good job, his father said, forgetting that back in the beginning, when Larry first drifted into the flower business, he was the one who was against it. It was girlie work, as he saw it, concocting little arrangements, making bouquets.

Now that Larry's father is retired, with only his

140

colostomy bag for company – so his daily complaint goes – he mourns the loss of his own work, swearing that the best and richest years of his life were spent in the Winnipeg bus factory where he was employed – and also honored, don't forget that – as head upholsterer. These days he wanders around the house, watches TV, and periodically rearranges his collection of corkscrews and bottle openers, though with less and less enthusiasm as time passes. Not working is lonely; it's too goddamned quiet, not working.

Larry's mother used to be at home all the time, a regular recluse, the family worried about her, but in the last couple of years she's become a member of the Winnipeg Agape Group, a soup kitchen housed in a nearby Anglican church. That's where she is every morning from eight-thirty till noon, stirring vats of creamed chicken or Hungarian goulash. She's ambivalent about Larry's change of job, unreeling the not very useful impartiality of the busily occupied. "I suppose it's an opportunity," she said when Larry told her he'd been asked to design a maze for a Chicago real estate giant, a millionaire with an estate in River Forest. "But it's a long, long way from home, and it's another country even."

"Go for it," his sister, Midge, said. "Get the frigging hell out of here. I only wish I'd done it when I had the chance and maybe I will yet. And, listen, if you want to hit me up for a loan, just say the word. I can live on my salary, if you call what I do living. God, I'm sick of that gift shop, the claustrophobia, Christ, and all the gifty shit we push on our dumb customers. But look, I've got poor old Paul's money growing mold in the bank, you might as well take a chunk. When he was alive he was such a cheapskate. He'd squeeze a nickel till the beaver shat. But you know something, he'd have wanted to help you out, he had a soft spot for you, you know. You never stopped shaking hands with him like a lot of people did toward the end, scared shitless. You even hugged him that once – that last week at the hospice. I was out in the corridor, I saw it happen but I didn't want to say anything at the time, I thought you'd be embarrassed. It's only money, for God's sake. You could consider it kind of like a scholarship or something."

Larry's ex-wife, Dorrie, took the news fairly calmly. She was thinking of making a change in her life too, leaving the car sales business and getting into retail clothing. A major chain had approached her; she was mulling it over. You could move sideways in her line, that was the beauty of sales. As for Ryan, he was eight years old now, old enough to be put on a plane and go down to Chicago for holidays with his dad. And there was always the phone. Rates before seven a.m. were a bargain; they could phone back and forth every day if they felt like it.

Flowercity, about to be taken over by Flower Village, a Japanese conglomerate, accepted Larry's resignation coolly, presenting him with a small severance payment and a lapel button in sterling silver, an enameled rose embedded in its surface. "You going to wear that thing?" Larry's father asked.

Big Bruce Sztuwark hosted a farewell banquet for Larry out at the West Kildonan Country Club, and all Larry's friends were there: Bob and Fiona Buxtead,

Gene and Liz Chandler, Larry's mum and dad and sister, Midge, Bill and Heather Herschel and their two kids, Lucy Warkenten, Jim and Jenny Carmody, Sally Ullrich (formerly Sally Wolsche) and poor falling-down-drunk Cubby Ullrich, on and on, even Larry's ex-wife, Dorrie, and little Ryan, all dressed up in a blazer and his first honest-to-goodness necktie. Thirty-five people sat down to roast beef and trimmings. Bruce, as emcee, delivered in his wet belchy voice what everyone afterward referred to as a eulogy. ("You'd of thunk you'd gone and died!" Sally whispered.) Larry Weller heard himself praised for his loyalty, his steadfastness, his honesty. "And I want to say," Big Bruce wound up, "that this man sitting here before you is a genius. You've all seen the maze he's installed out at our place, and that my wife, Erleen, and myself are so thrilled to death with. You've seen the photos in the paper and the colour spread in *Maclean's*. Well, my friends, this here is the guy who created it all. Let's have a toast, ladies and gents, to our great pal who's an artist of the true ilk. I give you Larry Weller, master maze maker and a good egg too!"

"Well," Sally said at the end of the evening. "Talk about being the celebrity of the night! I'll bet you had a double erection taking all that in. I'll bet you were in orgasm heaven."

Sally Wolsche was Larry's first. His first lay, his first fuck, though he never thinks of her in such terms – he's always been too tenderly grateful, too dazed at his good fortune. That she would look at him at all seemed an act of kindness, that she would offer him a course in

143

sexual first aid seemed a miracle. He thinks of Sally as a random force, a zephyr, who by chance crossed his path and – with purpose, pity, giggling a little as she unzipped his pants – rescued him from shame. There he was, a mere boy at eighteen, unkissed, untouched, unfucked, numbly average, bashfully unexamined. He'd scarcely ever talked to a girl. How this happened he didn't know. His skin was moderately good, which should have been something to trumpet in the trough of adolescence, but his body worked against him, that spindly trunk, those jointed legs and arms with their concavities, their long, mournful uncertainties.

After high school he'd registered for the Floral Arts Diploma, and because of his mediocre marks was accepted on probation. "You'll have to show us you can keep up with the curriculum," his advisor told him the first day of the course. Her hair was white and lustrous, as befits a floral arts teacher, and she transfixed Larry with a stern smile. Twenty-four women and two men were enrolled, although Larry didn't think in terms of their being men and women. He felt himself still a boy, and Marty Ross, with his stutter and his blue tractor hat plastered to the back of his head, was, if anything, even more of a boy. The girls, though, the twenty-four randomly shaped, differently scented girls, with their massed hair, their flowing blue-denimed bodies, their loose-leaf note-books shifting on their sweet shadowy laps – these girls brought a rollicking ease into the classroom that was exuberantly, intoxicatingly feminine. Was it their sense of their own overwhelming numbers that released the brakes? Whatever it was, Larry had never been exposed to such continuous wavelets of girlish laughter. Everything made them laugh, their instructors, their textbook illustrations, their own ineptitude as they struggled to put together those early flower arrangements. The sound of rising girlish laughter pleated the classroom air, charging the atmosphere with a rippling female power, and stunning the two male members of the class, who found themselves assigned, suddenly, to the not dishonorable role of class mascots, vaguely comic, poked and teased and helplessly adored.

Of all those girls Sally stood out as the prettiest. At nineteen she was a year older than Larry, but miles ahead in sexual experience. She fell into conversation with him at the first get-together party, an event advertised as "an opportunity to mingle with your peers." The evening consisted of coffee, donuts, and an enthusiastic greeting from Mrs. Starr, who urged them to linger and "develop a sense of your mutual concerns as young neophytes in our field."

"So how did you decide on the Floral Arts course?" Sally said, plumping herself down beside Larry in the general-purpose room where the party was being held.

He hadn't recognized this as a merely social question, and so he fell silent and serious, trying to recall why actually he *had* registered on the course, and wondering whether to tell Sally that it had been his mother's idea, and that this decision, like almost everything in his life, had presented itself without any easily available alternatives.

"You like flowers or what?" Sally put it to him more directly.

What should he tell her? His breath ran fast around his head. It had never occurred to him to take a position on flowers, to like them or not like them. He hadn't really thought much about flowers, their forms, their uses. A few months ago he'd finished high school, ingloriously, a C average, and now he was forced to ponder the question of how to earn a living. All this had happened faster than he'd imagined. His father was leaning on him to apprentice in sheet-metal work at the bus factory. His mother had got a bee in her bonnet, though, about floral design.

"Well," Sally said, crossing her long legs and tracing a lazy circle in the air with her foot, "I personally think flowers are the future. Like we've got all the basic stuff, people I mean. We've got houses and furniture and cars and groceries. So what we need is something to stick on top of all those basics. We need something non-essential. Something, you know, beautiful to look at. I've thought a lot about this. Another thing, I think people need something in their life that's perishable, so that when it dies you just go out and buy some more. You always know there's more out there to be had, and that feels good. See what I mean?"

She wore wide brown fringed pants and a vest edged in the same silky fringe. Larry found himself staring at the front of the vest, the way it tied over a white ribbed T-shirt. "Artificial suede," she said suddenly, as though this was something he needed to know. "Washable." Then she said, "I've got my mom's car. You want a lift home after the party?"

"Let's drive through Assiniboine Park," she said

when she was behind the wheel. "And see if anything's going on."

Later, her car parked in the moonlight by the entrance to the English Rose Garden, the window cracked to let in the soft, smoky autumn air, she said, socially, "Hey, you know something? – you've got all the luck. Two guys in the class and a bevy of girls."

Bevy. He wondered what that meant.

"I mean, you can have your pick. Just point your little lordly finger and she's yours. And you know what else? You could have Marty Ross too."

"Marty?"

"I see him giving you the eye. The come-on."

"Really?"

"Didn't you know he's queer as a kipper?"

"Well," he hesitated, "I wasn't a hundred percent sure."

"I can always tell," Sally said. "I look at a man's ass and I can figure out right away which way he swings."

In the darkness of the car Larry felt his face heating up and his penis glowing like a flashlight inside his dress pants. Sally Wolsche had looked at his ass. She had *appraised* his ass. He wondered what his ass looked like. He'd spent a lot of time thinking about his penis, its appearance, its relative size, how it responded to the pressure of his fingers whenever he thought of Megsy Hicks from back in high school, how it betrayed him with its sudden eruptions while he slept, how his best friend, Bill Herschel, referred to his own penis cheerily as a friendly trouser snake, a third leg, a turkey neck. It was baffling: when he looked at himself in the mirror it seemed his penis and testicles

147

were heavy and gloomy, yet they felt the lightest, hottest part of him – why was that?

But he'd never considered his ass as worthy of attention. Two tight cheeks packed in clean white underpants and blue cords, hidden from the world, but not it seemed from Sally Wolsche, who had looked, judged, and was now wiggling out of her pants and placing Larry's hand to the folded darkness between her legs, assuring him she'd been on the pill since she was fifteen.

Of course, he blew off too soon that first time – you stupid prick, he said to himself – but Sally only held him in her smooth, decent, girlish arms and told him in teacherly tones that it was okay, that it happened all the time, that next time she'd show him a way to hang on to it.

Next time! The words burned behind his eyes. When?

Sally paused, considering. "I've got a real busy week ahead," she said. "Other commitments. How about right now? If you can get it on, that is."

She gazed into the whiteness of his lap, and then, to his astonishment, ducked forward and flicked the tip of her tongue against his limp still-wet penis, bringing it instantly to life, so that he found his body all at once too glad to think, and too close to its melting point to remember afterward what it was he felt. He knew there was utility in this act of hers, a problem-solution briskness that sat on a different shelf than the act of love. Nevertheless he loved her, his sweet Sally, his beloved. (All his life he would be sexually aroused by the grayed air of autumn.)

And he was grateful, grateful. His excited heart beat like a floppy fish in a body that felt suddenly upended, emptied out, lost in a shrug of ecstatic ease. Acting out of curiosity, boredom, or some uncredited school of charity, Sally Wolsche had taken his puny, unamplified self and unlocked the door to his body and to that greater mystery of where he stood on the planet. He had touched the silken skin of a woman's inner thigh and had, with a little encouragement, placed his tongue inside a woman's mouth. His penis (his pistol, his wand, his root and rudder) had tumbled out into the world just as it was supposed to do and found itself an answering vessel, its first ride, its first rich wonderlandish satisfaction. In one night he'd gone from first kiss to first breast touch, and then he'd been taken "all the way," as people said in those days and maybe still do. He hugged himself for joy. Everything in his life could be revised now, given the hard waxed shine of pertinence and good faith. He could do what his fellow human beings did, what they were meant to do. He was like other people, he was going to be able to live in the world in the same way other people lived.

One week later Sally came to class with a diamond ring on her finger. She and a young man called Cubby Ullrich, a student in the Furnace Repair course, were planning on a spring wedding. "I guess it'll be like going steady for life," she told Larry, giving a helpless little shrug of apology and a not-quite wink.

"It is not exactly a thing of beauty," Beth said of her husband Larry's penis. "Now, breasts are beautiful. And lips. Even vaginas are nice and compact, all folded up so neatly, not showing off. But penises! I don't mean just yours, Larry, I mean penises in general. Their color and texture – you can't forget for a minute that they're made of veins and crepey flesh. And it's always there, hanging there. Dangling. Or poking out like a frying-pan handle. Don't you ever wish you could have a vacation from it? A day or two off?"

"It's not like that, " Larry assured her. "If you've always had it, you don't even think of it that way."

"What's odd is that you're obliged to use the same" – she paused – "the same system for peeing *and* for sperm delivery. Like a Swiss army knife, if you see what I mean. It's got these totally different functions. There must be a little brain in there, a little morsel of cerebral tissue anyway that says, okay, pay attention, it's insertion time. Or else, don't get excited, this is only a urination stop."

"It figures it out."

"It's beautiful."

"I thought you said it was ugly."

"The concept is beautiful."

"You're beautiful, Beth." He meant it. He said it again, overwhelmed – "You're beautiful" – against the hemstitched pillow case, under the shaded lamp that beamed a spotlight of heat on her bare shoulder. He loved her depths and mysteries, the sudden stretch of her smile, the sight of her quick oval face turning toward him, her head with the cutting contour brightness at the hairline, tapering to a point on the back of her neck. He wanted to sink his teeth into that point. Sometimes she sat on his chest, and he reached up with his thumbs, smoothing the place where her hairline sliced its clean way against the white of her neck.

When he was introduced to her at the Barnes' reception his first week in Chicago, he had been taken by the shaped hollow of her wrists. Later he came to love the knife-edged angle of her shoulder blades too, and her shadowy throat, her shoulders with their cool shelf of bone, her bent knees, the dark wedge of hair between her legs, the lovely lanky sprawl of her in bed. "Beautiful, beautiful."

He was always telling her she was beautiful.

"You know what St. Brigid had to say about beauty," she said to Larry abruptly one evening, catching his eyes on her body as she drew a sweater up over her head.

"Brigid?"

"Sixth century, Irish. Kind of a country girl, milk-maid type, but very beautiful, also extremely devout. She prayed to be made ugly so she could fend off her suitors."

"Why?"

"She wanted to marry God. Or Jesus, rather. And her prayers were answered. One of her eyes grew enormously big and the other one disappeared, so her father said all right, you can be a nun."

"A one-eyed nun."

"And then there was St. Lucy. Third century, late third century, but I'd better check on that. She was so sick of being told she was beautfiul that she plucked out her eyes and threw them in her lover's face."

"I guess that showed him."

"What these women wanted was spiritual purity. Of course, they were probably a little crazy and some of them were anorexic and dying to die. The shortest route to heaven was a quickie divorce between the body and the spirit."

"So sex was out of the picture."

"Was she beautiful?"

"Who?"

"Dorrie? Your first wife?"

Larry blinked. This seemed a trick question, arriving without preamble.

"Well, was she?"

"It's hard to say."

"Why, Larry?" Beth's voice bent sharply, and her eyes stared hard at the bony plate in his chest. "It seems to me that's something you would have noticed in five years of marriage, whether or not your wife was beautiful."

"She could be attractive."

"Fat or thin?"

"Skinny."

"A skinny car saleswoman. Wait, I'm getting an image. Lots of jangling jewelry?" She said this cruelly, which was not her usual way.

"Lots."

"Gobs of blue eye shadow?"

"I can't remember."

"Oh God, why am I jealous of her? Will you explain that to me please?"

"You shouldn't be. There's no reason."

"I'm mean. I'm pathetic."

"You're not."

"There is a reason, though."

"What?"

"Because you told me once, way back when we first met, that she was sexy."

"Did I say that?"

"You said sex was the only part of your marriage with Dorrie that worked."

"Well, except for the end, the last few months. At the end nothing worked."

"Oh, Larry, love, I shouldn't have brought this up. You look so tragic and sad all of a sudden. You look like you're going to cry."

Larry met Dorrie Shaw at a Halloween party in 1975. He came as a clown; she was a Martian. The Martian suit, with its spiky green antennae and pointed shoes, made her look full of sparks and suppressed laughter. Her breasts were small and round, and, he guessed, hard as tennis balls. When she danced she swerved her hips wildly, her feet moving like flints, but she held her upper body stiff with her elbows tucked in close. The effect was unexpectedly elegant. And sexy.

A week later he phoned her at work – she'd let slip that she was employed by Manitoba Motors – and asked her out to a movie. "I'm the clown guy," he reminded her. "Oh, yeah," she said. "You're the one who works in a flower store."

A few days later he was in her bed, sweetly, plumply, satisfyingly fucked. Dorrie had her own apartment on Lorraine Avenue, a miniature living room, a strip kitchen, and a surprisingly large bedroom with a double bed. Larry could tell she'd put some thought into the bedside lighting, which was soft and pinkish in tone.

He was twenty-five and had been to bed with five different women since his first encounter with Sally. Not a large number, but not a shameful zero either. At this time in his life he began to suspect that there was more ongoing sex in the world than he'd been led to believe, though he wasn't sure about Dorrie's sexual past. She was secretive, careful, clean, and skillful. Her personal contradictions kept him off guard; she was a distracted woman but one who possessed the gift of fierce concentration. She kept her eyes squeezed tight when she made love, her whole body taking him in its grasp and, afterwards, falling asleep under the dead-weight of happiness, the peace of the well-fucked – as she herself would have put it.

Fucking was her sole word for the act of love, and she was able to pronounce that charged, heated monosyllable with a calm neutrality, exactly as she pronounced such other activities as shopping or driving. How many other men had there been? He was always, before their marriage, and during, on the edge of putting the question to her, but when the subject loomed, some sharp movement on her part, a dismissive shake of her head, warned him to hold off. She kept her secrets, and he half admired her for leaving him to pluck them out by guesswork.

They made love in his father's car, on the floor in the backroom of the florist's where he worked, on the grass at Birds Hill Park, in an upstairs bathroom at Bill and Heather Herschel's, where they went to a house-warming party, in eleven different freezing hotel rooms during their honeymoon in England, on an airplane coming home to Canada, struggling under the Air Canada blanket and trying to keep their breathing inaudible. When they came together they were intense and silent, as though they'd been born to an age ignorant of the discourse of love. Endearments, curses, complaints closed themselves off when their bodies joined, a light switch doused. Only at the end of their marriage did Dorrie sometimes bark into his ear a command to hurry, that he was taking too long, and that was one of the ways he knew it was over between them.

Larry doesn't like to think of himself as being prim or prudish, not at all, and yet he never really got used to the way Dorrie said fuck instead of making love.

Plunge, prick, thrust, ram, split, screw, stab, and throb. Pulsate, stroke, bang, pummel. Hot beef injection. Slam, pierce, penetrate. Skewer, poke, drill, pop. Enter, entering into the darkness, the body, losing yourself in fire, in silence, in love.

When Larry was in his late teens he started jogging in the early evening after supper. "Ha," Larry's dad said with a lazy wink, "I'd rather do my jogging between eleven and twelve at night." As far as Larry knows, this was the only instance in which his father had referred to the act of sex.

But Mr. Herschel, next door, was full of sexual innuendo. An extroverted twinkly neighborhood man, a planner of block parties, the possessor of a full head of hair, pale-eyed, tie-clipped, he liked his jokes broad and raw and was always ready with a variation. "When the weather's hot and sticky," he recited, "That's no time for dipping dickie. When the frost is on the pumpkin, that's the time for dickie dunking."

Were penises funny then? Or such a serious business that they had to be roughly masked in back-yard humor. Was a penis an event? Was it history? Was it sacred or profane? As a boy Larry didn't know. And at age thirty-six he still doesn't know. The business of sex holds these questions in its mesh, like sequins or tiny beads.

How does a penis taste? He'll never know.

All he knows is that his penis is with him forever, doing more or less what a penis is meant to do. It's his to wash and tug at and dust with talcum powder and look after and use, and his to witness as it grows old along with the rest of his body. His partner in life, this extension of flesh, so creaturely, blind, and blundering, so friendly and willing in its puppyish moods, but which, in the future – he has no doubt about it – will be ready to betray him.

"Just tell me this," Beth Prior asked her new husband. "Did you love Her? Or should I even be asking this question?"

"You know you have every right to ask that question."

"Well?"

"Yes."

"What do you mean yes?" Her fingernails were flat and clean like little stained-glass windows.

"I loved her. But that was then. This is now."

"And there's nothing left, you swear?"

"It was a long time ago."

"Is that your best answer?"

"I think so."

"Shall I turn out the light?"

"Yes."

"Ready?"

"Ready."

Three years ago, when Larry's father started having pains in his gut, his wife, Dot, made him go to the doctor. Some tests were ordered, but the results were inconclusive. It was decided after some consultation that he should have a CAT scan.

The machine was a miracle but at the same time a disappointment. A big humming beer can, Larry's father had been led to believe. He thought he was going to feel like rolling into a science fiction story, but it wasn't like that at all. It was – well – like normal. Except that there in the silent half-darkness his body was chopped into transverse slices and photographed. A slice of pancreas, a slice of liver, a slice right through his lower colon where the cancer was eventually discovered. The sealed human body was, after all, a knowable country, with its folded hills and valleys laid open to view.

This is how Larry thinks of his life. He was born in the year 1950, and, given extraordinary luck, it's possible he'll live for a hundred years, right into the middle of the next century, in fact – ending his life in the year 2050. This span of years feels lucky to him and almost mystical in its roundness and balance.

But when he looks at that allotted time and the self he's been assigned, he is unable to focus. The sequential years shatter the minute he sets his glance in their direction. They lose their meaning, and fall instead into CAT-scan slices, brilliantly dyed and intricately detailed: his work, his friends, his family, his son, his love for his two wives, his bodily organs – and the few small bits of knowledge he's managed to accumulate so far.

His brain is always busy, and he wonders if other people live their lives in the same state of unfolding thought; it's as though a little man lived inside his head, a dancing stick figure who gestures and darts just behind the wall of his forehead, a loose-jointed professor jumping up and down with excitement, debating, questioning, and never sleeping except when Larry sleeps.

For the last few years he's been thinking of the *how* of mazes. How to design and install them, what shrubbery to select, how to maintain and control growth. Now, under the direction of Dr. Eric Eisner, he is thinking of the *why* of the subject. Dr. Eisner – sixty-five years old, bald, slit-eyed, portly – rejects, on the whole, the theory that the medieval garden maze constituted a holy pilgrimage in microcosm, a place where a pilgrim might wend his way to the maze's secret heart and therein find sanctuary and salvation. "It's an awful cute theory," Dr. Eisner tells Larry in his south Chicago accent, "but a little too neat." No. According to Dr. Eisner, the underlying rationale of the maze is sexual – this from a man who lives alone in a high-rise apartment and appears to have no sexual impulses whatever. A labyrinth, Dr. Eisner says, twists through the mystery of desire and frustration. It doubles back on itself, relishing its tricks and turns. It's aroused by its own withholding structure. In the center, hidden – but finally, with a burst, revealed – lies sexual fulfillment, heaven. "Or as close to heaven," Dr. Eisner concludes breezily, socially, "as any mortal man can come."

That's where Larry is now. At the site of that heaven. Forget the past, forget the future, the real music is spilling out of now, out of here. It's crashing on his eardrums. It's the lozenge on his tongue, the swelling of his penis, the shapes of women's eyes, the outreaching limbs of trees, the suck, the sniff, the saver of this minute – which will not come again.

Beth Prior, Larry's now-wife, likes to claim she's a third-wave feminist, which means she's anxious to understand the mysteries of men as well as women.

She's fond of quoting what Toni Morrison says about "the other" that Americans fear and envy and anguish over. Only it was never race for me, Beth says. It was men who were "the other." Who were they really? What did they want?

"Now let me get this straight," she asks Larry. (It's Sunday afternoon; they're lying naked except for a coating of sunblock, in the blaze of the enclosed deck off their townhouse on Harlem Avenue. She has her nose in a terry beach towel, and her fingers are tapping a tune on Larry's warm chest.) "When teenage boys go around having erections and daydreams and masturbating all over the place and *suffering*, what is it they actually *want*? I mean, do they just want to stick their penises *into* something? "

"You mean like in a knot-hole? Or a jar of liver?"

"I'm serious. I need to know these things."

"I don't think so. That's not all of it, not just sticking it into something."

"Or ramming it into something."

"You mean like punching someone in the nose?"

"Something like that."

"I used to go around wanting to punch someone in the face –"

"You, Larry? I can't believe it."

"It's hard to explain."

"Who did you want to punch?"

"It wasn't a who. It was – just the whole world."

"You're talking about ordinary male anger and aggression."

"Maybe. I grew up with a dad who was mad, remember."

"A mad dad. I don't see your father that way. What was he mad at?"

"At the government. His gas mileage. And, I don't know, he was mad at the newspaper, mad at the weather. Mad at everything. It could be I caught it from him."

"Like a virus."

"Or it could be just – just wanting to be noticed."

"And do you still want to punch someone in the nose?"

"Sometimes. Not as often, but sometimes. How did we get on this subject?"

"I was asking you why boys want to stick their

penises into things." She propped herself up on her elbows, her face peering at him sideways, earnest and avid and smiling into his eyes. "Tell me."

The rapture of another body, of a woman's body – that was it, he wanted to tell her, or the largest part of it. Wanting to know another body and knowing your own was never going to be enough. But to say this to Beth was to risk her feeling she was only a portion of a larger female tide that washes over him and makes his existence bearable.

And there's something else that Beth can never be told, which is that the wholly unexpected happiness of Larry's second marriage has created within him a new tide of love toward his first wife, Dorrie. During his and Dorrie's brief marriage the feeling between them had never been more than a ragged, stunted, starved impulse; the two of them lacked the imagination to bring anything more to life, and at the time of the separation he had come close to hating her. But now, since meeting Beth, he's been conscious of a rapid and steady mending of his old faulty attachment. In the mist of his subconscious his now-wife, Beth, and his then-wife, Dorrie, merge: a pair of sea creatures, sisters, all skin and clefts and tender seeking hands. The old resentments and angers of his life with Dorrie have faded from view, leaving a circle of radiance behind: their young, uncertain bodies, their heart-breakingly dumb silence, their wordless arrival at states of ecstasy, and the long sleep that followed, the happy, enviable, reassembling unconsciousness of children.

Sometimes Larry feels that Beth has taken over the old injuries of his first marriage and made them hers.

But how unjust for one person to unload his grief on to another! It was like the story Beth told him not long ago, how the one-eyed St. Brigid possessed the magic power to pass her chronic headaches along to a minor fellow saint, who willingly assumed them and who became known, for his troubles, as the patron saint of headaches.

"You never answered my question," Beth said sleepily, turning away from him. She reached around and tucked her hand between his legs. "About boys' penises. About what penises want to do?"

There were mysteries, Larry knew, snugged in the corners of the universe. No one knows, for instance, what keeps a bicycle vertical when it's in motion. No one knows why a man needs to show the world different versions of himself, and that one of these versions is the burrowing animal need to touch someone else.

"I'll have to think about that," Larry said to the smooth sheen of his wife's back, shutting his eyes against the sun and against Beth's ever-questioning voice, protecting her from the ratchety movement of his thoughts, knowing he was falling short of her expectations, and that he would always in one way or another fail her.

CHAPTER EIGHT

Larry Inc.
1988

A/MAZING SPACE INC.
Laurence J. Weller – Landscape Architecture
Specialty: Garden Mazes
982 Lake Street, Suite 33, Oak Park, Il. 91045
Telephone: 312 999 2888
Fax: 312 999 8884

At the age of thirty-eight Larry Weller finds himself a member of a rarefied and eccentric profession: he is a designer, and what he designs and installs are garden mazes. A simple maze maker is what he prefers to call himself; the alliteration of the label appeals to him, and so does the artisan directness and the hands-on assumption, even though he's obliged, every time, to stop and explain what a maze maker *is*, the insiderly scoop, and what he *does*. Larry's maze specialty twinkles at the edge of his world, often its only point of color; there are fewer than a dozen maze makers in the world; they're a rare breed.

He admits to anyone curious enough to ask that the North American market for mazes is small, minuscule really, since those who hanker for luxurious garden toys need to be both rich and intellectually quirky. In getting into formal gardening he has caught, entirely by accident, one of the generational updrafts: the realization that there is time at the end of this long, mean, skeptical century for leisure, time for the soul's adornment. Maze aficionados tend to possess an off-key imagination, a sense of history (be it warped or precise), a love for teasing mysteries or else a desperate drive toward the ultimata of conspicuous affectation. Such people are rare but they do exist. They can be ferreted out, as Laurence J. Weller has discovered, through word of mouth or by means of tiny, boxed, well-placed advertisements in the back pages of *Real Estate Gold* or *Architectural Digest*.

Larry, who grew up in a blue-collar family in Winnipeg, Canada, is still uneasy in the company of the rich, though he's dependent on them now for his livelihood. That was one of the points he and his wife, Beth, had to consider when he officially hung up his shingle last year. He's become a person adept in the dodge-and-feint department. (Yes, Mr. Barnes. Of course, Mr. Barnes.) A learned shamelessness is the cloak he puts on, having mastered the art of listening deferentially, head to one side, one eyebrow richly attentive, ready to absorb some new and astounding counter-proof – *absolutely, Mr. Barnes*. He is obliged to explain, patiently, pad and pencil in hand, such things as maze mathematics, maze aesthetics and conventions, possible maze construction, and finally, breaking the news as quietly as possible, the high cost of maze maintenance. Is this going to be his life, he wonders, articulating to the rich the particular ways in which they can part with their cash?

He's noticed that the heft of money makes the bodies of the wealthy more dense, more boldly angled and thus threatening, even when suited, dressed, coated – and wrapped in the soundlessness of their immense, padded, and luxuriously ventilated office spaces. The rich are underpinned by ignorance, he's noticed. They know nothing of the authentic scent of dust and dowdiness. They never knew a time when people bought winter tomatoes in little cardboard cartons, four of them lined up beneath a cellophane roof, twenty-nine cents, and how thrifty housewives – like Larry's mother, for instance – used only half a tomato for the family salad each night, so that the box lasted eight days, just over a week. The rich – except for the self-made rich – believe they're biting at the apple of life just because they know enough to appreciate pre-Columbian art and handpieced quilts. They're out of touch, they're out to lunch, they breathe the dead air of their family privilege.

Larry can't yet speak the many-branched language of money: the dizzying vocabularies of *commodities, equities*, or the running phrases that spill from the

165

mouths of the moneyed and then hook into a thick mesh of entitlement – what they want, what they expect. "This will all have to be done over," said Larry's most recent client, Phillip Jasper of the Jasper Foundation (tobacco, sportswear, plastics, cancer research). "The green of those hedges is too green-green. What I want is a blue-green. Deeper, more European like. A religious green, if you know what I mean. Oceanic. Big. But intimate too."

"Completely done over. You don't mean complete –"

"Cost? Don't worry about it. This is heritage we're talking about. What I'm leaving behind. A lasting monument. But it's also something I want my very, very dear friends to enjoy in the here and now."

"If you're absolutely sure –"

"Right. So, we're on, Mr. Weller? Terrific. Now if you'll excuse me I've got a meeting in exactly three minutes and –"

"I could show you some samples of the amur privet that has a dark-green leaf and does well in compacted soils –"

"I'll leave it to you, okay? You're the expert, Mr. Maze. Hey! How about that for a name! Mr. Maze!"

Larry now has nine completed projects in his portfolio, though he supposes he can't really count his first maze, which was a crude experiment in his own yard back in Winnipeg. He thinks of it often, though, even after all these years. The angled alignment of shrubs had completely surrounded the little house on Lipton Street, the mixed greens of cotoneaster, caragana, and alpine currant, hearty northern shrubs all of them, and it had driven his first wife wild. She wanted a lawn like other people had, not a bunch of snaky bushes running all over the place and giving her the heebie-jeebies.

Larry had copied the overall plan for that first effort out of a book of mazes he'd borrowed from the library, a design created by a sixteenth-century Italian architect named Serlio. Of course, he'd had to simplify the center of the plan, where his and Dorrie's two-bedroom house stood with its wooden siding and concrete block foundation. According to the diagram, the hedge corners were supposed to be crisply squared, but Larry, in those days, was always behind on the pruning, and his second-hand gasoline-powered hedge-trimmer was awkward to hold. "It's like living in a leaf pile," Dorrie said. "I'm ashamed for people to know I live here."

After supper on summer evenings Larry loved to take his small son, Ryan, by the hand and lead him from the maze "opening" at the front gate of his house to the "goal," which was next to the side door, a small grassy square where in the future he hoped to install a mechanical fountain. (When he had the time. When he'd saved up enough dough.) Ryan, already bathed for the night and in his pajamas, toddled by Larry's side, running his free hand across the top of the growing hedges, singing as he went and learning by heart, even at the age of three or four, the secrets of the various turnings. Turn on the first right, take the next two lefts, then right from then on. A classic formulation.

It may be that Larry has romanticized this particular memory. The soft kiss of the evening sun, the dizzy, unalarming purr of mosquitoes in his ear, his little boy's hand in his, Dorrie wearing shorts and a T-shirt glancing up from the front steps where she sat with the newspaper spread on her lap, the fragrance of grass and leaf, color and calm, an occasional car drifting by. He can scarcely believe, looking back today, that such innocence ever existed. And he can't imagine why he hadn't felt himself the happiest man in the world.

One day back in Winnipeg when Larry was still working in a florist's shop, he got a phone call from a man called Bruce Sztuwark, who said he wanted to build a garden maze out on his West Kildonan property. He'd heard about Larry through the grapevine, a mutual friend actually, and he'd heard good things. Was Larry interested in a commission? Great!

Larry, remembering how hard it had been to keep his own hedge corners in trim, especially the ferny caragana, designed a maze for Bruce and Erleen Sztuwark that was mostly circular lines and which employed as its principal planting stock the hedge maple (*Acer campestre*), which requires only light pruning. He worked the Sztuwark maze up from the ancient plan – another library book – of a man named Androuet du Cerceau, who was Catherine de Medici's architect, but added a few extra curves and teasing half-circles, his own invention, so that the whole plan undulated before the eye. There were beguiling shadows, or at least there would be when the plantings had had a chance to grow, but there were no long views, no *allées* – something most landscape architects feel is vital in maze design; Certainly Eric Eisner, the granddaddy of America's great landscape artists, believes the *allée* to be the *essence* of the formal labyrinth.

But the rich Sztuwarks were not formal people. They liked the relaxed circular plan. Larry did try to explain to them, taking his time, that every classical maze contains at its heart a "goal." This is the prize, the final destination, what the puzzling, branching path is all about. The goal can be a small mound or an ornamental tree or a topiary figure, or it can be a modest statue or fountain or even a reflecting pool. The famous Hampton Court maze has at the center two bench seats, each shaded by a tree. The choices are limitless, but there is always *something* to reward the patience of those who have picked their way through the maze's path and arrived at the chosen place.

Bruce, a lawyer and owner of a local radio station, and his silent, sullen wife, Erleen, listened carefully to what Larry had to tell them, and then they announced, or rather Bruce announced, that they had already decided on a "goal." It was to be a barbecue pit large enough to accommodate the big outdoor gatherings they liked to throw in the summertime.

Well, why not, Larry was able to say after a minute, after he'd sucked in his breath and got a grip on the situation.

Whatever the client wants. It was part of the deal, and Larry Weller, Mr. Maze himself, learned that lesson early.

The Sztuwark maze caught the attention of a local journalist-photographer, Mark Mosley, who tracked its construction from first plowing to the third year of growth. An exhibition of the Mosley photographs was held in Winnipeg's ACE Gallery, and *Maclean's Magazine* picked it up, running a feature article titled, not very accurately, BALD PRAIRIE TRANS-FORMED TO QUANT ELIZABETHAN GARDEN. There was a photo of Larry, too, looking taller and leaner than he was in real life, standing under a tree and poring over a set of plans. And no doubt about it, it was the *Maclean's* coverage that brought in his next client, the Saskatchewan Provincial Fair Board.

The Saskatchewan maze, dismantled at the end of the fair season, was constructed entirely from bales of hay stacked one on one to a height of seven feet and forming a meandering hay-fragrant tunnel that drew over one hundred and fifty thousand tourists toward its center, which was a wheel of earth tilted slightly forward and planted with prairie wildflowers, vibrant pie-shaped sections of blooming color.

Larry's own feelings about the Saskatchewan maze were mixed. On one hand, its carnival popularity was reassuring, though one visitor, an elderly farmer, became so hopelessly disoriented that he suffered an anxiety attack and had to be hospitalized overnight in Regina. Children loved it. Dogs and cats loved it. Cyclists found its tight corners a challenge, and a new sport, cycle-mazing, briefly, illegally, flourished in the small hours of the night. But the deadness of the maze material depressed Larry. Straw was tan. Straw was dusty and static. And what he loved about mazes was their greenness and growth, the vital plant tissue when it had been coaxed into new shapes, so that it offered up one surprise after another, confounding human perception – and presenting the opportunity to locate one's self in the living world. (Years later, working on the Great Snow Maze in Ulan Ude in Siberia, a structure composed of solid ice walls, he thought affectionately of the Saskatchewan project, its pervasive fragrance, its sweet heat and muffled embrace.)

At the beginning, while working on his early mazes, Larry kept his day job as manager of a small florist franchise in Winnipeg's West End. In those days mazes were his hobby so to speak, though, in fact, he never once pronounced the word hobby aloud – men and women of his generation, the so-called baby boomers, seldom employed that knobbly old-fashioned locution, speaking instead of their passions or pursuits or obsessions or sometimes, more guardedly, of their leisure activities.

His mother's cream jug collection, the ceramic cow she bought in London on her twenty-fifth anniversary trip back to the old country, the china shepherdess whose stiff skirt flipped sideways to reveal a spout – now *that* was a hobby. As was his father's corkscrew and bottle-opener collection, without a doubt one of the largest in the southern part of the province, 2000 specimens in total. Hobby people collected, mounted, displayed, and charted their finds. They were always, wherever they went, "looking out" for something, so that their weekend junkets or wider travels acquired a concentrated purpose and brightness.

"My husband is maze mad," said Dorrie, his first wife. Or, "He's got the bug."

The "bug" bit first when Larry and Dorrie visited Hampton Court during their 1978 English honeymoon. There the combination of arch formality and plotted chaos hummed to his young heart, and so did the notion that seedlings could be teased into dense, leafy, living walls so thick they baffled those who entered their midst. It caught him by surprise; it still does. When he looks into a set of garden specifications or rests his eyes on someone else's inventiveness, he becomes aware of a gentle snowstorm in his head – floating flakes on a blue sky, that take him out of his solitude and convince him he's a man like any other.

What a wonder, he thinks, that the long, bitter, heart-wrenching history of the planet should allow curious breathing spaces for the likes of mere toys and riddles; he sees them everywhere. Games, glyphs, symbols, allegories, puns and anagrams, masquerades, the magician's sleight-of-hand, the clown's wink, the comic shrug, the somersault, the cryptogram in all its forms, and especially, at least to Laurence J. Weller's mind, the teasing elegance and circularity of the labyrinthine structure, a snail, a scribble, a doodle on the earth's skin with no other directed purpose but to wind its sinuous way around itself.

Something else: the path to a maze's goal is always shortened by turning away from the goal, and this perversity, every time he thinks of it, brings a shiver of pleasure. He also loves the secret knowledge that a maze can never be truly symmetrical. These small oddities keep him reverent, awe-struck, faithful.

He plans, he constructs, he hires and subcontracts,

and mourns – but only occasionally – the fact that he no longer gets his hands dirty.

He has come to the point where he can glance at a maze diagram and his eye at once picks out the most economical path. He has a feel for intricacy and the clarity that cuts through it, "reading" maze design in the same way other people "read" machinery parts or the rumpled topographical folds of relief maps. This maze foolishness he's accidentally tumbled into gives him a privileged corner in the world, he knows that – his unique bird's-eye view, his only, only offering.

The Barnes maze in River Forest, Illinois (boxwood, inkberry holly), was Larry's professional break-through, a triumph in contemporary maze design – or at least "triumph" was the word used by the architectural critic in the Chicago *Tribune*.

Confined to a relatively small Augusta Avenue lot – but backing on to a forest preserve – it was both "classical in its suggestions and contemporary in its small postmodern gestures." (Larry had thought at first of placing a fountain at the center, but then remembered how noisy fountains could be. It was essential that those threading their way through shrub-lined paths be boxed in by barriers to their vision and enclosed, too, by silence. In a maze you had to feel doubly lost, with exterior sensation cut so cleanly away that nothing remained except for the sound of one's own breath and the teasing sense of willful abandonment.)

The half-blocked avenues of the Barnes maze, reminiscent of speed bumps, and a number of sudden intrusions – an iron gate with an electric eye, a near-vertical rookery – led straight toward a chevron-row repeat pattern (*Euonymus japonicus*) full of rhythmic Celtic echoes. "A triumph of integrated space," the *Tribune* review concluded. "This young designer understands that optical illusion is less about trickery than it is about the optics of the spirit."

It was at Rosie and Sumner Barnes' house that Larry first met Beth, his wife-to-be. He had arrived in the Chicago area a week earlier, having said goodbye, at last, to his florist's job in Winnipeg, emboldened by the Barnes commission and buoyed up by the hope that it might lead to others. "So," Beth had said, raising a glass of peach cooler to her lips, "you're the man who leads people astray."

He was unused to irony. He must have blinked or blown a puff of air up out of his throat.

"Professionally, I mean," she explained carefully, releasing the syllables like drops of mercury. "Leading people down the wrong path."

"Oh." He got it. Too late. She was turning to talk to someone else or else she was reaching sideways for another caviar on toast, the first caviar Larry Weller had ever seen. He took in the clean way her left ear lay against the darkness of her cropped hair. "And you?" he said quickly. "What do you do?"

"I'm unemployed," she said. Her finger touched a dull pewter disc that lay at her throat, suspended on a leather thong. "A sponge on society."

"Oh, God, I'm sorry. Sorry I asked, I mean. These days, in these economic times, we shouldn't go around asking people what they do –" He was blathering.

A pitying look shot in his direction, and he wondered how this pity had been secured. "I'm a student," she told him. "At Rosary, just down the road."

Her tone had changed. She'd had mercy on him. Her name was Beth Prior, and she was finishing her doctoral work on women saints and the nature of feminine goodness. Her parents were old friends of the Barneses. She'd grown up on this same street.

"Oh," he said. "So you live with your parents?" He was prying, but it seemed important to get the facts straight.

"No," she said, and now her tone was frosting over again. "They finally pitched me out on my twenty-fifth birthday. That is, they sold their house and moved to a condo in Hawaii. I sort of, you might say, got the message."

"I lived at home until I was twenty-six," he told her. Why? To spare her? To show her she wasn't the only one with infantile attachments?

"Really!" Now she did look into his eyes.

"Yes, really."

"In Winnipeg? That's what I was told. You're from Winnipeg up in Canada."

"Have you been there?"

"No."

Winnipeg was still his here and now, the black sphere that enclosed the pellet of his self, even though he now stood in a living room in suburban Chicago talking to this woman. She stood still as a deer with a look of mock innocence on her face. Now she was opening her mouth.

"Why?" she asked. "Why'd you live at home so long?"

"Well, I don't know exactly. Why did you stay home until you were twenty-five?"

"I was happy, I guess."

"So was I," he said. "Or happy enough anyway."

"How funny you should say that. That's what I'm going to call my thesis, if it ever gets finished."

"What?"

"Just what you said – 'Happy Enough.' "

"Why? "

"Because, oh I don't know. I've come to believe, I guess, that that's why so many people are good. They're good despite themselves. They're too lazy to be wicked. It's as if they can't be bothered. They may not be ecstatically happy or even moderately content, but they've got enough happiness to keep them from toppling over into the abyss."

He didn't know what abyss she was talking about. He wasn't sure be believed in an abyss.

A bead of caviar clung to her little finger and she sucked it off neatly. "Twenty-six years old when you left home," Beth Prior repeated. She seemed to be mulling this fact over. This was serious business and needed clearing up. "So what finally made you move out?"

She and her small silver earring awaited a response.

"I got married."

"Oh."

"And your wife? Is she here with you?" A feathery rise at the end of this question.

"We're divorced. She lives in Winnipeg."

"Oh." She twisted the pewter disc back and forth and dropped her eyelids. "Any children?" She had a smile that snapped with attention.

"A little boy, Ryan. Eight years old. He lives with his mother."

"That must be hard for you. I mean, you must find it terribly lonely."

"I do," Larry said, staring at her beautiful munching mouth. "I am." He was thinking how conversations just like this must be flashing all over the switchboard of North America, across the tilted rotating planet. Social interviews. The extracting of necessary information. The weighing of possibilities. *Married or not? And you?* Openings. Understandings. Bursts of confidence and reckless declarations. "I am," he heard himself say to Beth Prior, "I'm terribly lonely," and their eyes met. A direct hit.

Could he love a woman like this? A woman who, with her crispness, her cropped hair, and her direct straight mouth, was staring straight at him? Yes, of course he could. He shook his head in wonder at the thought.

"You look as though you're about to say something," she said. (Later, she confided that she had loved him on sight, his smooth, non-agenda face.)

He nodded, then glanced around the crowded room. The wall paintings with their little lights. The grand piano in the corner. The soft noise of conversation. "Why don't we leave?" he said. He wanted to bury his face in her white neck, and yet this suggestion of his to leave the party seemed lifted out of a bad old movie.

"Yes, why not?" she breathed through her surprised mouth. "Let's get the hell out of here."

He remembered later just how she pronounced the word hell – as though it were a real place full of breath, flame, and wonder, and crammed with exotic creatures and strange beguiling flowers, but a place not to be tolerated for one minute when the untested, unmapped world beckoned.

Their honeymoon (Larry's and Beth's) was spent outside Memphis, Tennessee, where Larry went to survey the site that Johnny Q. Questly, the retired country-and-western singer, had selected for his monster hedge maze. The design was to be universal, a simple winding snail without alternate routes − a sea shell, a coiled snake, the birthing journey − in whose center would be placed, once the plantings were installed, the marble Q-shaped tomb of Johnny's beloved late wife, Queenie. His darling, his dear heart.

To entertain the eye while the feet marched round and round, Larry had mingled pale spirea (once he had scorned spirea) with dark holly, and he had clipped the tops of those hedges into ruffs, turrets, spurs, a running travelogue of shapes and colors and an invitation to reach out the hand and touch.

"My Queenie was one of God's own marching angels," Johnny told them both over a vegetarian lunch on his immense, shaded, flagged-with-marble veranda. A solidly built man, he took a gulp of ice tea ("ass tea," he pronounced it) and wiped a tear from his eye. "Never took herself one look at another man in forty years of married life. Never a word of complaint when I was on the road, and I was on the road a helluva lot. If I took a drink too many, and I can't say it didn't happen on occasion, she'd look the other way. Forgiveness − she was a woman who knew the meaning of forgiveness. I messed up a couple times, real bad. Well! On our wedding anniversary one year I bought her a necklace. Diamonds, all diamonds. Like the fella says, diamonds are forever, but she only wore the damn thing – 'scuse my French – once or twice and then she got the cancer and passed away. She knew her Bible straight through. A simple life, that's what she liked, just the two of us out here at this place we bought after the kids grew up, watching the sun go down, a little TV after supper. That's all I need, she used to tell me, just the two of us loving each other. Hanging on to each other. Well, that's what our life was like."

In the last year, ever since Larry and Beth bought their house on Kenilworth Avenue in Oak Park, he's been troubled by middle-of-the-night insomnia. Three a.m. is the worst time, when he wakes and finds himself lying at attention between the sheets, his eyes scratchy with sleeplessness, and his thoughts crackling on a dozen channels. Hanging up your own shingle means worry, that much seems inevitable. There's the constant need to hustle, new commissions to track down, subcontracting to be arranged, and always the delicate matter of client relations, presenting design ideas in such a way that they seem suggested and not imposed.

To lull himself back to sleep, and keep himself from disturbing Beth – who sleeps a profound, saintly, and unsedated seven hours – he lets his mind wander through the seven spacious rooms of his house, the fastened doors, the square entrance, the stained glass in the hallway, the dining room weighted with its beamed ceiling and side lights, the living room and its twin bay windows and smell of cold ashes from the fireplace grate.

And then, if sleep continues to resist him, he flips through the files of his various completed projects: the tiny Presbyterian Center maze in upstate New York, the Barnes project with all its intricacies and inventions, the University of Maryland Governor's Garden, the Self-Realization Fellowship maze at their Colorado retreat, the Questly Curl, as it's come to be known, in Tennessee, and the St. Matthews maze, medieval in inspiration and high-tech in horticulture, which is confidently expected to win the Northenden-Eden Prize. And, finally, his thoughts drift and scroll along to that first venture in Winnipeg, his experimental maze that wrapped around and around the small bungalow on Lipton Street – originally advertised as a handyman special – where he and his first wife, Dorrie, lived in the early days of their marriage.

From the start the maze was a cause for conflict. Dorrie wanted green grass and flowers, not the dense, bushy fortress she was stuck in the middle of, and he wasn't sure he blamed her. It looked weird. It looked dumb. She resented the money Larry spent on plant stock, although he managed, through connections in the business, to get almost everything at wholesale prices. On weekends he was forever planting and pruning his shrubs instead of getting around to putting in the roof insulation the way he'd promised. The neighborhood was going downhill and the house was a dump anyway. They should put it on the market – as soon as the insulation was in place – and, what with her rising commissions at Manitoba Motors, buy out in the new subdivision in Linden Woods.

Over my dead body, Larry said, or words to that effect; he understood what she was saying, but he wasn't budging – not after all the work he'd done and what with the maze finally getting on its legs.

Linden Woods was all Dorrie could talk about. A big new house with a showroom kitchen and a whirlpool bath off the master bedroom, walk-in closets, the works. She swore she was going nuts living in Larry's crazy bush pile, and one day she really did go nuts, phoning a demolition company while Larry was at work and arranging to have the maze plowed up.

Half of it was gone by the time he discovered what was up. Wiped out, erased, the front yard levered.

She might as well have chopped his heart in two. That's how one of Larry's friends put it at the time.

But today, after all these years, the remaining half of the maze, neatly bisected, is still standing; its looped paths lie open at their ends so that you can enter at any point. Strictly speaking, it's not really a maze at all anymore, just a matrix of patterned shrubs filling the small space of the backyard. Dorrie, who is now Vice-President of sales for Nu-Cloz, a national sports-wear chain, arranges to have the quasi-maze pruned early each summer, and then again in the fall.

She and Ryan have not moved to Linden Woods after all, although they could easily afford it. The old neighborhood's picked up, for one thing, with young

181

families moving in and renovating. Her closest friend, Lucy Warkenten, lives next door, and she doesn't know what she'd do without Lucy. And there's Larry's mom, just a few blocks away; even though she and Larry are divorced, she likes to keep in touch. She phones or drops in often. Almost every day, in fact. Then, too, Dorrie thinks it would be a shame to take Ryan out of his school, with all his friends and how well he's doing. Stability matters, she thinks, and after Larry left her in the spring of 1983 she felt a need to cling to everything that was familiar.

Larry was back in Winnipeg just a month ago, July, for his father's funeral, and of course he stopped by the old Lipton Street house as he always does when he's in town, and, as usual, found himself surprised at how complete Dorrie's life seemed without him. He and Dorrie are on better terms these days, and he was impressed, visiting her, to see the glass-walled extension she's put on the kitchen; a solarium, she calls it. It's small, just a few square feet really, but the dark little house is filled with light now and a new dancing sense of space.

He doesn't know why Dorrie keeps the half-maze going. They've never once spoken of it; he feels it would be dangerous to mention it, even in passing. It grows, a truncated, chopped, mutable thing; it thrives; it's a curiosity. Larry often thinks on restless nights, lying beside his dear sleeping Beth, how this first maze may lack the enclosed secrets of the true form, but that its continued existence remains, so far at least, the most unexamined mystery of his life, a circling, exquisite puzzle of pain, and pain's consolation.

CHAPTER NINE

Larry So Far
1990

Turning forty opened a seam of panic in Larry Weller, and he had to admit, sadly, that there was nothing remarkable in this.

A fortieth birthday is twinned with anxiety, with mortal dread, it's to be expected, it's par for the course, at least among Larry's acquaintances or from what he glimpses on the commercials he sees on TV, which seem differently targeted for the post-forties, more sincerely sorry that "you out there" must be informed about the hazards of heart disease or hemorrhoids or depression triggers. Forty is on the side of the wealthy and the ailing – Larry sometimes burns with the shame of having "done well" – and the disequilibrium forty brings is all too well marked on the psychological road map; you shrug when it comes along, shrug and suffer in the shambling morning light and wait for your brain to absorb its juices. Forty invites a plague of spiritual fleas, but even these can be safely, dully predicted, especially when you know a wider stream of melancholy lies ahead. It's boring, the "age-forty trembles." Forty-year-olds are immobilized by the crud of doubt, but they've been warned, haven't they? Yes, they have. "Forty is the end of the party," says the laconic Eric Eisner, Larry's mentor, "and by the time you get to the cheese course of life, you've lost your appetite. What's left for us oldies is a freefall into hoary age and the thinning of imagination."

"I'm a forty-year-old man," Larry says to himself at least once every day, while putting his mouth to the rim of his coffee cup or starting his car or glancing up into the canopy of leaves over the street where he lives. And the thought – *forty years old* – hangs around and around, and forms part of the atmosphere. He understands at last the rather surprising, hard dullness of being an adult, and perhaps for that reason he's become a man too easily consoled by games and surfaces. And now, suddenly, having celebrated four decades of life, he is a sad man but without the sad history to back it up. What he needs is a good slap on the ear, but at the same time it seems to him that one wrong step would throw him off-course, and that what he would lose would be not money or friendship or intention, but his own self.

He can't complain, or at least he shouldn't complain. After a slow start in the world, and a life so frictionless he'd never learned to *push*, he's ended up in Chicago, a sought-after and relatively well-regarded landscape designer with a specialty in garden mazes. He's a man who's had a fair number of jump-cuts in his life, and it always surprises him how much he's accommodated, how much – from the other side – he's been allowed. You can have too much luck; it gets to look like clutter, like junk. At forty he finds his early engines of shyness reversed. His first marriage fizzled, a sputtering ruin before it began – he survived that – and he's found love, and its pungent oils and pleasures, with his second wife, Beth, who has a post-doctoral appointment in the religion department at University of Illinois Chicago, a brainy, speculative, sweet-tempered, supple-limbed young woman whose work on female saints often leads people to believe she is something of a saint herself, and, in fact, she does possess certain saintly virtues, most notably the ability to concentrate her mind so that her thoughts are knife sharp.

Together she and Larry have bought a heritage house on Kenilworth Avenue in Oak Park, set among the hush of other heritage houses along the deep-dyed greenness of rolling boulevards. He'd like a carload of kids, but he understands Beth's reservations about career and motherhood, and he does have a twelve-year-old son up in Canada, from his first marriage, and, besides, where would he, a man of forty, find the energy for fatherhood? Or the time? He and Beth seem to be busy all the time, either with work or travel or with their increasingly active social life, attending dinner parties, receptions, lectures, or free-floating events that defy categorizing but require their presence.

Their calendar is full. It still surprises him that he who grew up so shy and awkward as a kid should own a set of evening clothes which he climbs into more or

185

less unselfconsciously several times a year. His father, who's been gone two years now, would have been bug-eyed to see his only son zooted up in a penguin suit, which is what he almost certainly would have called it – his son, the high roller. A regular toff. Off to a cocktail party, out to an exhibition of architectural drawings. How had this happened? Was this the life that Larry Weller signed up for – Larry, son of the late Stu Weller, master upholsterer for a Winnipeg bus factory?

The fact is, he can never quite believe in his tuxedoed self, cousin to that phantom presence that lurks in his dreams, the guy watching the action, suffering, scared, and greedy in his borrowed, baggy clothes, but never actually stepping on stage and exposing his face.

Being self-employed – A/Mazing Space Inc. – gives Larry the kind of freedom that other people only dream of, and yet at forty he persists in feeling himself an inhabitant of a flat, bottomless, roofless world where all information is ingoing. Always, flickering at the edge of his vision, is something new he must absorb, and yet this flicker is accompanied by the apprehension of himself as a man condemned, no matter what his accomplishments, to be ordinary, and to pass slowly, painfully, through each of life's orderly prescriptive stages.

The evidence is in. Whether the cause is genetic or accidental, he knows himself doomed to live inside the hackneyed parentheses of predictability, a walking, head-scratching cliché: first the dreamy child, next the miserable adolescent, followed closely by the baffled young husband, and now, too suddenly, a settled forty-year-old white male professional who chafes at that number forty and lies awake wondering if he is about to enter a phase of banked authority and nostril-quivering sincerity – a cover, of course, for the trembling protein stew of his present incarnation. No one yet has noticed, but when they do Larry's certain that he'll be described as suffering from "midlife crisis" or "male menopause," those trumped-up diseases of trite and trivial contemporary man. He's right on time, too, stepping into the shoes of expectation as though they were made for him – angst-ridden at forty uh-huh. Right. Also self-doubting. Also emasculated, or at least veering in that direction. The old, old story. So what's new?

And where does he go, now that he's been smugly socialized down to his forty-year-old toenails? Delustered. Textureless. Inoffensive. Impotent. Ordinary. Any minute someone will take him aside and suggest he go and "see someone," insisting that the blue-footed flame that heats his perplexity is "statistically in line" for men of his age, that men have periodical cycles just like women, and that a strong surge of September air will blow his grief to dust. He should buck up and count his blessings. Meanwhile, has he, seriously, investigated the spiritual side of his nature?

Who is this guy? Give me a break.

"I understand what you're going through," Beth said to him some months ago after they had almost, but not quite, made love. A razor blade of moonlight streamed in from a crack in the curtains, neatly bisecting their queensize bed and its handmade (Appalachian) quilt. She kept her hand on Larry's collapsed penis, stroking it as one might a small woodland creature. "I blame myself for foisting that surprise party on you. Who wants to announce forty to the world. We should go into a cave at forty and meditate along with the hanging bats. Learn their echoing, reverberative secrets. Figure out how to live on the quiet side of ecstasy, just, you know, how to be at home in our environment, how to adapt. Forty's the age when we know we've already had half of what we're going to get, that's if we're lucky. You look down the tunnel and you see more of the same, and it's frightening, I can understand that."

Stop, stop, stop.

Larry's wife, Beth, is not yet forty; in fact, she won't be forty for another seven years, and a part of Larry resents her swift and accurate diagnosis of his condition. She accepts the Christian notion that darkness surrounds and threatens every glimmer of common happiness. She's oddly apologetic about it, as though she holds at least some partial responsibility. In a minute she'll be telling the story of some obscure Celtic saint with an unpronounceable name and the power to reverse sexual inadequacy. Yes, here it comes. Her intake of breath against his pajama-sleeve announces her strategy. Larry braces himself and thinks: she means to be kind, to be helpful, supportive, et cetera, a saintly wife with a statistically average mate.

"Well," Beth says, swerving into her narrative voice, its stretched vowels and pauses, "his name was St. Guignolé, sixth century or thereabouts." (This vagueness, this *thereabouts*, is simulated; Larry recognizes it as a ploy to defuse the consoling and positive message she is about to deliver.) "So," she continues, "there's this ancient wooden statue of St. Guignolé in a church in France, in Brest, I think" – more rationed vagueness, that carefully inserted *I think* – "and thousands of visitors of both sexes have made pilgrimages over the years in order to whittle away at St. Guignolé's upright member, carrying home the sawdusty bits, which they boil up in their broth and drink for supper."

"Go on," Larry says, knowing she will go on."

"Well, there are so many visitors scratching away that poor old Guignolé's dingie-thingie –"

"His dingie-thingie?"

"His prick, then."

"Oh, that." He loves the puckery, faintly acidic way Beth pronounces the word *prick*, as though, in fact, it pricks the roof of her mouth just to say it.

"Well, his wooden prick, his member, had to be replaced every twenty years or so. A new one had to be carved and stuck on. The priests finally got so exasperated that they encased him in plaster, only to find that the pilgrims scraped away at the plaster casing and carried *that* home."

"And so?" Larry asked his wife. "You're suggesting we make an emergency pilgrimage to –?"

"The point is that this, this thing – whatever it is that's worrying you – is an ancient and universal

189

concern. Potency, fertility. It's just the old fear-of-death image in disguise."

"Ah," he said, only half mocking. "So that's what it is."

"The point is that you're an absolutely normal and typical human being."

"Standard issue. Great."

"Well, what exactly do you want, Larry?"

If only he knew.

Their private word for Larry's condition was "it." Is "it" keeping you awake again? Is "it" still tormenting you? Tell me about "it."

But talking "it" over with Beth makes matters worse; she's too humidly helpful, too bent on swiftly applied intellectual therapy, too urgently determined to confine his sense of anxiety by placing "it" in a socially approved context, something men Larry's age experience, something they "go through." Beth believes that "it" is like a novel with its ups and downs of plot, and anyone's life is just that: a story about the fate of a child. What Larry's going through is a natural phase. A chapter. A passing condition, this inflation of sadness. She would like him to be burstingly confessional – at least this is what Larry senses – so that she can reverse the direction of his thoughts. Any minute "it" will blow away, she'll say. She said something like this only yesterday, in fact, making a bunchy flower of her lips and blowing against his cheek.

He doesn't want "it" to blow away, that's the catch.

When he wakes in the middle of the night, three

o'clock, four o'clock, he is immediately alert to the presence of "it" in the room, so close he could reach out and take it in his hand and marvel at the faithfulness and constancy of an "it" that has chosen him and now resolutely hangs on. "It" has the size and hardness of a walnut, a woody, fibrous shell with a few raised ridges, and a sense of packed hollowness within.

He tries to visualize his life – his life so far – and a grid rises up in his mind, neatly squared off, but oddly disassociated, as though its configuration originated in a dream. He possesses a dead father and a living mother. And a sister, Midge, in Toronto that he hardly ever sees, but who, if she suspected he was in despair, would sign off work for a week and jump on the next plane, ready to administer great bracing poultices of good cheer. His oldest friend, Bill Herschel, is engaged in the important work of saving the species of the planet; Larry's moist little whimpers of self-doubt wouldn't even register if set beside the endangered flora and fauna of the mid-continent. No, he definitely will not discuss "it" with Bill.

How much does the external world bear on Larry Weller? Wars, plagues, racial injustice, third world poverty, the oppression of women? Is this what wakes him in the darkness of his and Beth's bedroom? He wishes it were true; he would like to be a man who wrestles with giants. He would admire that man.

So far his anxiety seems merely to vibrate in tune with a saddened world. What he grapples with is the question of where he is in his life *so far*.

It's a safe enough game, a counting game, simple arithmetic: numbers set on that imagined squared-off grid. He needs to concentrate on the numbers, but he also needs to look at them sideways, through eyes that have been brought together in a squint. Too much truth, the same truth, becomes cheap. (He hopes this exercise isn't in the same category as "stocktaking" or, worse, "soul-searching.")

So. He has one parent, one sibling, two wives, one child.

He has a Diploma in Floral Arts (1969) from a Manitoba technical college, and a more recent and far more distinguished Diploma (honorary; Lasalle University) in Landscape Design.

He's lived in two cities, Winnipeg and Chicago. Make that two countries.

He's never missed a child support payment. His own hopefulness keeps him faithful to his self, that intermittently flickering self with its winking, provisional set of driving lights.

He's owned two Toyotas, an old tan Corolla that he traded in for a semi-new Camry. After the Camry came the deep silver Audi, and now the two-door Honda Accord. These cars are the clothes he puts on after he puts on his primary clothes. That's it in the wheels department. So far.

Houses. Three. The house he grew up in, a bungalow with a chainlink fence around its tiny rectangle of a yard, his boyhood bedroom (knotty pine) leading off the kitchen. Then the Lipton Street house, a fixer-upper, where he and Dorrie lived during their five years of marriage, and where she and Ryan continue to live. And now the Oak Park house, solidly two-story, gumwood trim in the hall and stairway, heavily mortgaged and in need of work – especially the garden which, so far, he hasn't touched – not quite a case of the shoemaker's children, but close. He's thinking of letting it go wild, flowers, grasses, but imagines trouble from the Neighborhood Association. In between owning the three houses there have been some apartments and townhouse rentals, mostly forgettable, mostly forgotten – those heartbreaking, desperate, intermediate addresses: 566 Calonia, 312 MacNair, 22 Ciscoe Bay, 2236 Harlem Avenue.

Health. Over the years he's smoked the odd bit of dope, but not any longer. He plans to start running again any day now. Cut down on caffeine. A mole on his back – is it growing? That rope of fat just below his belt. And the current middle-of-the-night insomnia. And that other thing. Had he ever been what the world calls a sexy man? Christ. He doubts it, it can't possibly be true, and he knows that no matter what evidence is brought forward he will continue to doubt it. You could call forth the first – sweet accommodating, generous Sally, and the five that followed, those rescue ships with their pantyhose, their jeans and mini- skirts, and then Dorrie, their ardent, private, rancorous, intense history, and then, after the separation, those two or three others – how careless not to know exactly! – and then, Beth, a safe harbor, a blessing, a continuance. This was his history, but none of it, it seemed, reflecting *him*. Was he a sexy man? Question unanswerable. Who is he, this shadowy, temporary self?

Hobbies. How can people think of hobbies when

their bodies are disintegrating and when their histories are in disarray.

Religion. If he'd ever believed in God, that Being has long since shrunk into the shadows of hedgerows. On a plane not long ago he sat next to a young man who was reading a crisp new Bible, pipelining straight to God, while Larry made do with the latest McMurtry. Once he heard the singer Curtis Hayfield performing a certain number on the car radio – he forgets which song it was – and felt a ripple across his flesh and wondered if that was what people meant by a spiritual experience. Making love, the sexual spasm – is that a part of religion? His dad's old joke was that church was for sinners. And that they were out to grab your dollars. His mother, though, has started going to Sunday services in recent years, but he's never heard her mention, either on the telephone or in a letter, the names of God or Jesus, the two main players. It looked for a time as though her sadness would last all her life, in the same way that furniture and china endure, but no, it began to crumble. She grew fervent and peaceful. He wonders if she prays. Praying must be like talking to the fairies, he's always thought, and yet he's done it the odd time himself – *Make this stop, make this go away, just let me have one more hard-on before I die, let me sleep, Jesus H. Christ.*

Once Larry heard a woman say: "I believe in silver. Sterling silver." His father believed in a clean basement. His mother, Dot, Believes, it seems, in guilt and salvation, and his sister in colonic irrigation. What shadow of the insubstantial brushes against Larry and instructs him to believe?

194

It's really when entering a previously unknown maze, especially a hedge maze, that Larry is brought to a condition which he thinks of as spiritual excitement. The maze's preordained design, its complications, which are at once unsettling and serene, the shifts of light and shade, the pulsing vegetal growth which is encouraged but also held in check – all this ignites Larry's sense of equilibrium and sends him soaring.

For his fortieth birthday (August 17th) his mother sent him a check for twenty dollars enclosed in one of those masculine birthday cards featuring a richly colored montage of armchair, pipe, highball glass, and Irish setter. He wonders how she imagines his life, his and Beth's. "Have yourself a celebration" she wrote in her near-illegible hand. And "Take it from me, life really does begin at forty!"

Beth gave him a handsome reprint of an eighteenth-century book, Batty Langley's *New Principles of Gardening*, 1728, which contains a number of extraordinary maze designs.

Lucy Warkenten, an old friend from Winnipeg, sent him a set of subtly marbled postcards she's made herself, and with a calligraphy pen she's written the single word "Onward!"

Bill Herschel faxed a surprisingly solemn message. "Let's promise to celebrate the next one together." (When they'd been boys back in Winnipeg they'd given each other on their birthdays dribble glasses or plastic dog poop.)

Larry's sister, Midge, and her latest live-in, Ian

Stoker, sent a jokey card with a play on the word forty. Four-T. Taste. Talent. Technique. Testosterone.

Larry's son, Ryan, sent, as usual, a necktie, which Larry knows has been selected, paid for, wrapped and mailed by his ex, Dorrie. These neckties have marched straight up the scale over the years. The fortieth birthday tie is Italian, deep-blue variegated silk, beautiful, in an all-over pattern which Larry, peering carefully, identifies as being based on the ancient Shandwick maze. Where had she found it, and had she realized?

The real surprise is a birthday card from Dorrie herself. There have been few cards or gifts or even letters between them since their divorce – Dorrie never was one for writing letters, and there was a six-month blackout period of angry non-communication just after he left her. Nowadays she and Larry see each other occasionally when Larry's in Winnipeg, and they talk frequently on the phone, conferring about their son, Ryan. His marks at school. His allergy to peanuts, and an emergency rush to the hospital last year. Orthodonture, yes or no. Travel arrangements for Ryan's three-times-a-year-trip to Chicago. Ryan's passion for athletics – was this a cause for concern? No, Dorrie thinks. Yes, says Larry, who has only a passing interest in sports himself.

They're on amicable enough terms after all these years, but the truth is they're really strangers to each other. Larry, looking at Dorrie's birthday card – a curling wreath of dark greenery with the raised number 40 in the middle – was startled to see that he had forgotten what her handwriting looked like, how small and fine and girlish it was, and how neatly it lined itself up. "Here's to being older and wiser," she'd written with what looked like a fountain pen, and then, "affectionately, Dorrie."

Affectionately. Such an after-dinner mint of a word. Affectionately smacked his heart. Not love, no, not love. Well, who expects love from an ex-spouse?

And then, just yesterday, he was struck by the thought that Dorrie, his Dorrie, would turn forty herself in a matter of weeks: September 24th. Impossible. Dorrie's firm, energetic flesh, now softened and creased and quietly discoloring. No. Never. Her small, talky, bossy breasts sagging and tinged with blue. He can't imagine it. Does she wake up in the middle of the night, does she sit rigidly on the edge of the bed, stare out the window at the chipped moon, and wonder at which moment her life began to drain away?

He blinked the image away, holding the lids of his eyes open against exhaustion, and letting those eyes fill with slow sadness. Getting older was to witness the steady decline of limitless possibility. That's all it was.

Emaciated, old Laura Latimer Moorhouse of the Milwaukee Latimers made an appoinmment to see Larry in his Lake Street office. He took her coat - some kind of lustrous fur – and offered her one of his rattan chairs, which she collapsed into, breathing hard and clutching the head of her cane.

Ancient, Larry thought. And in terrible health. Her chin had the tufted look of velveteen. Her skin was yellow.

"Are you comfortable enough?" Larry asked.

She nodded briskly, but the teased blond hair didn't move.

She wanted a hedge maze built in the grounds of the Milwaukee Memorial Children's Hospital. The design was entirely up to him. She'd heard excellent reports of his work, and she'd already consulted with members of the hospital board. The cost, of course, would be borne by herself. She was prepared to spend a good deal of money for the maze, and for the ensuing upkeep, since her time on earth was nearly over and she'd come to the realization that she had lived a stupid and thoughtless and selfish life.

"I'm sure you –" Larry felt compelled to protest.

"Stupid, thoughtless, and selfish," she repeated. Her mouth became a crumple.

"But we all –" Larry began.

"No. Most people live sensible and thoughtful lives. It's a fact. It's something I've noticed. Except for hardened criminals, most people manage to form meaningful attachments. They take care of one another. I've never had that opportunity, you see, to form a genuine attachment. My two husbands – what can I say? – they were perfect heels. And no, Mr. Weller, I have not had children of my own. Trouble in the woman department, and probably just as well. I was fat all my life. A fat girl, a fat woman. My mother would have loved me more if I hadn't been fat, I'm one hundred percent sure of that. She gave me a girdle when I was eight years old and made me wear it. What kind of a mother does that! You can imagine. My skin under the girdle was a mass of eczema, that was from the rubber probably. I was fat until one year ago when my cancer was diagnosed, stomach, liver, everywhere – that's why I'm thin and ratchety for the first time in my life. What you see before you is only half the person I was, only one-third of the old Laura Moorhouse, as a matter of fact. Hard to believe, isn't it? Three hundred pounds, that's what *she* was, and now she weighs in at ninety-nine. Call me perverse, but I'm proud to be a ninety-nine-pound woman. I'm brimming over with pride. Another sin, but a consolation too. Why a maze, Mr. Weller? I knew you'd ask. Because I've always loved mazes. Now, this may sound whimsical, but I've felt all my life that I was a kind of maze myself, my body I mean. There was something hidden in the middle of me, but no one could find it, it was so deeply concealed, and I don't just mean by fat cells. Why a children's hospital? A good question. Not because I love children. I don't think I do, really. It's because I long to *be* a child, even a sick child, a very sick child. I want my mother, my daddy. I want them standing next to my bed, one on either side, holding on to me, reaching out and putting their hands to my forehead, checking to see if I have a fever, soothing me, taking turns, first one, then the other. They love me so. You must excuse me. I'm trying not to go hysterical on you, Mr. Weller, and usually I don't, but it isn't often I speak out like this so frankly. Never, in fact. It could be the medication I'm on that's loosened my tongue. I've never told anyone this, that I long to have someone place a hand on my forehead and just hold it there. Pressing. Really, it isn't much to ask, is it? I've never discussed this longing, never expressed it, that is. How could I? I mean, it doesn't come up in ordinary conversation, does it? But then, how often does anyone have a real conversation, just talking back and forth the way we're talking, you and I, sitting in this little room of yours. Just these white walls. These green plants. With nothing getting in the way. Nobody putting a finger to my lips and saying stop, stop, enough, you're embarrassing me. Well, I can't say that it's ever happened to me before. No, not even once."

Two years ago, when Stu Weller was close to death, Larry flew to Winnipeg to be by his side. *By his father's side*, that scented phrase with its promise of resolution. What he actually felt when he reached the hospital was the helpless unease that the healthy experience in the presence of the profoundly ill.

His father's mouth looked large and lippy beneath the fleshy cave of his nose. The thick rind of a male body was still there under the hospital sheet, but inside was stinking rot. Larry could have sworn his father cringed as he entered the room and presented his preposterous healthy face. *So it's you.*

"He tires easily," Larry's mother said. Meaning, there will be no resolution. Larry immediately grasped that fact. No embrace. No prayers. Nor confessions. Nor blessings. Well, it was dirty pool to grill the dying, asking them to betray their secrets when they were down and out, and when they're about to go even further down.

To be alone, sick and unvisited, would be preferable, Larry thought, to the parade of visitors, neighbors, friends, and family who arrived at St. Boniface Hospital, all wanting a piece of final satisfaction from Stu Weller, critically ill, dying of cancer, smelling of shit, sucking in the gas of his last hours, already, in fact, out of reach.

"All I wanted," said Larry's sister, Midge, who had flown in from Toronto, where she owned a costume shop, "was to have one conversation with the old bugger." She was blubbering cold leaky tears. "We never did, you know, not once."

Larry dug in his pocket and found a Kleenex. "He wasn't much for words."

"Except to complain. Except to bitch at Mum because she was out at her Agape group all the time. It was different for you. He took you to all those football games when you were a kid. Hockey too."

"Hey, that's right." Larry was taken by surprise. He'd forgotten those outings. "That was a helluva long time ago."

"So did you do the father-son thing? Did you, like, really talk when you were sitting there in the stands, the two of you?"

"I don't think so. Maybe 'Great play.' Or 'Lousy block.' that was pretty much the extent of it."

"It figures."

"Once he asked me if I was in love with Dorrie. Before we got married."

"Really? He said it like that? 'In love'?"

"I couldn't believe it. The word 'love' coming out of his mouth."

"So what did you say back?"

"What do you mean, what did I say?"

"About being in love with Dorrie. Did you say you were or you weren't? "

"I can't remember."

"Yeah, I bet." She gave him a look. "Leave it to dopey Dorrie to get herself pregnant –"

"It's water over the dam, Midge. Jesus."

"Some dam. Ha. Anyway you got a great little kid out of the deal."

"Right."

"Even if you hardly ever see him."

"I know, I know."

"Anyway, I hope when you do see him that you talk. Really talk, I mean. I myself find it impossible to believe that a father would not once have a conversation with his only daughter. Even when Paul got AIDS, when he was in the hospice dying, our dear father Stu never once, he didn't even, he just – oh, Christ, why'd you get me started?"

"That's the way he was. That doesn't mean he didn't have the deepest feeling of –"

"I could kill him. No one should be allowed to be that inarticulate. People who won't talk to their own children should be put in jail."

"It's a generation thing." There was pain in this conversation with his sister, but Larry wanted it to continue. "Communication wasn't such a big priority in the folks' generation –"

"Do you think he and Mum ever had a conversation? I bet they didn't. I bet they just lived inside their dumb silence. All those years, eating, sleeping, looking after the house and yard, with never anything passing between them. At least Paul and I – but the two of *them*!"

"We can't know –"

"What do you mean you can't know? What's that supposed to mean? Do you honestly believe they had one genuine conversation in their whole married life?"

"It's possible," Larry told her. "Not that I could prove it."

Lately Larry's sad most of the time. Even when he's signing contracts or eating or laughing out loud or attempting to make love to Beth he feels the undertow of something missing. He'd like to shrink back to his old life, but the noisy amplitude of these recent years has to find someplace to go. And he's tired – tired of his name, tired of being a man, tired of the ghostly self he's chained to and compelled to drag around. He can't avoid the shame of his awful hopeful voice as he answers the telephone, too patently constructed to be a real voice, a voice to stay away from if you've got any sense. His mannerisms, his little ways, get on his nerves, his habit of placing a finger on the knot of his tie when he's under stress or clearing his throat unnecessarily before speaking. Here I am: a serious, likeable man scrolling through the flow of my life. A man – surely you can detect this – in a state of personal crisis. *Oh, that!*

But it's boring down there in the depths, and he senses that even his patient Beth has had enough. When was the last time she asked him how "it" was going? Maybe in the future she'll look back and resent all the energy she put into their supine bedtime conversations, cheering him out of his glooms, offering narratives from her vast storehouse, trying to patch him up and put his psyche in working order again. What dullness. Besides, she's busy preparing a lecture on the virgin saints, Cecilia, Margaret, Agatha, Mahya, Dorothy; virginity is strength, she intends to prove, a part of the body held in reserve, which must be seen not as passivity, but as the mask of a potent power over the self. She has it all worked out.

What do you do with private disappointment, Larry wonders. How do you fix it? He can't explain, not even to himself, but he's forgotten those things he used to take on trust, love's careless ease or lethargy, drowning in ordinary contentment. There's been a falling off of faith, which he presumes is temporary. Sooner or later a restoration will present itself, he feels sure of that – but when will it come?

Yet even in the midst of his present confusion he knows with certainty that the important conversations of his life will always be with women.

Tenderly, smilingly, he remembers Vivian Bondurant. Viv of the clear brown eyes and capable hands. They'd worked together at Flowerfolks for years back in the seventies, and the two of them had talked all day long. Their talk had been unstructured, loose, and capable of sustaining interruptions and uneven silences. She'd taught him, a tongue-tied kid just out of school, to open his mouth. He hasn't seen her in years. She'd be what? – forty-seven now. Almost fifty. Christ.

He and Dorrie hadn't known how to talk. No one had told them how it was with married people, how much they need space to let out the low, continuous rumble of their thoughts. The two of them exchanged consumer information; that's what he remembers anyway. They quarreled about trivialities, about hurt feelings, about money and in-laws, just as though they'd learned these topics of discord from reading Ann Landers. Mostly, especially toward the end, they were silent – though a part of Larry has come to believe that their silence held a sinewy richness of its own.

Right away it was different with Beth. Lying in the dark bedroom, their arms around each other, they'll talk for an hour or more before falling asleep, and Larry feels gladness swarming in his ears. Such ease, such unlooked-for happiness. One night in early October, the wind banging the north side of the house, Larry tells his wife about Laura Latimer Moorhouse's visit. Beth resettles her white limbs and murmurs into his ear: *No! That's awful! And then what? Oh, Larry.* Now she is wondering, aloud, what will happen to a world that's lost its connection with the sacred. We long for ecstasy, to stand outside of the self in order to transcend that self, but how do we get there?

Her tone is only mildly speculative. She has only to push the words out as her thoughts form, easy as air, exhaling against the blanket binding, against Larry's chest. Larry imagines the vibrations of her voice entering the wallpaper, passing straight through the retrofitted drywall, the ancient lath and brick, and traveling into black space and becoming flecks in the earth's vitreous humus.

And then he recalls, as he often does, lying in his boyhood bed and hearing through the plaster the sound of his parents talking in the next room. Their night noises, their bed talk. The woody rasp as they cleared their human throats or blew their noses. Sometimes it went on and on. The words were inaudible, a low, buzzing, reverberative music whose content, to their son Larry at least, was unguessable. First his mother, then his father, back and forth like a kind of weaving. There would be a pause, and then the murmurous resonance resumed. He would fall asleep, finally, to the rhythm of those strange voices: Stu and Dot Weller, his silent parents, coming awake in the soundwaves of their own muffled words, made graceful by what they chose to say in the long darkness.

Larry's busy these November days with the Latimer project, and he welcomes being busy, sensing that his freakish profession is the only thing that keeps him from disappearing; it also quietens the late millennial despair that drifts about the world these days, singing a version of: here we go again, and again, and again. He's done a preliminary set of drawings, thinking as he works how happiness lurks between the hand and the eye, and between the objective design and the abstractions that bloom in his head. A small untended space, but critical. Last week he drove up to Milwaukee and made a presentation to the hospital board.

A round of applause greeted his short talk, and the chair of the board expressed regret that wonderful Laura had not lived to see her dream realized, not even in blueprint form, but nevertheless, ahem, a worthy project was well and truly launched, and the necessary funding was solidly in place. Larry got the green light. He was to begin at once.

The winter would be taken up with planning and subcontracting, and by April the first hedges will be in place. He's decided on a combination of barberry, for its orange-red autumn foliage, and cornelian cherry, which takes well to formal shearing. A good June and July should double their growth in the first year, and by August – by August! And then a dazzling thought comes at him sideways – by August he will be forty-one! No longer forty, with forty's clumsy, abject round shoulders and sting of regret, but forty-one! A decent age, a mild, assured, wise and good-hearted manly age.

The number forty-one redoubles in Larry's head like a balloon of sweetness, which he shakes off roughly, as if it were a piece of foolishness he will not stoop one inch to acknowledge.

In the center of the Milwaukee maze he has designed a number of topiary figures grouped around a mirrored wishing-well, where children will be able to toss their pennies and whisper their deepest desires. To get better. To live. To grow up. To be like everyone else. Isn't that what we all want in the end?

The maze itself has a single entrance, but four exits, one in each corner. Why four? Most mazes have only one exit or perhaps two, but Larry, for the first time in his life, and for reasons he has not, so far, bothered to articulate before the hospital board, has designed a maze in which there is not the slightest possibility of getting seriously lost.

As for himself, he's persuaded that he's only been pretending to be lost at forty, a man on the verge of nothing at all. He's been rehearsing the condition, trying it on for size, as if he could with his sham despair propitiate the real thing – which will come, which will surely come. The arrow is already in flight, he knows that much.

For the moment, though, he's safe. A tide of balance has miraculously returned, and he's back to being Larry Weller again, husband, father, home owner, tuxedo wearer. An okay guy with work to do. So far, so good.

CHAPTER TEN

Larry's Kid

1991

Three times a year Larry Weller drives out to O'Hare International to meet his son's plane; Ryan is twelve now, almost thirteen, and he's been making these solo trips from Winnipeg to Chicago since he was eight – for spring vacation, for a month in the summer, and for a few days at Christmas.

Winnipeg lies at the dark curved end of the world, a world of snow, ice, and the imponderables of Mounted Police and paradise fishing and a socialist health plan – that's what Larry's Chicago friends think, but Larry knows better. It's a place much like any other. A medium-sized city, bustling, thriving, standing at the junction of two rivers, the wide Red, and the sinuous, somehow womanly, Assiniboine. Winnipeg is the place where Ryan was born almost thirteen years ago – a sunny day in late August, three-thirty in the afternoon, the Grace Hospital, an easy birth – and Winnipeg's the only place he's ever lived.

The boy's visits to Chicago are stressful for all concerned. Larry's second wife, Beth, a socially able and graceful woman in her mid-thirties who teaches a course in women's studies at Rosary College, is surprisingly awkward around children. Childless by choice, she is also the only child of elderly parents. With Ryan, she takes a Beatrix Potter approach one minute, tender and cosseting, concerned about what he eats, whether he's watching too much TV or getting enough sleep, then swerves erratically into a gear of cranked-up intimacy. She grins in his direction, even though she's not a grinning woman, and maintains the fiction that there is always a joke on the boil or a banana skin underfoot. The wrong words fall out of her lovely mouth, the wrong suggestions, and even her body, the easy, slender, shrugging body that Larry adores, tends to lurch forward and then collapse when Ryan's around; how do you hug a twelve-year-old boy? Perhaps you don't hug him at all. It's probably better, Beth's decided, to leave the hugging to Larry who is, after all, Ryan's blood parent. This summer she greeted her stepson with her broadest grin (*Hi there, partner*) and a vigorous downward-pumping handshake, a single determined-to-get-it-over-with gesture. She's noticed that the boy's hands are always sticky, and she's mentioned this to Larry two or three times. Is this sticky-hands thing something children have or is it just Ryan? Excessive sweat glands or poor hygiene? And he's so *quiet*.

"He's not really quiet," Larry says. "It's just that he doesn't know what we expect from him."

"Well, what do we expect?" They've been over this

ground before, but still she asks. Her voice at such times takes on a folksinger's deep quaver.

"The impossible."

"Which is –?" Her stepmother's pale distress.

"That he just act like a kid. Our kid. One of the family, one of us."

"I get it, okay, I *get* it. You mean he's supposed to relate to us without thinking about relating to us."

"That and, well, the other thing."

"What other thing?"

"The fact that when he was a tiny kid he was abandoned more or less. Remember, I was the one who walked out the door – at least that's how it must look from his point of view –"

"*And* there's also the fact that you've taken yourself a new wifie."

He stared at her; the word wifie felt false; he wondered what she was getting at, what kind of mood she was working up to. "All of that," he said finally.

"No wonder he's quiet." Beth's voice sheared off into a sympathetic sigh. "He must be always thinking, thinking, thinking. About what a raw deal he's been given, the poor kid."

"At least he's had *some* stability. Dorrie always –"

"When did you say he goes back to Winnipeg?"

"The twenty-second."

"That's ten more days!"

"I know."

As a landscape designer with projects across North America, Larry does quite a bit of traveling, and he often sees divorce kids on planes. They're easy to spot.

The flight attendant settles them in window seats and supplies them with crayons or puzzles before take-off, leaning over and speaking to them quietly as though to compensate for the emotional noise they've already suffered in their short lives. These children are clean and quietly dressed for the most part, with brushed hair, and faces that wear the fixed breakable expression of accustomed but uneasy travelers. Nevertheless, they manage, despite their youth and anxiety, despite the brutalities they've undoubtedly survived, to project a sense of earnest sociability. They've done the trip before. A whole lot of times. Mom's in Texas. Dad's in Toronto. Or the other way around. No, they never get air sick (this said in prideful, yet shyly confessional tones). They've been to Disneyland twice. They've seen the Blue Jays play. They're pretty good in math, especially since Mom's boyfriend's been coaching them in division. As for Dad's girlfriend . . .

It tears at Larry's heart. It half kills him!

O'Hare International Airport is a giant puzzle, with its various color-coded terminals, its concourses, its hundreds of gates – an immense sorting machine for the savvy, and a bafflement to strangers. Travelers emerge blinking at the exit doors, their luggage miraculously in hand, scarcely able to believe they've worked their way out to the benign freshness of the rooted world. Disabled passengers and young children are promised escort service by their respective airlines, but Larry, waiting anxiously for Ryan to emerge, always worries that these arrangements will break down. It did happen once, two years ago when

Ryan was ten. Disembarking, the boy had found himself suddenly alone.

He'd reacted, though, in a surprisingly calm manner for a kid his age, asking directions as he moved along the wide connecting corridors, finding his way from point to point. His hair had been sharply barbered for the summer vacation, and Larry, catching sight of him at last, came close to weeping: his son's pale Canadian face, the fragile shape of his skull exposed to the world, and the boy's small, bony body clad in shorts and T-shirt and dwarfed by the size of his canvas backpack. Were those tears in Ryan's eyes? – Larry couldn't be sure. The searing brightness in his glance of recognition could mean anything.

For Larry it's always the same when he meets Ryan at the airport. The anxiety of finding him in the crowd, then the drowning relief of his actual presence, then trying to catch his eye – yes, there he is, bewildered but waving dreamily in the distance. Safe. They move toward each other, and a moment later hug awkwardly, Larry bending down to fit his arms around the boy's rib-cage, Ryan uncertain about his role in this embrace, their two mismatched male bodies trying to come together, trying to prove something important to those others who surround them. One or two seconds of actual collision are all they can manage – Oh Christ, the fakery of it - then a rough pat-pat on the shoulder. *Hi there, fella.* Yes, well –

This is the way it's done, isn't it? This is how other people do it.

Larry's first sight of Ryan is inevitably blurred by the superimposed image of the boy's mother, Dorrie.

That name shimmers in the air, as distorting as a wave of heat, the face of his ex, and Dorrie's wiry body too, turning and bending, coping with what the world's dumped on her head, what *he's* dumped on her head. It's she, Dorrie, who sanctioned this child's cruel haircut. It's she, a thousand miles away in Winnipeg, who strapped him into his backpack at the crack of dawn, a backpack stuffed and weighted with matched socks rolled into balls tight as bombs. She's checked and double-checked the child's clean, folded underwear, the shirts and pants, a warm jacket in case the weather turns, a brand-knew toothbrush in a hygienic case – she's done it all; every atom of effort is hers. And see those metal bands on the poor kid's teeth. It was Dorrie, making inquiries, asking around, who found a competent orthodontist who wasn't out to rob her; she's the one who sits in the orange-and-beige waiting room thumbing through ancient magazines and Bible stories from a South African press while Ryan is put through the monthly torture of having his braces tightened. She'll buy him an ice-cream cone afterwards. And maybe rent a video to watch while they eat dinner, just the two of them relaxing over warmed-up lasagna, Ryan's favorite, and easy on the teeth and gums, too. Quiet. Peace. An evening like a thousand other evenings.

"So how's your mom?" Larry always asks on the drive to the house in Oak Park. This is his first real question.

"Okay," Ryan says.

* * *

In the summer of 1987 Ryan stayed on an extra week in Chicago. "I hope that's okay," Dorrie said to Larry on the phone from Winnipeg. "I have this chance to go to London and it's one of those eight-day bargains."

"Hey, that's great." His upgraded voice.

"You're sure Beth won't mind?" She pronounces the name of Larry's new wife with measured tact. *Beth*, she says, filling the word with blown air.

"Beth loves having Ryan around."

This wasn't quite true, but it wasn't untrue either. Ryan made Beth edgy, unsure of herself, that was all.

"So is this a business trip kind of thing?" Larry asked his ex-wife over the phone. Dorrie had a knack for sales – and had worked her way up to the vice-presidency of a large and expanding sportswear manufacturer. It could be they were thinking of going international.

"More of a holiday," Dorrie said. Then she added socially, "I haven't been across the pond since our honeymoon. How 'bout that! 1978."

"That's right," Larry said. He wondered if she was traveling alone but was careful not to ask.

"I'm going to be staying with a friend," she said then. "And I got to thinking that you really ought to have the address. Just in case, you know, something happens. Ryan's allergies acting up or something. Peanuts. He can't go near peanuts in any form."

"I know," Larry said.

"You have to watch out for peanut oil in particular. It's everywhere."

"I know."

"He's had these two emergencies –"

"I know."

" – and I just wanted you to be able to reach me –"

"That's a terrific idea," said Larry, who inevitably finds himself full of bloated compliments when talking to his ex. "I'll grab a pencil."

"It's number 7 Wellfleet Road. Hampstead. That's north of London or maybe it's a part of it, I'm not sure. Care of David Ellingwood." She spelled out Ellingwood carefully and rattled off a telephone number.

David Ellingwood. Larry wrote it down. Noisy heartbeats filled his chest, and his fingers burned at their pulse points. David Ellingwood. As far as he knew Dorrie hadn't had a serious relationship since the divorce.

"He's got an answering machine. In case we're out or something."

In case they're out. Dorrie and this man called David Ellingwood. Out! The phone sweated in his hand.

He and Dorrie separated back in 1983, and the divorce came through the following year. Marriage breakdown; the two of them had broken down, and it couldn't be fixed. Total agreement there. Now he was married to his beautiful Beth; she had come skating into his amorous longing at just the right time. So what was the matter with him, why was his scalp twitching and burning like this at the suggestion of a romance in Dorrie's life, and why was his heart banging like a spoon on a frypan? David Ellingwood, now that's a decent name. Probably a decent-*looking* man too. But then Dorrie had kept her looks; why shouldn't she attract the attention of a handsome man? A handsome *Englishman* who thought enough of her to invite her over to England for a holiday. Maybe he'd even sent her a plane ticket, he was so avid to be in her presence. So desirous of . . . what? How long had this been going on?

"Your mom phoned last night," Larry told Ryan the morning after Dorrie's call, "and said you could stay with us an extra week."

"Why?" Ryan said. He looked stricken. He bit back his lip.

"She's going to have a vacation with Mr. Ellingwood."

"Who?"

"With David." Larry floated the word innocently on the air, despising himself

"Oh, him."

"You know this David, then?"

"He's the guy who taught me how to play chess, but then he moved away."

"You know how to play chess?" asked Larry, who grew up playing chess with his friend Bill Herschel, but had never thought of teaching a kid Ryan's age.

"He taught Mom first, and then he taught me."

Larry tried to picture Dorrie hunched over a chess board; it was unimaginable. Not his Dorrie, who couldn't even manage to keep her Scrabble tiles in line.

"You mean your mother plays chess now?"

"She's real good. She even beats *him* sometimes."

"Who?" He wanted to make Ryan say the name out loud. He wanted the name to enter his heart like an arrow tipped with poison.

"David."

"Oh."

Larry and Beth had only been married a few months when Ryan made his first solo trip to Chicago. The early days were terrible for all three of them. Ryan stared hard at Beth, an only child's rapt attention, his mouth slack, and his smoothly combed hair enclosed in a protective bubble of apprehension. His head turned stiffly on his neck. Larry could tell he'd heard of stepmothers and that he was wary.

Beth was frightened too. This was a new role, and not one she'd expected to play in her life. "Just call me Beth," she said when it became clear that Ryan intended to call her nothing at all. "We're going to be good friends, I just know it." Her self-consciousness was such that she seemed forever reaching for matched sets of quotation marks. "Neato," she said about Ryan's Batman kite. Or "Wow" about his Save-the-Endangered-Species T-shirt. Or "Excellent" when Ryan unexpectedly came up with the answer to a radio quiz on baseball statistics.

Larry took Ryan to the Field Museum, which was a partial success, and to the Art Institute, which wasn't. He took him to see the topiary animals at the Chicago Botanic Garden in Glencoe. ("That's supposed to be a giraffe," he told Ryan, pointing to one of the foliage figures, and Ryan said, puzzlingly, "Why isn't it?") Another day he took him to see the Cubs play at Wrigley Field.

Beth begged off these excursions. She was writing a paper about an obscure medieval nun who kissed the seats of chairs where people had been sitting and drank the water in which they washed their feet; religious fervor lies side by side with insanity, she's decided, but she was carefully positioning the events in their historical context. It's altogether too easy to laugh at extravagant piety. Or extravagant anything, for that matter.

Both Beth and Larry have noticed that Ryan seldom laughs out loud. Surely he wasn't this solemn when he was at home with his neighborhood friends. Was it homesickness or was he mildly depressed? He didn't initiate conversations either, and answered Larry's questions with monosyllables, yes, no, uh-huh. What did he think of the movie Superman? It was okay. (Soda cracker crumbs hang on around his mouth as he speaks.) Wasn't that some catch! Yeah, great. So how about that octopus? He's all right.

Is it possible to love a kid this goofy and un-responsive? What does it mean to love your child?

Of course Larry loves his kid. He adds up the obvious. Ryan is quiet, tidy, well behaved, responds to suggestions, does well in school, listens attentively, and shows signs of physical courage – that moment on the subway when a crazy, armed, half-nude guy charged down the aisle of the car they were on and demanded that everyone fall on their knees and pronounce him Lord of the Universe. "Lord of the Universe, Lord of the Universe," Ryan had chanted, a smirking grin on his young face.

Every day during the visits Larry pumps up his fatherly love afresh, creates it artificially by stirring love's reasons into the dialogue and dust of his head – yes, I love this kid; of course I love him what kind of a parent fails to love his child? In this manner and by means of his own cunning, he calls on a stubbornly vital nerve located next to his heart or lungs or spleen, somewhere in there, then moving the words for love up into the emptiness of his cranium, so that they buzz their insistence and occupy the available space.

And occasionally – at least once during the course of each visit – a bright flare of authentic love bursts through and becomes for a moment or two an unstinting flow: the real thing. That time when Larry squeaked into a tight parking spot near North Beach, and Ryan, sitting next to him, had breathed, "Hey, great parking!" Or when he glimpses Ryan's clean bent neck as he leans over the *Trib's* comics page. (Oh, the power of a boy's bent neck!) Or the day Ryan emerged from the Underwater Adventure film at the Aquarium, his eyes so clear, clean, and lit with amazement, so open to the intensity of the uncomprehending moment, that Larry knew it was going to be all right between them – no matter what happened in the future, no matter how they would fail each other. At moments like this, love with all its firecracker madness goes off in Larry's heart. This child of his, this prize of his first passionate love. Flesh of his flesh. His dear son.

Ryan at six was underweight. He was a picky eater. He had allergies. He was afraid of the dark and occasionally wet his bed. He was always coming down with a cold or else getting over an earache. He cried easily, and couldn't bear to be scolded. He refused to look people in the eye, even the eyes of his father, especially the eyes of his father – the father who had left his wife and child, who'd packed a couple of suitcases late on a Winnipeg afternoon and moved out of the Lipton Street house, taking up residence in a crummy apartment over on Westminster Avenue.

Naturally Larry blamed himself for his son's various failures. Children of broken marriages get broken, it's as simple as that.

In the early days after the separation, when Larry was still living in Winnipeg, he phoned his son every evening, but what can you say to a kid that age? A child's world isn't conversation; it's a boneless rocking back and forth between what's allowed and what isn't. You have to be right next to that child to feel what he's feeling and keep track of what he's scared of at any given moment and what he's capable of bearing.

Five-year-old Ryan said a strange thing to Larry. "I've got voices in my head," he said, "and they're talking all the time."

This worried Larry at first, until he figured out what the voices were. They were nothing more than his son's interior thoughts. The beginning of self-consciousness. The start of that long, uncut, internal and endlessly repeated dialogue that would be with him for life.

"I don't believe in putting babies in daycare," Dorrie said after Ryan was born, but a few months later she did just that. Money was short, although they could have managed on what Larry was making at the time. Manitoba Motors, where she worked before Ryan was born, offered her a job in sales. Women on the showroom floor – it was something new, and Dorrie discovered she was terrific at inspiring customer confidence, she had a gift for making her clients feel like winners. "I always call them clients, not customers," she liked to say, "and I love to see them coming out of a deal happy."

Larry worried about daycare, he who'd grown up with a stay-at-home mother, but at age two, age three, Ryan gave the impression of being a reasonably contented child. In the evenings, after his bath, after Larry read him a story, he liked to run around and around the warm house in his pajamas. His squeals of glee and his brave toppling assurance mimed a happiness that Larry resisted. This can't last, he said to himself, but was unable to identify the cause of his unease.

Larry was with his wife at the hospital when Ryan was born. He'd gone to the birthing classes with her, and when the moment came he'd spent seven whole hours timing pains and helping her breathe, and then he watched as his son's small, hot, urgent head emerged from that unrecognisably red and fluid-dribbling oval between Dorrie's legs. After the head came the shoulders and then, with a wet rush, the tiny, wrapped-looking muscular body with its two dark stars at the centre – his son's testicles; a boy. Who would believe those twin markings could be so prominent from the first moment of life. (The penis, on the other hand, was tiny and folded, a rosebud as yet, a gesture.)

The doctor placed a pair of small silvery scissors in Larry's hand and showed him exactly where to cut the cord. Larry remembers, even today, the precise meaty yielding of tissue against the pressure he exerted. Happiness rose in his throat like a song. His son's few wet licks of hair were, he thought, a sign of perfection.

Then he knew, suddenly, what being a father meant. That savage desire to protect. To watch out for danger.

Dorrie Shaw got pregnant. This was back in 1978. She and Larry had been seeing each other for over a year – "seeing each other," that's what they called it – and during that time she'd gone off the pill and switched to a diaphragm. Her mother had had a slight stroke a few months earlier, and Dorrie was scared of the pill's side effects. Everyone was in those days.

At this time she had her own apartment, and wanted Larry to move in with her – he was still living at home, which was just a little bit nutty, she said, for someone his age. They mentioned marriage from time to time, but in a misty, abstract way, like a cozy fifties movie they put on for their own entertainment. "There's no hurry," Larry told Dorrie. He was frightened, but worked hard at keeping his voice steady and offhand.

"I want to be sure," Dorrie confided to Larry. "I don't want the kind of marriage my folks have, all that yelling and mess and kids all over the place."

Then, there she was: pregnant. Two missed periods, then three. They didn't even talk about an abortion, they'd come too far together for that, or else, not far enough. Neither of them knew the right words for the right kind of serious discussion or the right approach. And the ragged profile of acceptance – his folks, hers – kept them silent, fatalistic.

Even when Ryan was a tiny baby Dorrie worried about what they were going to tell him when he got older. "Like why's his birthday five months after our wedding anniversary? Kids ask those kinds of questions, you know. Kids notice."

"He'll have to learn to count first."

"They learn to count early these days. That *Sesame Street*!"

"He won't be the first kid born out of –"

"Don't say it. I hate that word."

"Wedlock?"

"You said it. I told you I hate that word, and you said it."

"No one uses it anymore. No one pays attention to that stuff."

"How about your sister Midge? She thinks I did it on purpose, trapped you, her darling baby brother, stuck a pin through my diaphragm or something. Well, I was the one that got trapped."

"Why worry about what Midge thinks?"

"What about your parents. How come they're always going around saying Ryan was premature, the darling wee little thing? Eight pounds. Uh-huh! Tell me about it."

"Because they don't know what else to say."

"Well, we're going to have to think of something to say to him, you and me. The day's going to come."

"We'll tell him," Larry said, "that we were just a couple of crazy kids."

"More like stupid," Dorrie said. She made a face. A suffering face.

He's probably known for years, Larry thinks. Ryan arrived in Chicago in the summer of 1991, having grown at least two inches since spring. A kid going on thirteen has got to know. Probably he's come across an old wedding photo or else something more official, some paper with a date on it, or maybe someone's said something to him, dropped a hint or even trotted out the whole story. And there was always the possibility that he'd just figured it out, letting a kind of slow logic drip into his veins, the whole picture coming together.

But how is a kid supposed to absorb this kind of knowledge? What if Ryan believes he's the sole reason his parents got married, that he was to blame for the whole fiasco?

Of course, that's what he must think, how the hell could he think anything else? Here he was, a little piece of protein in the wrong place at the wrong time, his cells multiplying day by day, and setting on course a stream of misery that ended in his parents' disaster. How does a boy of twelve stand it, walking around the world and holding to his chest the toxic secret that lies at the well of his life? What's he supposed to do? It isn't as though he can join a support group for early-arrival babies, or sign up for a twelve-step program leading to forgiveness of parents and their acts of dumb carelessness.

It worries Larry lately, it preys on his mind. Shouldn't you try to talk to someone's inner child while he still *was* a child? Larry's taken the month of July off, and he, with Ryan helping, has been attacking the neglected garden of the old Oak Park house he and Beth have bought, building a new fence, starting an espalier against the stone foundation – eastern redbud – and a row of young dogwood by the garage.

"So what's an espalier?" Ryan asked.

An espalier, Larry told him, is a plant that's trained on a trellis or wire. It wants to grow in three dimensions, that's its impulse, but you can force it to occupy a two-dimensional plane, flattening it out so it nicely covers a fence or a blank wall. "That sounds mean," Ryan said, voicing a thought that was so spontaneous and natural and so precisely what Larry would have said at the same age, that the words hung in the air for an instant, unanswerable. Larry debated getting into the issue of whether or not plants "feel," and decided against it. The day was too balmy and the moment too fragile. He shook his head and gazed at his son through softened eyes. "Maybe it *is* a little mean," Larry said finally, and was rewarded by a shy, jubilant smile.

Ryan's taken a surprising interest in the work. He's gone along with Larry to the plant nursery, he's offered good suggestions about how to give the fence along the east of the yard a weathered look – first a coat of grey paint followed by a coat of white and then a rough sanding – to make it look like it's "been there from day one." There's been plenty of opportunity for Larry to observe Ryan's feats of concentration and his

226

quick, quiet boyish courtesy – and interpret both, perversely, as a signal of pain.

The time has come, he decides, to have a talk with this only son of his, and to relieve the boy of the pressure of his privately stored suspicions. This will be one of the important conversations of his own life, he thinks, and possibly his son's life too; it thrills him a little to think of the truth spilling out and the clean space it will leave in its wake, though he knows that when the moment comes he'll have to struggle to find words. He'll manage, though. Where darkness and secrecy have hidden themselves, he'll plant openness and explanation.

But first he'll have to consult with his ex-wife, Dorrie.

He phones Winnipeg at eleven o'clock one night – after Ryan has gone to sleep on the sun porch, and after Beth, exhausted from teaching a summer course at Rosary, has gone upstairs to bed. (Why is it that Ryan's visits necessitate a double life of tiptoeing and covert conversations? It's always like this.)

Dorrie answers the phone sounding sleepy. She was sitting at the kitchen table, she tells Larry, reviewing a sales report for an early morning breakfast meeting. She plans to get away later in the week to Trois Pistols in Quebec, where she's signed up for a short French course. Rain's been falling all evening in Winnipeg after weeks of drought. There'd been lightning around suppertime and a change in the wind. How was Ryan getting along?

"I'm thinking of having a serious talk with him," Larry says, cringing at the melodramatic shading of his voice.

"About? " She's instantly alert.

"I think there are things he should know."

"He knows about sex, Larry, if that's what you're talking about. He's known for years. I bought him a book, and then we had a long talk. This was when he was, maybe, nine."

"That's great, Dorrie." His fake flattery.

"Not great." She's on to him. Is she ever! "Just necessary."

"That's what I mean."

"But if you still want to have a talk with him –"

"I want to – that is, I think we should tell him about us."

"What about us?"

"About our getting married, about his birth. I keep thinking he'll worry about it. That he'll put two and two together, if he hasn't already."

"Oh."

"I just wanted to know what you think."

A brief silence, then "I, oh –"

She's crying, he can tell. "Dorrie? Are you there?"

"No," she's saying. "No, I don't want you to tell him about *that*."

"But he's probably figured it out already."

"Then there's no need to –"

"I think he'll be lonely, that's all. Knowing about it all alone, living inside a question mark, if you know what I mean."

"I know what you mean."

"Well, don't you think –?"

"He knows. I know he knows. There've been hints. Questions."

"What kind of questions?"

"Like why we got divorced."

"What do you say to that one?"

"I said I was too dumb to be married at that time in my life."

"So was I. Christ. A regular doofus."

"No, Larry. We were both dumb, but I was also stupid and also –"

"You're too hard on yourself."

"– and also crazy. But then I got sane. I figured it out, after you left, all those years, I figured out how to stop being a coupon cutter and get sane and stay that way. One of the things I figured out was that you don't have to know every single particle of everything. Not every last shred has to be dragged out in the open. And I don't want Ryan to think – to think we had to, you know, get married, that we were forced to –"

Larry remembers suddenly how she used to stutter when she cried.

"We loved each other, Dorrie. That's the real reason we got married."

"Did we?"

He can't judge her tone, whether it's bitter or beseeching. "Yes, we did," he says, bringing a firmness to his voice. "I may have forgotten a lot, but I remember that for sure."

She's sniffling now, between her words. "He'll be all right, Larry. He can handle this by himself. He doesn't have to be told straight out. "

"You were the one who used to worry about explaining things to him."

"I was younger then, I hadn't got myself together yet."

"But don't you think it would help if –?"

"This one thing he can manage. Just this one thing. Please, Larry. Trust me on this one."

He lets a moment of silence go by, then says, "If you're sure –"

"I'm sure."

"He's turning into a great kid."

"He is, isn't he?"

"Thanks to you."

"You too."

"I shouldn't keep you."

"Bye, Larry." Tears in her voice; he can hear them. "Night."

Larry feels it the instant he puts down the phone: a guilty relief. And then, without warning, a potent electric shock of happiness so violent it seems to slice his body open from end to end. For a minute or two, all his senses are wired into this state of simple rapture. Dorrie's voice, its dying vibrancy. His tender white-limbed wife asleep upstairs. And his beloved child, whose name, for no reason he can recollect, is Ryan. He'll own this mysteriously bestowed name forever.

And what else? Larry asks himself. His own good luck, his dangerous history, his mistakes and promises, this dark silent capacious house, and the secrets and compromises that lie – serenely enough – beneath its roof.

CHAPTER ELEVEN

Larry's Search for the Wonderful and the Good
1992

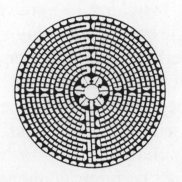

At the age of forty-two Larry Weller, a landscape designer with an office in suburban Chicago, gives the appearance of having found tranquility and ease in his life. He's not interested in breaking through the power firmament. He's already, in fact, come further along in the world than he ever expected to. Everything about him announces a man in a state of reasonable good fortune. His business card with its nicely enigmatic logo. His paid-up Visa bill. His tax receipts, which are squared, stapled, and neatly filed in a place where only Larry or his wife can find them. His clothes, his jeans, sweaters, his wide and narrow leather belts, his sports shoes and crisp socks – all these modestly wrap, enhance, and decently accommodate Larry Weller's middle-aged bones and attendant psyche, the relaxed apparel of good but not exclamatory quality. Moreover, his bodily flesh, his average face with its look of tightly woven canvas, his benign, slightly thickening trunk and limbs – these enable him to assume and maintain, when he chooses, a physical position of rare stillness, and his wife, Beth (his second wife, actually), has noted Larry's postural feats with a measure of pride: the way he can sit for an hour or more without twitching or scratching, composing his limbs so that he becomes a benign, amiable statue – at a backyard barbecue, for instance, or at a public lecture, it doesn't matter which – without crossing and uncrossing his legs in the tiresome way that more nervous, more self-conscious, and more appeasing men do, and how Larry is able to lean with just the right degree of incline into a gathering of people, his head angled forward, his frame subtly poised and attentive and eager to catch the least verbal breeze; he's endlessly appreciative, or so it appears, of what he's being offered, those scattered buds of suburban insight, or an obscure and mutually flattering joke, or perhaps an anecdote that wanders hither and thither across the sociological divide, but which Larry Weller, as signaled by his relaxed body messages, is anxious to absorb and applaud.

No one's taught him these things; it's just happened. You could call it Larry's good luck, the result of a few jointed behavioral neurons sewn into his spinal cord, unique as his blood type or fingerprint whorls. The curious rarefactions of his body – its stillness, its unconscious geniality – are always there, insistently present, along with the patient, subcutaneous question – have these been printed in his genes or did *he* imprint them *himself*?

His voice, too, radiates an impression of calm, seasoned good will. Low tones predominate and respectful pauses, and these are generally, and generously, attributed to Larry's Canadian Background, since it's well known among his and Beth's good friends that he was born and brought up in the Canadian city of Winnipeg. Just where this city is located is less well known: somewhere *up there*, somewhere northerly, a representative piece of that polite, white, silent kingdom with its aging, jowly Queen and snowy mountain ranges and people sugaring off and drinking tea and casting for trout and nodding amicably – much as Larry Weller nods at his neighbor across a backyard patio in Oak Park and sips his glass of California Chablis, and casts his glance fixedly up at the arch of maple boughs when asked for his views about the intentions of George Bush or about the exorbitant cost of National Public Radio. As for the politics of a universal health care plan, Larry is noticeably silent. A topic best avoided. Ah, but (changing the subject) the Canadian wilderness, the famed train journey across the western continent – this is everyone's dream, is it not? Would Larry agree? Yes. Emphatically. "Oh, yes, absolutely. Someday Beth and I hope to . . ."

Is Larry cool? No, impossible. His genes are bright and lively enough, but his social conditioning keeps him suspicious of coolness. He's recently filled out a pop culture quiz and scored in the "young fogey" category.

A comfortable man, comfortably settled, yet Larry himself would say, if asked – but no one so far *has* asked – that he's been parachuted into a life whose contours are monumentally out of whack with those he once knew. His Winnipeg childhood was inexpressibly uneventful – though perhaps no one's childhood can be described in such terms. He'd grown up the second child of a factory worker and a stay-at-home mother, whose primary leisure activities were attending Saturday morning garage sales in their immediate neighborhood or the occasional football game at the Winnipeg Arena. As a child, Larry was enrolled in public schools, and had, in fact, been ignorant, as were his parents, of any other kind of schooling. His marks were no better than average, and sometimes worse. After limping through MacDonald Secondary, he spent a year at a local technical college – no one, given his problems with math and the mess he made of exams, suggested he apply to the university. At Red River College he earned a Diploma in Floral Arts, and after that began a slow, spiraling drift: upward to manager of a Winnipeg florist outlet – and southward, eventually, to Chicago where he'd studied landscape design for a year under the great Eric Eisner and then made his way to the tight green parceled-out, shadow-strewn spaces of genteel and progressive Oak Park – ending up, much to his surprise, a qualified landscape designer (honorary) with a specialty in garden mazes. (In point of fact, he's done only one maze this year, for the Children's Museum in Muncie, Indiana, but he's been swamped by clients, especially from the American sunbelt, who want an Elizabethan knot garden crammed into their backyards, a squared lump of greenery and historic suggestion between the swimming pool and tennis court; a New Yorker, on the other hand, demanded a *faux* meadow on his Manhattan rooftop.)

He is, at forty-two – another surprise! – more or less solvent. He's getting along in the world, he and Beth.

But perpetually – every minute of every day, in fact – he prepares himself for exposure and ruin: he has no university degree to fall back on or boast about, he has never read Charles Dickens or Ralph Waldo Emerson, he'd be more than half-stumped if asked to locate the state of Nebraska on a map, he has next-to-zero brain-vibes on the subject of the American Senate, its contribution to American governmental stability or its menacing echoes of elitism. So how is it he projects such an air of confidence when, at the same time, living a fraction of an inch from public humiliation? Do other people exist this close to the flame of extinction? (Hidden there, on the back wall of his retina, is a quizzing caption in a flowing script, his own handwriting most likely, which asks: how did I get here? how did this happen?)

He has a mortgage, fairly sizable, on a seven-room house on Kenilworth Avenue in Oak Park. Three bedrooms! – as though a childless couple like himself and Beth could possibly need three bedrooms! The street he and Beth live on presents a sober stone and stucco frontality, though Larry knows how quickly the backs of these buildings dissolve, like movie locations, into weeds and garbage cans and evil-smelling alleys. (The word *alley* is not used in Canada; these not-quite streets are known instead as *lanes* – a beautiful word, Larry thinks, calling up a false image of quaint cobbled surfaces bordered by rows of sculptured evergreen plantings, miniature avenues which are insouciant, leafy, undeclared, and unnamed, and which lead inevitably to a distant moss-covered church, and couples wandering arm in arm toward declarations of love. Yes. Forever, yes. He is, has always been, a romantic, though it's only recently he's been able to identify and label the signs.)

And what else about Larry Weller? He is the middle-aged husband of a scholarly wife – "What does she see in me?" the querying script behind his eyes demands – who is a few years younger than himself, a woman whose specialty is women's studies (sub-specialty: religion), an area of inquiry that mildly perplexes Larry; he would like to understand more precisely the range and purpose of women's studies, but it seems he's left the question too late. When he first met Beth she was still working on her doctoral thesis on women saints; she was more lighthearted in those days about her chosen field; she seemed always to have one eyebrow raised above the other, signaling that what she "did" with her saintly women was part of a vast joke and not to be taken seriously. Lately she's changed, grown more hungry and avid, and certainly more anxious for publication. If her left eyebrow goes skyward now, it's more likely to ex-press frustration: no one cares, no one pays attention, academic success is a game of roulette or else vicious backstabbing.

His life has changed since his early, capsized marriage. Today, he and Beth spend long, settled, lamplit American evenings in their cozy back-of-the house den, baking their ankles before a newly installed gas fireplace; a kind of anxious boredom occasionally visits them as they read, sip decaffeinated coffee from flowered mugs, and now and then tune into Masterpiece Theater or else watch a rented video, and he knows now how, out of boredom, men and women nudge at their happiness in order to revive the intensity of early love. Glancing up from his book (something new off the press, perhaps, about formal gardens), Larry is most often swamped by the golden unreality and goodness of the scene he and his wife occupy, the shelves of stacked magazines that surround them, his wife's hands, slim as knives skimming over her lapful of manuscript pages. And of the other scene that is socketed directly into this one, himself and Beth later in the evening, climbing the stairs to their large square bedroom, the sheets tumbled crazily on the queensize bed, the walls tipped sideways, the only sound their hard breathing and tender, yet occasionally selfish, efforts, and later the moist gliding of her skin on his, coming heavily to rest, along with her muffled moaning of his name, *oh Larry, my Larry*. ("How did this happen?" a voice whispers inside his brain. "How do I deserve such recognition?")

Often, of course, they're out for the evening. He and Beth regularly attend performances of the Chicago Symphony, since Beth's parents, Belford and Ruth Prior – "Bells" was in securities before he retired to Hawaii, Ruth practiced tax law – send Beth and Larry a pair of season tickets every Christmas. Of course Beth and Larry go, despite the terrible parking problems in the Loop and despite the worry about leaving an unattended car, and despite the fact that

Beth is curiously bored by music and quite often falls into a doze halfway through the evening.

What does Larry Weller, formerly of Winnipeg, Canada, make of the concert series? To be truthful, he finds the symphonic strains largely opaque, he who grew up without ever once attending an evening of classical music, though a wealth of resources were readily available in that city, had he only known. On the other hand, the alternating rhythms of the symphonic movements are oddly, eerily familiar. They crash on his ears, loud and soft, ripply and smooth, sliding and stopping. These musical variations echo his own life: now happy, now sad, dipping, rising, fast and slow, up and down. Is it always going to be like this, he wonders, and is this all there is?

In January of last year Larry's wife at long last published her book about early women saints: *Happy Enough* by Dr. Beth Prior, based on her doctoral thesis of the same name; University of Illinois Press. $29.95. Illustrated.

A handsome, oversize book, it can be found turned outward on the shelves of all good bookstores, at least in the Chicago area, showing off its handsome, slick green-and-blue cover with the stunning portrait of St. Agatha (3rd century AD) holding forth a platter on whose shining surface are arranged her two breasts, nipple side up, which have been forcibly detached from her body as a punishment for zealous piety. The creaminess of these breast mounds reminds Larry of the cups of baked custard his mother used to prepare for him and his sister, Midge, when they were children. "It's good for what ails you," his mother used to sing mysteriously, setting the little glass cups down on the kitchen table, her tone at once apologetic and proud. A sprinkle of golden nutmeg was strewn across the top, and he and Midge scraped this damp, dimpled crust away in a flash, popping it on to their tongues and grinning at each other as though they had somehow outwitted their mother.

The reviews of Beth Prior's book were uneven, as they tend to be for such academic studies, but generally positive. "Dr. Prior has the good sense not to mock the excesses of early Christian ecstatics, but to view them in the context of their female powerlessness in early Western societies" (*Northwestern Arts & Letters*, Vol. XVI, May 1992, pp. 24-5).

On the strength of the *Northwestern* review and also a favorable mention in the April issue of the *Women's Book Review* ("learned, humane, innovative"), Beth has applied for a Guggenheim Fellowship, knowing that they – whoever *they* are – wouldn't dream of turning her application down. She has youth on her side, after all; she has a fresh new-minted (almost) PhD; she's widely read in a number of areas, she's committed and clear-eyed, and, furthermore, the feminist/deconstructionist revamping of history is a hot topic at the moment. She can't miss.

The thought of obtaining such a fellowship was exciting to her – this much was clear to her husband, Larry, who observed the intensity with which she filled in the forms, pushing her pen down feverishly into the allotted squares and agonizing over which of her colleagues she could count on for a letter of recommendation: Dr. Rosemary Stanley from U.I.C.? – no, too conservative. Felix Zuegler, who'd written an introduction to *Happy Enough*? – he was perhaps too closely connected with the project to be thought objective. Whoever she thought of was too important or else not important enough. A whole night's sleep was lost over this matter of supporting letters, though in the morning she announced to Larry that she didn't think the letters would carry much weight after all, not when set beside her curriculum vitae, that fifteen-page closely spaced document (soon-to-be-a-major-motion-picture, as Larry likes to say).

It worried him a little to see his wife counting on the fellowship so much – her fever of intelligence was once something else – and he wondered what he could do to cushion the blow, should it come. It was important to have an alternate plan, he told himself; he would have to put his mind to it; he would have to think sideways, perhaps even apply for a grant himself, not that there was much chance of getting one.

It's my turn, Beth said blithely, as if temporal justice accompanied the presentation of awards. A Guggenheim, she explained to Larry, is almost a guarantee of a tenured position, a tenured life, and she's been bouncing around long enough from one post-doc post to the next. It also carries sufficient for a whole year of travel and research, and perhaps the promise of another book, this time a contemporary study of the feminist perspective on the Annunciation, that moment, historical or mythical, when the angel

240

Gabriel announced to the Holy Virgin that she was chosen to be the Mother of the Messiah. "The greatest imposition ever perpetrated on a woman," declared Beth Prior, aged thirty-five, beloved and baffling second wife of Larry Weller.

"You could always shut down the office for a few months," she told him, "and join me halfway through. You know you've always wanted to see the European mazes. And, listen, Larry, I think we should list the house with a good rental agency right now. You have to start early with these things, you have to plan ahead."

When the letter from the Guggenheim Foundation came, informing her that she had not, unfortunately, been awarded a fellowship – "An unprecedented number of applications were received this year" – she went quiet; the bones of her face froze sharp as stone, than collapsed to tearful rubble. She wept and raged, slamming her hands on the oak coffee table so that it rattled on its legs. She reviewed her qualifications. She railed against the application process, then against the ignorance of the jury who were, she suspected, all men, white European men, with men's circumscribed and testosterone-limited bias; the Guggenheim game was infamous for favoring male candidates; she should have known she'd get shoved aside. Screwed, shafted.

The next day there was a second envelope from the Foundation, this time for Larry. His application had been approved, the letter said, and hearty congratulations were offered.

"You didn't tell me you'd applied," Beth said stiffly. "You never mentioned it once."

"I didn't think I had much of a chance."

"It isn't as though you've actually published anything."

"And I certainly don't have a PhD."

"Damn, damn, damn, damn."

"Look, Beth —"

"It isn't fair. Even you can see it isn't fair."

"No," Larry said. It pained him to look at her trembling hands. "It isn't fair, you're right. But we can share it. Who was it who said two can travel as cheaply as one?"

"That's ridiculous. And I wish you'd stop trying to cheer me up. It's making me crazy. I find it —" She stopped herself.

"What? "

"Humiliating."

"Why humiliating?"

"That you would have done this behind my back."

"I didn't think of it that way."

"A breach of trust. That's what it really amounts to."

"I'm sorry. You know I'd never —"

"No, I don't know that. And I'm not sure you're sorry."

"It isn't as though I lied about it."

"You have to admit, Larry, that what you did doesn't exactly represent full disclosure on your part. And full disclosure is what we've based our whole —"

"I just thought —"

"What did you think? I'd be interested in knowing."

"You seemed to want to go so terribly much."

242

"It wasn't just the going, Larry. God! It was – I don't know – the having."

"But in a way we're both having."

"You just don't get it, do you?"

Maybe he didn't. He saw that now. There was so much that he didn't "get." And he wasn't sure he believed in the possibility of full disclosure either. He thought of Dorrie. He thought of his mother and father. The gaping silences. The missing wire of connection.

"Look," he said. "If we got busy we could be in England in a month's time." This came out, he realized, in the practiced, oily, diverting tones of a fond uncle. "Or how about we just pack our bags and go tomorrow?"

"Tomorrow's not possible. How could we possibly–?"

"Next week, then."

"I don't know."

"Of course we'll go."

"Anyway," she paused, "it's a good thing I listed the house. You wanted me to wait, remember? I told you we should go ahead."

"We'll have a terrific time."

He said this loudly into the air, speaking in a falsely ringing male voice that cantilevered, it seemed to him, over a swamp of dishonesty – but whose, his or Beth's? The balance between himself and his wife had shifted subtly, that much was clear. He had in some way betrayed her. And she would be a long time forgiving him.

"Damn, damn, damn," she muttered into her knife-like hands. Cursing him.

* * *

243

They landed at Shannon, rented a bright blue Ford Fiesta and headed off to see the the original site of the Hollywood stone, the oldest dateable labyrinth in the British Isles, 550 AD. Rain poured straight out of a blackened sky, and silvered the sides of their little bouncing car. "I feel damp right to the middle of my American corpuscles," Beth said, shivering in the front seat. Twenty minutes later the sun came brightly to their rescue, leaving the green cultivated Irish countryside glistening all around them. "Like top-of-the-market broccoli," Beth observed with a wave at the hedgerows.

What was important, Larry explained, was the location of the Hollywood stone. It had been discovered some years earlier at the beginning of a circuitous fourteen-mile pilgrims' path through the Wicklow Mountains, the start of an approach to Glendalough, an early Celtic monastic community.

The Christian maze so clearly incised on the rounded, brownish lump of stone suggested two conjoined messages. One of those messages informed travelers that the road to the Celtic sanctuary was convoluted and difficult, much as today's generic zig-zag road signs give warning of hairpin turns ahead. A more profound reading of the maze related to the difficulty of life and life's tortuous spiritual journey.

That this double message could be conflated into one symbolic sign seemed wonderful to Beth. "It's like a naive form of perspective," she marveled. "No absolute rules and no worry about the confusion between the elemental and the spiritual."

Her face was flushed with happiness, as it always was when she was in the proximity of holiness. An avowed agnostic, believing the sacred has been taken over by psychology, she nevertheless was someone who melted toward the vision of God's grace, seeing it as a storm of sunlight, the most powerful force in history.

The Hollywood stone itself, unfortunately, was no longer in its original position beside St. Kevin's Road, but had been moved to the Museum of Antiquities in Dublin where Larry and Beth saw it later that day.

"It's a rotten shame," Beth murmured against the glass case, "to take something sacred away from where it belongs. A sign for pilgrims. Encouragement for the road ahead."

"Or discouragement maybe."

"That too." She has been in an agreeable, speculative mood all day, though both she and Larry were wobbly with jet lag.

"Its surface would be rubbed away in no time," Larry reminded her. "By tourists like us. Or by the rain and wind."

"You're right," Beth sighed, her good humor vanishing. "We do have to make the necessary compromises, don't we?"

In England the weather was exceptionally fine. The time was late June. Lobelia bloomed all over London, over the doorways of houses, in public parks and squares, and Beth was awed by the thought that this once smoky old city, with its layers of history and pollution, could support so delicate and fragrant a flower, and in such profusion. The sharply sweet fragrance entered the window of their hotel in Pembridge Gardens in Notting Hill. They breathed in its druggy, weighted scent, and spoke again and again about how fortunate they were to be in this peaceful, green, deflowered city, so far from the scorched flatlands of Illinois where (as they had seen on last night's news) a drought was threatening this year's corn crop.

Immediately after breakfast each morning Beth travels by tube to the National Gallery or to the Victoria and Albert Museum. It is her intention to see and take notes on every representation of the Annunciation she can find. Almost always the composition of this sacred encounter is the same. Mary on the right of the tableau is calmly seated with an open book before her. At the left stands, or rather crouches, the angel Gabriel, with his feminine, overly saccharine face and flowing locks, and immense, gaudily painted, backfolded wings, holding in his arms a strongly shaped phallic lily. Between the two figures lies the artist's blurred suggestion of a civilized society, a tower or two or else a stone archway leading into an enclosed garden, that symbol of virginity, and always, somewhere in the blue air, a bird with his beak pointed sharply toward Mary, delivering the tumultuous news: she, of all women, has been chosen.

Beth writes these details down in her spiral scribbler and later enters them into her laptop. She watches for variations, rejoicing when they occur. Such anomalies represent to her ruptures in the traditional narrative, and indications of interpretive privilege – a privilege she intends to avail herself of once she begins her new book. A book written under the *aegis* of a Guggenheim Fellowship; *aegis*, this is how she more and more often thinks of it.

Larry, searching his way through the wonderful and beautiful mazes of Europe, did Hampton Court first, to get it over with. He was among the earliest at the gate on a soft, breezy Tuesday morning, and he walked through the corridors of the maze in twenty minutes flat, reciting the classic formula to himself, right, left, left, et cetera, and taking the turns on automatic pilot. Birds twittered overhead in the morning light; the glossy banked hedges of yew were still damp with moisture, giving off the air of expensive upholstery, rigorously propped up.

In the last few years he's seen several American reproductions of the Hampton Court trapezoid: at Deerfield in Pennsylvania where thousands of six-inch boxwood seedlings have grown slowly to maturity, and are brilliantly set off by azalea borders. Then there is the maze at Williamsburg, executed in holly with geometric topiary and preached hornbeam; a smaller version of Hampton Court, it was a little jewel.

He had anticipated that the Hampton Court pilgrimage would turn a significant key in his consciousness, filling him with the bloom of recollected happiness or else nudging at failure. This was the place, after all, where he and his first wife, Dorrie, had come on the final day of their honeymoon, fourteen years earlier, and where he had undergone between the teasing avenues of yew what he supposes he must call a transformative experience. He has never been able to identify what happened to him during the hour he wandered lost and dazed and separated from the others, but he remembers he felt a joyous rising of spirit that was related in some way to the self's dimpled plasticity. He could move beyond what he was, the puzzling hedges seemed to announce; he could become someone other than Larry Weller, shockingly new husband of Dorrie Shaw, non-speculative citizen of a former colony, a man of limited imagination and few choices.

But today, turning the hedge corners briskly and appraising the tricky dead-end shadows, he remained stubbornly unmoved. Sixteen nodes, sixteen branches; it seemed a little too neat. He noticed that the old plant stock was in need of thinning. He felt the strengthening sun and wished he'd worn a hat. A party of schoolchildren had arrived, and the voice of their teacher attempting to keep them in check was full of hard, braying, authoritative tones. He observed the essential monotony of the ancient maze – if 1690 could be termed ancient – and the way in which the twin trees at the center seemed, somehow, out of scale and rather prim and silly, as though the maze traveler were being taunted instead of rewarded. Important design possibilities had been overlooked, he saw, though he supposed he should admire the innovative "island" that lay within the perimeter hedge, something that had not been fully appreciated in its day. He paused to take a deep breath, inviting a wave of strong feeling, but none came. Two schoolgirls stood giggling at the end of a shrubbery wall and casting curious, flirtatious looks in his direction.

He caught the first bus back to London.

The Leeds Castle maze, set on two islands in the middle of a lake, was something else. Beth, who was quickly growing tired of her Annunciation project – too many vapid virginal faces, too much male presumption on the part of the painters who immortalized them – joined Larry for a day at Maidstone in Kent. The maze, designed and executed just four years earlier, was stunning in its intricacy and verve, and Larry, working his way through the clever passages, recovered something of his old sense of a maze's connection with more elementary human scramblings. "A maze," he told Beth, quoting from something he'd read not long ago but whose source he'd misplaced, "is a kind of machine with people as its moving parts."

"But," Beth asked, "surely we don't want to be part of a machine? " Her old quizzing curiosity had revived wonderfully after weeks of insomnia and gloomy note scribbling in the British Library. Only yesterday she'd exclaimed to Larry how happy she was to be a woman who'd chosen not to run with the wolves. Today her face glowed with the afternoon's heat, and the expensive pumpkin-colored sundress she'd bought in a London boutique showed off her slender, sharp shoulders – so that Larry was thinking already of their hotel room back in London, the wide double bed and its cool, uncreased sheets.

Beth repeated her question. "Do you honestly think people want to be a part of a machine?" More and more her face has the stretched look of someone trying to stay "interested."

"Yes," Larry said, surprised at the speed of his response. "At least I do." He waved a hand toward the crowds of holidaymakers pressing around them. Children. Lovers with their arms linked. Families. Groups of Boy Scouts, smart in their uniforms but reassuringly unruly. There were immense touring parties of tentative Japanese moving rapidly to and fro like starlings, and chuckling Germans with cameras at their bellies and bottled water in their backpacks. Americans drifted by in groups of three or four. "Pretty snazzy," one of these elderly Americans pronounced.

"A maze is designed so that we get to be part of the art," Larry told Beth.

"So you think this is an art, do you?" She gestured broadly. Her tone was only half mocking.

He ducked the question; the word art made him nervous. "The whole thing about mazes," he said, "is that they make perfect sense only when you look down on them from above."

Beth took this in. "Like God in his heaven, you mean. Being privy to the one authentic map of the world."

"Something like that."

"So what kind of a God wants us to get confused and keep us in a state of confusion?"

"Isn't that what we've always had? Chaos from the first day of creation? But mazes are refuges from confusion, really. An orderly path for the persevering. Procession without congestion."

"You read that somewhere."

"Probably."

"At least they provide a way out."

"One exit anyway."

"Salvation or death? Or more confusion. An unsolvable maze has got to be invalid."

"Some people would say there's amusement in confusion." More and more, lately, he lets his thoughts come out in words, these same thoughts he'd once kept shyly locked up in his head.

"Would you say that, Larry? That confusion is *fun*?"

"Not fun exactly, but a little time off. And God knows we all need time off."

"You aren't by any chance trying to tell me something, Larry."

"You're working" – he looked for the words – "awfully hard."

"Too ambitiously, you mean."

"Not that exactly. Too –"

"Desperately?" she supplied.

"That's not what I mean."

They'd reached the underground grotto by now. All around them were walls decorated with sea shells. Grinning statues and cascades of water. A fun fair with the fun twisted grotesquely sideways, and something larger and more primitive hinted at.

"I just think," Larry went on, "that we need little stopping places now and then to crawl into. It's our scared animal selves pushing forward. Making burrows and then trying to find our way out again."

"Who was it who said life is mostly a matter of burrows?"

"I don't know," Larry said. "Did someone say that?"

"Auden, I think."

Larry only vaguely divines who Auden is – his hideous ignorance! A poet? He nodded non-committally.

"Or maybe it was Camus."

They had arrived in an underground passage ninety feet below the maze hedges. A flooded cave stood before them, and also the maze's goal, the seat of the nymph. They'd come this far, part of a wave of other maze walkers, and there was a sense that they were about to ascend into the sunlit world once again where struggle and confusion ceased, at least momentarily.

Beth, turning suddenly, reached over and gripped Larry's hand hard in both of hers. "I'm glad we're living inside the same burrow," he said, speaking in an intense, urgent whisper.

"Me too." His wet voice. He could hear himself swallow. His reasonous saliva. His thundering ardor dissolving in its own juices.

"And sharing the same Guggenheim too." Her tone had turned rich. She gave Larry a quick look to check his expression.

He smiled down into her eyes, and then into the parting of her crisp dark hair, and felt himself, temporarily, forgiven.

They settled in, renting a small Wandsworth flat and buying their own groceries. A certain amount of peace came with this decision, since both of them were domestic by disposition.

They never lost, though, the sense of being travelers.

All around them they could see similar men and women; the modern inhabitants of the world were wanderers, pilgrims, and the labyrinth was their natural habitat. Each weekend Larry and Beth went mazing, as they called it, starting off with the largest hedge maze in the world at Longleat House in Wiltshire, 380 feet by 175 feet, composed of yew and a series of six wooden bridges. Designed and built in 1978, the maze employed spiral junctions and a species of psychological teasing that directly addressed and manipulated the visitors' compulsion to conserve time and energy. "A beauty," Larry said at the end of the day. "My feet are killing me," said Beth, "and my arm's going to need a week in traction." (Her Annunciation work was once again progressing.)

They visited, on various sunny or rainy weekends, the brick pavement maze at Kentwell Hall, the symbolic hedge maze at Blenheim Palace, a yew construction at Hever Castle in Kent with structured buttresses, the serious-sounding Environmental Maze in Wales (rhododendron, birch, and oak), a massive battlemented hedge at Knightshayes Court with alcoves for statuary, and the turf maze at Saffron Walden. "I've got a feeling I've been here before," Larry said when he and Beth arrived at the picturesque main street. "Not the maze, but the town."

"So what's this supposed to be for?" Beth asked about the turf maze, which was a series of circles cut into the ground back in medieval times. The Saffron Walden design was Christian and traditional, but it was thought, Larry said, reading from his guidebook, that the maze provided a kind of bawdy sport for young men and maids. "Marvelous," Beth breathed. "You can imagine them, can't you, racing around after each other, tripping on their petticoats, stealing kisses."

"The turf wears away," Larry explained, "so the chalky ground becomes the path and the turf the divider."

"You're sounding pedagogical, Larry. You're sounding like *me*."

The foot-shaped Bicton maze in Devon was the creation of Randoll Coate and Adrian Fisher, the genius of contemporary maze design, and Larry and Beth traced their way through each toe of the foot, and arrived breathless and full of delight at the roundabout in the heel, where they were spun toward the maze's solution. "So this is what mazes are about," Beth said. "You kept telling me they were about love or sex or death or God. But really they're just fun."

"I told you they were fun. You've forgotten."

This seemed to him something that had happened often. Beth had a way of reconstructing their life together, reassembling their conversations, their various arrivals and departures and chapters of marital history. It worried him, but only occasionally. Half the time he thinks how fortunate a man he is to be married to a woman of imagination. A flag of persistent untruth flutters in his head, but he chooses to ignore it.

In August Larry and Beth went to France, where they were joined for two weeks by Larry's son, Ryan, who was thirteen now. He arrived at Roissy airport, it seemed to Larry, with a new lanky look about him. (It

254

was one of Larry's own secret sorrows that he would never himself be described as being lanky, having passed directly from weedy adolescence to full-fleshed adulthood.)

Their first stop was the Jardin des Plantes in Paris itself to see the recently restored eighteenth-century maze, with its central summerhouse and bell. Then they drove (a rented Renault 19) to Chartres to have a look at the pavement maze in the great cathedral. "This floor design," Larry said to his son, more loudly and teacherly than he intended, "happens to be the oldest surviving medieval Christian labyrinth in the world."

"You're supposed to look at the windows too," Beth said. She was an uneasy stepmother, and never knew quite what tone to take.

This gift to his son, this sight, this slice of holy silence, struck Larry as a rare privilege. How often are we able to give openly the treasure of surprise? But Ryan was busy staring at a couple kissing behind a statue of Saint Joseph. "Tonsil hockey," he murmured to himself, or perhaps to his father and his father's wife, who were standing a few feet away.

"This particular maze is from the thirteenth century," Larry continued. It seemed important to make the boy understand the unicursal marvel he was looking at, that this wasn't just a piece of hopscotch on the floor, though, in fact – and he couldn't resist explaining further – the game of hopscotch is based on cathedral architecture. "That's back in the twelve hundreds."

"The *trèizieme siècle*," said Ryan, as nonchalantly

as though he were blowing out a balloon of bubble gum.

Larry's ex-wife had insisted on registering Ryan in the French immersion stream of his school, right from the age of six. Now, at thirteen, he was startlingly fluent, able to interpret for his father and stepmother, inquiring about the price of postcards, making table reservations in hotels, and even, in one case, talking a policeman out of a parking violation in Aix-en-Provence, where they'd gone to see the magnificent three-hundred-year-old Chateauneuf le Rouge maze. Beth has a formal understanding of French grammar, and Larry remembered a few phrases from high school, but neither of them could comprehend the language as it was spoken on the street, much less spout it back in the slangy, unselfconscious manner that Ryan assumed.

At Chateau de Villandry (something of a disappointment), at Madame Arthaud's maze in Rennes, at Chateau de Balleuil where a modern maze was planted as recently as 1989, at La Commanderie de Neuilly *en* Oise (circular, hornbeam hedges) – at each of these historic stops or the maze trail, thirteen-year-old Ryan took the lead, asking directions, translating pamphlets, and, if there was a guide, doing a shrugging, half-embarrassed precis of the official spiel.

Always before, the vacations he'd spent with Larry and Beth had been awkward. Visiting the Oak Park house during spring vacation or at Christmas, he tended to fall silent – or sullen, according to Beth – unable, it seemed, to relate to either of them in a natural, spontaneous way; but now, here in this strange country, he quickly made himself part of a three-way ongoing irony, the twist being that two helpless adults were being led by a cunning young kid across the bewildering hexagon of France.

Beth relaxed for the first time with the boy. They even exchanged jokes.

"So what do you call a man who loves another man?" Ryan demanded.

"Duh, I dunno," Beth gave him back.

"A Christian."

Was this funny? Beth looked uncertain, but then laughed uproariously. "Who told you that?"

"Pierre."

"Who's Pierre?"

"My mom's boyfriend."

"I thought it was David," Larry said carefully.

Ryan looked confused. "That was way back. Pierre's her boss. More of a boss than a boyfriend."

"But he tells good jokes?" Larry persisted. He knew better than to pursue this. Careful.

"Yeah."

"Know any more?"

"*Oui mon père, mais en fançais.*"

Mon père; the words struck Larry in the heart. The lighter-than-air mateyness, the straight-in-the-eye punch. This was more than he deserved, much more. With a stab of love he watched his son watching him — a grown man who stumbled, fell into error, got lost, made a fool of himself, but was willing, at least, to be rescued. Something good was bound to come of this.

* * *

Beth loved Madrid. Its sunshine and bright disorder and, especially, the dozen or more Annunciations she found at the Prado. Fra Angelico's was dazzling, so simple, curved and direct, so suffused with tender piety that Beth stood helpless for a moment before it, swept with doubt about the validity of her enterprise, and its mocking thrust. The El Greco was a whirling triumph, with Mary eccentrically posed on the left instead of the right as though the artist had cocked his brush at the world and said: dare me. (Beth scribbled all these thoughts rapidly into her spiral notebook.) The fifteenth-century Mateu was just plain weird and almost as enchanting in its way as the Sopetran. The Picardo, early fifteenth century, was a gem, possessing not just a single book for the Holy Virgin to read, but a whole bookcase. ("As if they had bookcases in Nazareth," Beth murmured.) Dieric Bouts, the Dutch painter, depicted Mary overcome with humility, her eyes closed in the best saintly manner. In the Moraley, sixteenth century, Mary was pretending not to hear the angel, who had a ribbon of speech emanating from his right hand, destined straight for her ear.

But Beth's favorite was the fourteenth-century Robert Campin painting in which Gabriel is standing outside Mary's chamber preparing to enter. Mary, for once, is really reading, her not-yet-holy eyes fixed to the page, absorbed, composed, happy, with not the faintest idea of what is about to burst in on her.

In Barcelona Larry and Beth spend a whole morning wandering through the Laberint d'Horta where they are the only tourists. The old gardens are romantic, even sentimental. There is even a corny, fake facsimile of a farmworker's shelter, and near it, a false cemetery. "All the furniture of the romantic imagination," Beth commented approvingly. "Poverty and death made pretty and cute."

The labyrinth itself was closed. A short, stout man, whom Larry and Beth took to be the head gardener, hurried toward them in his crisp, slightly mismatched green pants and shirt, and gestured with chopping hands toward the workers inside the maze, busy with their shears and clippers.

Larry made a motion of supplication, bowing slightly, the palms of his hands brought humbly together, and the gardener smiled abruptly in response, shrugged, and waved them through the cypress archway. He held up the fingers of his two hands. "I think he means ten minutes," Beth warned.

The deep green cypress walls rose all around them to a height of two meters plus, and led with relative ease toward the goal, which was a circle surrounded by eight leafy arches, and at the center Eros himself, gleaming whitely in the mottled Spanish sunlight, about to release an arrow of love.

"I'm glad you persevered," Beth said afterwards. "I'm glad you did that thing with your hands. I've never seen you do that before."

They would travel in the following weeks to the mirror maze in Lucerne. The richly enigmatic Scandinavian mazes lay ahead of them; Finland alone had over a hundred stone-lined labyrinths. In the spring of the following year, they would find themselves in Japan's teasing, contemporary wooden mazes, and then on to Australia. So many wonders to see, and so much of it destined to blur and soften in Larry's memory.

But he would remember, always, walking through Barcelona's Laberint d'Horta, where he and Beth had been given gracious permission to enter, how still the morning had been, how the good, clean, single-minded offering of cypress perfume rose to meet them, low musical was the splashing fountain and the sound of manual clippers all around them and the brooms of the workers resettling the gravel paths, and how Beth had reached out and stroked with her hand the smooth marble skin of Eros, turning toward him then with a look of perfect wonder in her eye.

CHAPTER TWELVE

Larry's Threads
1993-4

Innocence is a slippery substance. It seems you can't possess it and at the same time *know* you possess it. Yet Larry Weller feels himself to be an innocent man, and one who has little aptitude for irony. Which is why, he suspects, people trust him, hire him, pay him, and remember him with words of thanks and with mild greetings carried back and forth by distant friends or former clients. If his life were a stage, its wings would be airy, capacious, and open to the light. His crosshatched look of bewilderment is half his charm – he knows this, but persuades himself, and others, that he doesn't. The worse that can be said of him is that at age forty-four both his marriages have failed. Is this, then, a man incapable of holding a woman's love?

The series of events that led to the end of his second marriage began on the March morning ('93) when Larry's wife, Beth, received a phone call from the University of Sussex in England, inviting her to apply as head of their Women's Studies department. Larry remembers that she laughed out loud at the thought. Impossible, that hoot of hers said. She and Larry owned a house in the Chicago suburb of Oak Park, a house with seven spacious rooms and a garden that, with its newly planted shrubs and ornamental fruit trees and perennial beds, was on the very cusp of becoming "established." Larry had his office just around the corner on Lake Street, ten minutes' walking distance, and Beth, besides teaching part-time at Rosary College, was trying like crazy to get pregnant.

Nevertheless, she packed her bags and crossed the Atlantic to see what was being offered.

"It's a terrific place," she said, phoning in the middle of the night and waking Larry from a sound sleep. (She's never been good at working out international time differences.)

"The salary's not bad. God, it's amazing, in fact. And the benefits! I wouldn't be expected to do any teaching at all, unless I specifically wanted to, which I'm mulling over. Secretarial staff of three. Three! And five teaching staff plus four cross-appointments. They think my religious studies area will bring a needed balance to the department. Everyone here's read my book, the whole committee, I mean, and they ask *intelligent* questions. I'd forgotten there were articulate beings in this world. The housing market here is steep as hell, but – well, what do you think, Larry?"

"It's the middle of the night here. Can I call you back tomorrow?"

"Tomorrow I'll be in London. They want me to talk with the former head, she's retired, a real sweetheart, living in Hampstead, writing a book about women mill workers at the turn of the century and the deprivations they suffered under –"

"Call me Sunday then." He knew how hysterically fluent she was about to become. An image of her hot brown eyes radioed straight through to his optic nerve.

"I love you."

"I love you too, but –"

"But what?"

"But let's not rush into anything, Beth."

By Sunday she had accepted the job. ("This kind of thing doesn't come along all that often.")

They would commute. Lots of couples did these days, Larry knew that perfectly well, though he'd never heard of a cross-Atlantic marriage and had his doubts. They could try it for one year and then put everything on the table for discussion. If Larry timed his UK visits with Beth's fertile periods they'd be winners all around. They'd have cash in the bank, a bun in the oven, and a glittering set of opportunities before them. For example, they could spend seven months in England and five in the States; they could work it out.

October. Larry packed a week's clothes in a carry-on bag. His duds. His threads. (It was his boyhood friend Bill Herschel who used to say threads, a term he must have lifted from old motorcycle movies or maybe a Harold Robbins paperback – and after all these years Larry never folds a shirt or a pair of pants without Bill coming to mind, and the larky, back-street, cool-talk word: threads.)

"Business or pleasure?" the immigration officer asked at Heathrow. "Stud duties," Larry thought of saying, but instead murmured, "Pleasure." Pleasure after two celibate months, pleasure after knocking around his and Beth's half-furnished house – those long cloud-streaked evenings – and eating pick-up meals at the Calypso Cafe on Marion Street. Pleasure.

He was shocked when he saw the place Beth had rented. He'd expected it to be small, since they had agreed to economize. But this was spartan. A third-floor flat with no elevator. A cupboard for a kitchen. The only bedroom was tiny, white, and windowless, and contained a narrow white bed. A nun's bed. "There's the fold-out couch in the living room," Beth offered, apologetic, flustered.

She had acquired a wardrobe of nun's clothes too. A severe black suit. A smart black wool dress. A rippling black silk tunic-kind-of-thing that she wore over black tights. A long-sleeved white Viyella nightgown. Her new threads.

"I hope you brought a suit," she said to him. "The vice-chancellor and his wife are having us to dinner, they're dying to meet you."

"No," he said, "I didn't."

"Oh, Lord, then we'll have to go and buy you one."

They settled quickly on a solid dark-grey double-breasted suit, laughably expensive. The woolen material was heavy and the weave exceptionally tight. The jacket, and the trousers too, fit more closely to his body than he was accustomed to, so that when he moved he felt the nagging tug of restraint. He was obliged to go back twice to the shop to have the necessary adjustments made, and these were done by a fox-terrier of a boy/man who sighed through his nose when taking Larry's measurements. Larry looked in the mirror and thought: a burial suit. Grave clothes.

"Smashing," said Beth. "And you'll get all kinds of wear out of it."

In fact, he never wore it again. He carried it back to America on a hanger, sheathed in black plastic with the shameful words Gentlemen's Own Choice displayed diagonally across both sides.

November. One week after winning the State of Illinois Award for Creative Excellence, and for all practical purposes clinching the Midwest Pride-in-Accomplishment Medal, Larry Weller packed his threads once again – his stone-washed jeans, perfect for a man feeling stone-washed and stone weary – and climbed aboard a 727 for Boston, where he was to meet with the mayor of that city to discuss a million-dollar landscape project which would never come into being.

Beth, when he phoned to tell her, was understanding. Maybe it was just as well, in fact. A blessing in disguise. She's been invited to join a group of pilgrims who were walking from Guildford to Norwich to visit the famous Julian shrine.

"Who's he?" Larry asked.

"It's a she, and she's a sort of saint, only not a canonized saint. Fourteenth century, I told you about her before."

"There's always December. You are still planning to come home for Christmas?"

"You sound testy, Larry, or else this is a bad connection."

"I'm not testy. I'm lonely."

"It won't be long till December. We can copulate daily for a whole month. Nightly too. Egg and sperm in joyful, continuous union."

He resented the cajoling tone in her voice. He resented her need to ripen her soul on a pilgrimage. "Right," he said.

"But you are managing. I mean, you're feeding yourself sensibly. You're looking after your laundry and so on."

And so on and so on.

His first wife, Dorrie, had done all the laundry. They never discussed this arrangement; she just did it.

Those were simpler times, the late seventies. People fell more easily and with less rancor into traditional roles. Dorrie carried his soiled underwear down into the black cobwebby basement of their little Winnipeg house and dumped it in with the whites. (Today he has a wardrobe of black, red, and bright blue underpants, but in those days he would never have imagined anything but white touching his lower body.)

Dorrie slung these same laundered jockey shorts on to the length of clothesline Larry had strung between the water pipes – no need for clothes-pegs, gravity did the trick – and there they dried stiffly in the heat from the furnace. She collected them quickly after a day or two, plucking them down from the line and tossing them into the plastic laundry basket she held under one

266

arm. With a kind of wonder he watched her do this: it was like harvesting, so speedy and essential. Later she sorted the underwear on their tufted bedspread, her own pile of nylon briefs and bras, and his jockeys, smoothing them quickly with the flat of her hand, and folding them into neat thirds. He found this act of hers almost unbearably intimate, despite the fact that her movements were swift, economical, unhesitating, and devoid of emotion.

He'd brought these garments unthinking to his marriage, and it was she, Dorrie Shaw Weller, a policeman's daughter, who looked after them, who washed, folded, and put them away in the darkness of a dresser drawer. Marriage was full of mysteries, and this was one of them.

The first Christmas after they were married, Dorrie splurged and bought him an expensive Italian shirt at a designer warehouse in the North End of Winnipeg. It was blue. Indigo, Dorrie corrected him. The shirt was unlike any he'd ever worn, looser in its cut, the sleeves, the yoke, the collarless neck – all these announced a kind of theatricality that embarrassed him. Where would he wear such a shirt? And would he spend the rest of his life tripping over new forms of self-consciousness?

He pushed the shirt to the back of the closet and hoped everyone would forget about it.

"Je-suss!" his sister, Midge, said the first time she saw him sporting it – at a family dinner, Thankgiving – "What an absolute beaut of a shirt."

And more and more he did wear it, each time protected by a kind of previous inoculation against shock. "Wonderful material," his mother said. "I'll bet it irons like a dream."

"Looks like you went and forgot to take off your pajamas," his father said.

"Where'd you get this?" said Beth some years later. "This is – my God, this is beautiful."

Beth doesn't wash and iron the blue shirt, as Dorrie had once done. She sends it out to be professionally done; "This is the kind of shirt that has to be looked after," she says, meaning Larry is incapable of doing so himself and so is she, but she does, on the other hand, appreciate quality. She runs her hands along the seams, fingers the stitched flap that conceals the buttons. His special shirt, his non-Larry shirt.

Both my wives have touched this shirt, Larry thinks.

The thought is covert and suffused with sly humor, as though the man he is has never quite disconnected from the boy he was.

At enormous expense Larry and Beth spent a week in Paris. It was February. The room at the Hotel Auber was small, and not really all that warm. When they weren't walking along the Seine, when they weren't visiting the Corot exhibition, when they weren't exhausted from shopping at the conveniently located Bon Marché – where Beth talked Larry into buying a pair of silk pajamas – when they weren't doing any of these things, they lay on the large, flat bed with their clothes off and laboriously attempted the act of procreation. The track of syllables between them grew shorter and more brutal, as though they'd decided with their simple grunts and cries to consecrate all their energies to this purposeful act. Beth was cold and tense with anxiety, her big-clock ticking behind her shut eyes. Larry's eyes, on the other hand, were wide open. "Is this a good idea?" he asked the coved ceiling, the bedside lamp, the bottle of mineral water on the dresser, the imperfectly captured voices of people rising from the street below, shopping, strolling. "Is this what we really should be doing? "

"I think that was it!" Beth said every time. Or, "I really felt that little ping of connection. That spermy arrow arriving right on target."

The silk pajamas from the Bon Marché were colored a deep maroon and made him feel like someone in a porno film. "Manufactured in Bangkok" the label said. The material rippled coolly against his chest, though he seldom wore the bottoms.

The chambermaid folded these pajamas beautifully each day and put them under his pillow, nesting them there like a secret she and Larry held in common. He found himself tossing them more and more carelessly on to the floor in the morning, and imagining this unseen woman bending to pick them up, then stroking the material smooth, then the perfect arranging of sleeves and buttoned front.

Was there something perverse about the pleasure he took in this act of imagination? He knew the answer. (These wayward chips of himself are hard to look at, so mainly he doesn't.)

He slept badly in Paris, and blamed, first, jet lag, then the slipperiness of the new pajama tops or elsc a species of suspended regret, so partial, veiled, and colorless he was unable to fix his eye on its center. He switched on the light one night, four a.m., motorbikes squealing in the distance – shouldn't that be church bells? – and stared at Beth, sleep-drugged by his side. What to do? He fumbled in the drawer of the night table for the Gideon Bible, thinking he might try a page or two to see if its tight dull print would lull him to sleep.

But there wasn't any Bible. All he found was a slim, stapled pamphlet which, on examination, turned out to be the telephone book for the town (village? municipality?) of Hancock Mills, New York. He leafed through its twenty or thirty pages. A single phone number was circled: Jas Wolford, 27 Cuttler Ridge Rd, 377 8999.

The area code listed at the front of the book was 518. The world around Larry shrank, or rather zoomed, to the smallness of 518, a mythical forested kingdom in the eastern United States, and then contracted even further: to Jas Wolford, whoever he or she (Jasmine?) might be. Someone sitting by a telephone, that much was certain, someone like himself, waiting and wondering. And hoping any minute to be called.

He was going screwy, consoling himself like this with the fixtures of gloom, begging for it. It was time to go home.

Larry's mother bought his jockey shorts when he was a boy, half a dozen pairs each year on her annual shopping trip to Fargo, North Dakota. Fruit of the Loom, that majestic trademark, so full of poetry and promise, but no different really than any other underwear.

She bought all his clothes, in fact – bargain hunting in Eaton's basement or else the Bay, his school pants, his shirts and sweaters. These clothes were never quite right. Once when he was about twelve she bought him a red-and-black checked wool shirt that gave him "the scratchies," and which she then laboriously lined with rayon taffeta. Humiliating. His high-school cords were a putrid shade of brown. His jeans were too wide in the seat and too bright a blue, not one of the approved makes, not even close. He hated these clothes, but loved his tireless mother, and wouldn't have dreamt of showing his disappointment. Chiefly, he didn't want her to know that he cared about such things. It was her belief that men shouldn't pay attention to the clothes they wore. Men were above such concerns. They lived outside the secret knowledge of women, of weave and wear, of color, quality and laundry instructions and the small intuitive grasp on buttonhole excellence or failure.

She did not understand shoes. Or socks. Or the fine points of collars and the way a pair of trousers should fall.

When Larry was nineteen, though, she talked him into buying a Harris tweed jacket for his graduation. Her face was a mask of twinkly approval. She liked the weight of the English cloth and the fact that it wouldn't show the dirt.

He loved that jacket. He wore it for years, living inside its rough, safe embrace, and finding himself for the first time in his life able to walk around the world and knowing he looked like a normal person. The right set of threads at the right time. They saved him.

* * *

271

For his 1978 marriage to Dorrie he wore that comic costume of young romance, a navy-blue suit. The lapels were hilarious, the pants were flared, the material was shiny. His necktie sat on his chest, wide and red, but blessedly unpatterned. In the photo taken in a corridor just outside the marriage court he is smiling dazedly and appears to have no idea of how badly dressed he is. (Dorrie wears an off-white wool suit with pink roses snugged at her wrist, and you can tell she knows she looks good.)

For his wedding to Beth – in the ballroom of the Oak Park Arms, 1986 – he wore a tux. He actually bought, rather than rented, this get-up. (A clever salesman at Fields pointed out to him that owning your own tux costs exactly the same as six rental occasions, and this turned out to be good advice.) There are so many pieces to put on, the trousers, suspenders, cummerbund, shirt and studs, the devilish tie, the princely satin-edged jacket – and to his astonishment he has mastered each of these curious inventions. He whistles to himself as he dresses for a formal evening, as though assuring the striped wallpaper and full-length mirror that he is an ordinary man after all, and one who isn't the least intimidated by important threads.

Like everyone else, Larry's heard about men who like to dress in women's clothes. Transvestites. He wonders what it would be like to do this kind of thing, especially how the smooth press of fine-mesh nylon would feel running up against his calves and thighs.

Years ago, when his father was in the final stages of

cancer, Larry came upon him at the hospital wearing a woman's shiny pink quilted robe. "It's your mother's," his father had grunted apologetically. "She thought it'd be warmer for me." Larry remembers feeling a flare of anger toward his mother. He had wanted to run to the nearest mall and buy his father a man's robe, something in a dark, quiet color and simple design, neatly belted and invisible. "Why waste money?" his father said. "I'm not going to be around much longer. I'm used to this anyway, the funny-bunny looks I get."

Now it was April, 1994, a cold rainy night, and Beth had recently returned to England after spending a sexually strenuous Easter week in Oak Park. Larry stood naked in his and Beth's large square bedroom with its air of stale eroticism. It was late, and he was about to go to bed when his eye caught the hem of one of Beth's flowing nightgowns hanging in the closet, pale icy blue with a sprawl of white flowers, a scoop neck and short sleeves. He slipped it over his head and regarded himself in the mirror.

His mouth twitched. He allowed himself a lewd wink before taking it off again. What precisely had he felt with the silky fabric swishing around his knees? Nothing much. Shame perhaps. A kind of satisfaction too.

It was a record, the rainiest spring Chicago had ever had. Larry and his old friend and mentor Eric Eisner were sloshing along side by side down Woodlawn Avenue on a mid-May morning, having just come from a meeting with a wealthy philanthropist who had awarded them a joint commission for the restoration of the old garden surrounding the Humanities Institute.

Chicago streets feel sorry for themselves in the rain. They cry sooty tears, they squeak and cringe. Dr. Eisner, who was in his seventies, carried the same umbrella Larry Weller carried, the large, black ubiquitous umbrella of the male species. Their raincoats, too, were identical. Larry was somewhat startled to see this, the same threads worn by a man in his forties and one in his seventies. Beige, of course. Tabs at the shoulders. Concealed buttons. That little curved what-do-you-call-it rain reinforcement over the back shoulders.

Underneath the two coats a few inches of dark trouser leg showed, four of them to be precise. The same black socks and polished shoes slapped down on the rainy pavement, left, right, left, right. This was frightening, a grotesque doubling of images, and he felt himself suddenly drained of blood, a tattered, thready garment of a man, snagged in a beveled mirror.

Quickly he breathed in a gulp of comforting air. In one week's time he would be in England, where, according to Beth, the sun had been shining day after day, a miracle of an English spring, a record for this century. The British breezes were soft and mild, and she'd bought herself a new flowered "frock." "It'll do as a maternity dress, too," she'd said. "In case we get lucky next time."

He owns only four pairs of shoes, and he loves these shoes. (Other men have a closetful of shoes, ten or twelve pairs, but Larry draws the line at four.)

His evening shoes, shining slippers, don't really count. They're glossy black, they're frivolous in a Fred Astaire way, they'll never wear out, but they continue to wrap around his feet when he needs them, to carry him lightly into evenings that sit starred on the calendar but which fade quickly in the memory.

The black Oxfords. These are the shoes he was wearing when he looked down and realized Eric Eisner, a man thirty years his senior, was wearing the same: the same cut and make and invisible soles, the same laces neatly looped into bows. If you were allowed only one pair of shoes, you'd probably choose these – they're generic, they're *shoe* shoes, they announce the presence of a man coming forth in all his adult sobriety and good sense and prudence and leather-enriched masculinity.

His tasseled loafers. He calls them his weekend shoes because he's embarrassed to mention, or even think, the name of the Italian manufacturer. He's worn these soft loafers for years on lazy Chicago Saturdays – they match perfectly the red-copper mood of weekend mornings. They're made of brown calfskin, rich as mahogany, more expensive by three hundred percent than any of the other shoes in his wardrobe. The designer's name is etched discreetly on the uppers, but Larry cares nothing about this, he really doesn't. (A former prime minister of Canada owned dozens of pairs of these beauties, before public disclosure and a rapid sinking into shame.) In September Larry wore his tasseled loafers to England. (They make ideal flight wear, since the expensive leather has a yielding forgiveness.) He was wearing these very shoes – in a restaurant in Southampton, Italian food, crowded with good smells and noisy conversation – when his wife, Beth, looking nervously alive and beautiful, leaned across her plate of grilled polenta and Dover sole and announced that she didn't want to be married anymore. It wasn't a question of another man. There was no one else in the picture. It was where she was at this time in her life. The dream of mothering a child was gone. The thought of their life together was gone. Oak Park, Illinois, was a dot on another planet with a different set of gravitational rules, and these she no longer comprehended. The loss of sex would be a sorrow to her – he, Larry, had always been the most tender of lovers, really, she meant it – but renunciation has its own excitement, even an erotic excitement, a kind of fascinated suffering, not that she expected him to understand any of that. She hardly understood it herself. But he mustn't worry, she was happy, yes happy. He might find it foolish, her little white room, that narrow bed of hers, but she'd made her choice.

His running shoes, Nikes, are ten years old.

It was funny how everyone in the second half of the twentieth century suddenly started buying these large, lumpy, sculptured, multicolored shoes. It was as though people discovered overnight that their footwear didn't have to be black or brown, and didn't need to conform to what was streamlined and quietly tasteful. The traditional shoe was challenged, and it collapsed at the first skirmish. Shoes could trumpet their engineered presence, their tread, their aggressive padding; they could make all manner of wild claims, converting whole populations to athletic splendor and prodigious fitness. Larry's running shoes are red and white, with little yellow insignias located near the toes. Each of the heels has a transparent built-in bubble for additional comfort and buoyancy when running on hard pavement.

For Larry Weller the threadiest part of his life is his hair.

There are men (not Larry) with receding hair who, in defence, grow an informal rat-tail or plume at the back and seem dumbly oblivious to how weedy and wasted this makes them look. Hey, but it's real hair, they seem to be saying, I can still get hair to grow out of this skull of mine, even if it's only this wisp, this gesture at having hair.

Other men, Eric Eisner for instance, clamp a wig on their bald pate, and there it sits, stiffened and thick in the shape of an artichoke. These men can't see how funny they look, especially from behind, and so they persist in believing they look just fine.

Larry, whose forty-fourth birthday is coming up, pretends indifference when it comes to his hair, but there isn't a moment when he isn't at some level conscious of his various sproutings, his long, sparse leg hairs, the wavier, thicker hair on his chest, his pubic extravagance for which he is endlessly grateful, his underarm thickets, the dark whorls at his wrist nudging his shirt cuff, the light, modest sprinkling on the tops of his hands, the coarse bristle across his face, and, most important of all, his head threads, which are thinning evenly, neatly, all over.

He thinks of himself as a lucky man in the hair department. He's had his good hair innings, and that hairy part of himself has given him a richness of enjoyment that he would be reluctant to admit. His wife, Beth, from whom he is separated, would no doubt be ready to offer a range of theories, psychological and mythical, about male hair and its importance to a man's self-image, but Larry isn't interested in any of these theories, not these days.

His body hair came early, age thirteen, fourteen. It grew in quickly, secretly, a solace, covering the approved areas and convincing him that he had resources he would one day be able to call upon.

From 1970 to 1978, like every other North American male, he had a heedful of shoulder-length hair. He kept it clean with daily shampoos – daily shampooing was an invention of the seventies, or perhaps the late sixties, and no one, it seems, died of it. His folks hated his long hair, though. His father, especially, grumped about hair in the bathroom drains and how he couldn't tell if his son was a boy or a girl from behind. Larry wondered himself about the pleasure he felt when turning his head quickly and feeling that silken ride of hair kissing his face.

After the break-up with his first wife he grew a beard. It started with a lazy feeling of sadness – too sad to move around much or talk, too sad to shave. His friends, hesitant about offering sympathy or advice, were given the opportunity, instead, to comment on Larry's beard, how well it was coming along, how there were glints of surprising red amongst the brown, how some men could wear a beard and others couldn't. "Jesus Christ himself," his father commented. Finally, the hay-fever season did Larry in; ragweed pollen moved into his beard and drove him crazy at night. He rose one September morning at five o'clock and shaved himself clean. "Hello there," he said to the young chin in the mirror, and made a face.

These last few weeks, late summer, he's been growing a moustache. It's only an experiment, to see if he can do it, to see what shape it's going to take. It's also a present he's given himself. No money invested. Just these self-produced hairs popping out of their hidden hair pockets and making themselves known.

His dressed self. The sum of a thousand misunderstandings.

Beth, Beth, you should see me now.

His hand at first traveled frequently to his upper lip, finding reassurance in the roughness he found. His moods were diagonal and time-warped. He felt as self-conscious as a boy, but surprisingly no one commented on the pathetic early days of the moustache, the peculiar discolored scruff between nose and mouth that looked, oddly, like an undressed wound. Perhaps hair is no longer a topic of social interest, perhaps it no longer signifies. People do what they want with their hair these days. Anything goes; that booming cliché. – The fact is, nothing quite goes.

As the bristles of his moustache grow out they soften into little paintbrushes. He trims it (them?) once a week now, with a kind of love, like pruning shrubbery, like facial sculpture. He's not sure, though, if he likes what he sees. His mouth has been transformed into a smirk, and now that his house is on the market he wonders if the moustache makes him look shifty and unreliable as a vendor. Would you buy a used house from a man with a . . . ?

But under the moustache is the old Larry and also Larry's sense of touring in his own life adventure: The Larry Weller Story. No one else knows it, but he does, and that's what matters. And beneath his clothes is Larry's old body, the body he was born with, the value-added body that's housed him for forty-four years, his thickening walls of flesh, his thumping conduits of blood and electricity. He's keeping it cool and secret for now. (*Oh, Beth, my dear one.*) He's keeping himself alive in there, his skin, his skull, his dressed-up face with precisely woven shadows – doing what everyone tells him to do, which is to take care of himself, endlessly pardoning himself as he stands there at the edge of his consciousness, letting himself off with echoes and explanations – *we had some good years together, not everyone can say that* – and hanging on to the threaded filaments he's collected along the way, which will either bury him alive or give him a chance to catch his breath.

CHAPTER THIRTEEN

Men Called Larry
1995

Larry could be someone else, but he's not. He's Larry Weller, an ordinary man who's been touched by ordinary good and bad luck.

Laurence John Weller, forty-five, is a man who shelters under the kicking cadence of a nickname – which is, not surprisingly, Larry. Except for rare occasions – his christening, his two weddings, his various diplomas and awards for landscape design – he has always been known as Larry, and probably always will be.

The world is divided, he sometimes thinks, between the nicknamed and those who remain tied all their lives to their formal designation, the indissoluble Williams, the Andrews, the serenely intact Marys and Marthas. The bearers of nicknames are asked to walk around in the world with their hands in their pockets;

they invite themselves to be imposed upon – either that, or they reach out and claim special privileges. Larry's Oak Park neighbor Ace Hollyard comes to mind: "Call me Ace, as in ace in the hole." Or Larry's former client, the Irish showbiz czar "Bacon" Malone.

There are names, of course, that refuse to open up to variation. Larry thinks of his friend and mentor Eric Eisner; what can you do with the name Eric? Or Garth. (Garth McCord, the well-known Toronto industrialist and land developer, has recently – just last week in fact – contacted Larry Weller of Chicago with a major landscape proposal, and Larry is thinking seriously of taking it on, even though it means moving to Toronto for the better part of a year.)

Larry's late father had a nickname too: Stu, for Stuart; his elderly mother is Dot (Dorothy), and his only sister, Marjorie, has been called Midge (or sometimes Pigeon or Widge) since the day she was born back in the late forties. That tells you something; a whole family surrendering to the diminutive. It suggests that the Wellers are not quite grown-up folks, but more like a diagram – pop, mum, sis, bro – of what a more robustly named family could be.

Larry grew up in Winnipeg (the 'peg) next door to the Herschel family: Hersh and Gert, and their kids, Bill and Toots. It was as though the Herschels, like the Wellers, failed to earn the full dignity that people named Jonathan or Ann-Marie or Clark or Susanna insist upon. On the other hand, you could argue that the nicknamed population possess greater adaptability, turning toward the world their sunny freckledness and their willingness to "go along."

They're the planet's guys and gals, they're hands-on friendly, they let you know just by the nonchalance of their names that they've already relinquished a little morsel of their DNA, their panic and their pride. They stand there as though they have no secrets. As though they don't know how to grow up and leave their oatmeal behind, that special gift bowl with their name incised on the rim.

Being called Larry means that a part of Larry is always going to be that boy hanging around the house on a summer day, waiting in the stopped August light for something to happen. On a piece of paper, out of boredom, that kid will print his name over and over again, Larry Weller, Larry Weller, until it dissolves into nonsense. A pencil's rough squiggle.

By coincidence, both Larry's ex-wives had nicknames. His second wife's name was Beth, short for Elizabeth; she could just as easily have been a Liz, but then she would have been a different person with a different set of arrangements. His first wife, Dorrie, had been christened Dora by her parents, a name that in Dorrie's opinion reeked of old-maidishness, smelly-footedness, and typing-pool ambitions. As a matter of fact, Dorrie continues to use the name Dorrie, even though she's recently been appointed chief executive officer of SkyBlue Greetings, the Canadian branch of an international card company. She started out selling cars (Manitoba Motors), then moved to sportswear (Nu-Cloz), working her way up to vice-president in charge of sales, and now, since last December, she's into stationery products; she's been moving up the ladder all these years, but dealing,

Larry's observed, with merchandise that is increasingly smaller and lighter and more ephemeral.

Not long ago, Larry happened to catch her on a national TV news show: Ms. Dorrie Shaw-Weller, as she calls herself now, was making a public apology for a tasteless Father's Day card her firm had produced. The offending card was flashed on the screen, a girl's flat cartoonish face and a balloon over her head containing the words: "Thanks, Dad, for not drowning me at birth."

"We do vet our new lines carefully," Dorrie Shaw-Weller said into the microphone. Her voice was head-shakingly sincere. Her grey eyes held a suggestion of personal distress but were clearly prepared to level with the viewers' outrage. "We at SkyBlue Greetings are proud of our reputation for being sensitive to women and to minorities, and we deeply regret that this card somehow slipped through our focus group. We have, of course, already withdrawn it from the retail outlets."

Of course, of course.

Larry had been surprised and even impressed. Had Dorrie prepared this statement herself, then memorized it? Her voice, which might have grown company-cool over the years, was instead packed with warm tones. This was an empathetic person speaking, a person Mr. and Mrs. Consumer out there could trust. He remembered that she'd done a three-week management course in Vancouver a couple of years ago; it's possible she picked up a few public relations pointers.

"Thank you so much, Dorrie Shaw-Weller," the

twinkly-eyed TV host wound up, "for agreeing to come on the show and offer our viewers an explanation."

"Thank *you* for giving me the opportunity," said Dorrie in her persuasive manner. Her hands rose straight up before her, framing a box of crisp air, then falling open slightly as if offering a shrugging embrace, a gesture that said *look, we all make mistakes, so please, please forgive me, all you understanding folks out there.*

A lot of people are named after someone, but not the casually disentitled Larry Weller. His folks just liked the name Larry a lot, that's all, but they had the good sense to realise it would have to come enclosed in the more formal Laurence – this was back in 1950. Larry was the name they dressed him in. It was sweet, perky. "I just thought it sounded like a real boy's name," his mother told him once. "Like Jack. Now that's another name I like. It's, you know, masculine. There's nothing silly about it, but at the same time it isn't one of those stuffed-shirt names."

"Are you sure," his second wife, Beth, asked him, "that you weren't named after St. Laurence?" Beth had written her PhD dissertation on the early female saints of the church, and was able to describe for Larry the brave deeds of St. Laurence and his fiery death, how the prefect of Rome had demanded to see the treasures of the church, and how Laurence, in response, gathered together the poor and infirm who lived on the alms of the faithful. "Here," Laurence announced, gesturing at the tattered crowd, "are the treasures of the church." For his trouble he was roasted over a sort of hibachi; Larry's seen the nineteenth-century woodcut in Beth's *Pictorial Lives of the Saints*. "I'm cooked enough," the irreverent Laurence is believed to have shouted. "You can eat me now."

Much as Larry would like to be associated with this hero of legend, he doubts very much that his parents had the early Laurence in mind. They weren't Catholic, for one thing, and didn't know diddly-squat about saints. No, he was just one more citizen of the Larry nation, those barbecuers, those volunteer firemen, those wearers of muscle shirts. Men called Larry have to be brave, while other men are allowed lapses.

His middle name, John, was also randomly chosen. "I wanted you to have a middle name," said his mother, Dot, who had none and deeply resented the blank in her life, "and John had a nice royal ring to it."

So there he was, Laurence John. Larry. His chance to show the world other sides of himself was curtailed by that fact.

Men, unlike women, live with their family names all their lives. A name settles with all its appropriate weight on their chests, like an X-ray apron, and there it stays. Larry's second wife, an ardent feminist, wouldn't have dreamt of changing her name to Weller, and Dorrie, who assumed it automatically back in 1978, has now reestablished her maiden name, Shaw, bolting it with a hyphen to Weller. This sounded strange to Larry at first, but now he's used to it.

The name Weller itself has two possible origins, as

Larry discovered when he looked it up in a book of Beth's. There are some sources going back to the twelfth century that describe Weller as meaning a "boiler of salt." A later version, and the one that Larry prefers, has Weller as one who dwells by a stream or spring, a sort of professional water overseer.

Like a lot of people, Larry's never really liked his first name much; its Larryness has alway seemed an imprisonment, and a sly wink toward its most conspicuous rhyme: ordinary. His middle name, John, is a blank of a name, occupying space. But the name Weller he's learned to love: one who lives within the sight and sound of running water, a water man, a well man, a custodian of all that is clear, pure, sustaining, and everlastingly present.

There are some men, mostly jocks, who get called by their last name all the time. No one understands how this gets started, calling someone like Bill Jones, say, Jones or Jonesy, and never Bill; it's a little like those houses where people either use the back door all the time or the front door, and no one knows why.

Larry almost never gets called Weller; when it happens, he wants to laugh. The name shatters against his ear into flakes of grammar: well, weller, wellest. Sometimes his sister, Midge, phoning on a Sunday night will address him, tenderly, as Lare-Bear. Bill Herschel used to call him Square-Lare, but that only lasted a short time and now he calls him Lorenzo. Wary Larry, Beth sometimes called him when he was having trouble making decisions. But mostly he's just Larry.

Larry, Larry. It's a word that's grown a skin of pure

transparence. He doesn't see or hear it anymore. It's absurd. As absurd as the pointless flowers and trees, the wave action of the sea, the stones and stars that gape at each other through blind air. Useless, all of it. A disordered abundance.

No one gets named Larry anymore. It's had it as a name. Think of someone called Larry and you automatically conjure up a guy drinking beer in a sixties rec room. He's wearing polyester pants. He's watching the ball game on TV and belching softly. Next he's reaching under his T-shirt and scratching his belly hairs and doesn't care who sees him do it. He knows he's at the end of the Larry line, so what the hell. (It was Beth who provided this profile of a "typical" Larry type. That was years ago, soon after they met. ("I can't believe I'm kissing a man named Larry," he remembers her saying, her voice full of honest wonder and her mouth tight like a fold of paper.)

But there are a lot of leftover Larrys out there. Not as many, maybe, as there are Mikes or Tonys or Als or Gregs, but enough so that no one blinks when you say your name is Larry. No one asks you how you spell it.

There's Larry on the Larry King show, who's sneery but oddly sane, and who sometimes shows surprising restraint. There's Larry Holmes, the boxer. There used to be Larry Olivier, the great actor, but he was really a Laurence at heart; you didn't get to call him Larry unless you were one of his inner circle, which you weren't.

* * *

Larry Weller of Chicago, soon to pull up stakes and relocate in Toronto – he's decided to make it a permanent move – knows only three Larrys, personally that is. Larry Liddle from Windows Incorporated comes out to the Weller house with his crew of men on the first Saturday of each April to take down the storm windows and put up the screens. In the fall he comes again and does the whole thing in reverse. He's a red-faced man with long ropy muscles and a heedful of tight solid-grey curls. Every time Larry hands him a check he stares at it for a minute, then gives a little whistle of appreciation. "Hey, another Larry, what do you know!" He seems to find this coincidence exhilarating, something to celebrate, although Larry Weller knows that by next fall Larry Liddle will have forgotten their shared name and that they will go through the whole ritual of recognition, astonishment, and fellow-feeling once again.

Except that there won't be another fall. He announced this to Larry Liddle last week when he came to take down the storm windows. The house has been sold; he and and his wife are soon to be divorced, and he himself is heading off to Toronto to set up a design office. "That's up there in Canada, isn't it?" said Larry Liddle. "Yes," Larry Weller said, and then added apologetically, "That's where I come from originally." "Well," said Larry Liddle. "Well, well, well." He stared at the check, seemingly stricken at the thought of Larry's departure and at a loss for words. Finally he said, "That's going to make one less Larry around here for company," which was true enough.

Larry K. Wellington is a Chicago architect who's

widely known for the pink office tower that cantilevers like a stack of cupcakes over Wacker Drive and also for a dozen dazzling summer-houses he's designed in the Michigan dunes. People get Larry Weller and Larry Wellington mixed up all the time. There have been a couple of misattributions in journals, and clients sometimes phone the wrong number and need to be redirected. The two Larrys met only once, at a fundraising dinner for the soon-to-be-demolished Wardlaw Gardens off Washington Boulevard. Larry Weller loathed Larry K. Wellington from the moment Larry K. Wellington addressed him through his long narrow nose: "So you're that garden maestro, huh." The silk knot of his tie stood out criminally. Like a small animal. Like a grenade ready to go off. His handshake was overly long, damp, and probing, and there was a wet look to his chin as though he had dribbled his red wine and couldn't be bothered to mop himself up. "So," Larry K. Wellington said with leering familiarity, "it seems the two of us are stuck for life with the same sobriquet. You know what they used to call me in school? Scary Larry. I had this way about me. Even then. The look of success. It made people jealous, see what I mean. They could tell I was going to get ahead and they weren't. What a crappy world. It's all crap in the end."

It seemed impossible to Larry Weller that such a man was allowed to walk freely on the streets of Chicago. And that his name happened to be Larry.

Thank God for Larry Fine, who lives on Kenilworth Avenue across the street from the Weller house. Larry Fine is a psychologist, or a behavioralist as he's quick to tell you, who teaches at the University of Chicago. This Larry has thick, thick wrists covered with mats of hair, but he's a good mile and a half from being a traditional hetero type. He bakes, he wears aprons, he sews his own curtains. Last Christmas he made Larry Weller a shirt out of green linen. He names everything he owns. His kitchen stove is called Eleanor. His car is Jacqueline. His computer is called Gertrude, daughter of a previous Gertrude. Larry Fine is probably a little in love with Larry Weller. They both know this, but it doesn't matter and it doesn't stop them from enjoying a beer together on Larry Weller's screened porch – especially on lonely evenings since Beth's taken off – and talking about sports, sex, theology, AIDS research, the meaning of garden mazes, and the importance of names.

"We'll look back on this century," Larry Fine says, "and we'll see that one of the big social changes in America was the claiming of our own names. We stopped letting other people name us. You can own your name the same way you own your breath. You can shorten it or beef it up and it's still yours. Have you seen those ads for the Lois Club? All the women in Chicago named Lois get together once a month. I don't know if they bawl their eyes out or perform Lois chants, but they're dishing straight into their randomly assigned names. On the other hand, you want to look at the evolving nature of the baptism ceremony. Our rituals tell us everything, and the old patriarchal laying on of hands is out the window, there's no more of this 'I christen thee Elvis Presley' or whatever, and expecting it to last. There's a whole different emphasis now. We get to name ourselves if we want to. There've always been a few oddballs who did it, but they were showbiz types or else people on the run. Now it's as mainstream as the stud in my navel. Did you know that it's out on the west coast, the frontier, where people go to court the most often to change their names? They want to be something else, and they know they've got to get rid of the old moniker for once and for all. For me it's different. At one time, ten years ago maybe, I was ready to be an Abraham or Ezra, something with a little biblical zing, but I made up my mind I'd hang on to the name Larry. I'd force it, by God, to take a new shape. I'd give it some gender stretch, some fiber, a few brain cells even. It's a dopey name, let's face it, but it's ours and we can learn to love it."

"Just sell the furniture," faxed Beth from the University of Sussex, where she's beginning her second year as head of Women's Studies. "Or keep what you want."

And now it's gone, every stick of it, except for his and Beth's queensize sleigh bed which was seized upon by the couple who have bought the house. They loved it; they had to have it; they were willing to pay whatever Larry had paid, and more. Their name is Halfhead, Wilford and Stacey Halfhead, and Larry's been wondering, ever since he signed the documents, what it's like to live with a name like Halfhead. Would you have to pump yourself up with fresh resolve every time you introduced yourself? Every time you made a phone call? "Hello, this is Halfhead calling." Wilford

Halfhead is in computers, as everyone seems to be these days, and she, Stacey, the brave, or else insane, woman who has taken the Halfhead name for her own, weaves blankets. Larry supposes that this bed and all its disintegrating erotic ether will soon be covered over with one of Stacey's cheerful woolen creations.

He couldn't bear to part with the pine refectory table and its ten chairs, and so he had them sent by van to Toronto. He and Beth paid too much for them at a downtown auction – they'd never get the investment back. That's part of it, but not all. Here on this beautiful table he's often spread his working drawings, most recently for the Malone maze in County Mayo; here is where Beth, having run out of desk space, spliced together the revisions on her dissertation. Evenings, the two of them sat across from each other at one end, talking over plates of grilled fish or else pasta, depending on whose night it was to cook. Talking, talking. He'd married a talking woman; and now, in his last week in Oak Park, the last night in fact, he feels the house's deep silence.

The TV has been sold, and the VCR; there seemed little point in lugging out-of-date electrical gear all the way to Canada. Two sofas went quickly through an ad in the *Trib*, one of them recovered only weeks before Beth took the job in England and decided she didn't want to be married anymore, at least not married to Larry Weller. The stone-topped coffee table went to Larry Fine across the street. An antique dealer drove over from La Grange last Saturday – his business card identified him as The Lone Granger – and snapped up two wing chairs and Beth's oak desk and then, at the last minute, decided to buy the rugs as well. Larry's feet echo on the shining floorboards. Without furniture, without the lamplit islands he and Beth brought into existence, there is only rectilinear space and cold air. What he feels on the final night in the Oak Park house is love's booming vacuum. No, it's more like love that's been replaced by a frantic sadness; he has a long drive ahead of him tomorrow, but he knows he won't sleep tonight. How had he recovered from his first marriage? Maybe he hadn't, maybe all this failure was cumulative.

Larry Weller stars in his own life movie, but in no one else's. This is hurtful to admit, but true. His ex-wives are into new stuff and don't really need him, not even his money. His mother's installed in an Anglican care facility in Winnipeg, where she's bathed and diapered by an ever-changing roster of sweet-faced nurses and praised for her wonderful disposition and ardent prayerfulness.

Larry's sixteen-year-old son by his first marriage is up in Winnipeg too. Ryan lives with his mother in the same house he's always lived in, 234 Lipton Street, and goes to MacDonald Secondary, the same high school Larry attended. Unlike Larry, though, who never excelled at sports, Ryan runs the 100 meter event for the school track-and-field team. Last March he qualified for the Manitoba Allstars, and Larry wouldn't be surprised if he harbored Olympic ambitions. Until a year ago Ryan had never possessed a nickname, but now he's become Flyin' Ryan, at least in the local papers – a name so loaded with tribute that it hardly qualifies as a nickname. What a way to imprint yourself on the world. What a way for the world to stamp you for life. Leapin' Larry, that would have been a good way to go through the years, that would have given Larry Weller a head start.

Larry's sister, Midge, lives in Toronto where she runs a costume business, rent or buy. The truth is, he doesn't know his sister all that well these days, but nevertheless Midge is half the reason Larry's decided to relocate in Toronto; he's been alone for months, and he's figured out what he needs in his chilly life, or the slow drizzle his life's become. He needs the warmth of blood connection, something he's never really required before. Maybe this is what happens when you hit the mid-forties mark. He wants someone to keep tabs on him, someone who'll phone him just to shoot the breeze: so how'd you sleep last night? how's that cold of yours?

Not long ago he asked himself what there was to keep him in Chicago now that Beth had pulled out. He could do his maze design work and consulting from any major city in North America. Electronic outreach, instant communication; this was the nineties. He's decided, too, to change the name of his one-man firm. Since 1988, when he first hung out his shingle, he's advertised himself as A/Mazing Space. This name, with its coy slash and double pun, won't do for Toronto, he sees that clearly, and it absolutely won't begin to do for the year 1995. He's dropped the old Laurence J. Weller, too, from his new business cards. Now it's a simple: Larry Weller, Mazemaker. Clean.

Direct. Stripped down. (He's reminded tonight of another April night almost twenty years ago when he stood on a cold street in his shirt-sleeves, inviting the rest of his life to come at him, to take him in its embrace.)

A happy marriage, whether it's long or short, gathers a kind of density around it, the easy verbal slippage of "my wife," "my husband," and the swing-in-the-garden sense of "we always" – fill in the blank – "we always take vitamin C when we're coming down with a cold," "we always stay home Sunday night," "we always cancel the newspaper when we're away for a week." And the collected hours of joined sleep, they add up to certain assurances about love too: that even if you leave love alone it forms a cocoon around you. Which is why in the last year Larry's been unable to adjust to the animal grief of stirring in his sleep and finding himself alone. He wonders if he's acquired that sad body smell of lonely people, old cologne bottles, mothballs, broken shoes.

Tonight he tries to put himself to sleep by thinking of Beth breathing by his side, improvising a crude shelter for his thoughts, but he's incapable of capturing her image. Instead he tunes in to the vagaries of her voice, her scent. None of this works. Every memory flash leads to a supplemental twinge. He is a man going through a bad time, he knows he is, but he avoids looking at that man, the self he frightens away with loud thoughts, grotesque images. His jalopy of a life. His Larry life, which is projected tonight on the ceiling of a stripped-down second-floor bedroom, a square of streetlight shining through an uncurtained window and reminding him of failure's potent fumes. (If you're living a life without sex, you start talking to yourself.)

A kind of sleep comes eventually. Sleep's dark tower, windowed, locked. His dreams boil with green swamp water and sharp words waving their long leaves against his face.

The morning light is explicit and cruel, its first slapping steps on the floor grotesque. There lies his suitcase, open. There is the bed with its bare mattress ticking and rimmed stains, blood, semen, sweat, his and Beth's, but now the bedsprings are preparing for a transfer of power. He himself will be on the road in an hour, Toronto bound. Yes, he will – Larry Weller, a forty-five-year-old white male, an endangered species if not rare, will be on his way to the next thing and the next. He longs for something, but what? (That infant in his highchair, he started all this.)

There's a comic side to human striving, he knows that, and something pathetic about smiling too willingly into the camera and babbling on to yourself about the widening of life's sensuous possibilities, but nevertheless he feels as he backs out of his driveway for the last time, a sudden jolt of brightness, which he supposes is ardor and disinterest stirred by the same stupid spoon. What a gullible dope he is. Larry. Larry Weller.

And then he remembers, as he drives south down Kenilworth Avenue and on to the ramp of the Eisenhower Expressway, an evening last week when he and Larry Fine sat on the screened porch together watching TV. This was the occasion of an international track meet beamed from Munich. One of the American runners was being interviewed. A bull of a man. Immense, muscled, with stunned-looking blue eyes. "I've had this dream since I was six years old," he whimpered into the camera. "I've got this dream of gold for my country. The American dream, it's still alive in the hearts of athletes. But hey, it's not about winning, it's about, uh, doing your best out there and paying your dues, you know, standing up for this country of ours that's the only free country there is, know what I mean? – in the whole world."

"Christ," Larry Fine said, reaching for the off button. "Christ, why are guys such dumb pricks?" Then he said, sadly, "You know something? There's a sense in which, deep down, all the men in the world are named Larry."

CHAPTER FOURTEEN

Larry's Living Tissues
1996

At forty-five years of age Larry Weller has lost a number of his excretory "units," or nephrons – despite the fact that he has never been a heavy drinker. His liver, like most people's livers, has been shrinking since the age of forty.

His ancestors, of course, sleep in his blood and brain, their packets of DNA neatly arranged and pretending not to matter as much as they do. Larry's bone mass, which peaked in his twenties, has also been declining in recent years, or so he suspects. He keeps meaning to get that test he's heard about. As a landscape designer he spends a fair number of hours hunched over a drawing-board, and he's sure this hunching and bunching of his spine, plus the natural tension that accrues, is responsible for the lower-back stiffness he feels in the morning. An occupational hazard, you might say. (He's sometimes suspected that in that space between his skeletal frame and his thin muscles there lurks a kind of private joke.)

The separate bony plates of his head became fused shortly before his first birthday, shutting off any effective access to the primordial hum of the universe, the breath of a larger, more generous life, the smell of possibility – this is a loss, but one that Larry only occasionally senses: in the midst of ardor, in the face of unexpected beauty or mystery, while running his palm across the trimmed top of a green hedge or between the thighs of a woman, that narrow envelope so bravely opening itself to dramatic shifts of scenery.

Two minutes with his electric toothbrush each morning, and he is a better, braver man. He has twenty fillings in his teeth. Also two bridges. No caps so far. A very slight yellowing, especially of the bottom teeth. His lower left gums have receded so that the roots of the teeth are close to being exposed. His dental hygienist, last time he went for a cleaning, gave him a tiny doll size toothbrush with which to poke into the problem area each morning and night. This adds another minute, or at least thirty seconds, to the time he must devote every day to looking after his body. He wonders what Charlotte Angus, who frequently spends the night at his apartment, thinks of this miniature brush hanging there in the bathroom next to his regular toothbrush. Maybe she believes it represents some weird fetish, and for that reason has, so far, withheld comment. He himself sees it as a nod in the direction of his eventual death, one more signpost on the way out.

Larry's testosterone, if he follows the normal pattern for North American males, has probably been in decline since his thirties – this worries him, but it doesn't worry him every minute of every day; he prefers to think his occasional episodes of sexual failure are psychological, and that a total reverse is possible. How many times has he felt the skin of his scrotum tighten? – a million? – and isn't it reasonable that this involuntary mechanism wearies eventually? Since he moved to Toronto a year ago and met Charlotte Angus, he feels he's operating on three out of four cylinders. Charlotte is the same age as he is. It might be different if she were twenty-five. But different in what way? He's not sure.

The thickness, color, and sheen of Larry's hair is at risk. He knows that about fifty percent of men of European descent suffer some balding, which ought to be a comfort but isn't. Charlotte thinks that men are pathetic in their fear of baldness. As long as the emerging skull is clean and not too bony or warped with veins, what does it matter how much hair there is? And what about Yul Brynner?

Like everyone else, Larry's skin started to lose its elasticity during his teens. His life range of expressions can be found on his face, etched there. A small brown spot sits in the middle of his upper left cheek, and another on the side of his neck. Are these caused by exposure to the sun, or could they be liver spots? He remembers hearing his mother talk about liver spots, how they arrived when she was still in her thirties and how she learned to sit with her hands folded like a basket in her lap, palms up, so that these unattractive blotches were hidden. Larry's first wife, Dorrie, had rather rough skin, healthy but at the same time prickly. It could be that this roughness was caused by the extremes of the Manitoba climate rather than genetic factors. Beth, his second wife, had soft Irish-looking skin – her face, her arms, her legs and buttocks – made even softer by the nightly use of oils and creams. Charlotte Angus treats her forty-five-year-old body to a monthly massage at a Queen Street salon, followed by a salt bath and "body polish." Each treatment sets her back seventy-five dollars, but she thinks of it as an investment in her mental health.

Presbyopia is something else Larry Weller suffers from; in plain English this means that his ability to focus on nearby objects has declined, and that he now requires reading glasses. Blues, greens, and violets are often difficult to distinguish. His eyes also adjust more slowly when he comes into a dark room. Last week he returned to his St. Patrick Street apartment after a late-night meeting with the McCord Foundation Board – Garth McCord is a Toronto land developer – and almost stumbled across Charlotte's overnight bag in the bedroom. (He had forgotten to phone her to say he'd be late, and this forgetfulness is, he suspects, the most troubling part of his aging.)

His hearing, as nearly as he can tell, is stable, and he feels fortunate that he was never a heavy metal fan or had to work in a noisy factory like his father and thereby suffer irreparable damage. Would he wear a hearing aid if he had to? Probably not. Well, it would depend on how severe the loss was. He'd have to think about it. His life, he feels, is not so much a story as a sequence of soundings – real soundings, bouncing in his inner ear.

If the medical statistics tell the truth, Larry's brain weighs less than it did when he was thirty. He can no longer balance a number of ideas in his head at the same time, and, in fact, he's refused to take on new clients until the McCord project is completed. This is the largest garden maze he's ever designed, a three-dimensional showpiece, and the mathematics confuse him occasionally in a new and worrying way. What's happening inside his head? What became of the ease with which he could hold on to a visual concept? He likes to think, on the other hand, that he's accumulated some experiential knowledge: wisdom, that is. He's read recently that the human brain weighs almost exactly the same as the human foot, and this thought with its compacted unreason makes him shiver.

His lung cells have stiffened – which is absolutely normal at forty-six – so that his former capacity is now deflated by about twenty percent.

Larry's arteries have also started to stiffen, but only slightly; this is not surprising when you remember that his heart muscle has contracted close to two billion times in his life. He tries not to worry too much about professional problems and he stays away from fatty food. His sister, Midge, and her live-in boyfriend, Ian, have become fanatics about fat and have cut out all butter, margarine, and oil from their diet. Lemon juice diluted with water is what they dribble over their salads these days.

His mother and father both suffered in their time from constipation and piles, but Larry has avoided these maladies. A few tablespoons of All-Bran every morning keep this department of his life workable. Flatulence is another problem altogether. He can't imagine what Charlotte thinks when he rips off. Don't women fart? He doesn't remember either of his wives losing control except perhaps in deep sleep, and then it was only a soft, rather endearing burble. He'd like to ask someone about this, but he can't think who. He's up twice a night, lately, to urinate. (In his thirties, it was once; in his fifties, will it be three times?)

His ratio of muscle tissue to fat has shifted slightly, and he's thinking of getting into some serious weight training. He's heard that the Toronto Athletic Club has a good lunchtime program, but he often attends meetings over the lunch hour or else he and Charlotte grab a sandwich – turkey breast, never cheese – at the addiction center where she works as a counselor. Larry's decided to donate his organs to science after his death, and has declared this intention on his driver's license. He's ashamed that such a small, painless act should make him feel virtuous.

On the whole he's in decent shape. His body is an upright walking labyrinth, and he feels the miracle of it. In his earlobe there are capillaries that connect to his heart. On the surface of his skin live nerves so sensitive that his brain knows the instant a microscopic insect lands on the back of his hand.

There are things he'll never know about human bodies, particularly that side of the world that's tipped away from him and curtained in darkness: menstruation, birth, certain jokes and griefs and hormonal explosions. There are men who stuff their fists up other men's assholes – he'll never know how that works or how it feels.

Temperamentally he seems to have settled for a convivial melancholy, the rather lumpy psychic matter of perplexity; the problem is, he doesn't know how to be the person he's become, but this could change tomorrow. For the moment, there he sits behind his own face. He's dressed, he's on time. What a surprise. What a bad surprise too. The parts of life that used to offer comfort more and more seem an illusion or a deep difficulty. This is what Larry's old friend Eric Eisner calls the paradox of plenitude. It seems that once there's enough money, enough recognition, enough love – not that he loves Charlotte Angus, exactly – then there's nothing to look forward to except the next minute.

Larry got sick. It was summertime. He was sitting in his airconditioned office on St. Clair Avenue, talking to a subcontractor on the telephone. They were dickering back and forth, but in a friendly way, about the cost of globosa seedlings for the McCord project. Larry felt he was entitled to a more substantial discount for so large an order, and he attempted to put this into words. Instead he felt a river of nonsense gush past his lips. It seemed more of a tune than a sentence, more of a joke than a serious counter-proposal. His voice, even to his own ears, held the quacky noise of a cartoon creature; where had *this* come from? "Are you all right, Mr. Weller?" he heard from the other end of the line. He felt a stirring of nausea which was accompanied by fading light. Then he collapsed. A

305

recently hired part-time secretary heard the thud of his body on the carpeted floor and came running.

Three weeks later, a noise like a tractor passed through his brain. (But no, it was only the dinner trays being wheeled down the hospital corridor.) Other images swam into view and then quickly fled. Once, making an enormous effort, he lifted his arm sideways and encountered an object that was both familiar and strange. A rectangle, cardboard, sharp cornered – a Kleenex box, in fact, though he couldn't have named it. He pulled out a tissue, and felt, with a spasm of surprise, its clean rasp against the cardboard slit. He let it drift to the floor, a white floating bird, beautiful, though he viewed it with detached curiosity, knowing what it was and not knowing. Then he pulled out another and then another. The scratching sound of the tissues through the opening told him he was alive, and he felt his wrist fall into a circular rhythm, into a kind of dance. A buzzing sensation of joy accompanied each pull, until finally a hundred tissues, the total contents of the box, lay in a heap by his bed, a drift of soft snow. Voices swam through the air around him – *he's moved, he's waking up* – then throbbed into silence.

These twitches, these nightmares – this is who he is.

He opened his eyes. He was alone in a hospital room, flat on his back, frozen into a primordial stiffness. There was an astringent smell in the air like corn cooking. The rectangle of hard light from the window smacked his eyes, which felt peculiarly dry. He moved experimentally on the sheets, only to find that his arm, his nose, his penis were socketed into plastic piping. Then someone rushed a cold cloth to his face.

Three weeks had passed. He couldn't believe it. Yes, his sister, Midge, said. Twenty-two days. We thought you were done for. My baby brother in a coma. A deep coma.

The decision was made, after Larry's collapse, not to alert his elderly mother in Winnipeg; why worry an old woman who was semi-comatose herself and half the time couldn't remember her son's name? Larry's two ex-wives, of course, were contacted, and Larry's seventeen-year-old son, Ryan, flew to Toronto from the University of Pennsylvania where he was enrolled in the summer track-and-field Champ-Camp. Midge reported to Larry, with dampened eyes, how the boy had sat by his father's bedside for six straight days, talking to him continually, trying to call him back.

It seemed almost indecent to ask, but Larry had to know: what were the exact words that had come out of Ryan's mouth during this period of one-sided intimacy? Words of encouragement? A serenade? Reminiscences? Words of love? A lullaby? "Well, what he did was, every day he read you the newspaper from end to end," Midge told him. "The *Toronto Star*. Everything but the obits. It took him all day to get through it."

Ryan, his son. It was unimaginable, even shocking. Once a mere flake of consciousness, the boy had been recast into this ghostly benevolent presence by his father's bed, stumbling through the editorials, the sports scores, the stock-market report – this was the same blameless little boy Larry had walked out on when he and Dorrie split up back in 1983. And now this kid had actually – no, Larry couldn't bear to think of it. Not for the moment anyway, not in his present state of weakness. (Several times a day he finds himself inexplicably close to tears.)

What is a coma exactly? Sick unto death, according to Midge, though the patient sometimes survives. A state of profound unconsciousness caused by – but at first no one knew the cause. Encephalitis was suspected and later confirmed. Probably carried by a mosquito. That weekend he'd spent fishing with Ian Stoker at Rice Lake. There would have to be tests. Brain damage, yes or no? The situation was unclear. More tests.

The two ex-wives had *not* rushed to his bedside. Beth, of course, was in England, but he would have thought Dorrie might have made the trip from Winnipeg, especially since the two of them have been on amicable terms in recent years. There were, however, wifely cards, wifely flowers, faxes and notes. The dozen roses that Beth sent through Interflora had bloomed and died before Larry got around to waking up. Dorrie's more practical potted mums were doing well, sitting on the TV that Midge had rented after the great day of awakening, July 20th, 1996.

The great day of awakening – that's how Larry thinks of it. No one can explain why or how, but a switch had flipped in his numbed brain: time to wake up, buddy. For the first few days he suffered from headaches and confusion, those tractors again, patrolling the corridor and sliding up the snake of his central nervous system, giving off little yaps and cabooms. His body felt inexpressibly exhausted after his long sleep, his joints sore as an old man's. "Can't you remember anything?" visitors asked. Their faces made it clear that they found Larry's fall into the void incomprehensible. He had journeyed to "the other side." There must have been something he brought back. Dreams? Lighted tunnels? Booming voices? Some memory surely slept there, like a white dwarf in his brain.

No, there was nothing. And this confirmed what Larry had always believed, that there were no final instructions attached to death, not even to this near-death.

"Charlotte sat up with you almost every night," Midge told him. "She slept in that chair, or at least she tried to sleep. She didn't want you to be alone when you woke up."

"But I was alone," Larry said. He wondered if he sounded petulant.

"She's a remarkable woman."

"Yes."

"A ve-ry loving woman." Midge's tone was affectionate, yet flinty. Two years older then Larry, she was having one of her big-sister days.

"I know, I know."

"Just reminding you."

He was alive. And it began to look as though he was not going to suffer permanent damage. How to clothe his naked relief? The sudden fissure in his life had closed over, joined smoothly by the bright daily thread of renewed consciousness. His appetite picked up. The trays of mashed potatoes and slabs of onion-flavoured beef seduced him back to life. Appetite, fullness. His ongoing Larry self. Yes, said the particle accelerator chamber of his brain: feed me. The newspapers, so immense and pungent, were overflowing with thrilling surprises, and the best of these surprises was that the world was continuing in its usual plugging-along pace. Yeltsin persevered with his impersonations, the killing in Ireland started up again, the miniature theater of Bill and Hillary opened for another muddied round, and Bob Dole grumped from the TV screen and showed his sorrowing, baffled face to the nation. All this felt freshly miraculous to Larry, and everyone, including the neurologist, told him how lucky he was, how fortunate that prompt medical assistance had been available, how unstinting the efforts of the coma team had been, and how the wonders of anti-inflammatory drugs and steroids had preserved his living tissues.

He was grateful, he really was. But something tugged at him in those quiet minutes just before or following visiting hours, some filament of desire. He knew what it was and he resisted it. He yearned to go back to the silent, unreachable place he couldn't remember, to cradle his consciousness in a nest of softness. Safety, sleep, insensibility. He wanted to embed himself in that channeled obscurity, which he dully recognized as his true home. Darkness. No, not darkness. More like the color of rainy daylight. A maze without an exit.

No, he will not be torn loose from his life this easily.

It was the Olympic Games, finally, beamed from Atlanta, Georgia, that saved him. The feverish down-south clamor burned up the days and nights of his convalescence. Running, jumping, splashing, it went on and on, a carnival of muscle and precision, crude salutes and embracing coaches, while all the while he lay back on his pillows, absorbed, transfixed. His old friend Bill Herschel flew in from Winnipeg to spend a few days with him. They could have talked; they'd seen little of each other over the years other than rushed visits, and there were all sorts of things they might have said, but instead the two of them huddled by the hour in Larry's hospital room, the multi-hued TV screen bringing them the hectic grunting drama of diving, gymnastics, weight lifting, rowing, volleyball, soccer, wrestling; these curious human flailings it seemed to Larry, and became one immense game, an invented supersport composed of rushing air, gravel, and water, possessing stringent rules and a series of bizarre obstacles that had to be overcome, the contrived hurdles, the hoops and crazed dangers of novelty. Music swelled toward applause and back again; thick-sounding buzzers and starting guns punctured the air, and all the while the moving, tilting, straining, leaping, sweating men and women delivered him, at last, back to his own body.

Not wanting to miss anything, he and Bill channel-hopped madly. Watching Donovan Bailey run the hundred meter dash and take the gold medal, they filled the room with little yips of joy. Bill whipped off his T-shirt, waving it like a flag over his head, and performed a mad hopping dance at the foot of the bed, two hundred pounds of gesticulating male flesh, and Larry, still connected to his tubes and wires, felt the bright juice of euphoria surge through his deadened tissues. Breath, beginnings. He was on the mend, as his mother would have said. The moment overflowed with itself, its massed perfection. The air in front of his eyes became tender. He was alive again in the housing of his skin and blood, and for the moment that was enough.

He'd met Charlotte Angus soon after he moved his office from Chicago to Toronto. It was not, he discovered, at all difficult for a single man, even a single man in his mid-forties with two divorces on the books and carrying ten extra pounds of belly fat, to meet women. Available women abounded; everyone he knew kept a list of attractive, intelligent single females who were eager to find a male partner. But where were the attractive, or even unattractive, middle-aged single men? "They've either gone gay," says Larry's sister, Midge, "bless their dithery dinks. Or they've hooked up with younger women. Or, number three, they're selfish jerks you wouldn't want to foist on anyone."

She herself, after one sad early marriage, has ended up living in North Toronto with a man called Ian Stoker, a fifty-year-old designer of sidewalk hoardings, who works, at least when work is available out of his basement office. They've been together eight years now, riding the vertical grooves of a so-so relationship. "Perfect is not what I'm after," Midge has confided to Larry. "I know that at my age there're bound to be compromises. For one thing, I never really fancied pressing my tender lips up against a moustache, and by the way, I'm glad you've got rid of yours, Larry. You look younger and cleaner without it. Actually, though, there's not all that much pressing between Ian and me these days. Of any kind. I don't think he's seeing anyone else during the day, but I wouldn't rule it out. How do I stand not knowing? Because I'm busy as hell down at the store, that's how. I get home from work, and Ian's got something in the oven, usually something decent, and he's got the table set, sort of, and I can, you know, put my feet up. He's not about to go bowling or drinking, not him, it's not in his genes. He's already patted out our potato patches on the couch and we just fall into them for the evening, a kind of TV trance that isn't as bad as you might think. At least he isn't forever switching channels, that's one thing in his favor. And what else? – let me think. Oh, God, what else? He goes fishing now and then so that I get the house to myself, and is that ever heaven! He has a shower every morning. I'd rather he showered at night, but what can you do. He doesn't go in for strong-smelling toiletries. Ten points for that. Hmmmm. When he's got money he spends it. One tight-fisted man was enough for me. You remember what Paul was like. I did love the guy though, especially toward the end. And in the beginning. Lordy! Ian, on the other hand, understands the worth of a good bottle of wine. He knows chocolate from chocolate. He doesn't gobble peanuts or pretzels, any of that stuff, and he gets his teeth attended to twice a year. Now that's enough to build a relationship on, don't you think? In my opinion he does good work. His hoardings for the Smithsite Building were a lot more interesting and lively than the building itself. Everyone said so. He doesn't talk mean about his ex either. All he says, and this is only now and then, is that she was always burning toast and blaming the wiring in the apartment. This toast business was sort of symbolic. Like she had this habit of redirecting the blame for every small disaster. When she lost her job she blamed the alarm clock. Honestly, she went and threw it in the garbage. When she had her miscarriage she blamed Ian, she actually said his indifference must have made the fetus 'nervous.' I admit he's no Adonis. That chest of his, yikes. Those round shoulders. Nothing to sing about. But I've been looking around and I've noticed there really aren't that many good-looking men anymore. Not over the age of, say, forty. Men get the sags pretty early in life. Whereas women! Women look after themselves. I mean, look at Charlotte. Mid-forties and she's a peach. Her skin, her manicure, that funny laugh of hers. She has a very, very positive attitude. And good taste in scarves, also hair coloring. I just hope you appreciate what you've got, and I mean that, Larry."

Charlotte is a widow. Her husband, Derek, an accountant, died four years ago of prostate cancer and left her reasonably well off. She doesn't have to work, but how else is she going to fill her time? – that's what she says. Especially with the two boys grown up, one in Alberta, the other on the coast. Besides, she has her diploma in counseling; it would be a waste not to use it.

She and Larry met at a dinner party given by mutual acquaintances. Everyone else around the table was part of a couple, and it was clear from the forced exuberance of the conversation that match-making was in the air: a good woman on her own, and, that rare thing, an available single man. The two of them were seated side by side, and so closely that Larry's elbow, cutting into his roast chicken, slid silkily against the sleeve of Charlotte's blouse. "Sorry," she said, smiling down at her plate and withdrawing her pink swathed arm. (She was, he later learned, devoted to shades of pink and rose, as well as the softer reds.) The talk at the table was general, but it tended to flow strongly, Larry noticed, in the direction of the two unattached guests, himself and Charlotte Angus. Did he like Toronto? How did it compare to Chicago? Had Charlotte seen *Showboat*? No? What about you, Larry? You really shouldn't pass it up. Either of you.

A week later they were in bed together. That first night – they went to Larry's apartment rather than Charlotte's house in Deer Park – they were both shy as virgins. Larry had not had a night of sex since his wife, Beth, left him, and for Charlotte it had been years. In fact, she confided – this was later – that she'd only ever had one partner. She and Derek had married young and they'd both been old-fashioned when it came to monogamy. At least she had been.

Her skin had the powdery softness of a cared for but unexercised body. "Oh," she said, drawing in her breath sharply, as if pierced by an old recollection, "oh, oh."

He was not so much excited as at home in her flesh, its willing tenderness, and that chorus of reassuring, breath-filled "oh's." She had not wanted the light left on. "Please," she'd said, gesturing toward the lamp.

Darkness covered them like a cool sheet. He prized it, drank its richness in. As for Charlotte, she was trembling, her arms and legs, a luxurious shudder he reached out to embrace.

It's happened before in his life, lying at attention beside the body of a lovely woman – midnight, a summer breeze at the screen, crickets stitching up the darkness, the rumble of occasional traffic in the street – and always he's felt a flood of gratitude so sharp, so sudden and powerful that it resists the confines of language or gesture or even the rough and tentative modeling of thought. What is this paradise? Touching. Being touched. The unburdened self, half-conscious once again of primitive melodies playing offstage. The unearned privilege of a human hand on his human body. A willing caress, that leaping increment of knowledge locked in the skin, yes, oh, yes. His throttled, misshapen, and discontinuous life might yet be rescued. As it was this very minute by a woman called Charlotte Angus. When he least deserved it.

Sometimes he thinks Charlotte loves him, though he may just be reading the flickering shadow of shared boredom. Certainly they haven't spoken about love, not yet.

She was curiously maternal in her ways. And, why not? She'd been a mother since she was twenty-five years old. (The thought of the twenty-five-year-old Charlotte, her shy smile, her earlobes innocent of jewelry, swamped his heart.) Some days he objected to her mothering and some days he didn't. He should take zinc tablets, she suggested. If only Derek had taken zinc. He should try using foam innersoles in his shoes, they made the most remarkable difference. When he had trouble sleeping, all he had to do was imagine he was writing his own name on a velvet blackboard; write it slowly with the pad of your middle finger, thinking each loop and serif in your head; if you make a mistake you can erase it and start over again.

He feels he must respond by saying something aerobic and jaunty: "Great." "Terrific."

Well, he thinks, maybe this is how it goes between forty-five-year-old lovers. At this age the body needs every available encouragement. Attention to diet and exercise. Recipes for relaxation. Forty-five-year-olds aren't out rolling in the autumn leaves, for God's sake, they aren't making impromptu snow angels in the park or frugging the night away. No. They're concentrating on improvements to their domestic arrangements; it was time, for instance, that Larry went shopping for some comfortable furniture; the dining table and chairs he'd brought from Chicago were utterly beautiful, Charlotte had never seen anything like them, but the rest of the apartment needed, well, cheering up. She offered helpful hints about window coverings. Also advice on spot removal and invisible mending – that light grey suit of his, though, really should go to Neighborhood Services. He was working too hard, throwing too much of himself into the McCord maze, driving himself toward a deadline that was, when it came right down to it, completely arbitrary.

Larry listened and nodded. That was the trouble

with middle age: you forget what you had at stake. You just plain forget.

It is not the time, and they both feel this instinctively, to talk about living together. But two or three nights a week they end up in either Larry's bed or hers. These nights are long and sumptuous. He wakes and watches her, asleep on her heavy side. They both remark, often, about how much better they're sleeping, how generally more relaxed they feel. Larry even drifted off to sleep one Sunday afternoon on Charlotte's living-room couch. It was a cool spring day, and Charlotte, seeing him there, covered him with a mohair blanket. (She was a woman devoted to texture and to small exacting shifts of comfort.)

He felt the feather touch of the blanket as it dropped around his shoulders, and, without quite waking, knew himself to be in the embrace of profound tenderness, that second cousin to passionate love. His breathing deepened, carrying him – with lowered pulse rate, the dim headlights of a dream beckoning – toward the coastline of perfect sleep.

His dear Charlotte. This is something new. This is sweeter in a way than the lies, theater, and staged manipulation of marriage, but he can't quite move his bones all the way into it. He's caught between a rock and a soft place; that's how he feels when he thinks about Charlotte Angus, whose shame and goodness is her eagerness to please – that softly dropped blanket, her generous mouth and tongue, the way she barges straight through uncertainty, toughing it out. For no reason that he can imagine, she's reached toward his living body and offered herself.

Larry's father, who died in 1988, left instructions to have his body cremated. This surprised everyone, that Stu Weller, a stubborn traditionalist, was capable of forming so progressive and environmentally responsible a decision. Now, October 1996, Larry's mother, Dot, has joined her husband in death. "A grand old lady," said the head of the nursing team in Winnipeg. "She was ready to go," said Midge Weller. "Yes," agreed Larry's ex-wife, Dorrie, "those last few months were really terribly sad." "I suppose she would want cremation?" Larry said. He posed this as a question. "Absolutely," Midge answered.

Midge and Larry flew to Winnipeg, row 23, seats A and B, a pair of middle-aged siblings, both stocked with their dead parents' store of genetic tissue and something of their dead parents' perpetual confusion. Suddenly they had been orphaned. Midge leafed through a copy of *Victoria Magazine*, sniffling, red-eyed. The exquisite table settings, the photographs of antique linen, the recipes for violet marmalade reminded her not of her mother, but the distance her mother had always stood from such things. "She was so goddamned plain," Midge told Larry. "She never allowed herself to swing free. To be extravagant and silly." Larry, reading the latest *Newsweek* – more confused threats from the Middle East – felt unworthy of this insight. He had loved his mother, he was certain of that. In fact, what he felt for her went beyond love. A woman of uneven moods, of bursts of physical energy and slow tears, who, late in her life, found peace in the liturgy of the Anglican church and the love of Christ. Dot Weller had given birth to him, he'd nuzzled at her breasts, flesh of her flesh. But these scenes belonged to the background music of Larry's life – there, but not pressingly there.

It was decided between Midge and Larry that they would scatter Dot's ashes the day after the funeral on the waters of West Hawk Lake where their father Stu's ashes had gone. (Larry's son, Ryan, gave the eulogy at the simple Anglican ceremony, and Dorrie, who had been with Dot at the end, holding on to her hand, served coffee and sandwiches in her Lipton Street house. And it was Dorrie who lent Midge and Larry her car for their ash-scattering expedition.) They drove eastward. The day was windy, and the fields and rocks had the stubbled, deadened, monochrome look that precedes the first snow and the freezing over of the lake. "We're just in time," Midge said.

"You mean she was just in time," Larry said.

His mother had said to him as a child – and this discussion he now musingly recalls – driving along the flat Manitoba highway, the trees stripped of their leaves, the snow fences bundled here and there along the shoulder, soon to be erected for the winter – that human bodies turn to dust. He remembers that he doubted the truth of this statement. Dust was that dry accretion under his bed. A human body rotted, spoiled.

But dust was what he and his sister carried in the trunk of Dorrie's car, a box of dust. Larry has recently learned that it takes hours of intense heat to reduce a human body to powder. Even so, there were pieces that refused to break down, hardened bits, bones perhaps or teeth. It was astonishing, the durability of bodily atoms.

Midge switched on the radio and turned up the heat so that the car became a little cave with its own soothing weather. He knew she was dreading the moment when the two of them would stand by the lakeshore – for one thing, neither of them was sure whether this was a legal act or not – and plunge their hands into the dry remains of Dot Weller, their mother.

The moment didn't happen, not that day anyway. Arriving after a two-hour drive and parking at a deserted scenic lookout, Larry opened the trunk of the car and found – nothing. "I thought you put it in," he told Midge. "I thought you did," said Midge, weeping openly and hugging herself against the cold.

"Christ. She's still back on Dorrie's front porch."

"I can't bear this."

"We don't have to put her in the lake. It was only an idea. I mean, Dad's ashes have long since –"

"It looks too cold anyway."

"Those waves."

"What if we –"

"Take her to Toronto?"

"On the plane?"

"I don't know."

"We could, you know, put her in our backyard. That nice place by the peonies. Or are we just being lazy, Larry, not wanting to drive all the way back to Winnipeg for the ashes and then back here to –?"

"She really did like peonies. Remember how she'd –"

"I'm sure Ian wouldn't mind. Or do you think it's too ghoulish for words? Putting your mother's remains in your yard."

"No, I don't think so. I mean, we may not want to admit it, but she's only –"

"Ashes."

"That's right. Dust."

"No," Midge said, an hour later. They still had sixty miles to go before hitting Winnipeg. She punched off the car radio with a snap. "We can't do this, Larry. We can't take her to Toronto. We'd never feel right about it. We'll have to come back to West Hawk tomorrow and put her in the lake."

"Yes," said Larry, wishing he'd been the one to say it.

Last summer, when Larry Weller lay unconscious in a deep coma, a coma that was possibly irreversible – the doctors would make no predictions – his body received meticulous care and almost constant surveillance. He slept his dreamless sleep and never knew – never felt, sensed, registered – that the integrity of his bodily organs was being maintained. He was fed intravenously during this period since his gagging and swallowing reflexes were non-operational. Frequent suctioning was required in order to remove the secretions of the mouth and throat and keep his airway open. Of course, his oral hygiene was attended to, his gums and teeth swabbed twice daily with lemon-glycerine.

Every two hours he was turned so that the pressure on his skin was relieved and his lungs aerated. It required a male nurse to move a body as heavy as Larry's, or two female nurses working together. He had to be carefully placed, his spine aligned, in order to avoid future orthopedic deformities. The function of his joints was maintained by daily motion exercises. An indwelling catheter handled the urine which he continued to produce in his unconscious state, and the digital removal of his stools from his rectum was regularly performed.

Electronic monitoring recorded his vital signs and attempted to measure his level of consciousness – even though little is understood about coma and its curious halfway position between life and death. Does a comatose body think or dream, does it hear noises and sense the tensions that surround it? His chin and cheeks were shaved, and his fingernails and toenails trimmed. His feet were bound to an L-shaped plastic board in order to provide support. Without this foot board his feet would have "dropped" to a planter flexion position, permanently shortening the muscles and tendons at the back of his ankles, so that, should he survive, he would be unable to stand upright.

Hundreds of hands had touched him during the twenty-two-day period of his unconsciousness. The hands of professionals, doing their job, ticked off items on his chart, keeping his blood-filled tissues alive and elastic. His most private orifices, his nostrils, his anus, were kept free and clean. The faces of the strangers who performed these acts are utterly unknown to him, and this seems to him to represent a fundamental imbalance in the world. His two failed marriages, the distance he feels between himself and his dead parents, his inability to understand his son, or to will himself in love with Charlotte Angus – all these failings speak of the separateness of human beings, with every last person on earth withdrawing to the privacy of his own bones.

But it isn't true. It is impossible to live a whole life sealed inside the constraints of a complex body. Sooner or later, and sometimes by accident, someone is going to reach out a hand or a tongue or a morsel of genital flesh and enter that valved darkness. This act can be thought of as a precious misfortune or the ripest of pleasures. The skin will break open, or the cell wall, and all the warm fluids of life will be released – whether we wish it or not – to pour freely into the mixed matter of the world, that surging, accommodating ocean. Larry Weller is disturbed by this notion, but oddly comforted, too. He is recovering; in a sense he's spent his whole life in a state of recovery, but has only begun, at age forty-five, to breathe in the vital foreknowledge of what will become of the sovereign self inside him, that luxurious ornament. He'd like that self to be more musical and better lit, he'd like to possess a more meticulous sense of curiosity, and mostly he'd like someone, some *thing* to love. He's getting close. He feels it. He's halfway awake now, and about to wake up fully.

CHAPTER FIFTEEN

Larry's Party
1997

Before the Party

Unless your life is going well you don't dream of giving a party. Unless you can look in the mirror and see a benign and generous and healthy human being, you shrink from acts of hospitality. Which is why Larry Weller has not given a party in some time. He can't, infact, remember the last time. Anti-social is what he's been since his second wife, Beth, left him three years ago.

But now Beth is going to be in town.

And so, by chance, is Larry's first wife, Dorrie – spending a few days here on business.

Two ex-wives in Toronto on the same weekend. A coincidence.

Beth faxed Larry from England to say she'd love to see him after all this time. ("It's been far too long, and I've got some wonderful news.") And Dorrie wrote one of her postcards. "I've got meetings all Saturday morning, but the rest of the weekend's free. Why don't we try to get together for old time's sake?"

"It's really the perfect occasion to give a party," said Larry's friend Charlotte Angus, as though the matter were already settled. "And I promise to pitch in and help." Then she added, more tentatively, "If you'd like me to, that is."

"Of course, I'd like you to. But how? What can we –?" He feels lost in this too sudden social thicket; it's been so long. "When? What kind of? What time?"

"Saturday evening? Dinner. Seven o'clock is good. It's early, but that way you can count on everyone leaving before midnight."

"You really think this is a good idea? It seems –"

How did it seem? He put the question to himself. A forty-six-year-old man (forty-seven in August) hosting a party? You don't see it happen often, a single man, twice divorced, paying off his social debts, inviting his friends not to a restaurant, but into his own space for an evening of conviviality. A table set. Talk, laughter. Food and drink raining down. Most men in Larry's position receive rather than dispense hospitality. That's Charlotte's opinion. Such men receive and receive and receive. It can go on for years, this social imbalance, before anyone thinks to question it. Some state of emergency must occur to make a reversal seem inevitable.

And now that moment has come. Two ex-wives arriving on the same weekend and both of them – Larry can't help but be pleased, even flattered – both writing ahead, seeking his company. This is civilized behavior, this reflects well on him as a man, as a former husband, and so on and so on.

"What I can't believe," Charlotte said to Larry, "is that they've never met each other. I mean, wouldn't you think that once, in all those years, they would have –?"

"Chicago's a long way from Winnipeg," Larry told her, not very convincingly. "They did talk on the phone once or twice."

"Politely, I'm sure."

"Very."

"Both of them right up to the minute on post-marital etiquette, I suppose."

Larry had to think about that. He's seen Beth's jealous side, how irrationally disparaging she sometimes was about his first wife, and he also remembers Dorrie's rough edges. Still, that was ancient history, the temperaments of his spouses; he was in his twenties when he married Dorrie, in his thirties when he and Beth got together; his marriages seem far away to him now, inventions of another, younger, less solid self. He knows so much more than he did twenty years ago, at least he likes to think so. A billion bytes of information weigh him down. "I think," he told Charlotte, "that you can depend on them both."

"Good. Because it does hold plenty of potential for–"

"I know, I know." The fact was, he was excited now by the prospect of the party, and excited by his excitement.

It was over lunch on a Wednesday when he and

Charlotte had this conversation. Larry's noticed lately the way in which restaurant eating enlarges his sense of himself, and how he and Charlotte probe over their small public tables possibilities that they shrink from in private.

Earlier in the day he had given a short press conference about the launch of the McCord maze, a project that has engaged him for the last two years. In exactly five weeks' time the maze will be opened to the public. It is a relatively low-key piece of work, but one that Larry nevertheless feels is the most creatively adventurous of his life. He's pulled the rug out this time, but subtly, softly. Instead of the stiff, formal plantings of traditional mazes – holly, box, yew – he's employed dozens of dense but informal hedges – such gently sprawling plants as five-leaf aralia (tolerates polluted air well), amur maple, honeysuckle, ninebark, which bears up against wind and cold, winterberry for its bright red berries and dark leaves, Russian olive, rose of Sharon, caragana because of its feathery lightness, winged euonymus, and forsythia. (Garth McCord has gone on record as saying forsythia is too "suburban" a shrub. He made quite a point of it, it was his money after all, but in the end a compromise was reached.) Larry hopes, and this was the view he presented to the press this morning in a prepared statement – that the maze will incorporate the essential lost-and-found odyssey of a conventional maze, but will allow the maze walker to forget that the shrub material is a kind of wall and think of it, rather, as an extension of a dreamy organic world, with the maze and maze solver merging to form a single organism.

The McCord ravine property, generously donated to the city parks system, slopes toward a small stream, and the maze's path, downward and then up on the return journey, is intended to mirror the descent into unconscious sleep, followed by a slow awakening. (Three reporters attended the press conference – Larry admits to himself, if not to Charlotte, that he was disappointed at the turnout – and each of them scribbled down the phrase: *extension of the dreamy organic world.*)

Larry and Charlotte Angus were seated at an outdoor table in a cafe called the Blinking Duck, off King Street, sharing a seafood salad and discussing the still-abstract notion of Larry's dinner party and glancing up at a curiously blank sky. This is Canada, that cold crested country with its changeable weather and staunch heart. Today, though, is exceptionally warm for April, and Larry had made the mistake of wearing his grey wool blazer and a tie. "Why don't you slip that off," Charlotte advised in her thoughtful way, and he did.

We might have either eight or ten at the table, Charlotte was saying, but why not make it an even ten since the table seats that number beautifully. Simple but elegant food. A light red wine, Italian maybe. An early evening.

A breeze rolled across the terrace, a thrusting April breeze, lifting the twin points of Charlotte's scarf by a fraction of an inch. Everything Larry knows about women informs him that she is at a place in her life where a scarf at the neck is presumed to do wonders in the perking-up department. "Actually," she announced, fingering the scarf's border, "a dinner party isn't quite the same as an ordinary party."

"Why is that?" He felt his own sleepy smile drift over the pink paper tablecloth. He's been seeing Charlotte for more than a year now, and they've grown easy with each other. At least part of this ease springs from a habit of half-hearted teasing, as though each has made a pact to claim a certain amount of ironic territory from the other.

"Oh, I don't know. A dinner party's safer somehow. It's more of an event." Charlotte's voice had taken on an arc of singing confidence. She is a shy woman, but given to bursts of energy. "A staged event. You can keep a dinner party under control."

"With small talk you mean?"

"Well," she said, shrugging, "thank heavens, I say, for small talk. Small talk's better than big talk. Big scary talk. Aesthetics, societal values. And people stabbing you to death by mentioning authors you've never heard of. Quoting from Kierkegaard. I mean!"

Larry's smile widened. He is not a man given to dinner-table quoting, though he sometimes wishes he had the capability.

Charlotte was not finished with the subject. "Have you ever imagined how silent the world would be if we couldn't talk about the weather or the price of real estate? Or about the squirrel nuisance in our back- yards? What if we didn't have our vacations to babble on about? Or what our children are doing? My God!"

"Even that's not a safe topic." Larry took in Charlotte's mobile mouth and swinging earrings, remembering that his own son, Ryan, had recently been accused of doping up before a race, steroids, that the matter was under investigation.

"And another thing," Charlotte went on, "you can't ask people what kind of work they do. It's considered intrusive nowadays. I mean, what if they happen to be out of work? Or what if they work for some company that makes porno films or sanitary napkins or something? It's all right for you, Larry, you work with lovely green living things."

"So," Larry said, "you think a dinner party's safe? In terms of conversational neutrality."

Charlotte's eyebrows go up. "Well, keeping control's somewhat important, isn't it? I mean, the dynamics. It might be, you know –" She sliced a hand through the air in front of her.

A pause followed. Larry couldn't have said whether it was a long pause or a short pause. He glanced about and saw that the restaurant was beginning to fill up with young couples, most of whom looked like lovers. Twenty-year-olds, thirty-year-olds, their hands meeting over the table tops, little sexual wavings of their fingertips.

"I'm a rotten cook," Larry said, shaking his head and thinking about his friend Bill Herschel, who smokes his own trout and regularly bakes bread for his family. "Beth used to insist we take turns doing dinner –"

"Really? You never mentioned that."

"It was one of her things."

"As a feminist, you mean."

"But all I could do was pasta."

"Pasta? Hmmmm. No, I don't think so. Not for ten people."

"Then we're in trouble."

"I did promise to help." Charlotte was speaking more loudly now that the noise level has risen. "But, look, how exactly would you, you know – introduce me to the ex-wives? I mean, what words would you use?"

"We-ll." He paused, uneasy, warning himself to put on his safety brakes, knowing how sensitive Charlotte could be. "I'll just say we're friends."

"And we are, aren't we, Larry?" Her eyes met his, making a pledge. Or asking, it seemed to him, for a heightened confirmation.

"We're good friends." He kept his gaze guarded, tapping light as a fingertip on the word *good*, but it seemed to satisfy her.

"Maybe," she said, wrinkling her forehead, "we should have eight instead of ten. Or better yet, nine. That way we can talk asymmetrically around the table. Asymmetry always brings a better focus to the conversation."

How does she know such things? "Are you sure that's what we want? Focus?"

"Of course it is."

"Instead of a nice out-of-focus blur? Like that French movie we saw, where we didn't know what was going on?"

"We can buy some of the stuff for the dinner already made," Charlotte hurried on, taking a small notepad out of her bag. "Dessert, for instance. Everyone does nowadays. Yes, definitely a bought dessert. Something chocolate. From Dufflet."

"Speaking of dessert –"

"Exactly what I was thinking. Why don't we split a slice of cheesecake. The almond looks good."

"Why not."

They've fallen into the habit in recent months of sharing portions of food – some insufficiency in their appetites, Larry thinks, or else the geriatric equivalent of holding hands. He regarded her fondly. The bravery of her lipstick banner. Her eyes. Placating, eager eyes; how did she manage to keep such eagerness alive? (A gleam of green eye-shadow, expertly applied. Quizzing brows. The droop of one eyelid when she was tired.) Her bright silk scarf evoked blazing images of Central America, but Larry knows she bought it in Provence – or was it Spain? – last summer. It must be hot, he reflected, having something like that tied around your neck.

Charlone's a woman who always "does her best," who "throws herself into things," and perversely it is this, he thinks, that keeps him from loving her with the same warmth she directs toward him. Something – perhaps the death of her husband five years ago, perhaps her genetic make-up – compels her, it seems to Larry, to bite harder than most at the biscuit of life. To bite and to keep on biting.

"If you decide on lamb," Charlotte Angus said to Larry one week before his dinner party, "you really ought to serve beans."

"Why beans? No one likes beans. At least no one I know."

"That's how they serve lamb in France. Very rare,

pink in the middle, and with white beans. It's traditional. Or those littlee lima beans. You can buy frozen ones."

"Beans are indigestible."

"Big piles of beans are indigestible. You're absolutely right. The thing is to serve just a *few* beans alongside the meat. More of a garnish, really, than a serving."

"How many is a few? Twelve beans? Twenty?"

"You're lying on my arm, love. There, that's better."

"So we get some beans to garnish the lamb. Does that mean we don't have to garnish the beans?"

"A little parsley sprinkled on. Or fresh sage. They have it at St. Lawrence Market. Sage would do very nicely now that I think of it."

"And to garnish the sage?"

"You know what, Larry? You're being awkward and jocular. Male jocularity at this hour isn't –"

"Appropriate," he supplied. Beth, too, had objected to jocularity.

"Exactly."

"When is the proper time for male jocularity?" He fitted his body to hers, drew a leg up around her soft hip.

"Never. I thought you knew. There's a new by-law. Oh, God, look at the time. I've got to be at work early this morning. Meetings. The trauma team's doing a presentation."

"What do you mean I'm being awkward?"

"Did I say you were awkward?"

"Yes."

Menu - Larry's Party

Champagne (Cartier Imperial Canadian?)

~~~

Butternut squash and ginger soup

~~~

Leg of lamb with rosemary
   Baby lima beans / carrots
(Beaujolais)

~~~

Salad

~~~

Bavarian
   Austrian chocolate cake
(Muscat de Frontignan?)

~~~

Coffee / brandy

"Because you're – you're trying to trap me into saying things that are wifely and trivial and presumptuous. So that I'll look like a domestic bully when all I am is the girlfriend who's trying to help you out."

"I love the way you say that. 'The Girlfriend.' With capital letters."

"More like italics. I mean, at age forty-six, anything associated with the word girl is completely in-congruous and – good God, just look at this skirt of mine. What comes over me when I spend a night at your place? – at home I *hang up* my clothes, I look after myself. I'm going to have to press this, and fast. I don't suppose you have such a thing as distilled water on the premises?"

"I'll buy some today. When I'm out buying the lima beans."

"You'll need about three packages. For nine people that should just do it nicely."

"Is it nine? I've lost track."

"You know very well we said nine. Why all of a sudden are you trying to make this party seem all my idea? And, Larry, look, if you want to serve the lamb with the bone out, and I do recommend it, you'd better order it now. Today, I mean. Olliffe's does a gorgeous job. They'll marinate it too. Olive oil. Lemon. Rose-mary. Lovely."

"Anything else?"

"Well, you could – no, that's enough girlfriendly advice for this morning. Although maybe, on second thought –"

"What?"

"Nothing."

"Will I see you tonight?"

She paused and gave him a look. An unreadable look, but he knew there was punishment in it somewhere. "How about tomorrow night instead," she said. "At my place."

Beth abandoned Larry, finally, in 1994, leaving behind in their Oak Park house a closetful of soft clothes and a bathroom cluttered with high-tech hairbrushes and miniature perfume bottles.

Otherwise she left him carefully, tactfully, *psychologically*. There was her first calm face-to-face announcement in a Southampton restaurant, followed a few days later by an expansive letter.

> Darling Larry,
>
> All this will be easier for you if you think of life as a book each of us must write alone, and how, within that book there are many chapters. I think we both know that our chapter, yours and mine, has contained pages of ecstasy, of reciprocal growth –

On and on it went. He found the prose hard to follow, as though it had been written during a bout of drunkenness, but that was impossible since Beth never touched anything stronger than spring water – her allergies, her fear of gaining weight. The closing paragraph went:

> Your spiritual signature, sweet Larry, has illuminated mine, and I like to think that our combined epigraph has sent shooting stars, sexually

as well as intellectually, across the synapse of our stitched together leaves, igniting the kind of authenticity that lives on after separation. I do feel it is time, though, to get going on a fresh sheet of foolscap, as it were, and write our way to understanding and forgiveness.

Dear bossy, pedagogical Beth. Heartbrokenly he read this letter, at the same time feeling his face ease into a smile.

Wait a minute. Whoa there. *Heartbrokenly smiled?* Surely not. Perhaps he smiled *around* his heartbreak. *Under* it, *through* it.

Larry, more and more the observer, the critic, stepped back and watched himself picking up his wife's letter and attacking it with a surgical red pencil. C-minus. And that was being generous.

Understanding and forgiveness, uh-huh! So that's what she prescribed. Was that all?

When Beth left him, not for another man but for a teaching job in England, he had been close to his forty-fourth birthday, a man in his mellow season, or so romantic fools would have him believe. Understanding and forgiveness should have come easily. Like rolling off a log. With the softened shrug of an unmuscled shoulder. Where, after all, is it written that love is more potent than a fresh career opportunity? "My adorable Larry," his smooth-skinned Beth had penned in a postscript, freshly oxygenated it would seem by the transports of her own rhetoric. "You have been translator to my unformed soul, attentive reader to my body and mind, and lastly, editor and publisher of my fumbling love. Let's you and me together, turn over our separate pages. And read on!"

Yes, well. What else was there to do?

Unless a man has himself abandoned a wife, he will be unable to understand-and-forgive. Instead he'll see those twinned verbs as miniature implements – spade, hoe – on a woman's charm bracelet, fanciful and decorative, and not stop to consider for a minute the immensities of charity they demand. Nor – sweet Christ! – the seesaw of guilt they bounce into view.

Larry and his first wife, Dorrie, had been married for five years when he left her. Five years, one child, a house in the process of renovation, a fully occupied width of time – and yet he has trouble remembering what their life had been made of. The two of them came together, it always seemed to him, back in the time of the old poetry, 1977, when the world rhymed and chimed and the ceilings were higher or, even if they weren't, the possibility of height was felt.

"What was she like?" Charlotte Angus asked Larry once; this was after an episode of lovemaking in Charlotte's white and cream bedroom.

"Who?"

"Dorrie. The first."

"You won't believe this, but I can't remember."

"Was she terrific in bed?"

"Hmmmm. Hard to put into words."

"Meaning you'd rather not say. Meaning it's none of my business."

"Sorry."

"I'm the one who's sorry. My big mouth."

"She could be funny. She'd do imitations of her boss at the Toyota dealership. And of my dad, too. She was good at it. Before everything fell apart."

"And did everything really fall apart?"

"Everything. Well, everything except Dorrie."

"Why didn't you go to a marriage counselor?"

"It wasn't in our vocabulary."

"Did you think there was a stigma attached to –?"

"Not a stigma, not that. It really *was* a question of vocabulary."

"If Derek and I had had problems, I'm sure we would have sought out professional help. It would have been the most natural thing in the world."

Mention of Derek, Charlotte's dead husband, tended to make Larry feel slightly sick. "Maybe you and Derek had that kind of vocabulary," he said carefully.

"Are you sure you mean vocabulary? You honestly didn't know what a marriage counselor was?"

"We knew that. Everyone knew that."

"Well then?"

He thought of his mother, who had been depressed for long stretches of her life, but had never dreamt of seeking psychiatric counseling. "I didn't know the words around the words," he told Charlotte. "How to get there."

"Sometimes, Larry, you say something and I don't have any idea what you mean."

"Sometimes I don't know either," he said, swallowing.

It seemed to him that what he swallowed was the bitterness of his own essence. He was not the man he started out to be. He's richer and sadder now, and he's lost the trick of keeping track of himself.

"Well? What do you think?"

"Looks nice. The tablecloth was a good idea."

"It pulls everything together, doesn't it? And I'm glad you thought of those dark green candles, Larry. White candles look churchy."

"Thanks for bringing flowers."

"I remembered," Charlotte said, "what you said once – about not having roses on a dinner table, the smell getting into the soup."

"My days as a florist!" He let out a sigh. "We must have learned that in the first term. It's with you forever." He looked around at the set table, the gleam of forks and knives, the shining wine glasses, the dining chairs standing at attention. "It's all with you forever, isn't it. Every bit of it."

"You're not going to get maudlin, are you, Larry?"

"I might. I'm beginning to have doubts about this whole –"

"It's nerves, not doubts. And it's perfectly normal. When Derek and I used to have dinner parties, I always panicked at the last minute. Like maybe I'll burn the main course, maybe nobody'll come, that sort of thing. You did hear from everyone, though, didn't you?"

"Both the wives faxed."

"How odd."

"That's what I thought. Midge phoned. She and Ian are going to be a few minutes late. And Sam Alvero left a message – he might be a few minutes early, something about picking up his car at the body shop."

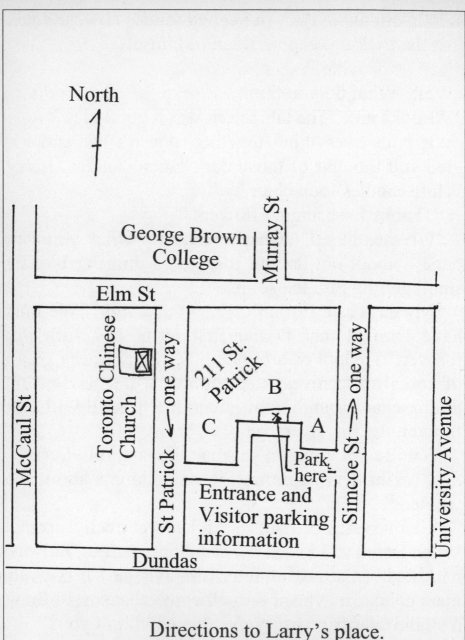

Directions to Larry's place.
See you April 26 @ 7.p.m.
Ask for 211 St. Patrick, Apt. 788.

"The McCords?"

"His secretary phoned. She wanted to know if it was black tie or what. I said casual."

"Now, that'll be interesting. I wonder what he thinks casual means. Speaking of which, are you going to change?"

"Don't you like this sweater?"

"I do. You look all wrapped up and safe."

"That was the idea."

"Whereas I feel exposed as hell in this dress. Exposed to the gaze of the ex-wives. Their darting little eyes. Inquisitive. I was going to wear a scarf but —"

"You look perfect."

"Not too mysterious or menacing? Here she is, folks — Larry Weller's new woman friend. Hmmm. Now who might she be, how does she fit into the picture? Not exactly a spring chicken, is she? Oh my God, I'm babbling."

"Nerves."

"Hold on to me a minute.'

"Hmmmm."

"That's better."

"It's going to be fine."

"Actually I can smell the lamb, can you? Heavenly, heavenly garlic. I hope they're all hearty garlic eaters. Well, too bad for them if they're not."

"I can't smell anything."

"That's because you've been here all afternoon. And you got the carrots ready, I see."

"And the soup. But maybe you'd better taste it."

"We've still got half an hour. We could do place cards."

"I don't know. That sounds awfully –"

"Formal? Maybe you're right. Well, let's at least figure out the seating. Commit it to memory."

"Why don't we just let everyone sit where they want –?"

"We can't *do* that, Larry! What if the two wives ended up next to each other? I mean, we want to keep this informal, but having them side by side might be asking for" – she paused – "for trouble."

"What kind of trouble? They're not going to pull each other's hair out. It isn't as though they're rivals."

"Oh, Larry!"

"What do you mean – 'Oh, Larry'?"

"I don't know. It's just that sometimes you're such an innocent."

"The two of them occupied completely separate slices of time. No overlap at all. I don't see how how they can be rivals. They're really – I don't know – fellow escapees."

"Oh, Larry," Charlotte said again, shaking her head. "You don't – you don't get it, do you?"

"I guess not." In a way, though, he did.

"Anyway, they're going to be here any minute and we really should put some thinking into the seating strategy."

"Well," Larry said, "we could put one wife at each end – that way they'd be as far from each other as possible."

To his surprise she took this seriously. "Hmmm. Too obvious maybe. And not really correct. They're the guests of honor, remember."

"And you and I certainly don't want to be at the ends, playing Mum and Dad. At least I don't."

"No, I chucked that idea right away. Too self-conscious and hierarchical. As though we were out to control the evening."

"So what do we do?"

"I thought your sister and Ian could take the ends. Keep it in the family kind-of-thing. As a matter of fact, I hope you don't mind, Larry, but I made this little sketch while I was at work today, a sort of seating plan." She drew a folded sheet of paper from her bag and laid it out flat on the table. "Now you see where I've got Midge and Ian. I'm afraid I couldn't work out the boy-girl thing perfectly but –"

"That's okay."

"And here you are in the middle of the side between Samuel and Marcia McCord. I'm only guessing, but I don't see them as having too much in common from what you've told me about Sam. His being new in this country? His English? And so forth. Now, Dorrie's right here next to Midge – you did say they liked each other."

"They didn't used to, but now they've really –"

"And Garth McCord's across from you, with Beth on his left. I figured they'd both have all that spiritual stuff in common."

"You've really thought this out, haven't you?"

"Am I being too hostessy? Too managerial? Tell me if I am."

"But wait a minute – where are you sitting, Char?" He didn't often call her Char. "You're not here on the plan."

"Me? I'm not? Oh my God."

"You've only got eight places. There're nine of us."

"I don't believe it. That I did this."

"Why don't you sit here?" Larry said, pointing. "Between me and Sam."

"Or maybe between Garth and Dorrie."

"You choose."

"What do you think it means?" Charlotte said. Her voice had become a wail. "Subconsciously, I mean. Absenting myself from the table. Pretending I'm not here."

"The doorbell!"

"You get it, won't you? It's probably Sam Alvero. I'll go and turn down the lamb."

"Well, this is it."

"Yes. This is it."

"In a few hours it'll be over. We'll be on the other side. Just us."

"Right." She smiled up at him.

"One kiss. For luck."

"For luck. For lucky us."

Larry went toward the door then, taking a deep breath, and releasing it into a stream of pulsing desire: let this evening be soft and open, let us be kind, give us everything we want.

The Party

Beth was beautiful. He'd forgotten just how beautiful. The cold spring night had given her a touch of color, and her green velvet coat with its silver buttons swung out dramatically when she came through the

346

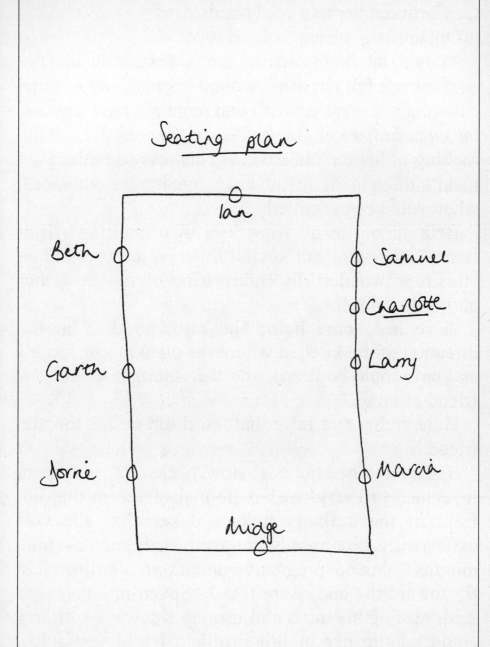

Seating plan

Ian

Beth

Samuel

Charlotte

Garth

Larry

Jorrie

Marcia

Midge

apartment doorway. "Larry," she said, and took his face between her two cold hands.

Oh, the ashy incense of old love!

"You're the first to arrive," he said absurdly, and the next minute felt her arms around his reck and her lips covering his, pressing with that remembered firmness, but even firmer tonight because of the cold. He felt the rocking of his own heartbeat. This was something he hadn't thought of in advance: greetings, embraces, what would be permitted.

Beth sprang away from him then, smiling. "But, Larry," she sang out socially, her voice crystalline, "this is so wonderfully enterprising of you. A dinner party!"

"I've had some help," he said, nodding in the direction of the kitchen where the clanking of spoons and pots could be heard, and then thought to add, "A friend of mine."

How grainy and false that word felt on his tongue: friend.

She unbuttoned her coat slowly, then threw it open, it seemed to Larry, with a flourish. Even in the dim light of the hallway he could see that she was exuberantly, bloomingly pregnant. Eight months, nine months? – but no, pregnant women weren't allowed to fly toward the end, were they? "Seven months," she said, reading his mind and turning sideways so Larry could admire her in full profile. "I told you I had wonderful news."

He opened his mouth. What was this? Who? When? But the doorbell went again, followed immediately by a crash from the kitchen.

Just five minutes into his party and he was already lost.

"Samuel Alvero, this is Beth Prior. Sam's been working with me on a project here in Toronto, he's a horticulturist, recently arrived from Spain. Seville, isn't it, Sam? Beth here has just come from London. She was starting to tell me that she's –"

"I am enchanted to meet you."

"A pleasure."

"Oh, how do you do! I'm Charlotte Angus. Sorry, I was busy in the kitchen when you – you must be Beth. Well, well! It's so good to see you, so wonderful you could come, I mean. And you're Samuel. Larry's been telling me about you, what a marvel you've been these last busy weeks, working day and night getting ready for the opening. Is that the doorbell again, Larry? I wonder if you could get that, there's something I've got to check on in the kitchen."

"Let me introduce Garth and Marcia McCord. You already know Sam, Garth. You met on the site – only last week, wasn't it? And this is Beth Prior, just off the plane from England. I should explain before the others get here that Beth and I were once, well this was years ago, but at one time – oh, and this is Charlotte Angus. Charlotte, I think you've met Garth, but not Marcia. Marcia's from New York originally, if I'm not mistaken."

"Virginia. Richmond, Virginia."

"Oh, that's right. Virginia."

"But I did actually live in New York."

"I see."

"For a little over a year. Eighteen months, as a matter of fact, or maybe it was seventeen. That's probably why you thought –"

"Can I take some drink orders?"

"I love New York, but these days I love it tragically."

"Love it how?"

"I'll give you a hand with those drinks."

"I think I can manage, Charlotte. Why don't you –"

"There it goes again, the doorbell. That must be –"

"I'll get it."

"Dorrie."

"Hello, Larry."

"No trouble finding the address?"

"I took a cab."

"Come in, come in, let me take your coat. A cold night for April."

"A little windy."

"And yesterday it was absolutely –"

"It's wonderful to see you. But –"

"But?"

"This feels so strange, somehow."

"Being here?"

"Yes. Being here. I don't know why."

"You're looking – lovely." It was true. She looked nervy, expectant, clear-eyed.

"So are you."

"Older anyway."

"Lucy Warkenten sends her love."

"Lucy. How does she like being a city councillor?"

"She's never been happier. She told me to tell you so."

"I'll phone her tomorrow."

"It sounds like you're having quite a party."

"Just a few actually. Nine altogether. But before we go in, there is something I should maybe tell you, Dorrie. I should have mentioned it in my note."

"Yes?"

"Beth's here. Visiting from England."

"Beth. Oh."

"It was sort of a coincidence, you both being here at the same time."

"Oh."

"I hope this isn't going to be awkward for you, Dorrie. It just seemed like a chance to get together –"

"Oh no. Not awkward at all. Not a bit, Larry. Heavens no."

"This is Dorrie Shaw-Weller. Let me introduce you around. Garth and Marcia."

"How do you do."

"Love your earrings. I once had a pair almost exactly like them except in silver. And maybe just a little bit smaller. I absolutely cannot wear large earrings, they swamp me. My face."

"Thank you."

"And this is Samuel Alvero who's been working with me on a maze project."

"Ah, so you are a Weller also? Part of the family. This is enchanting. I hadn't expected. To be at a family party."

"It's very nice to meet you, Samuel."

"And please meet a good friend of mine, Charlotte Angus."

"How do you do, Charlotte."

"We're so pleased you're here in Toronto."

"And this is Beth Prior."

"Well, well. So you're Dorrie."

"So you're Beth."

"This is – I don't know what to say – it's incredible."

"It is, isn't it? That we're meeting each other at last."

"Do you mind, Dorrie, if I give you a big hug."

"I'd love it, but . . . but – "

"He's got his own swimming pool in there. It's perfectly safe."

"Now that almost everyone's here, maybe I could suggest champagne."

"Champagne!"

"Tonight, well, tonight's a sort of special occasion."

"Shouldn't we wait for Midge and Ian, Larry?"

"They can always join in when they get here."

"I'm afraid I'll have to pass, Larry. Champagne and fetuses don't mix, and of course I never was one for –"

"I'd be happy to accept a glass of champagne."

"And believe me, Garth does love his champagne. Once we went to the most amazing party, it was on a boat anchored off Cape Cod, and they had the darlingest little man in these bright red boots who hopped around pouring –"

"Yes, please, Larry. Hmmmm, beautiful."

"Just look at that color"

"Smooth as silk."

"Well, naturally we all got high as kites and a woman, you'd recognize her name if I told you, she's everywhere these days, she said to Garth that he had the sweetest earlobes she'd ever seen on a man, and Garth, red as a radish, said –"

"I have not drunk champagne since I said goodbye to my good friends four months ago. And I see this is made in Canada. Astonishing."

"You'll find it a little fruitier than –"

"Was that the doorbell, Larry? Why don't you let me get it this time?"

"Midge, Ian! You're just in time."

"We let ourselves in."

"Larry was about to propose a toast."

"You look stunning, Charlotte."

"You too."

"Take a glass. And one for you, Ian."

"This isn't a real toast. I only want to offer a warm welcome to you all. And to wish you health and happiness."

"And here's to the opening of the McCord maze."

"Yes, let's not forget that."

"The what?"

"I'll tell you all about it later."

"Here's to us."

"Cheers."

"Happy days."

"Onward!"

"And now, let me refill your glasses before we sit down at the table."

* * *

"This is the most glorious soup. Do I detect ginger?"

"And a hint of lime too, that's my guess."

"Who do we congratulate? Who's the maker of the soup?"

"Speaking of limes, Garth promised me a lime soufflé for my birthday. You haven't lived till you've had the Four Season's version of lime souffle. Well, we made a reservation but the most awful thing happened just as we were sitting down –"

"Actually Larry made the soup."

"Larry!"

"Now, why should you sound so surprised?"

"Ah, we've wounded his pride."

"I just can't imagine Larry making soup. I do remember he was a pro with the can opener, but –"

"And if I recall it was Campbell's tomato soup."

"Exactly. That was his specialty. I'd almost forgotten."

"Later, of course, he graduated to Campbell's tomato soup with Parmesan cheese sprinkled on top. Moving up on the culinary scale."

"Now why are you women giving Larry such a hard time tonight?"

"I was going to explain that our guests tonight, Dorrie and Beth –"

"One thing I absolutely cannot eat is clams. My allergist says it could be deadly. Convulsions, a rapid lowering of blood pressure, and I already have the lowest blood pressure this side of the moon. He says that –"

"Times have changed. Men aren't ashamed to say they make soup nowadays. Ian makes the most delicious cream of broccoli –"

"It's a good way to use up the stalks, actually."

"Shame on you, Ian. You sound positively pious."

"Good God, I do, don't I?"

"Eco-smug."

"Greener than thou."

"Even in Spain these things are changing. Spaniards love their soup, and most men, younger men that is, know how to chop up a little cabbage and make it to boil."

"Well, it's not exactly a big deal when you put it that way, is it?"

"It's just that we're still struck with incredulity that a man can actually pick up a paring knife."

"That it even occurs to him!"

"My husband Derek never once —"

"My father, Midge's and mine I should say —"

"Ah, I do not understand. Midge here is your sister, Larry? You did not tell me."

"His big sister, let me add! And Ian at the other end of the table is my partner."

"Your husband. I see."

"In a manner of speaking."

"This really is a family party. I see. I am honored to be included."

"Almost a reunion, Samuel. But I was going to say that my dad occasionally would make tea —"

"Are you sure, Larry? I don't remember your dad lifting a finger in the kitchen."

"But tea was absolutely all he did."

"So that makes you the first generation of male soup makers."

"Garth's never made soup."

"Neither have you."

"What's that supposed to mean?"

"I was just saying –"

"You don't even like soup. Remember that time in Santa Barbara. You sent the soup back. You said you thought it was idiotic to fill up on peasant slop instead of waiting for –"

"Marcia means to say that –"

"I remember having the most wonderful sorrel soup in Tennessee. Remember, Larry, it was during our honeymoon."

"Your honeymoon? Ah, in Spain we say *luna de miel*. Direct translation. I always feel happy when I find direct translation. *Luna* is moon, you see, and *miel* –"

"When Derek and I were married we said that we'd postpone our honeymoon until –"

"When I find direct translation, I feel the world is more small."

"True, true."

"There's this restaurant in Saskatoon that serves lemon meringue soup!"

"What? Where?"

"I understand, Beth, that you live in England. Marcia and I try to get to London twice a year, and, in fact, that's where we first developed our passion for garden mazes. We saw three or four –"

"At least four! I'm a mad fanatic for keeping track of details, ask anyone, and I'm sure we visited at least four, maybe five –"

"In the abstract, there's no reason for these mazes. They're wrapped in privilege, they do nothing –"

"And we were so taken by the, the mystery of them, all they stood for, symbolically, transcendentally, that we thought we'd try to bring the tradition home to Toronto."

"A maze is not culturally specific, that's what Garth believes."

"So this is the McCord maze you mentioned earlier?"

"To be officially opened in a few days."

"Mazes are like – they're like thumbprints on the planet."

"The tighter the whorl, the higher the blood pressure. Did you know that?"

"Tighter the what? Higher the what?"

"One of our culture's flipped pancakes, completely useless except – "

"The mayor's going to cut the ribbon."

"And she'll lead the first party through."

"The way we see it, at the center of the maze there's an encounter with one's self. Center demands a reversal, a new beginning, a sense of –"

"– of rebirth. In the turns of the maze, one is isolated and then comes alive again."

"Which speaks to the contemporary human torment of being alternately lost and found."

"You can see that Garth's become a convert."

"Wait'll you see the seven-point node – it's got a magnolia tree and –"

"The thing about a maze, there can be one route or many. If you think of that symbolically, it means that our lives are open –"

"Most of the city councillors will be there, officials

and so on. Marcia and I'll be there, of course. Samuel will do the interpreting of plant types. And Larry here will accompany us in case we really get lost."

"We've always needed the idea that history moves forward, toward improvement of some kind, at the very least renewal. But this maze of Larry's hints at the circular journey which is really, when you stop to think about it – "

"Edmond Carpent says that the maze –"

"Take the Ore algorithm –"

"Controlled chaos and contrived panic."

"That's exactly right, Dorrie. Wonderful. But how –?"

"I read an article on it. A whole book, in fact."

"Oh! The Spellman book?"

"You look surprised."

"You do surprise me, Dorrie. You always have."

"I live with a maze, remember? Right outside my window. Well, half a maze anyway."

"And you've kept it going. I've always wondered why –"

"It wasn't an act of penance, if that's what you think. I guess . . . I've got used to it. I love it, if you want to know the truth."

"What are you two whispering about?"

"Can I offer a little more of Larry's soup? Dorrie? Garth?"

"Just a smidgen."

"So curious this language, English. Smidgen!"

"But does anyone really get lost in a maze?"

"Larry did. On our honeymoon."

"The Versailles maze, destroyed unfortunately, had thirty nodes and forty-three branches and –"

"*Your* honeymoon? I do not understand. Did you not say –"

"I wasn't *really* lost –"

"Weren't you, Larry? At Hampton Court? I remember how we waited for you. How we were worried when you didn't come out with the rest of us."

"A person doesn't need any particular knowledge to solve a maze. You're born with the necessary navigational equipment."

"So this was *another* honeymoon."

"Ah!"

"I haven't had a chance to explain that both Dorrie – and Beth – well, by coincidence they both –"

"– happened to be here in town, and that's why Larry and I decided to have a few friends in to dinner at Larry's place and –"

"And Derek? Is he –?"

"Dead. Some time ago. Cancer."

"I'm so sorry, I shouldn't have –"

"Terribly sorry."

"Cancer, a scourge."

"My therapist believes that most cancers are caused by anger, by not recognizing and embracing your anger. He says I'm a case in point, not that I have cancer, not yet anyway, but he says I really have got to attempt to claim –"

"Do you have a family back in Spain, Samuel?"

"My brothers, my sister –"

"But are you married?"

"She has been dead one year. My wife. It was a depression. She took some sleeping pills."

"My therapist says – "

"That's one reason I accepted to take this project in Canada. To make some air between my sorrow and myself."

"To put some distance."

"Yes, precisely! To put some distance."

"Who was it who said 'only disconnect?' "

"Forster, wasn't it? But I think he actually said –"

"If no one would like another helping of the soup –"

"Let me give you a hand, Charlotte."

"No, Larry. Let *me* give Charlotte a hand. If I sit any longer this baby'll get a permanent crick in its neck."

"Ah hah! that looks like a leg of lamb."

"I thought I smelled lamb when I came in the door earlier."

"I adore lamb!"

"Larry, this is a night of surprises."

"He shops, he cooks, he carves."

"And sets a mean table."

"No, really, I –"

"And he gets himself lavishly praised."

"Men!"

"It's not their fault that we love and patronize them in the same breath."

"Good heavens. I just noticed! This is our old table we're sitting at. Larry and I bought this table in Chicago, at an auction!"

"Beautiful."

"Men! The praise men get just for being men!"

"What's it like being a man these days?"

"Yes, what's it like? In the last days of the twentieth century?"

"Tell us."

Larry, slicing through the pink lamb and serving second helpings on to still-warm dinner plates, is struck by a thought. That he's hardly ever given a party before. He grew up in a house that, except for family dinners, never once resonated with the chimes of party noise and festivity. No children's birthday parties, nothing happening on New Year's Eve except the TV, Times Square, New York City, and a glass of sweet sherry at midnight. Had his mother and father simply lacked the gene for hospitality? Or, and this is more likely, had they been too shy, or else ignorant of the shaping impulse that blows a party into being? It should be such a simple, natural thing, really, the gathering of a few friends under a roof, the offering of food and drink and warmth and also that curious tensile and sometimes dangerous platform of opportunity for *something to happen*.

But, of course, it isn't simple at all – and he realizes this now, looking around the softly lit table, his friends, this gathering of strangers and kin – and three women he has known so well, *known* – and feeling the party, his first and only party, slipping sideways, collapsing, turning rigid. Shouldn't a party loosen ordinary human bonds? Good question.

At this moment Larry is feeling the opposite, that the membrane between people is tougher than he'd imagined. Where was the tonic glitter of personality he'd imagined. Perhaps he should open another bottle of wine. Wine the great loosener. Yes.

"Yes," his first wife, Dorrie, is asking from her end of the table, "tell us what it's like being a man these days." Her mouth is crisper than he'd remembered and now it shapes itself into the beginning of a smile, or perhaps another question.

Dorrie's idea of giving a party had been to invite another couple over to the house for pizza and TV. He remembers those late seventies evenings, Dorrie in jeans and a sweater and her thick hair brushed smooth around her small face, setting a bowl of chips-and-dip on the coffee table, and another of peanuts, muttering to herself about whether the rug needed a quick vacuum. Then thawing the frozen pizza for heating up later, checking to see that there was a bottle of wine in the fridge, worrying about the baby waking up. How many such evenings had there been? – probably only a few, Larry thinks. And where had he been in the preparations for those joyless, weary, two-couple gatherings? Nowhere. It seemed nothing had been expected of him.

He wonders what kind of parties Dorrie gives now. She lives in the same house, but both the house and her life have changed dramatically. She's stronger now, but she's also softened; he supposes some people would call this change a mellowing, but it goes beyond that. He can tell by the way she's cutting her lamb, the neat, sure strokes of her knife, the alert look of pleasure on her face, that she's more comfortable in the world than she once was. None of which should surprise him. But it's not her skill with a knife that holds his attention. No, it's her eyes, those wide, remembered grey eyes, that seem to be tipping the whole room in her direction. Her neck rising out of the collar of her dark dress and that wide strip of silver at her throat – has she any idea how she looks?

"Are we talking about young men?" Beth asks. "Or men who grew up convinced they belonged to the dominant culture?"

"I think," Midge says, "that we're talking about the men at this table."

Beth sits back in her chair, registering delight. She has already cleared her plate of vegetables. "In that case, who's going to go first?"

"This question. Do you mind – my English is so slow – do you mind saying again this thing, this question you have asked."

Contentedly, Beth laces her hands across her abdomen. "We want to know what it's like being *you*, at this time in *our* history."

She's happy tonight. Larry remembers that she always loved parties, that she had grown up with parents who hosted a dinner party every week or two. Beth, when he married her, took for granted a chest of family silver, enough for twelve. Also several sets of china, and individual saltcellars, each with its own tiny spoon. She sailed into married life with a calm regard for well-cooked, traditional food, immense roasts carved into thick slices and accompanied by the passing of a silver gravy boat. These were the very parties she always talked about giving, she and Larry in their Oak Park house. That, after all, was why they'd bought the house, and the table with its ten beautiful chairs, a table whose edge she is now fingering through the heavy cloth, perhaps calling up its smooth grain and luster.

These parties, though, hardly ever took place. She was too busy with her dissertation, her lectures, too preoccupied to dive into serious arrangements, the phone calls or written invitations, the menu, the kitchen work. Besides, she'd given up meat, and found the thought of preparing fish for eight or ten too daunting. "We owe everyone," she used to moan to Larry, but with a sly catch of amusement in her voice. "We'll never catch up."

"Lima beans," Garth McCord says happily. "I haven't had lima beans since was a kid at school."

"In France they –"

"In our family we never had beans. It's a long story."

"More wine, Marcia?"

"Lovely wine. It reminds me of the time Garth and I –"

"This table. If you find you don't really need it, Larry, I wouldn't mind having it back."

"Being a man at this moment of history means –"

"Go on, Ian. What does it mean?"

"It means – are you sure you want to hear this?"

"Yes!"

"Well, we're certainly no longer providers and guardians. That went years ago."

"For the most part, not for everyone –"

"And we don't belong to male lodges anymore. That used to be part of the male support system. The Elks, the Moose, the Lions, the Rotarians."

"I can't picture you belonging to –"

"And hunting and fishing? – forget it. Women sneer when we men talk about hunting and fishing."

"That's not true, Ian. I love it when you go fishing."

"Because you want the house to yourself Admit it."

"All right, I admit it."

"A man these days is no more than an infrastructure for a penis and a set of testicles."

"That's not true! Tell me it's not true."

"That's all that's required of us. Our bodies are just walking, talking envelopes designed to contain our paltry store of genetic tissue."

"Who says we've come to that?"

"Well," Beth offers, somewhat irrelevantly, "an apple's no more than a thickened ovary wall that – "

"Next time I bite into an apple I'll remember that."

"A man today –"

"What we all really want is to marry the men we'd be if we were men."

"Pardon?"

"Be serious, Ian," Midge says. She joins her palms to form a basket. An empty basket that wants filling. "You can see we really want to know." She's leaning forward so that the candlelight, flatteringly, colors half her face. Larry remembers that his sister is about to turn fifty. Her tone is only mildly mocking.

"All right, then. I'll be serious. But you ought to be warned that I wouldn't call myself a typical man."

"And I'm certainly not one either."

"And I wouldn't say that I am –"

"Typical, never."

"Methinks thou dost protest too –"

"We're waiting, Ian."

"All right, all right. Today, and I think you'll agree, a man's position has become entirely reactive. We have to take our signals from women or we're out of the game."

"Backlash! Hmmm. But go on."

"Being a man in 1997 means walking on eggshells. I don't dare tell a women that she looks nice anymore. That I like the color of her dress or the way she's changed her hair. They'd have me up for sexual harassment."

"Whoever they are."

"But this isn't what it's about, is it? Compliments. Courtesies. Whether or not to open a door for a woman."

"Oh, I don't know. Partly that *is* what it's about."

"It's a smoke-screen."

"I've found the most marvelous hairdresser, the nicest, most brilliant little man, I'd be happy to give you the name –"

"I'm a little tired," Ian says, "of men always being buffoons. They're buffoons on TV, buffoons in movies, and in books – they're goofs, they're weak in the balls, they're the butt of every joke."

"But maybe they really are. Buffoons, I mean."

"What ever happened to men who had dignity and courage?"

"Oh, they're still around, those men, but they're . . . they're just a little bit –"

"Corny?"

"Yes, exactly."

"And that's why," Ian continues, "I've been walking on eggshells since about 1980."

"But," Dorrie says, leaning forward, "how much do you *mind* walking on eggshells?"

"Good point."

"I agree with Dorrie. You shouldn't damn well mind at all."

"That's not quite what I mean. I mean –"

"What do you mean?"

"Well, that walking on eggshells just means – ordinary kindness."

"And respect!"

"For women –"

"And men."

"Eggshells all around, you mean."

"Something like that."

"It could just be that it's men's turn to *major* in eggshells."

"Male sensitivity. Hmmmm."

"I'm not sure I go along with that, Beth. Aren't you being just a little bit sweeping in your –?"

"I mean it."

"So do I."

"Me too."

"Maybe you misunderstood me. It's not a question of minding. It's a question of confusion. Of being off-balance half the time."

"What do you think, Garth?"

"I haven't thought much about it, to tell the truth."

"I knew you'd say that, Garth. I could absolutely depend on you not to have thought about it. Let me tell you what Garth thinks about. He gets up in the morning and he starts –"

"Easy does it, Marcia."

"But it's to be expected," Beth perseveres. "Confusion is the natural climate – the only climate for the post-feminist age."

"I wonder why people always talk about the post-feminist age," Charlotte muses. "As though we're already there. As though we've already got there –"

"Good point, Charlene."

"It's Charlotte."

"Right, sorry, Charlotte. But my point – well, it's not so much a point as a –"

"I would so very much like to hear your point. "In Spain we –"

"My point is that we – both men and women – ought to cherish this period of confusion. Our present period of discomfiture – well, it's a great and ecstatic gift. We've had 5000 centuries of perfect phallic clarity. Everyone knew the script. Men buttoned themselves into their power costumes –"

"But at least we all knew who we were and what was allowed."

"Will you shut up, Garth, for God's sake. You don't know what you're talking about."

"Lighten up, Marcia."

"What if I don't want to lighten up?"

"– the first half of the century was packed with evil, the second half with emptiness –"

"So men stood in their upright posture –"

"Erect!"

"Ha."

"– and –"

"And womans? What about womans?"

"Women walked around the edges."

"Very, very quietly."

"*Tell* me about it. Garth always –"

"Women *tiptoed* on eggshells."

"Ouch."

"Is that all you can say, Larry? Ouch."

"I just meant – "

"Do you know what my mother told me before Larry and I got married? She said, 'If you want to keep him from straying' – I was wife number two, remember – 'don't gain more than ten pounds. In your whole married life. Ten is the maximum allotment.' "

"Omigod, I've already –"

"*My* mother – this was before Derek and I got married – she said a wife should send her husband off to work every day with a clean white handkerchief that she'd washed and ironed herself. That was his calling card to the world. And the handkerchief was her contribution to his success."

"And did you? Do the hanky thing?"

"I did. Oh, lordy, I bought all the bromides. There was a steady parade of handkerchiefs until the day Derek died, damn him. And goddamn all those handkerchiefs too. If I had it to do over again I'd do a ritual burning –"

"Bromide! A good Scrabble word."

"Did you know that if you put all the world's Scrabble tiles in a row, they'd go twice around the earth."

"My mother said to me that there was one thing a husband wouldn't tolerate and that was pantyhose dripping on the shower rail. So when Larry and I got married back in seventy-eight, and bought our house on Lipton Street, I made a trip down to the dark basement every single night, just before bed, so I could hang my pantyhose on the clothesline."

"Whisked out of sight!"

"I never knew that, Dorrie. I wouldn't even have noticed if you'd –"

"Maybe not consciously, but Dorrie's mother knew how these things accumulate –"

"And get added to the resentment that's already in the bank. The inexorable adding machine."

"What resentment is this?"

"Yeah."

"The natural hatred men feel for women once the women have done their reproductive duty. It's Darwinian."

"I love women."

"So do I. Marcia and I –"

"But have you noticed the way men hog the armrest on airplanes? Sorry to be so petty, but it's like women don't have an arm that they'd maybe like to – rest."

"I must say, if you kind people will permit me, that I find the sight of a woman's, how do you say it? – pantyhose? – I find this sight quite, well very –"

"Erotic?"

"Ah, yes, indeed, e-ro-tic."

"And so my lucky brother's virgin eyes were never once assaulted by the nasty and unbearable sight of dripping –"

"*My* mother gave me just one piece of advice before Garth and I got married. Don't ever embarrass your husband in public. No husband will stand for it."

"Oh."

"So that's why we're in therapy as I speak."

"Marcia, for God's sake –"

"I can't seem to stop embarrassing him. It's like an addiction. Something I've got to do."

"We all have some form of addiction. Where I work we –"

"But you haven't heard the worst part. The worst part is that he loves being embarrassed in public. He sort of, you know, solicits it. He thrives on it, as you've probably noticed. That's *his* addiction."

"That's not true."

"Well, my mother didn't give me any pre-marital counseling –"

"Lucky you, Midge."

"Oh, I don't know. I might have done a whole lot better with a little sage, targeted advice."

"More lamb?"

"It's absolutely delicious."

"It's the marinade."

"All I meant to say is that men and women at the end of our century should treat this period of uncertainty as an experiment. We can try things out. Men can cook up a batch of soup if they want and not have to give up their penises."

"They can even stir it with their penises."

"Ouch."

"I don't believe this! We're back on the subject of soup."

"And penises."

"I only meant it as a metaphor."

"If only we could live our lives backwards, taking

advantage of our accumulated knowledge. Wasn't it Kierkegaard who said –?"

"Who?"

"Yes."

"I'm not sure, I'd have to look that up."

"I have to agree with Beth. In the company I work for – we make greeting cards –"

"Dorrie's being modest. She heads up this company that –"

" – we're trying to move toward a less gendered kind of thing. Our baby cards, for instance. The old pink and blue standards are giving way to yellows and greens. A baby's a person, not a he or she. And as for valentines, we're attempting to enlarge the market for women-to-men cards. Or cards for the gay sector."

"Who?"

"More wine, Marcia?"

"Just a little. Just half. I have to be careful not to –"

"That's certainly the way I intend to bring up this child of mine when it's born. I hope to treat it like a person right from the beginning. And by the way, it's a boy. I had the test. A boy who's going to grow up to be a man, whatever that means. He's pencilled in for all that raw male aggression and rage – "

"I don't know that that's true, that men –"

"Well, I distinctly remember Larry telling me when we were first married that he spent great swaths of time wanting to punch people in the nose."

"Swaths? Did I say that? Maybe now and then, but not –"

"I don't think, as a man, that I've ever wanted to punch people out –"

"That's what you say, Ian, but why is it when you're at a traffic light and the light turns green, you insist on being the first car off the mark?"

"Not the same thing as a nose punch."

"I'm not so sure about that."

"In my country we never –"

"Is it just testosterone or something even more embedded? I mean –"

"Oh, my God, the secrets men keep from women. And women from men."

"It breaks the heart."

"But does it really? I mean really?"

"Maybe it's better that way."

"No. No, it's not."

"A man's journey is different than a woman's –"

"Anyway, this baby of mine is going to be a person first and a man second."

"Good luck. But let me warn you, it's like trying to climb up a grass blade to achieve what you're looking for."

"What an anxious society we are. Anxious about politics, about gender roles, about –"

"Tell us about – about your – your baby, Beth."

"You mean who the father is?"

"Well, yes."

"Sperm bank. I've wanted a baby for years, as Larry knows. But, well, it didn't happen. And so last year I decided to apply for, for technological assistance."

"Amazing what they do these days – but how, how does one go about choosing?"

"You get a little catalogue with all the donors listed.

It describes racial background, height, education, one or two special interests, and so on."

"Just imagine if we applied for marriage partners like that."

"Go on, Beth."

"The first one I applied for was out."

"Out?"

"Out of stock."

"Oh."

"I hope you people won't mind if I put my head down on the table for a few minutes, I've got an excruciating headache."

"Marcia's had a rotten week."

"Don't give me that suffering squint – pu-lease."

"Maybe you'd like to lie down. In the bedroom."

"No, no, the table's fine."

"At least let me move your plate out of the way."

"Out of stock, you said."

"So I found another donor I liked almost as well."

"But won't you always wonder what that other would have produced?"

"I don't think so. I'll be too busy to think. That's what everyone tells me."

"To bring up a child alone, well, that can not be so very easy. In my country, we –"

"At first I thought I could handle it. I was invincible. Then I started to wonder."

"Second thoughts. That's certainly understandable."

"But I can't really allow myself second thoughts, can I? I have think of workable strategies now that I'm getting into the motherhood business.'

"Larry says you're here for meetings."

"In a way. But I've got an interview on Monday morning. At the University of Toronto."

"Really?"

"They're looking for someone in Women's Studies."

"So you mean – you mean you'd actually consider leaving England and moving to Toronto?"

"It's a beautiful city."

"Fabulous."

"Why'd you come here, Larry?"

"My sister. Midge."

"I didn't know that, Larry. You moved for me?"

"And you?"

"I wanted to open my own costume shop, and this seemed the perfect place."

"– everyone wandering around in costumes, that's for sure."

"I was born here. My father was born here."

"But, Beth, wouldn't you be, well, lonely in a new city?"

"I'd have Larry."

"Oh."

Larry is surprised how loud that "oh" sounds. And surprised he'd been the one to utter it. It rolls like a small marble across the sudden silence at the table and falls among the scattered plates and breadcrumbs, the half-eaten leg of lamb on its pool of dull-glazed *jus*, then bumps against the bent sleeping head of Marcia McCord, with her tideline of make-up snaking across the side of her long, thin, elegant neck.

This, Larry thinks, is a party in its ruins. An idea that should never have come into being. If this party were a play the curtain would come down. If this were a movie there'd be a fade-out. Right this minute. Now.

But no. He knows the evening isn't finished. There's more to come.

He's been waiting all evening for that something more, without knowing what it is, but now he sees across the table that Dorrie is smiling directly at him. What is she saying with that old, wise smile, its utter knowing and familiarity?

Indecipherable, but nevertheless he smiles back, a smile full of messages: here we are, the two of us.

Something has happened in the room, he understands that; there are two densities present, suspended one inside the other, and the air around the table, candlelit, soft, breaks up into shimmering bars of heat. A perceptual accident perhaps, a mirage, but here they are, suddenly, Larry and Dorrie, the Wellers, husband and wife. This is their party. They are, in this alternate version of reality, partners in a long marriage, survivors of old quarrels long since mended. The journey they appear to have taken separately has really been made together. After all, after all. So this is what has happened. Their parents are dead, the years have flown, and they themselves are parents of a beloved son who is in difficulty. It is they, Dorrie and Larry, who have brought this evening into being, and here, arrayed around them as though in a holographic image, are their friends and family, warmly invited, encouraged to talk, comforted with food and wine, adored, embraced.

The hour is winding down. Soon the old friends will be gone. Soon they will have only each other.

Evening's end. An engulfing dream, dissolving. A vision, a blur of what rightfully is theirs.

The chocolate cake is perfection. That's what Charlotte deems it – perfection! She would be mortified to know that a smear of chocolate has parked itself at the left-hand corner of her upper lip, making her look unbalanced. Wicked, in fact.

Señor Samuel Alvero has just declared that he will not speak on behalf of the male sex and how it defines itself to itself. "I am, after all, the stone guest tonight. Do you know this phrase? *Invatado de piedra*. From *Convidado de Piedra*. Perhaps it is only for Spanish people. A stone guest is one who is invited to occupy a place at the table, to fill a slot. He is not expected to say much. Or do much. He is just –"

"Just there."

"Precisely."

"A stone."

"I'm feeling like a stone myself," Beth says. "After all I ate."

"Gorgeous cake," says Marcia McCord, who has revived and is now patting her hair smooth. "It reminds me of the time Garth and I went to this place in Vienna and I had three pieces of chocolate cake for lunch, psyching up my courage to have my ears pierced."

"In Spain we always –"

"You know, I've never had my ears pierced," Beth announces with a note of awe.

"Because of your political principles?"

"Because I'm a total coward. So it's clip-ons or nothing."

"And clip-ons kill!"

"Tell me, why would an intelligent women want to mutilate her –?"

Midge Weller begins a long story about being fourteen years old and sneaking off to a shopping mall in Winnipeg where free ear piercings were being offered, and how she'd spent that night with her head wrapped in bath towels and her earlobes bleeding freely and fiercely.

"I was forty when I got around to *my* ears," Charlotte tosses in, her voice droll and aslant. "Which is late, late, late, but I thought, what the hey, I have to celebrate this event somehow."

"A small puncture for womankind."

"Two small punctures."

"Ha!"

"My own mother did mine at home," Dorrie contributes. "I was about twelve. She got me down on the couch and started in with a hot needle. I fainted after the first ear, and the minute I revived she went for the second."

"Did you ever forgive her?"

"Of course. But then I'm at a place in my life where I've forgiven everyone. Except myself maybe."

"In my country it is the custom to –"

"Why is it we never forgive ourselves?"

Larry looks up. Who is it who's said this? – who? It's Marcia McCord. She's staring straight into the side of her second slice of cake, and Larry sees that her eyes are crowded with tears.

He's always known he was a man with a few loose parts: a brain, for instance, with a hinge he can flip open. And now he thinks: Oh, these women, these beautiful women. He regards them with wonder. These women are separate selves, but also part of Larry's self. And it seems they are in league together, attempting around this simple rectangular table, suddenly, to refloat the evening with their generous mouths and gesturing hands. He loves them all – he does! His bossy, loyal, suffering, unpredictable sister with her salty tongue. His two magnificent wives – just look at them! They are brilliantly alive in the flickering candlelight, in a way he never would have guessed – graceful, articulate, earnest, kind. And his gentle Charlotte, yes. And he loves even Marcia McCord, who has just this minute parted her bitten lips and launched into a description of Garth's true opinion of Austrian hotels – cute, dull, expensive, flat, and flavored with burnt milk.

The voices of these women form a cloud of lightness over the table. Now they're talking about the importing of unpasteurised cheese. Now they've switched to the benefits of train travel over air, to the national breast cancer movement, to David Cronenberg movies, to Karen Kain's retirement. This is a kind of intricate dance they're conducting, or else it's a spider's web. Where would his life be without women? A stone guest at his own party. That's the truth of the matter. Filling a slot.

The men around the table are silent for the moment, characters observed by a badly managed camera – digesting the rich cake, Larry thinks, or listening, or else pondering – pondering that unanswerable question that they've so carefully avoided – what is it like to be part of the company of men at the end of our millennium? What do they want once their names are inscribed in the book of life? Wait a minute – there isn't any book of life.

Men. These curious upholstered assemblages of bones, the fearful mortality that attends them, the clutter of good luck and bad, the foolish choices, the seeds of the boys they'd all been – and those seeds sprouting inappropriately even as their hair thins and their muscles slacken. Fighting for a little space in the world. Needing a little human attention. Getting it up, getting it off. When does it stop? Does it ever stop?

Larry recalls a photo someone had taken of him as a very young child. He is propped up in a rather elaborate highchair and is staring straight ahead, his infant face full of hurt and knowing. Is it his future as a man he's seeing? That stumbling being who knows now that every single day something will be taken from him, and that one day it will be too much?

Some twenty years ago it was different. Yes – it would be almost twenty years ago, the end of April, a cold night just as this. Walking alone on a Winnipeg street, twenty-six years old, he'd seen, perhaps for the first time, the kind of man he could be. He'd felt the force of the wind, and impulsively he'd whipped off his tweed jacket, offering himself up to the moment he'd just discovered, letting it sweep him forward on its beguiling currents. Love was waiting for him. Transformation. Goodness. Work. Understanding. The enchantment and liberation of words. The discovery of his own clumsy body and how it yearned to connect. And children, too, if he were lucky, but he was going to be lucky, that question was no longer in doubt. The wind that blew against his exposed body informed him of his good fortune. All he had to do was stand still and allow it to happen.

"I am so sorry about your wife," Charlotte is saying to Samuel Alvero. They have carried their coffee cups into the living room and are sitting near the bay window on two rather stiff chairs. "My own husband, Derek, it was the same thing for him. Sleeping pills. An overdose."

"Perhaps an accident —"

"He left a note."

"But I thought you said — did you not say it was a cancer that —?"

"It was being treated. He was doing fine. But he was too sad. Or mad at the world. Or maybe at me. I haven't told very many people."

"I am so sorry."

"I haven't said anything to Larry. I don't want him to know."

"You can trust me."

"I can tell from your eyes that I can trust you."

"And I can tell from *your* eyes that — "

"Did Larry tell you how much I loved Spain?"

"So! You have visited my country!"

"We started in Madrid, three terrific days and then —"

"The weather, it was good?"

"It rained one evening, the fattest raindrops I'd ever seen. Not many, just a few, but each one was so full and perfect, and they fell on my bare arms. It was heaven in a way."

"My therapist," Marcia McCord says to Ian, "has this theory that I act out because I feel I'm doomed to act out."

"You mean like a self-fulfilling prophecy kind-of-thing?"

"I know nobody likes me. People can't stand me, and that's a fact. And so I make sure they really and truly can't stand me."

"I like you."

"But the way you say that. Men are liars, aren't they? And they're always making women glue the little emotional pieces together for them."

"Relax, why don't you?"

"All right. I will. Oh, Jesus!"

"You're crying."

"Not really, it's the smoke."

"No one's smoking."

"Oh."

"Let me take your hand for a minute. Let me."

"Thanks."

"You're trembling."

"I know."

"It's not true that I'm never embarrassed," Garth McCord tells Beth. He stirs his coffee with great thoroughness, even though he's taking it black. "I'm embarrassed as hell all the time."

"But why do you –?"

"I love her. She's – difficult. She's had problems all

her life. I knew that when we got married. She needs a lot of, a lot of – tending. But I love her."

"You're lucky then."

"And it seems you're lucky too."

"You mean – this? The baby?"

"You've made a real choice. This didn't just happen."

"Yes."

"And now you're thinking about moving to Toronto."

"Thinking, yes, but there are so many considerations. Like, would it be awkward for Larry if the baby and I were in the same city?"

"Hmmmm."

"I suppose I thought that maybe we could, you know, even reach a new understanding. The two of us? But, of course, I didn't know about the existence of Charlene –"

"It's Charlotte."

"And I don't have an inkling about how serious their relationship is. You can see what a mess I'm in."

"And it's so easy to do damage. Take my word for it."

"What did you say?"

"Damage."

"That's what I thought you said."

Larry is walking around the room refilling coffee cups, bending, pouring, taking in snatches of conversation. Midge and Dorrie sit crowded together on the small sofa by the artificial fireplace, and Dorrie is explaining why she is in Toronto for the weekend.

"I'm apartment hunting," she says into Midge's ear, but Larry, bending forward, hears too.

Midge puts down her cup. "I can't believe it. That you'd ever leave Winnipeg."

"I'll hate giving up the house. All those memories."

"But why?" Larry asks.

What's the matter with him? He's overfilled Dorrie's cup.

"The company's been wanting me to relocate, but I didn't want to move until Ryan finished high school. His friends and everything."

"You've given him real roots."

"I'm just so surprised, that's all."

"That nephew of mine! He's a peach."

"He is a pretty nice kid. The drug episode, it was all his coach's idea, it seems."

"What an influence!"

"It's a damn good thing he's transferring, then."

"Thank God it's over," Larry says. Over, yes. But his son, who is only technically involved, is nevertheless stricken for life, tainted anyway, the world for the moment spoiled. "Lyin' Ryan" is what he's been called in the press. A knife in the chest.

Midge changes the subject abruptly. "Maybe Ian and I can help you with your apartment hunting, Dorrie."

"I might take you up on that."

"Maybe I could help too," Larry says.

"Hey," Midge says. "You sit down, Larry. Let me do the coffee refills."

"Are you sure?"

"I'm your sister, the boss. Remember?"

"Larry," Dorrie says. "You're looking stunned. What is it?"

"I'm not stunned. I'm just –"

"Just what?"

"I don't know. Glad. That you'll be here in Toronto. We'll get a chance to catch up at last."

"Do you think we ever will? Get caught up?"

"Probably not. But we could talk anyway."

"Don't look now, but Marcia's crying. She and Ian over there in the corner. There're tears in her eyes."

"I thought she was, but I wasn't sure."

"Should we do something?"

"I don't think so."

"I used to cry a lot, Larry. After you left I cried for two years."

"I'm sorry, it was –"

"You don't have to be sorry. I didn't know how to be married back then. By the time I figured it out, it was too late."

"And you never married again."

"There were a few . . . friends. Men friends. But not many. I've been busy. Working. Being a mother. And mostly –"

"Mostly what?"

"Mostly figuring out how to be a person. I needed to stay home to do that."

"I cried too."

"Did you?"

"In a different way, maybe."

"How different?"

"Not very different. Not at all, in fact."

"Charlotte – she's –?"

"A friend. A good friend."

"Did you mean what you said at the table tonight? That you weren't really lost that time we were at Hampton Court?"

"Not exactly. I was lost, but I wanted to be lost."

"Why didn't you tell me?"

"I wasn't sure you'd understand."

"I would have understood. But I wouldn't have known how to tell you that I understood."

"Was that our problem? That we didn't know enough words?"

"Or what we were allowed to say."

"We could have said anything. We should have learned."

"Learning to talk can be taken two ways. There are the words themselves and –"

"– and what's behind the words."

"Tell me, Larry – do you still want to be lost?"

"No, not any more. I want –"

"What?"

"To get myself . . . found." This is not quite true, but what's true he doesn't yet trust.

"I was just thinking a little while ago, Larry, when we were having dessert – how everything is different now. And yet everything's – somehow –"

"– the same."

"Yes."

"I love you. I've always loved you."

"I love you too. I've been waiting. Only I didn't know I was waiting."

Larry slept, but woke several times, dreaming, or perhaps not dreaming, of the comforts offered in this world: humor, fatalism, change, acceptance, an understanding of statistical truth. We will probably die of heart disease, we will probably suffer marital or sexual failure, we will have nightmares in our childhood. We will read 4.3 books each year. Our children will end up in emergency wards with scars on their faces and darkened front teeth. And we will go round and around. Watching where we're going. Where we've been.

Dear Larry,

I had to go into the office this morning, these damn bureaucrats don't believe in sabbath rest, and I thought I'd just slip this note under your door. I feel rotten that I didn't stick around to help clear up last night, although, to tell you the truth, Larry, I had the feeling that maybe Dorrie would stay and give you a hand.

I think we were all tired, and when Sam offered to drive me home – he lives just around the corner, it turns out – I couldn't resist. He's got some wonderful CDs of Spanish music, classical guitar, that he said he'd like me to hear. You remember how taken I was with their music!

Great party, by the way. We did it! Whatever "it" is.

Charlotte

Hi darling brother. It's just Midge here, pouring my scattered thoughts into your voice mail. It's ten-thirty Sunday morning, and do I ever have a hangover. Ian too. Never mind, though. I expect you're sound asleep and can't hear the phone ringing. Or don't want to hear the phone ringing. Just thought I'd say thanks for the great party. Marcia McCord is a very naughty girl, isn't she? Actually, she's a mess. Poor Garth. Why are men such sops? And by the way, this question does not require an answer. Ian and I thought your soup was a smash – and naturally he wants the recipe. Also you get points for your roast lamb and the dessert, which I'm damn sure did *not* come out of La Cuisine Weller. An interesting evening. Your stone guest was – hmmmm – a bit stony, playing his role of visiting foreigner so straight and tight and hand-kissingly charming. But somehow I warmed to him in the end. Maybe because he was nice to Charlotte, who was looking a little – baffled. Or did you notice? What idiots women are! Yours truly included. Beth was – how shall I put this? – herself. Full of herself. Full of baby and self. One compacted self-referential sphere of flesh. She'll be fine. Hope you've figured that much out. And Dorrie. I always wondered what would happen if you and Dorrie got together again. Well, I had a hunch she was waiting for a second ride on the merry-go-round, even if she didn't know it herself. So long, kiddo. Talk to you later.

From: samero@mccordworks.com
hello friends. this is to say hello on this sunday afternoon. i insist to thank you for dinner last night. I

was content with good friends at table, good food and wine. and talk what more could anyone ask for. you have all been so kind and Charlotte also. your friend sam

Garth here. Sunday afternoon. Sorry to miss you, but I'll leave a brief message on your tape. Two-twenty-two or thereaboutish. Great party. Marcia and I had great time. Just great. Great food and company. Marcia slept right through the night – no sedative or anything. First time in ages. Great sign. Sorry about rough bumps. But it was great. Marcia says thanks. She says it was an authentic experience. She says don't worry about her. Thanks from me too.

FAX: From Beth Prior, Hart House, University of Toronto
To: Larry Weller
Dear Larry,
Just to say thank you for a wonderful party. And I was most grateful to Midge and Ian for dropping me off here afterwards. I wish I could say I slept well, but, in fact, I was up all night thinking. And coping with heartburn – not your lovely dinner at fault, just "the wee babe" registering objection to surfeit and pleasure.
In a way this is hello and goodbye, since I've just this minute managed to change my travel arrangements. I'll be heading back to London tomorrow morning. The whole Toronto expedition now seems something of a fool's errand (I'm the fool, of course, who else?) and I'm anxious to get back

home before the hormonal gods punish me with a premature *accouchement*.

Dear Larry. I always knew you loved her. And that she loved you. I knew! From your silence I knew. From that totally noncommittal card she sent you when you turned forty. I noticed you kept it, at the bottom of your underwear drawer. It seemed to me that all that was required was the right time frame or mood or circumstance. Or just taking the right corner at the right moment – like one of your beautiful mazes.

your loving Beth

p.s. Thank you for inviting me to your party. If you're in my neighborhood I'll give a party for *you*. Any time, I mean it. RSVP. Regrets only.

Some run the Shepherd's Race – a rut
Within a grass-plot deeply cut
And wide enough to tread –
A maze of path, of old designed
To tire the feet, perplex the mind,
Yet pleasure heart and head;
'Tis not unlike this life we spend,
And where you start from, there you end.
(Bradfield, Sentan's Wells, 1854)

The publishers hope that this large print book has brought you pleasurable reading. Each title is designed to make the text as easy to read as possible.

For further information on backlist or future titles please write or telephone:
In the British Isles and its territories, customers should contact:

ISIS Publishing Ltd
7 Centremead
Osney Mead
Oxford OX2 0ES
England
Telephone: (01865) 250 333 Fax: (01865) 790 358

In Australia, and New Zealand customers should contact:

Australian Large Print Audio & Video Pty. Ltd.
17 Mohr Street
Tullamarine Victoria 3043
Australia
Telephone: (03) 9338 0666 Fax: (03) 9335 1903
Toll Free Telephone: 1800 335 364
Toll Free Fax: 1800 671 411

In New Zealand:
Toll Free Telephone: 0800 44 5788
Toll Free Fax: 0800 44 5789